PART ONE

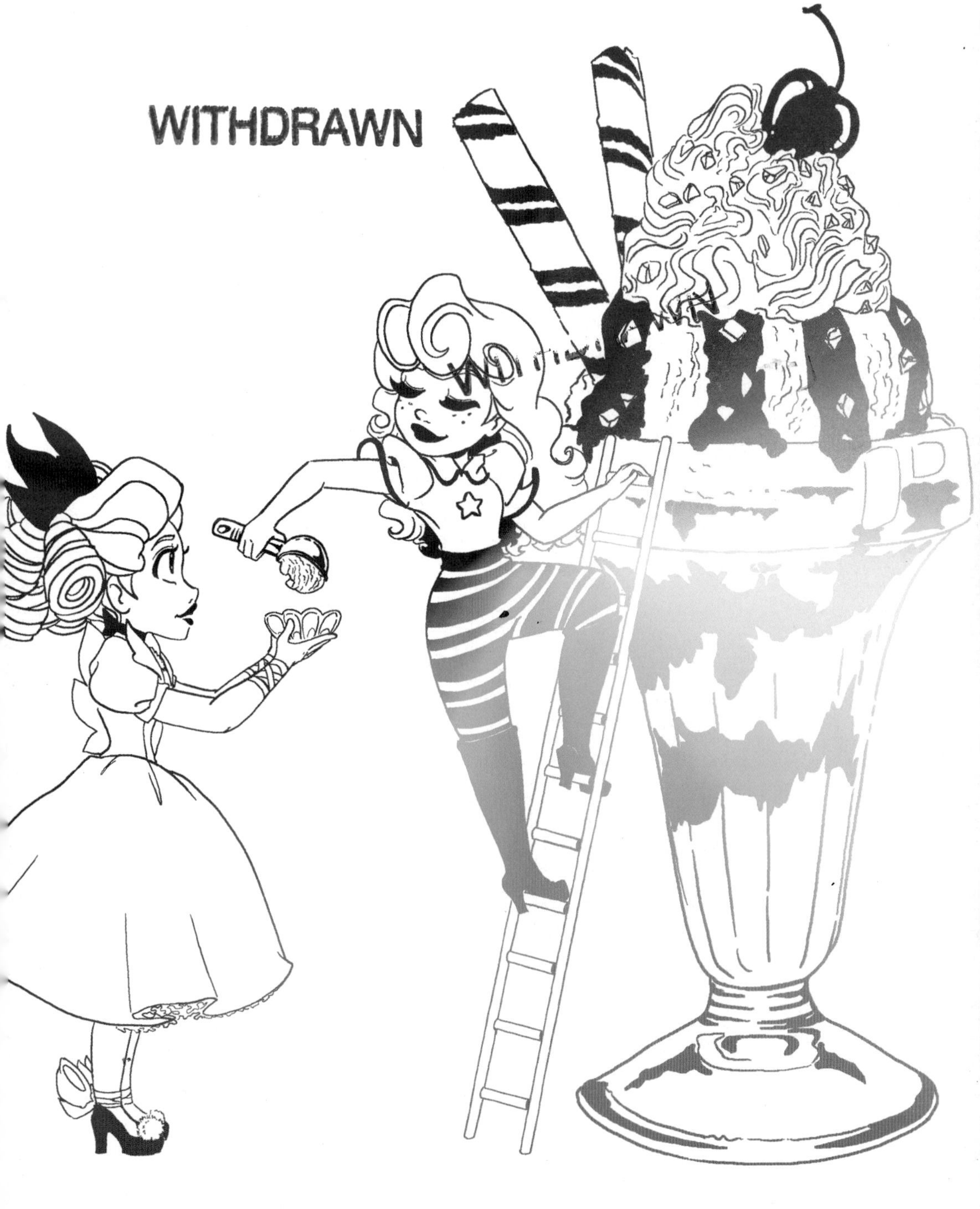

TOYETICA 5

STORY AND ART BY MARTY LEGROW

LETTERING
Justin Birch

MY NEW YEAR'S RESOLUTION
is to eat even more pizza

Bryan Seaton: Publisher/ CEO • Shawn Gabborin: Editor In Chief • Jason Martin: Publisher-Danger Zone • Nicole D'Andria: Marketing Director/Editor
Danielle Davison: Executive Administrator • Chad Cicconi: Action Lawyer • Shawn Pryor: President of Creator Relations

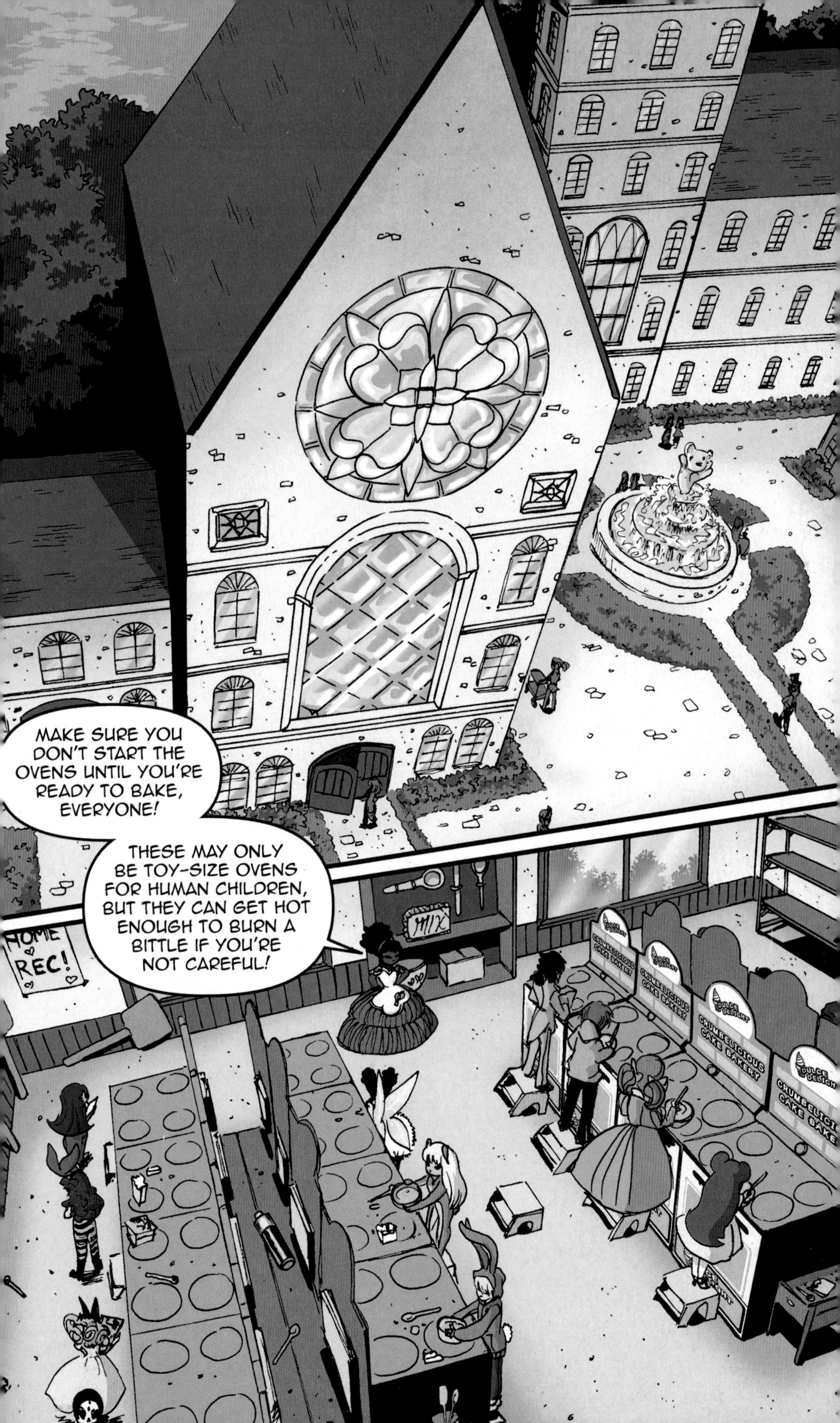
MAKE SURE YOU DON'T START THE OVENS UNTIL YOU'RE READY TO BAKE, EVERYONE!
THESE MAY ONLY BE TOY-SIZE OVENS FOR HUMAN CHILDREN, BUT THEY CAN GET HOT ENOUGH TO BURN A BITTLE IF YOU'RE NOT CAREFUL!
HOME REC!
MIX
DULCE DELIGHT
CRUMBELICIOUS CAKE BAKERY

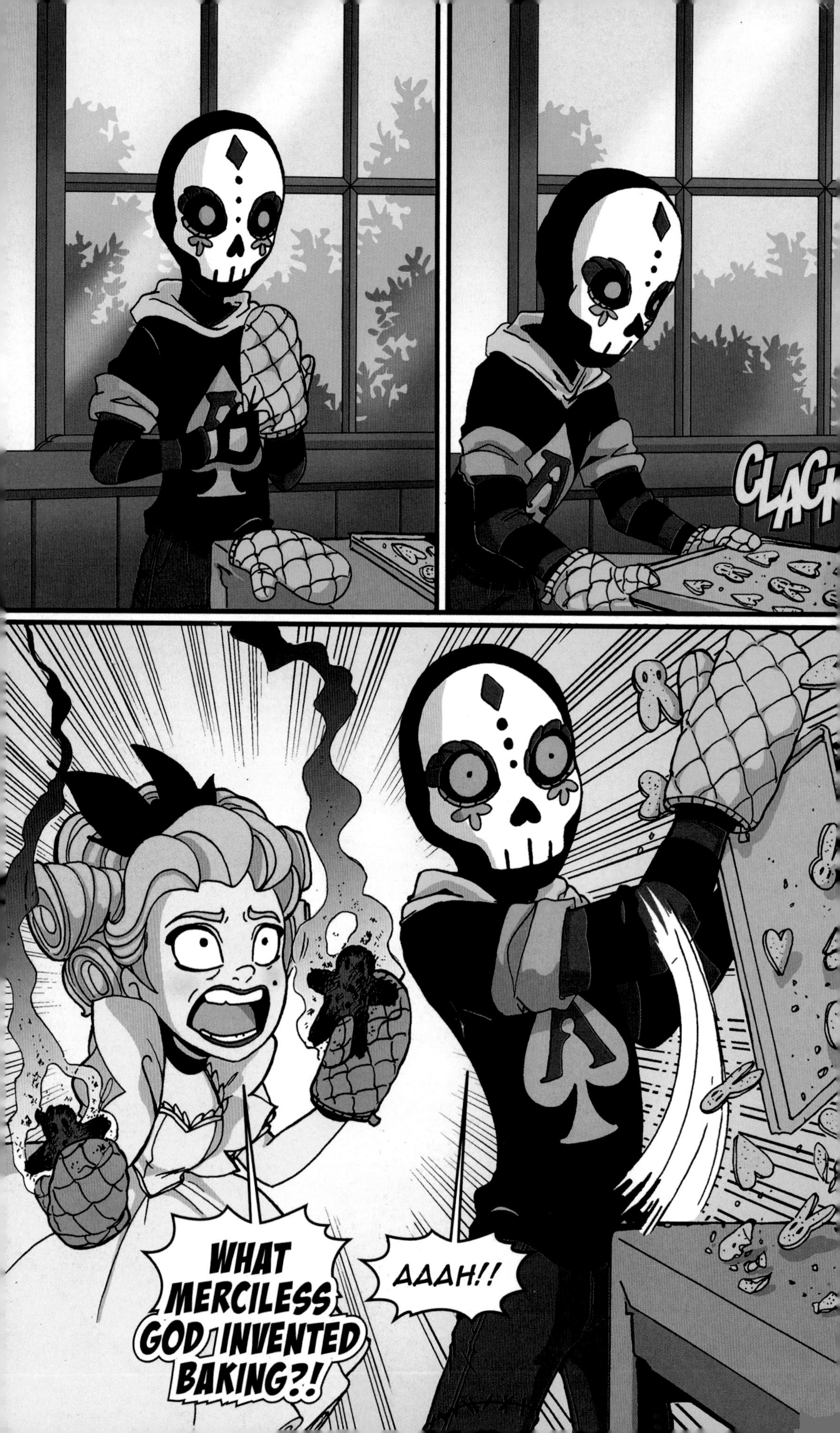
CLACK
WHAT MERCILESS GOD INVENTED BAKING?!
AAAH!!

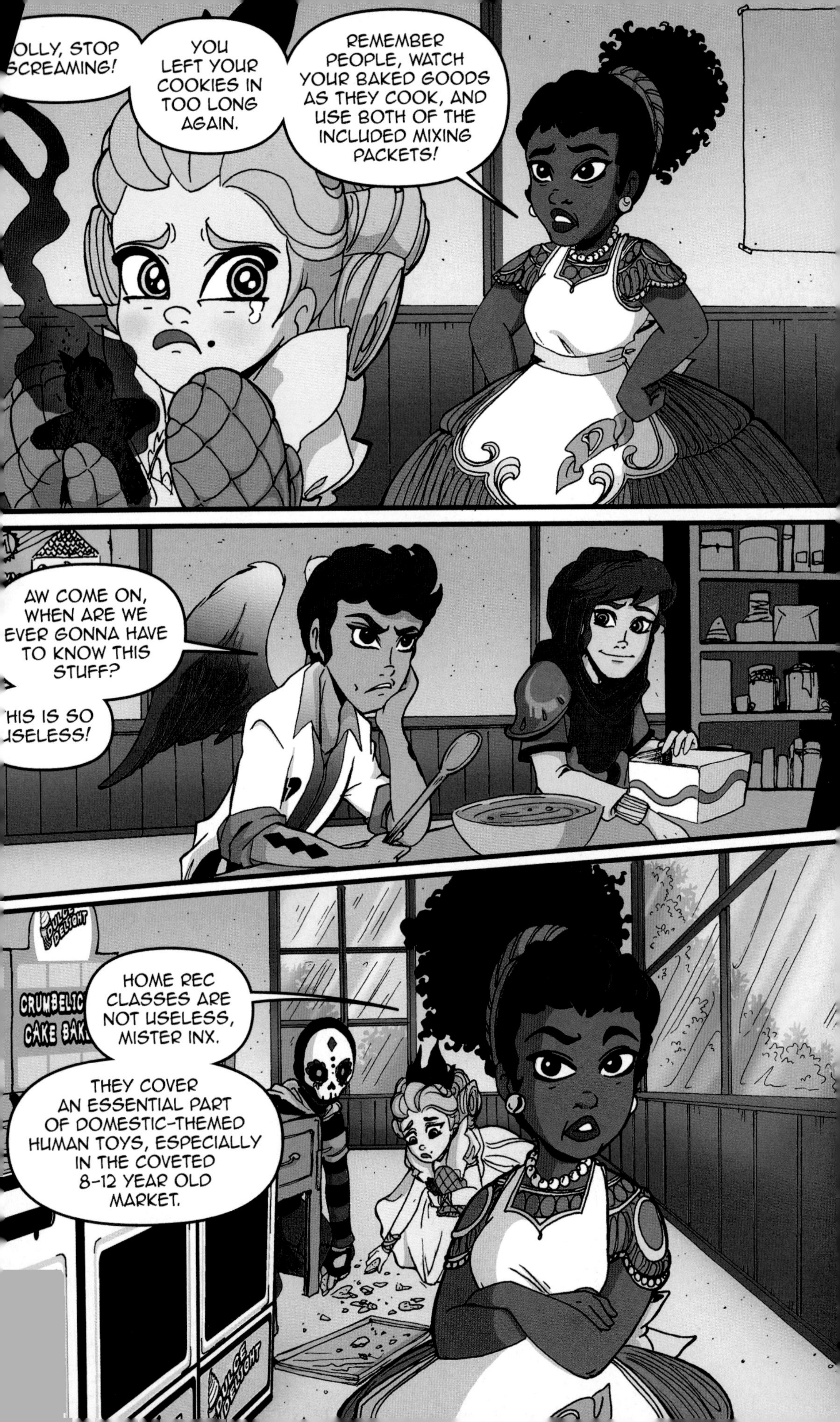
OLLY, STOP SCREAMING!
YOU LEFT YOUR COOKIES IN TOO LONG AGAIN.
REMEMBER PEOPLE, WATCH YOUR BAKED GOODS AS THEY COOK, AND USE BOTH OF THE INCLUDED MIXING PACKETS!
AW COME ON, WHEN ARE WE EVER GONNA HAVE TO KNOW THIS STUFF?
HIS IS SO USELESS!
HOME REC CLASSES ARE NOT USELESS, MISTER INX.
THEY COVER AN ESSENTIAL PART OF DOMESTIC-THEMED HUMAN TOYS, ESPECIALLY IN THE COVETED 8-12 YEAR OLD MARKET.

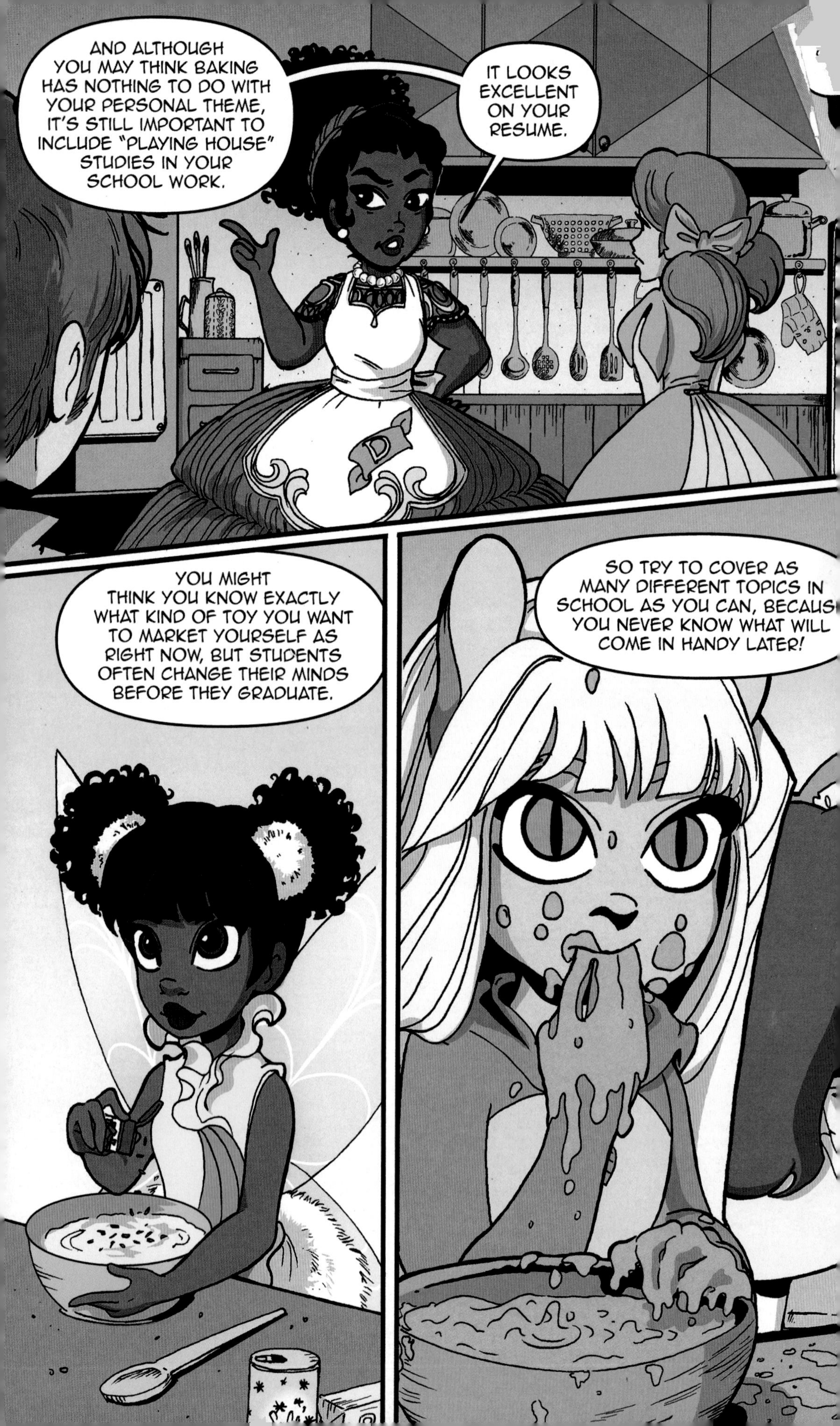
AND ALTHOUGH YOU MAY THINK BAKING HAS NOTHING TO DO WITH YOUR PERSONAL THEME, IT'S STILL IMPORTANT TO INCLUDE "PLAYING HOUSE" STUDIES IN YOUR SCHOOL WORK.
IT LOOKS EXCELLENT ON YOUR RESUME.
YOU MIGHT THINK YOU KNOW EXACTLY WHAT KIND OF TOY YOU WANT TO MARKET YOURSELF AS RIGHT NOW, BUT STUDENTS OFTEN CHANGE THEIR MINDS BEFORE THEY GRADUATE.
SO TRY TO COVER AS MANY DIFFERENT TOPICS IN SCHOOL AS YOU CAN, BECAUS YOU NEVER KNOW WHAT WILL COME IN HANDY LATER!

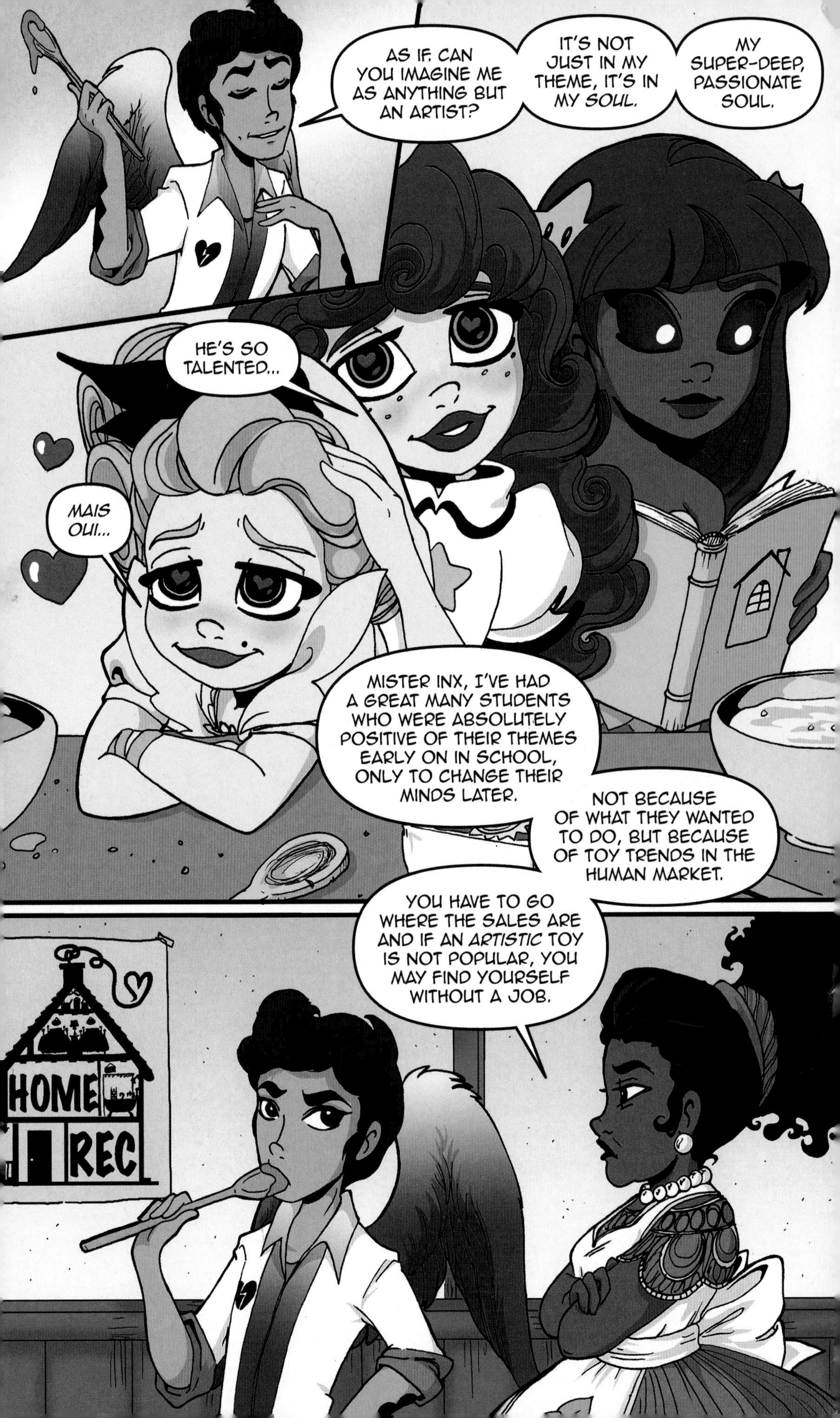
AS IF. CAN YOU IMAGINE ME AS ANYTHING BUT AN ARTIST?
IT'S NOT JUST IN MY THEME, IT'S IN MY *SOUL*.
MY SUPER-DEEP, PASSIONATE SOUL.
HE'S SO TALENTED...
MAIS OUI...
MISTER INX, I'VE HAD A GREAT MANY STUDENTS WHO WERE ABSOLUTELY POSITIVE OF THEIR THEMES EARLY ON IN SCHOOL, ONLY TO CHANGE THEIR MINDS LATER.
NOT BECAUSE OF WHAT THEY WANTED TO DO, BUT BECAUSE OF TOY TRENDS IN THE HUMAN MARKET.
YOU HAVE TO GO WHERE THE SALES ARE AND IF AN *ARTISTIC* TOY IS NOT POPULAR, YOU MAY FIND YOURSELF WITHOUT A JOB.
HOME
REC

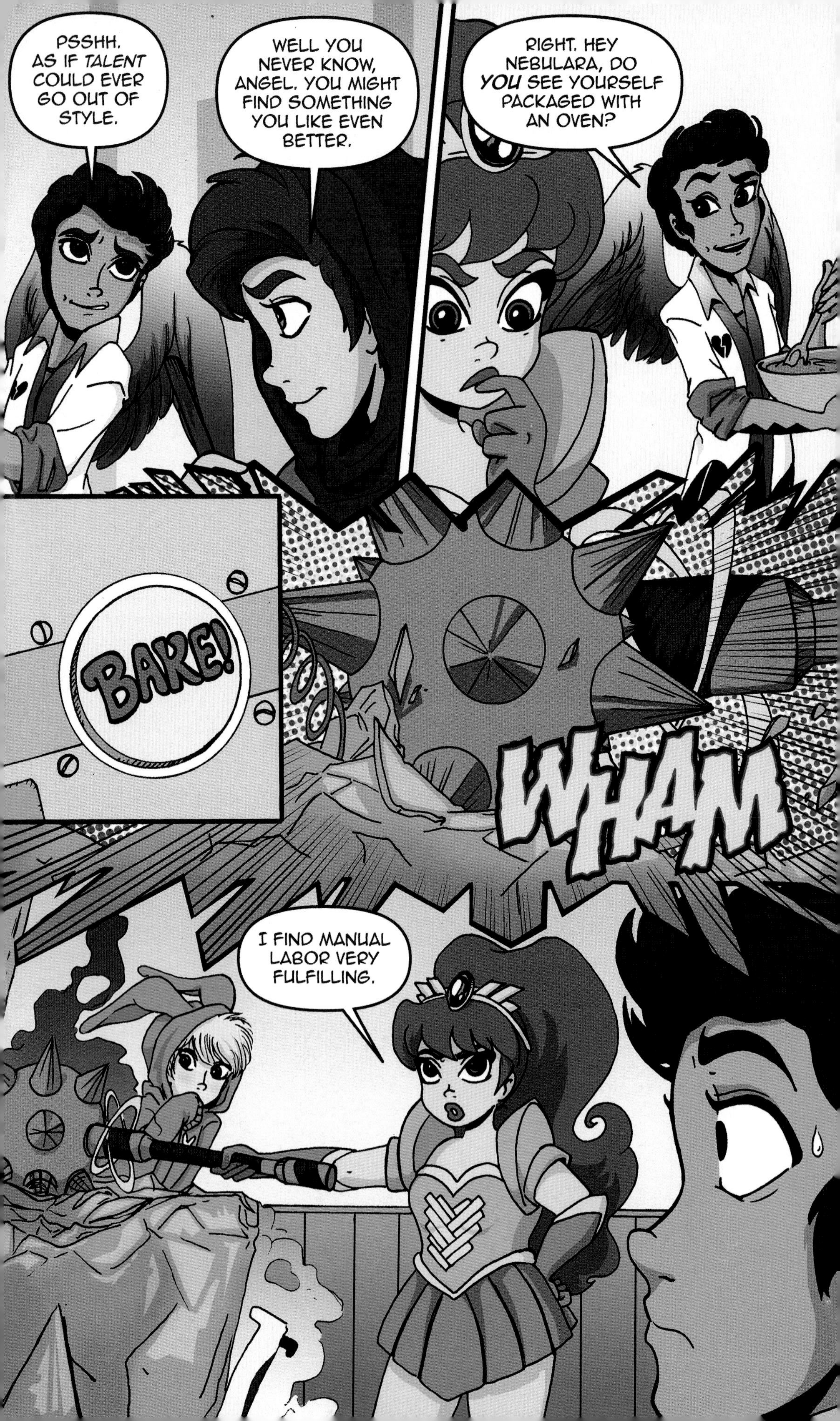
PSSHH. AS IF TALENT COULD EVER GO OUT OF STYLE.
WELL YOU NEVER KNOW, ANGEL. YOU MIGHT FIND SOMETHING YOU LIKE EVEN BETTER.
RIGHT. HEY NEBULARA, DO YOU SEE YOURSELF PACKAGED WITH AN OVEN?
BAKE!
WHAM
I FIND MANUAL LABOR VERY FULFILLING.

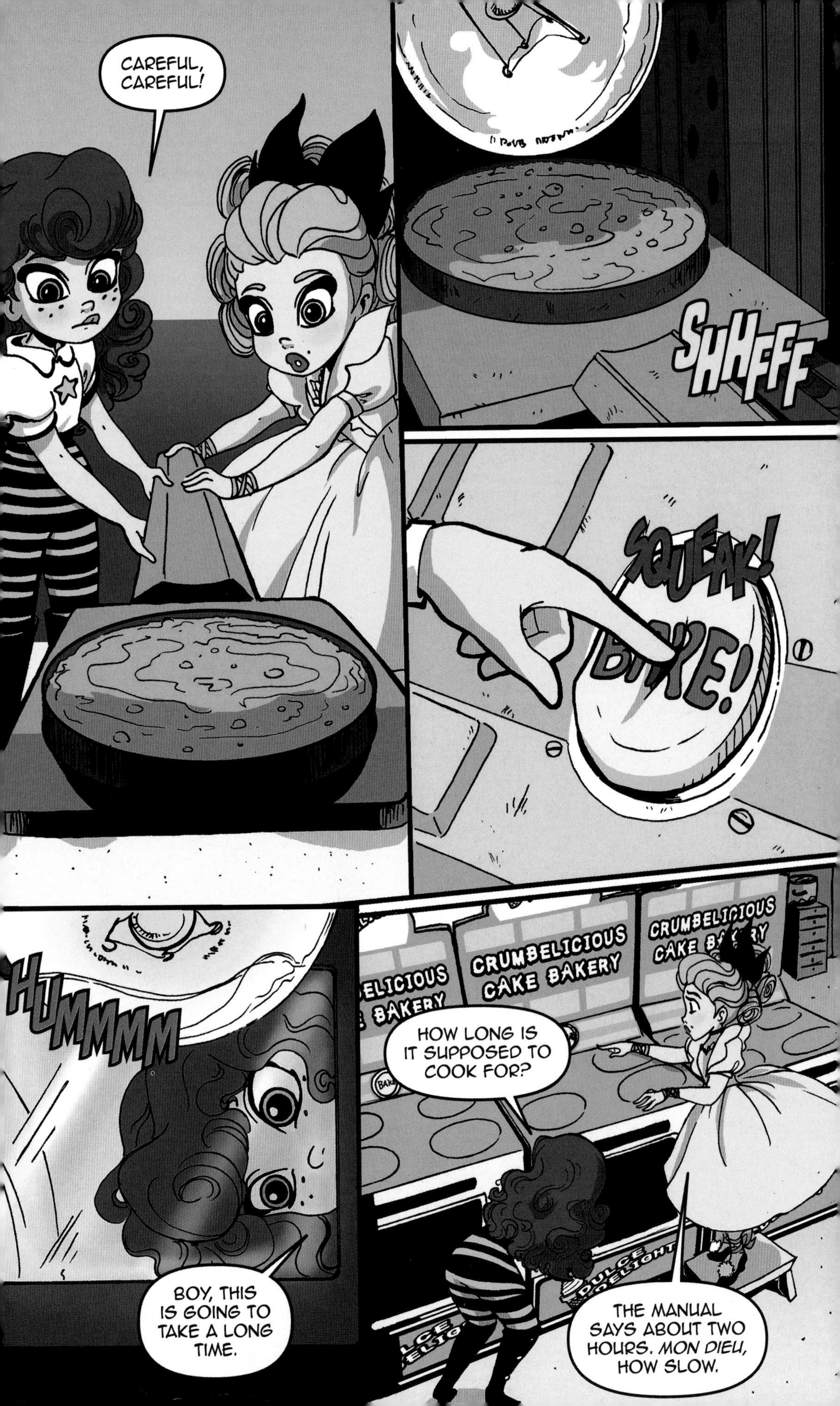
CAREFUL, CAREFUL!
SHHFFF
SQUEAK!
BAKE!
HUMMMM
BOY, THIS IS GOING TO TAKE A LONG TIME.
CRUMBELICIOUS CAKE BAKERY
CRUMBELICIOUS CAKE BAKERY
HOW LONG IS IT SUPPOSED TO COOK FOR?
THE MANUAL SAYS ABOUT TWO HOURS. *MON DIEU*, HOW SLOW.

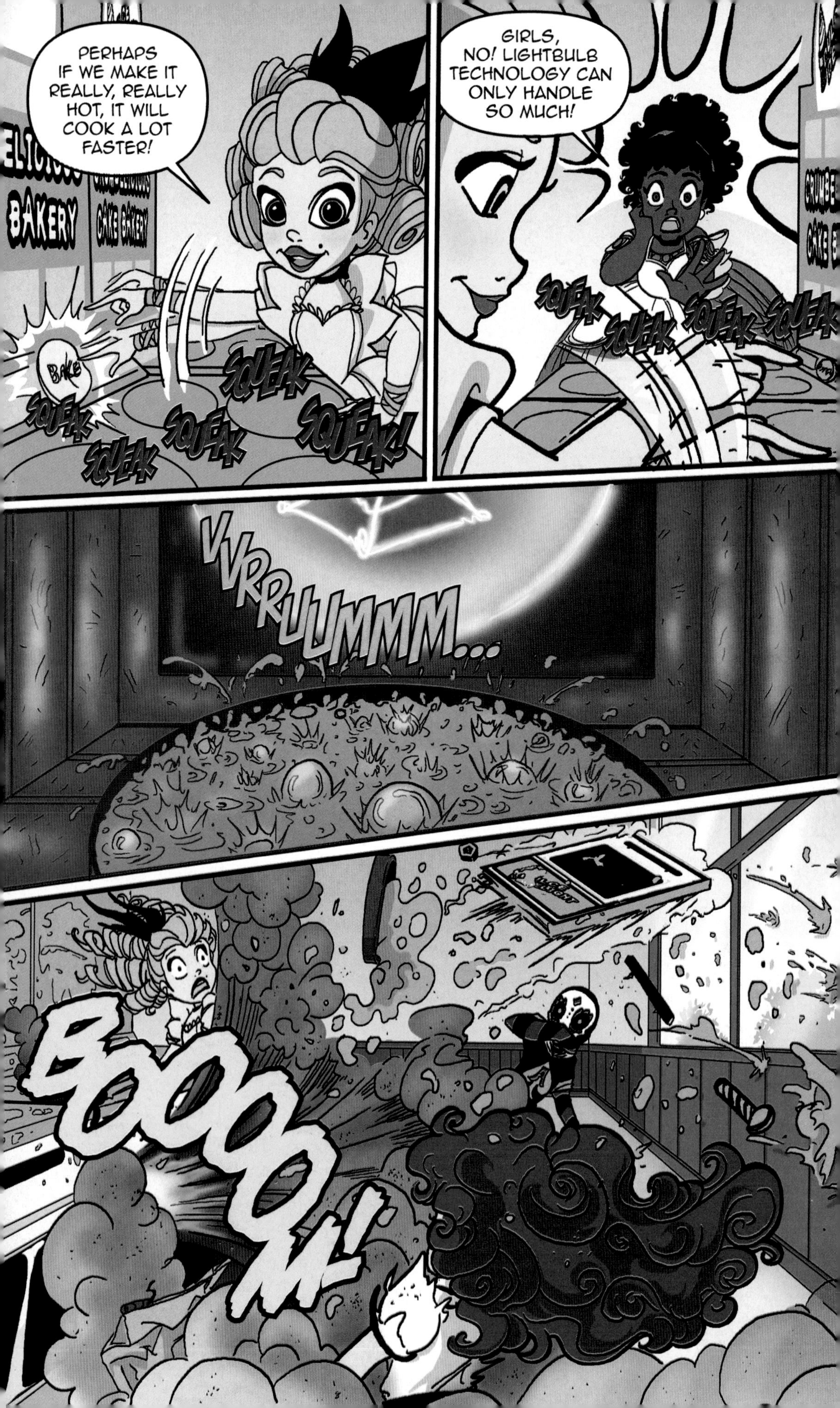
PERHAPS IF WE MAKE IT REALLY, REALLY HOT, IT WILL COOK A LOT FASTER!
BAKERY
CAKE BAKERY
BAKE
SQUEAK
SQUEAK
SQUEAK
SQUEAK
SQUEAK!
GIRLS, NO! LIGHTBULB TECHNOLOGY CAN ONLY HANDLE SO MUCH!
SQUEAK
SQUEAK
SQUEAK
SQUEAK
VVRRUUMMM...
BOOOOM!

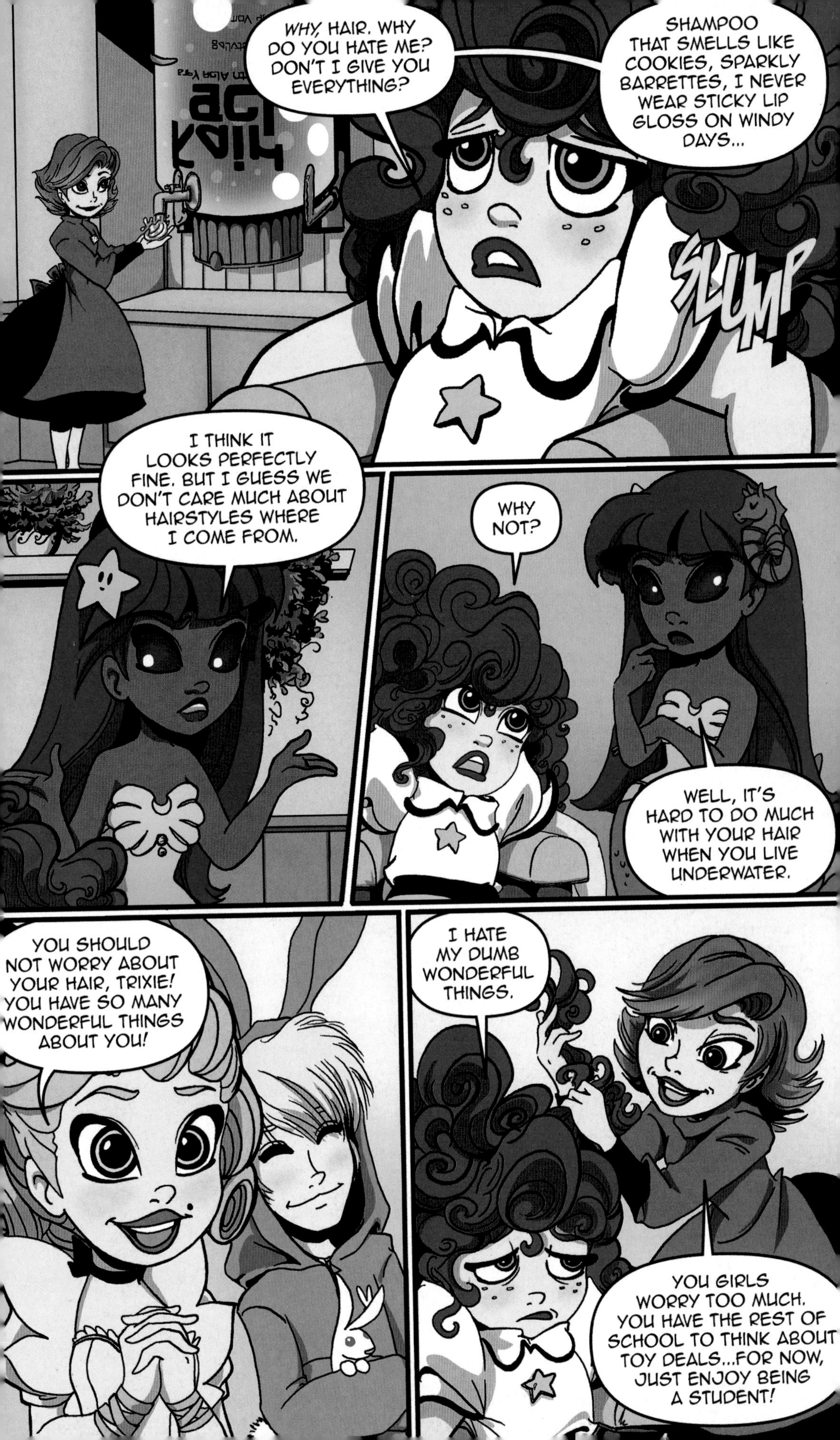
WHY, HAIR. WHY DO YOU HATE ME? DON'T I GIVE YOU EVERYTHING?
SHAMPOO THAT SMELLS LIKE COOKIES, SPARKLY BARRETTES, I NEVER WEAR STICKY LIP GLOSS ON WINDY DAYS...
SLUMP
I THINK IT LOOKS PERFECTLY FINE. BUT I GUESS WE DON'T CARE MUCH ABOUT HAIRSTYLES WHERE I COME FROM.
WHY NOT?
WELL, IT'S HARD TO DO MUCH WITH YOUR HAIR WHEN YOU LIVE UNDERWATER.
YOU SHOULD NOT WORRY ABOUT YOUR HAIR, TRIXIE! YOU HAVE SO MANY WONDERFUL THINGS ABOUT YOU!
I HATE MY DUMB WONDERFUL THINGS.
YOU GIRLS WORRY TOO MUCH. YOU HAVE THE REST OF SCHOOL TO THINK ABOUT TOY DEALS...FOR NOW, JUST ENJOY BEING A STUDENT!

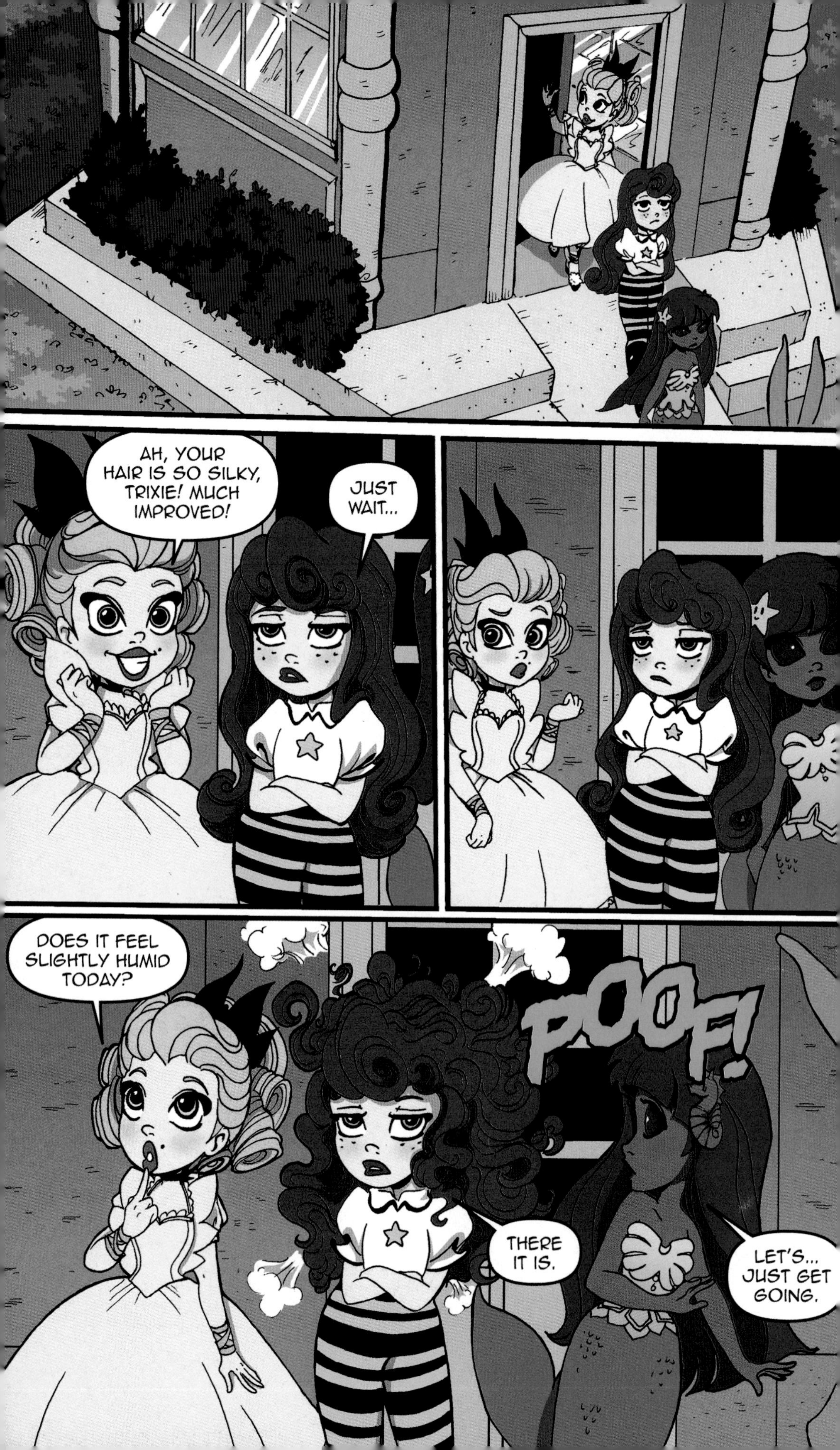
AH, YOUR HAIR IS SO SILKY, TRIXIE! MUCH IMPROVED!
JUST WAIT...
DOES IT FEEL SLIGHTLY HUMID TODAY?
POOF!
THERE IT IS.
LET'S... JUST GET GOING.

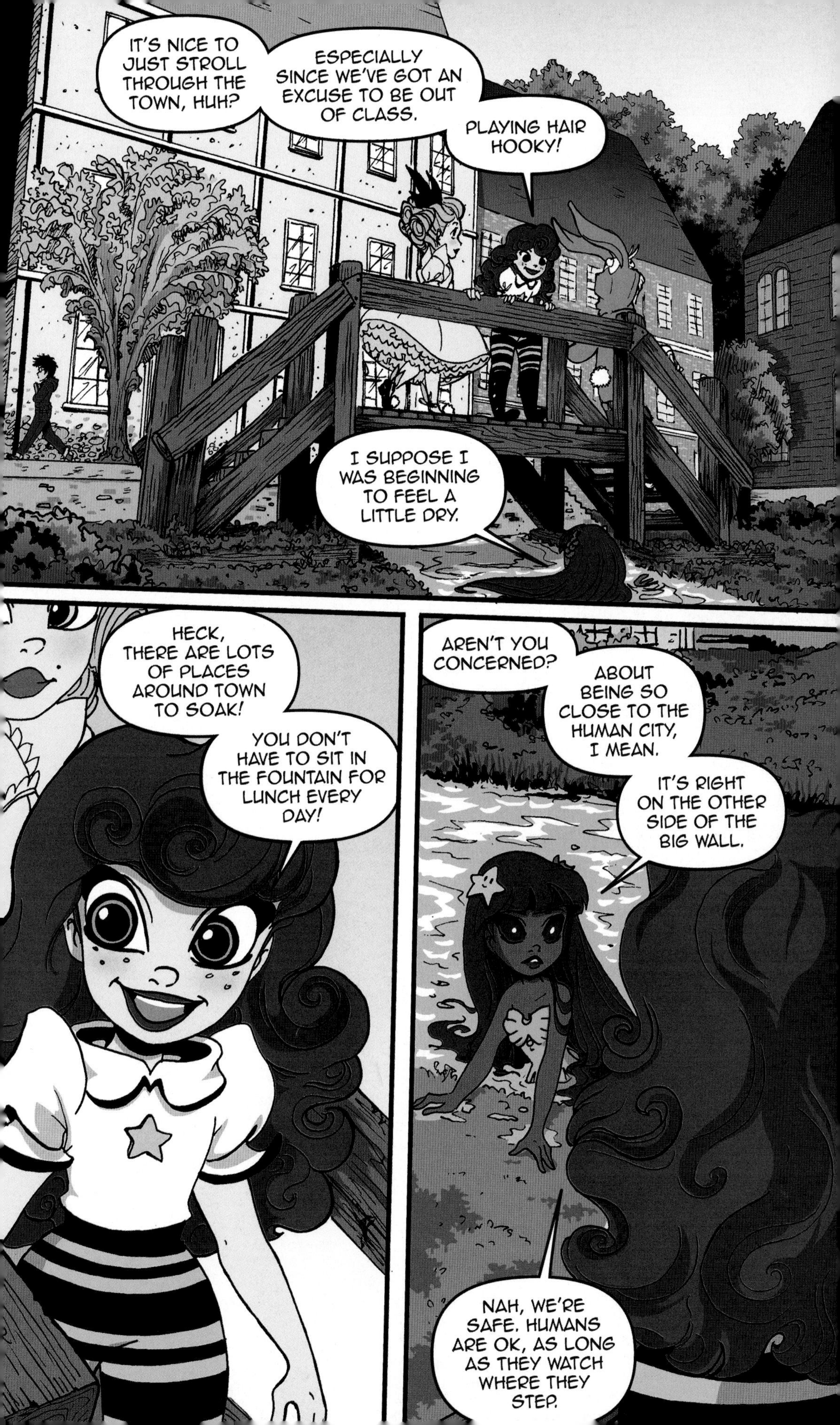
IT'S NICE TO JUST STROLL THROUGH THE TOWN, HUH?
ESPECIALLY SINCE WE'VE GOT AN EXCUSE TO BE OUT OF CLASS.
PLAYING HAIR HOOKY!
I SUPPOSE I WAS BEGINNING TO FEEL A LITTLE DRY.
HECK, THERE ARE LOTS OF PLACES AROUND TOWN TO SOAK!
YOU DON'T HAVE TO SIT IN THE FOUNTAIN FOR LUNCH EVERY DAY!
AREN'T YOU CONCERNED?
ABOUT BEING SO CLOSE TO THE HUMAN CITY, I MEAN.
IT'S RIGHT ON THE OTHER SIDE OF THE BIG WALL.
NAH, WE'RE SAFE. HUMANS ARE OK, AS LONG AS THEY WATCH WHERE THEY STEP.

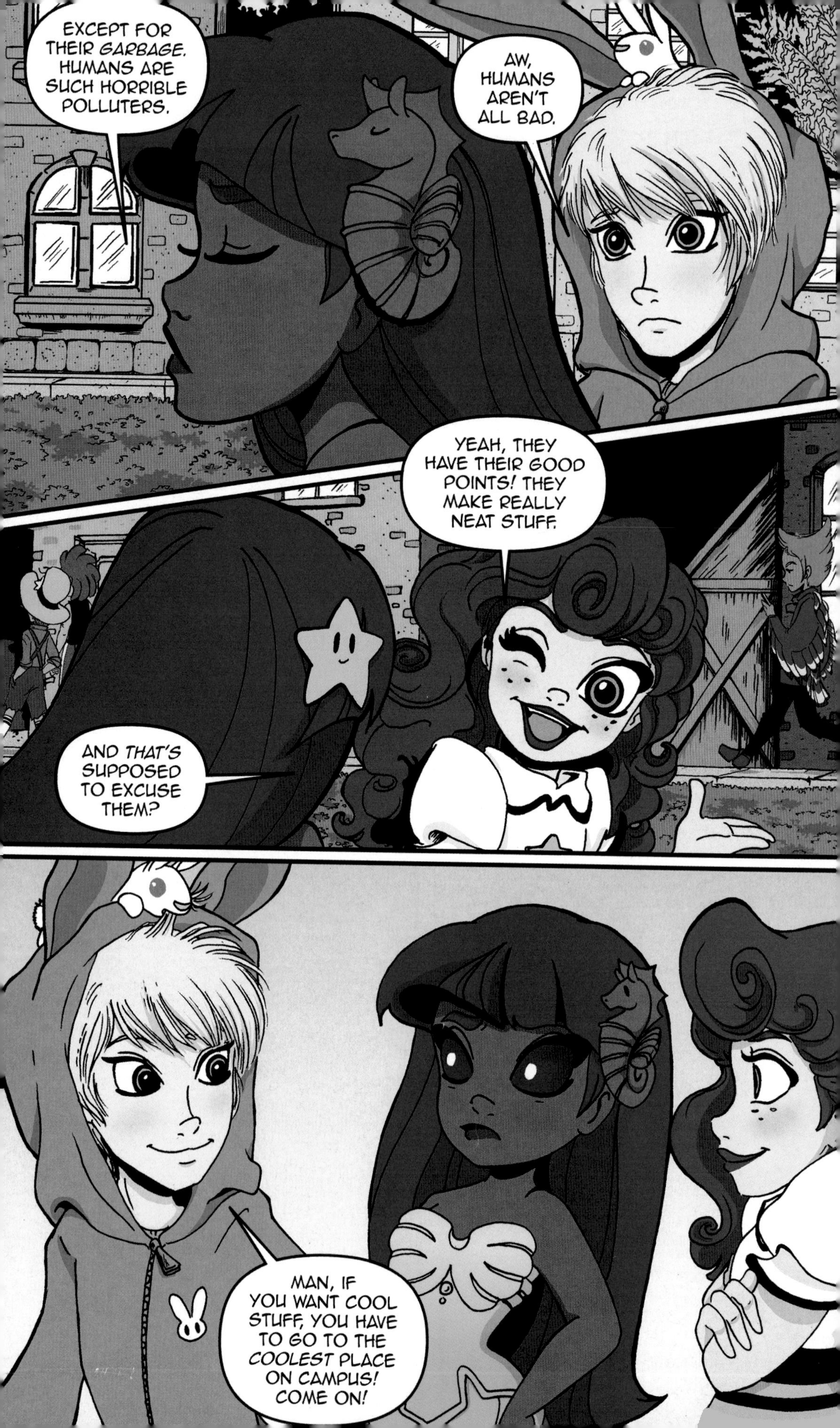
EXCEPT FOR THEIR *GARBAGE*. HUMANS ARE SUCH HORRIBLE POLLUTERS.
AW, HUMANS AREN'T ALL BAD.
YEAH, THEY HAVE THEIR GOOD POINTS! THEY MAKE REALLY NEAT STUFF.
AND *THAT'S* SUPPOSED TO EXCUSE THEM?
MAN, IF YOU WANT COOL STUFF, YOU HAVE TO GO TO THE *COOLEST* PLACE ON CAMPUS! COME ON!

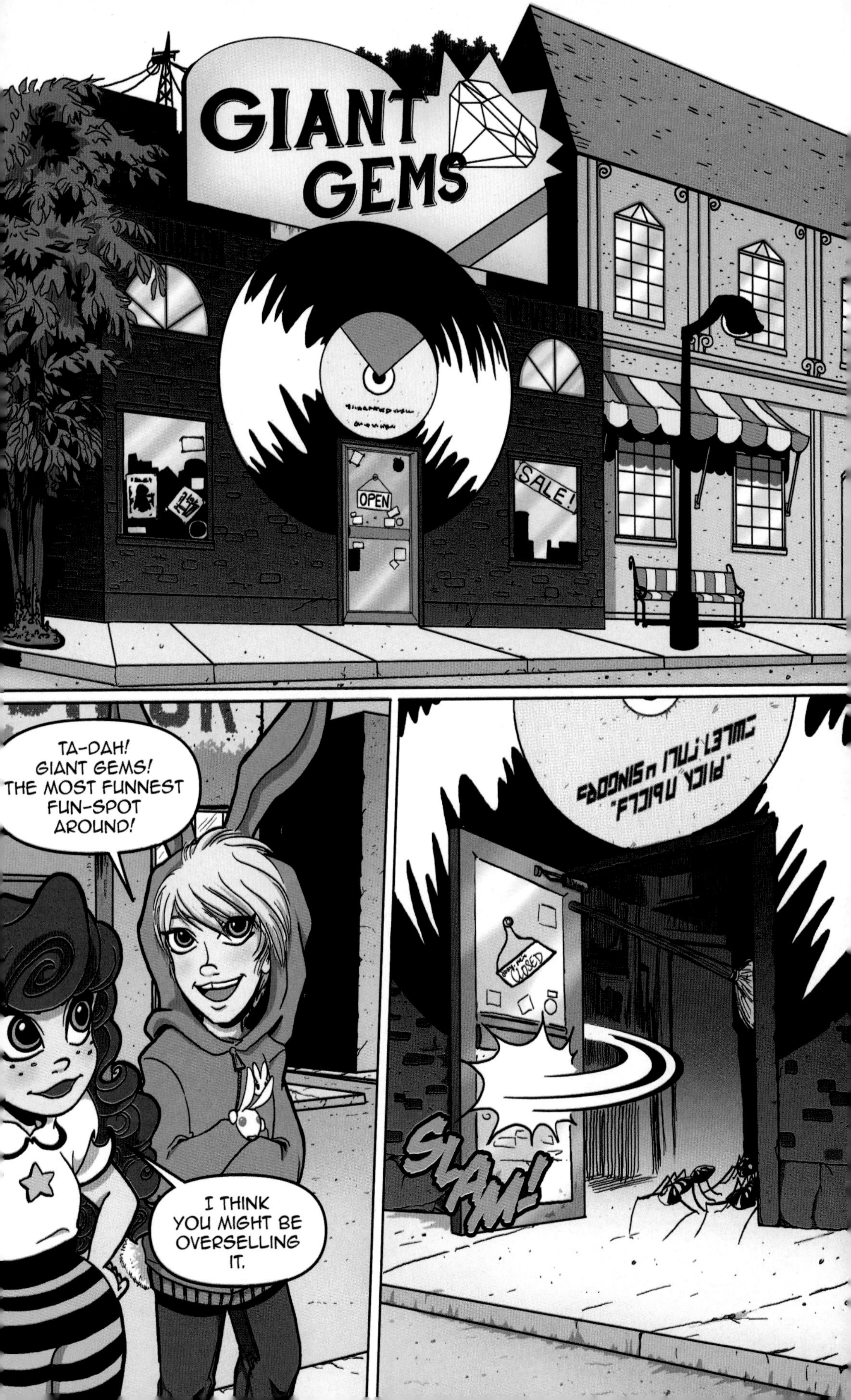
GIANT GEMS
OPEN
SALE!
TA-DAH! GIANT GEMS! THE MOST FUNNEST FUN-SPOT AROUND!
I THINK YOU MIGHT BE OVERSELLING IT.
CLOSED
SLAM!

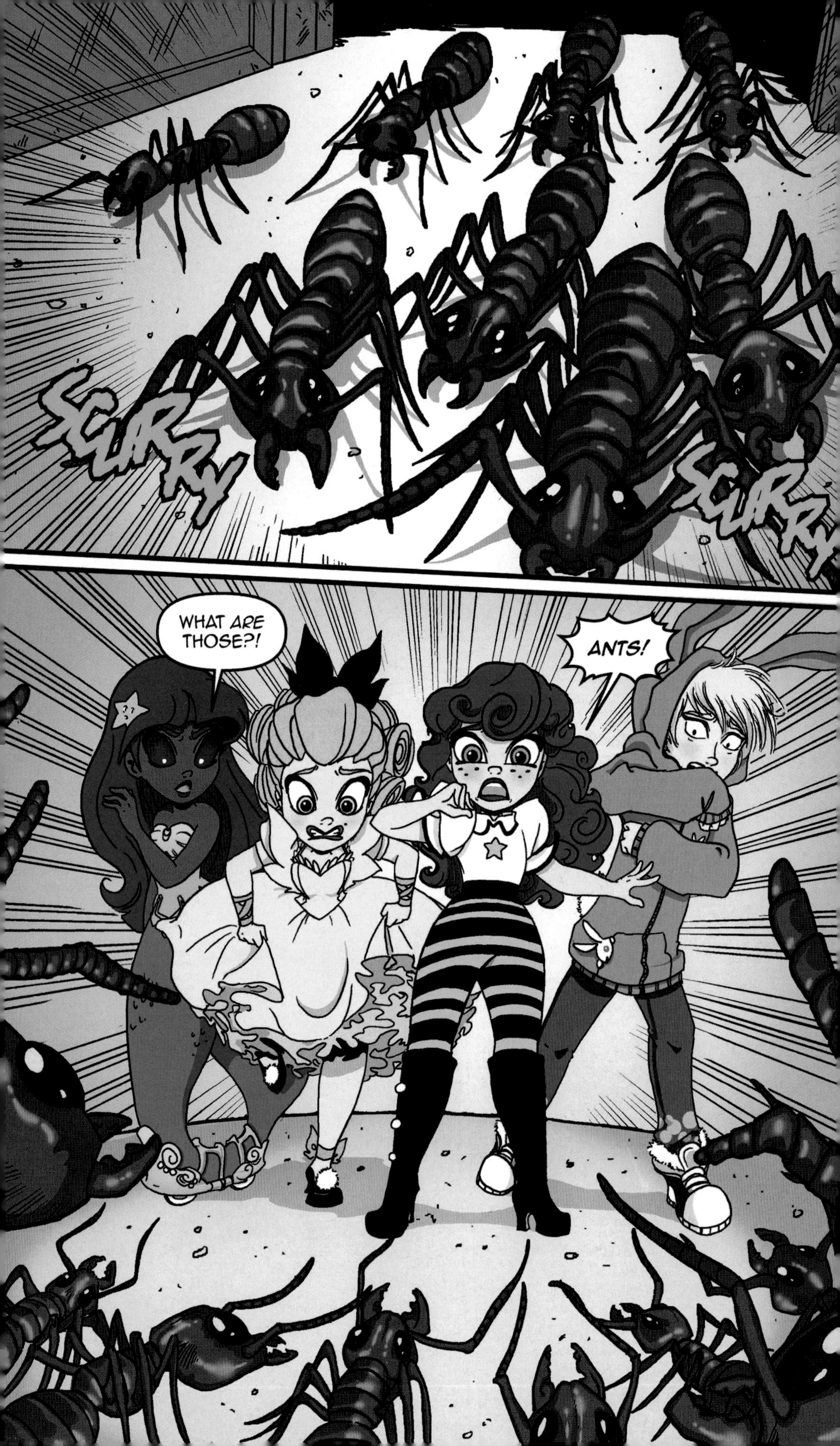
SCURRY
SCURRY
WHAT ARE THOSE?!
ANTS!

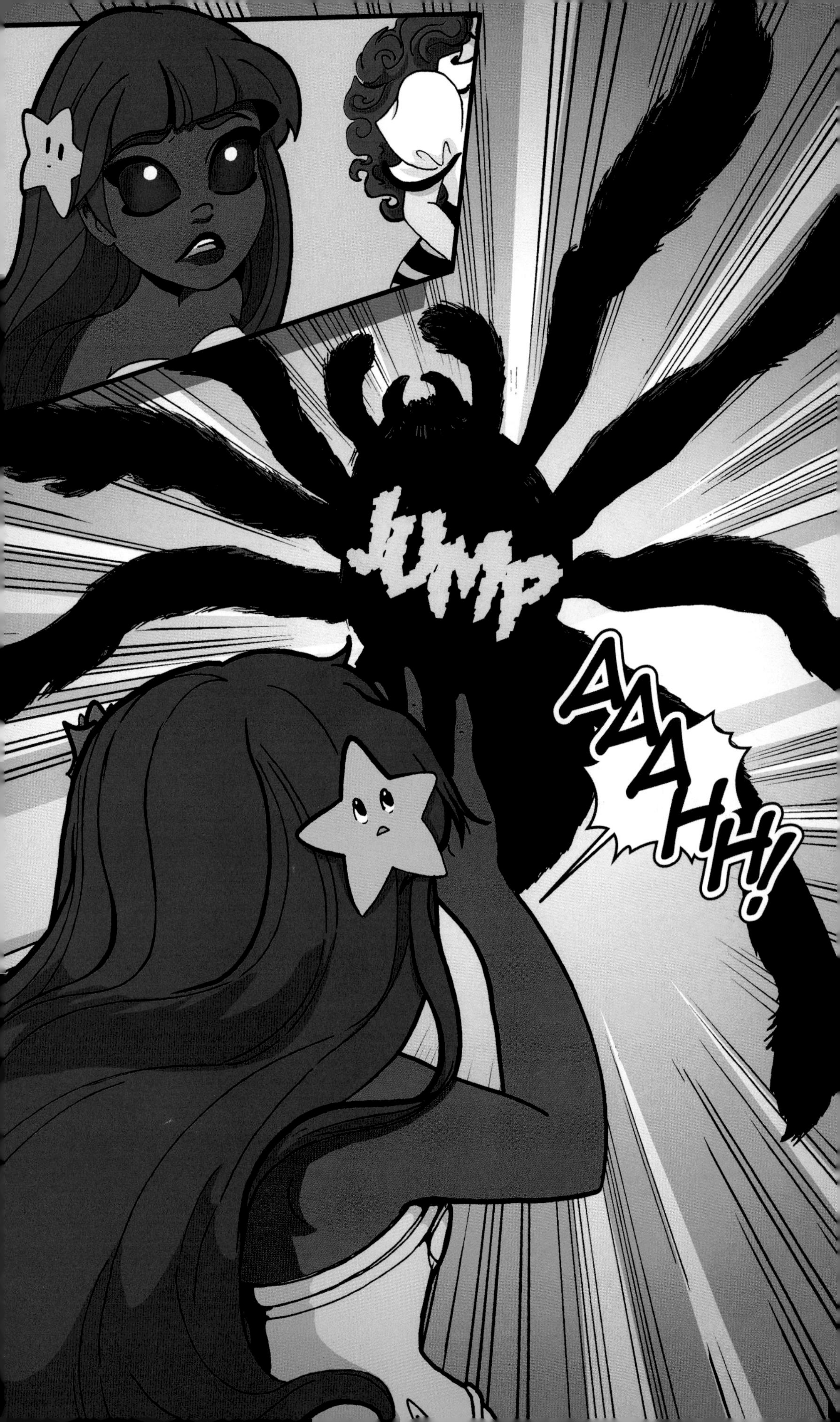
JUMP
AAAHH!

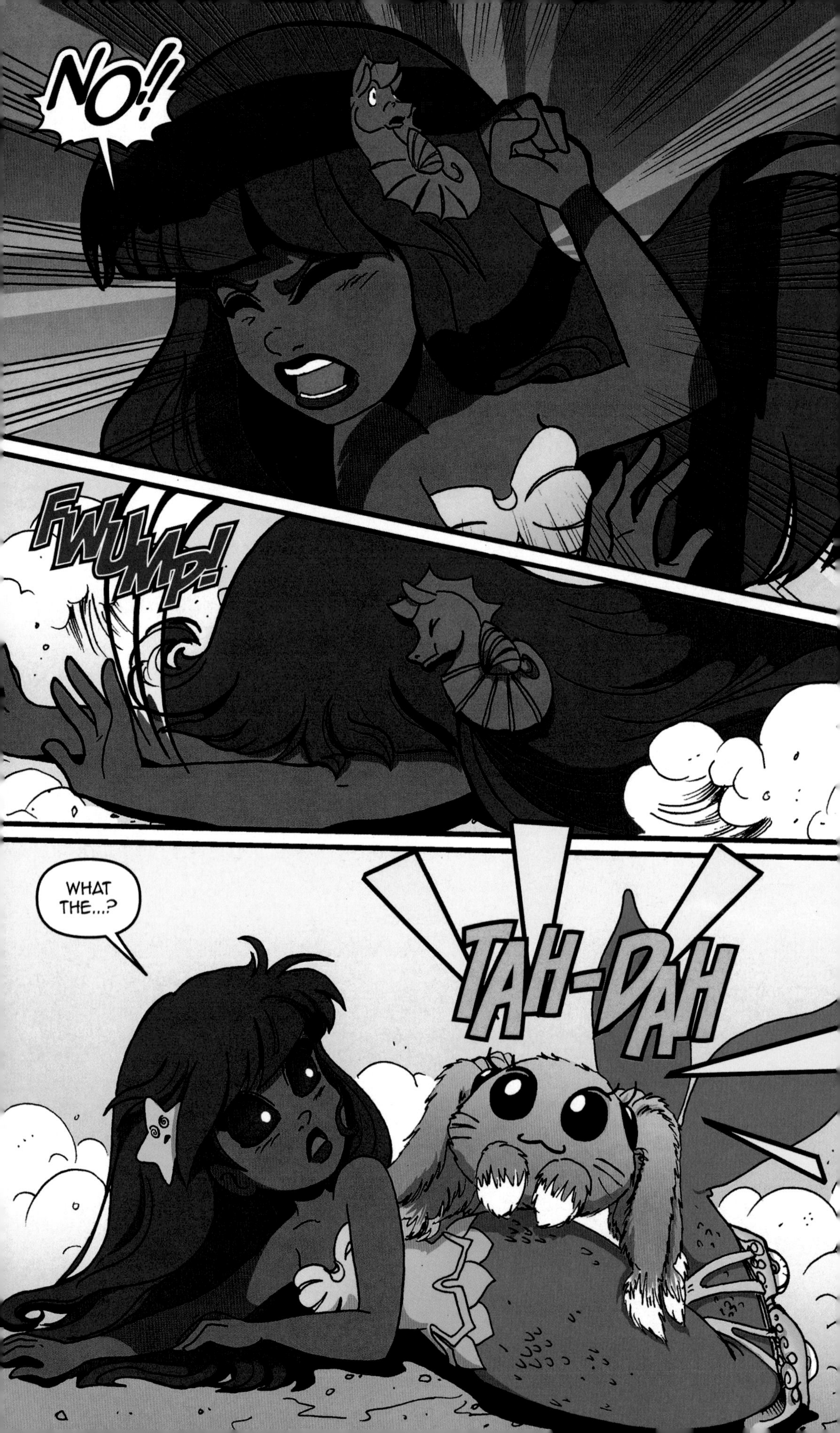
NO!!
FWUMP!
WHAT THE...?
TAH-DAH

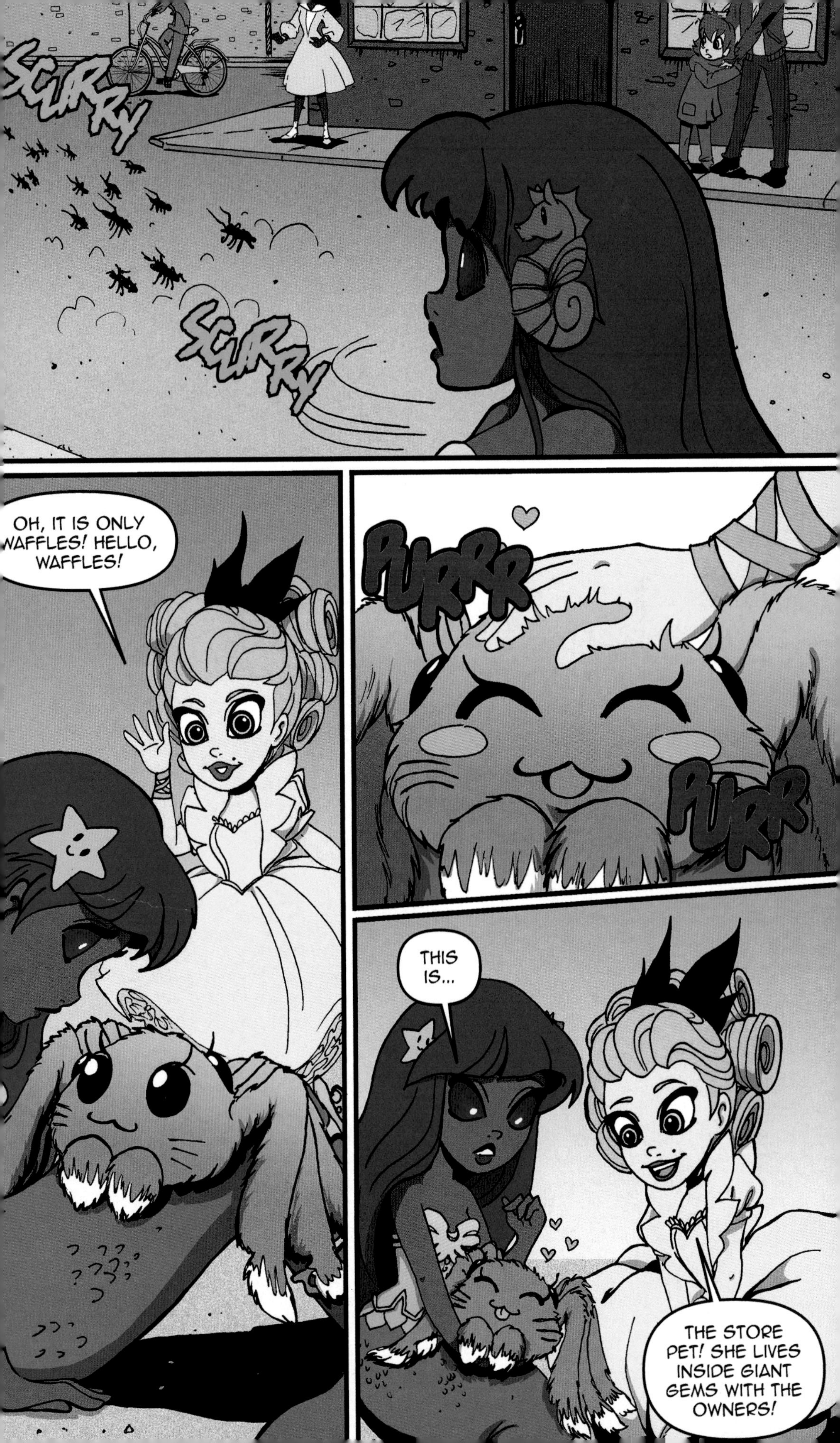
SCURRY
SCURRY
OH, IT IS ONLY WAFFLES! HELLO, WAFFLES!
PURRR
PURR
THIS IS...
THE STORE PET! SHE LIVES INSIDE GIANT GEMS WITH THE OWNERS!

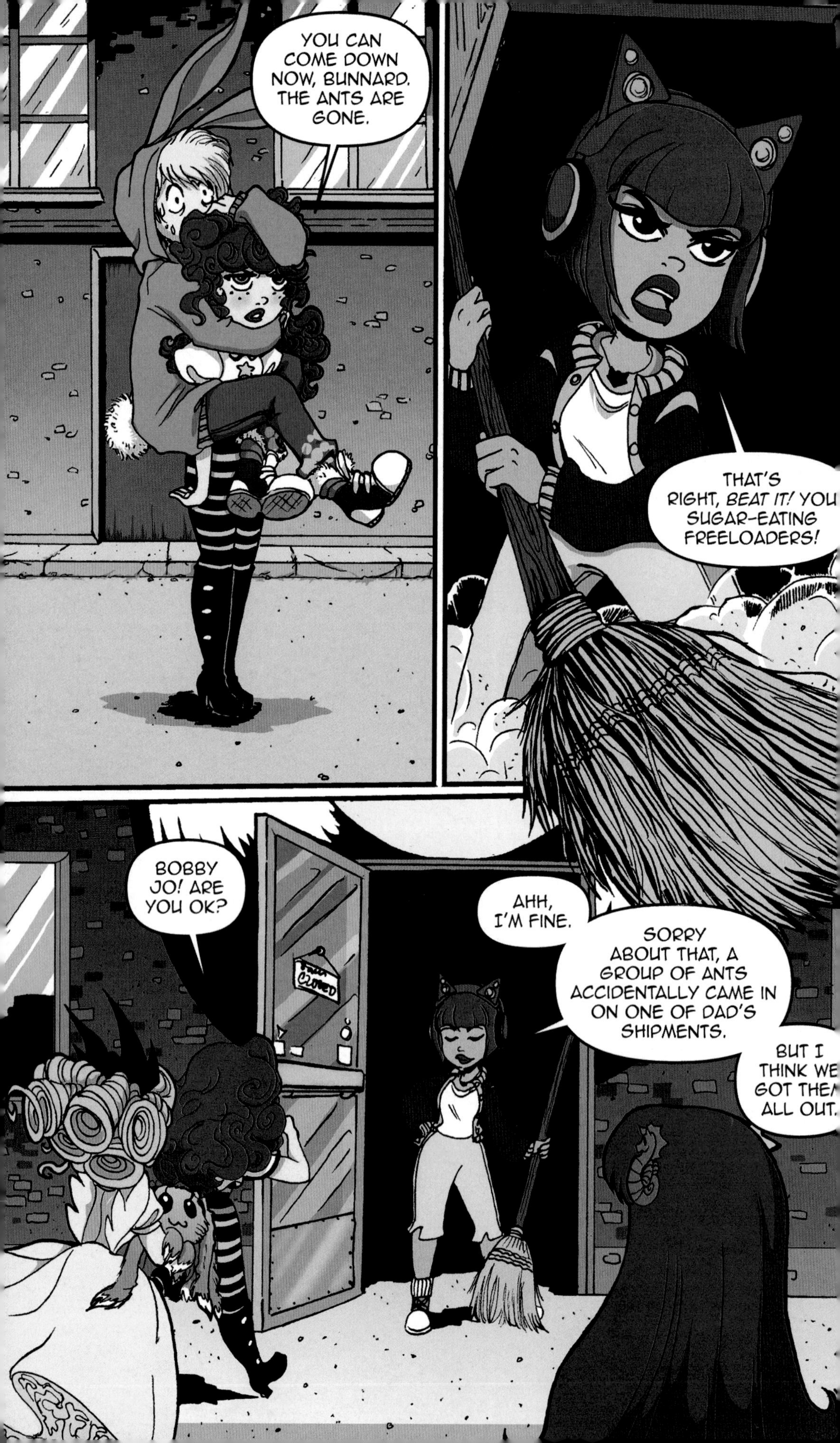
YOU CAN COME DOWN NOW, BUNNARD. THE ANTS ARE GONE.
THAT'S RIGHT, *BEAT IT!* YOU SUGAR-EATING FREELOADERS!
BOBBY JO! ARE YOU OK?
AHH, I'M FINE.
SORRY ABOUT THAT, A GROUP OF ANTS ACCIDENTALLY CAME IN ON ONE OF DAD'S SHIPMENTS.
BUT I THINK WE GOT THEM ALL OUT.
CLOSED

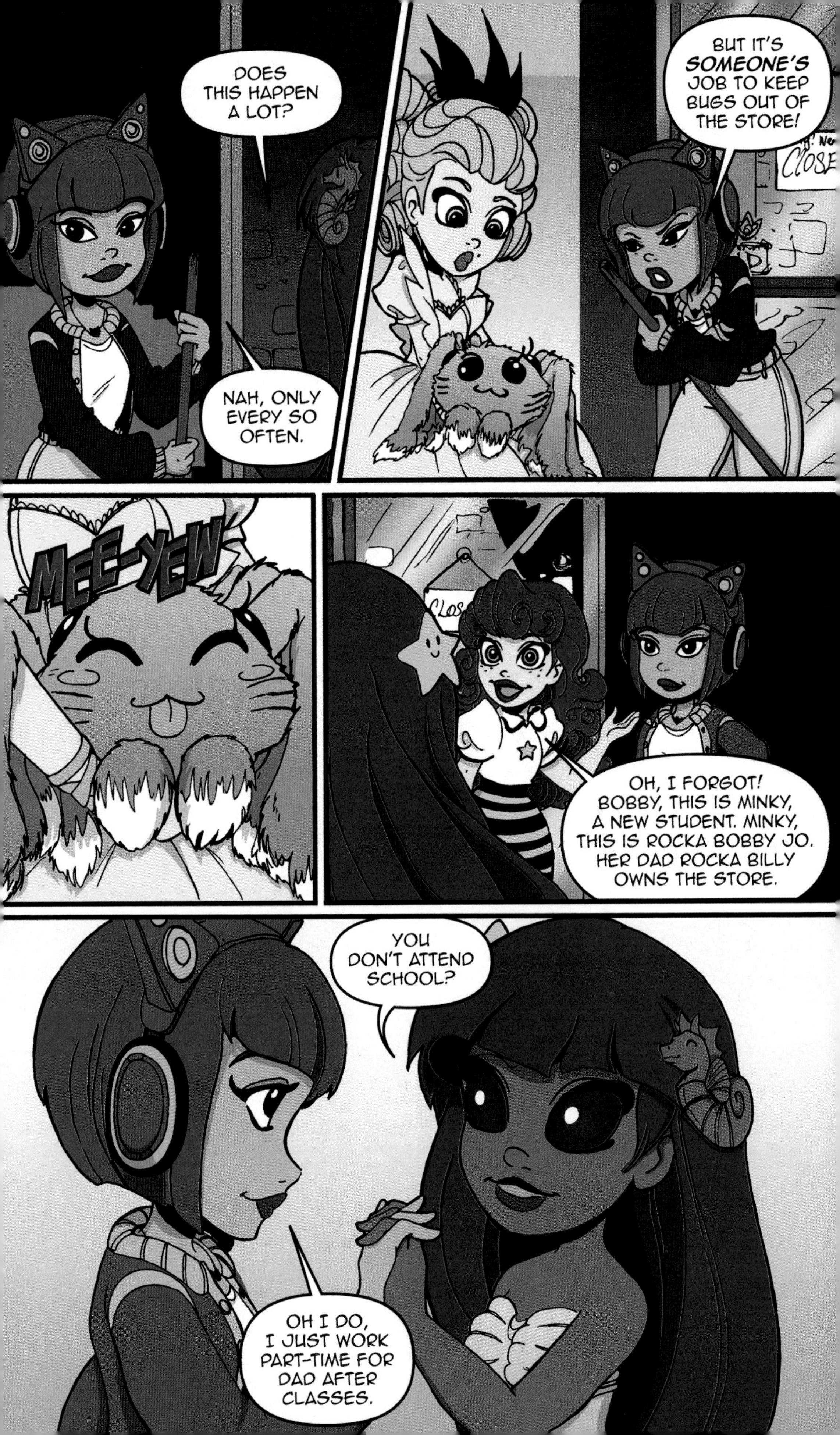

DOES THIS HAPPEN A LOT?
NAH, ONLY EVERY SO OFTEN.
BUT IT'S SOMEONE'S JOB TO KEEP BUGS OUT OF THE STORE!
CLOSE
MEE-YEW
OH, I FORGOT! BOBBY, THIS IS MINKY, A NEW STUDENT. MINKY, THIS IS ROCKA BOBBY JO. HER DAD ROCKA BILLY OWNS THE STORE.
YOU DON'T ATTEND SCHOOL?
OH I DO, I JUST WORK PART-TIME FOR DAD AFTER CLASSES.

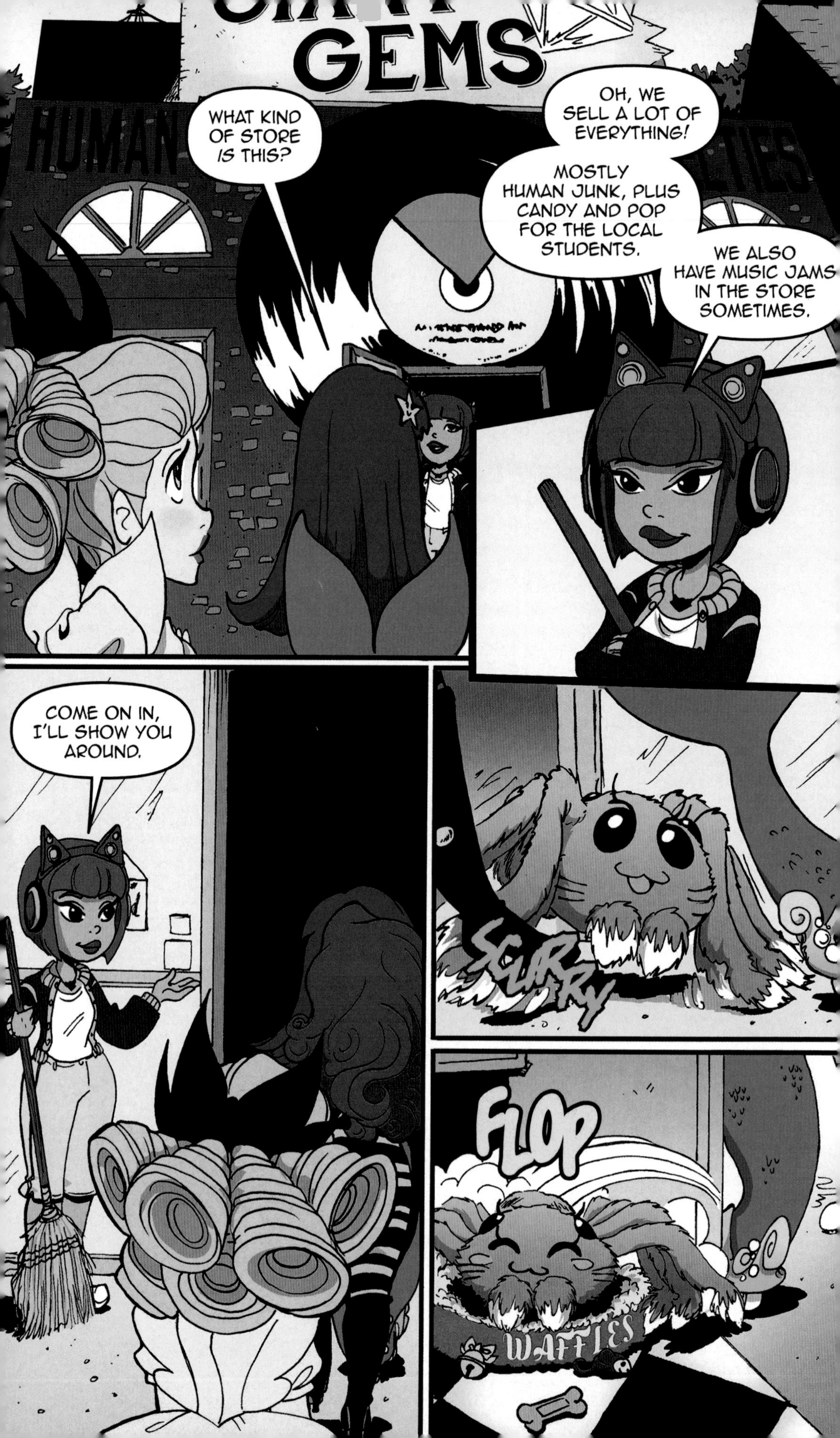
GEMS
HUMAN
WHAT KIND OF STORE IS THIS?
OH, WE SELL A LOT OF EVERYTHING!
MOSTLY HUMAN JUNK, PLUS CANDY AND POP FOR THE LOCAL STUDENTS.
WE ALSO HAVE MUSIC JAMS IN THE STORE SOMETIMES.
COME ON IN, I'LL SHOW YOU AROUND.
SCURRY
FLOP
WAFFLES

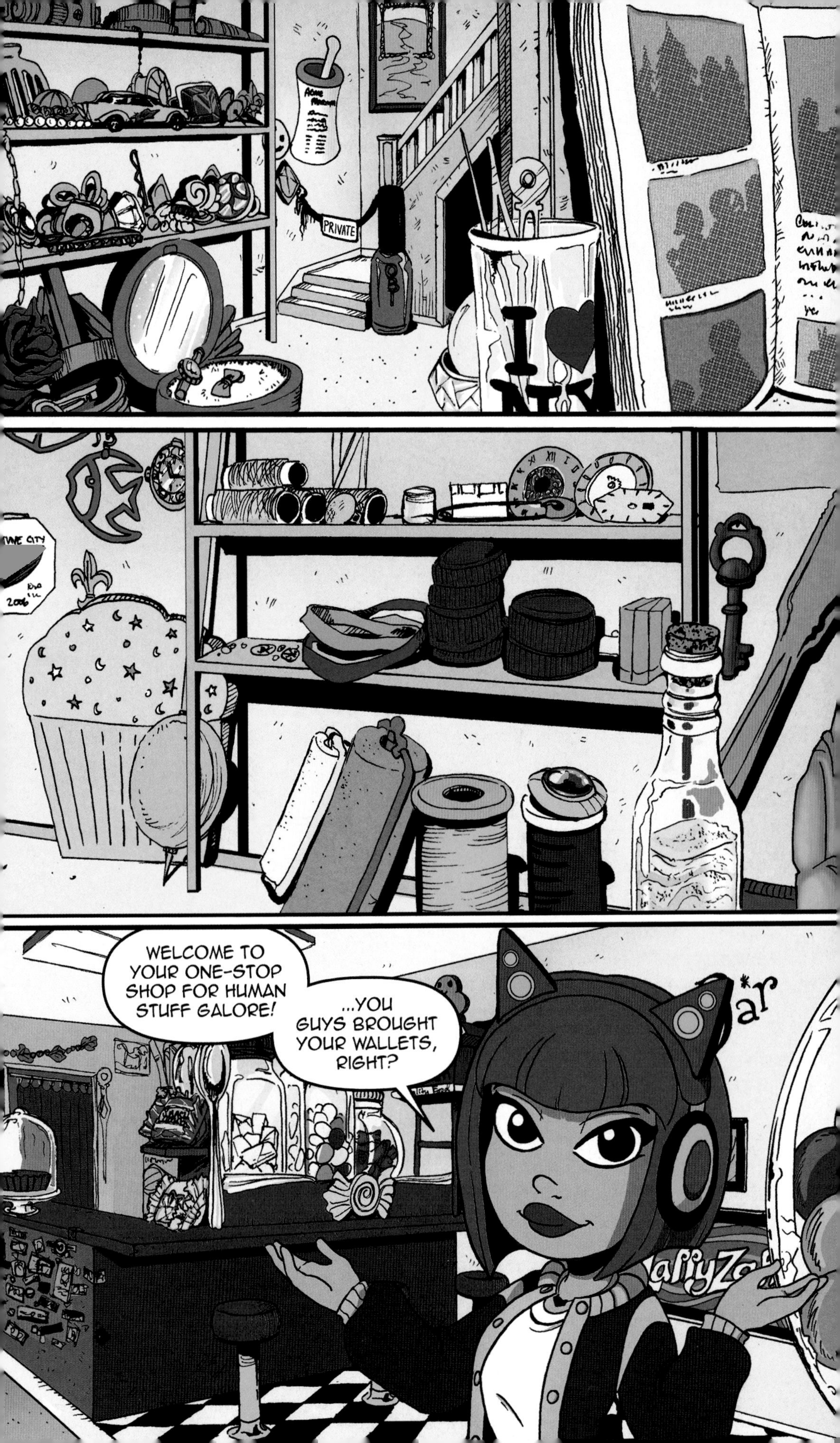
PRIVATE
I ♥ NY
WELCOME TO YOUR ONE-STOP SHOP FOR HUMAN STUFF GALORE!
...YOU GUYS BROUGHT YOUR WALLETS, RIGHT?

pages in progress

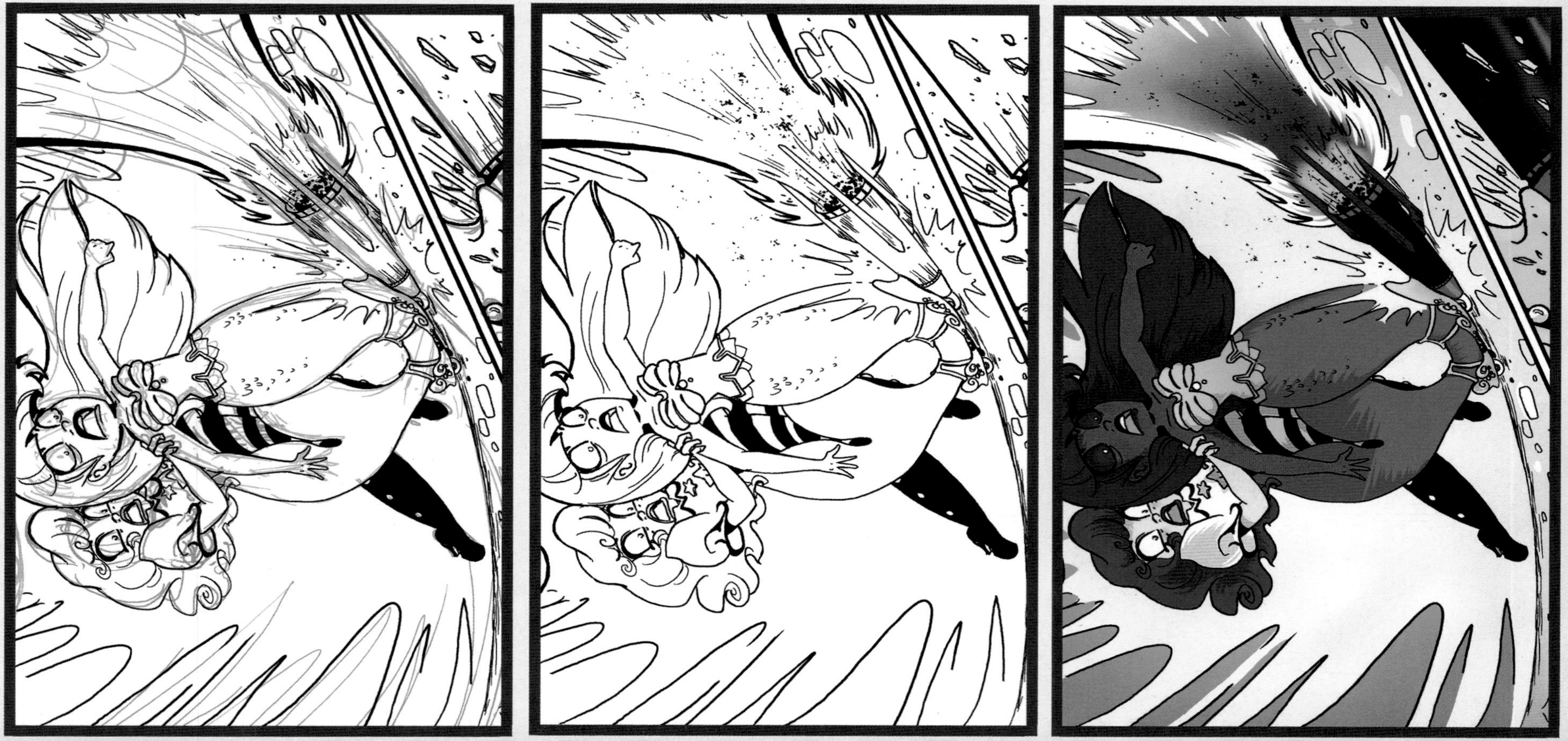

GIANTS

PART TWO

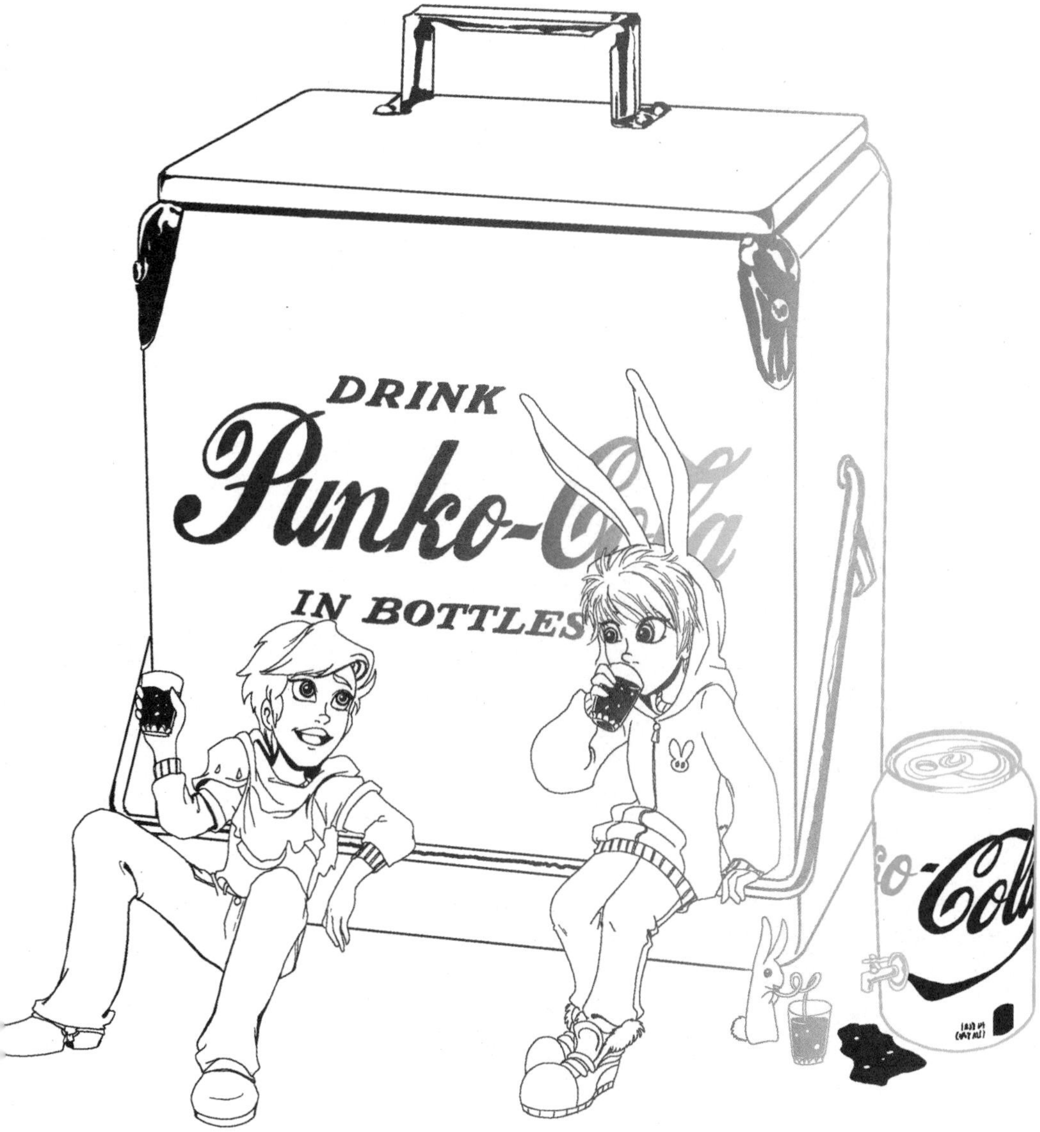
DRINK
Punko-Cola
IN BOTTLES
o-Cola

STORY AND ART BY MARTY LEGROW

LETTERING
Justin Birch

BOBBY JO BY
Kayla Cutillo

Bryan Seaton: Publisher/ CEO • Shawn Gabborin: Editor In Chief • Jason Martin: Publisher-Danger Zone • Nicole D'Andria: Marketing Director/Editor
Danielle Davison: Executive Administrator • Chad Cicconi: Action Lawyer • Shawn Pryor: President of Creator Relations

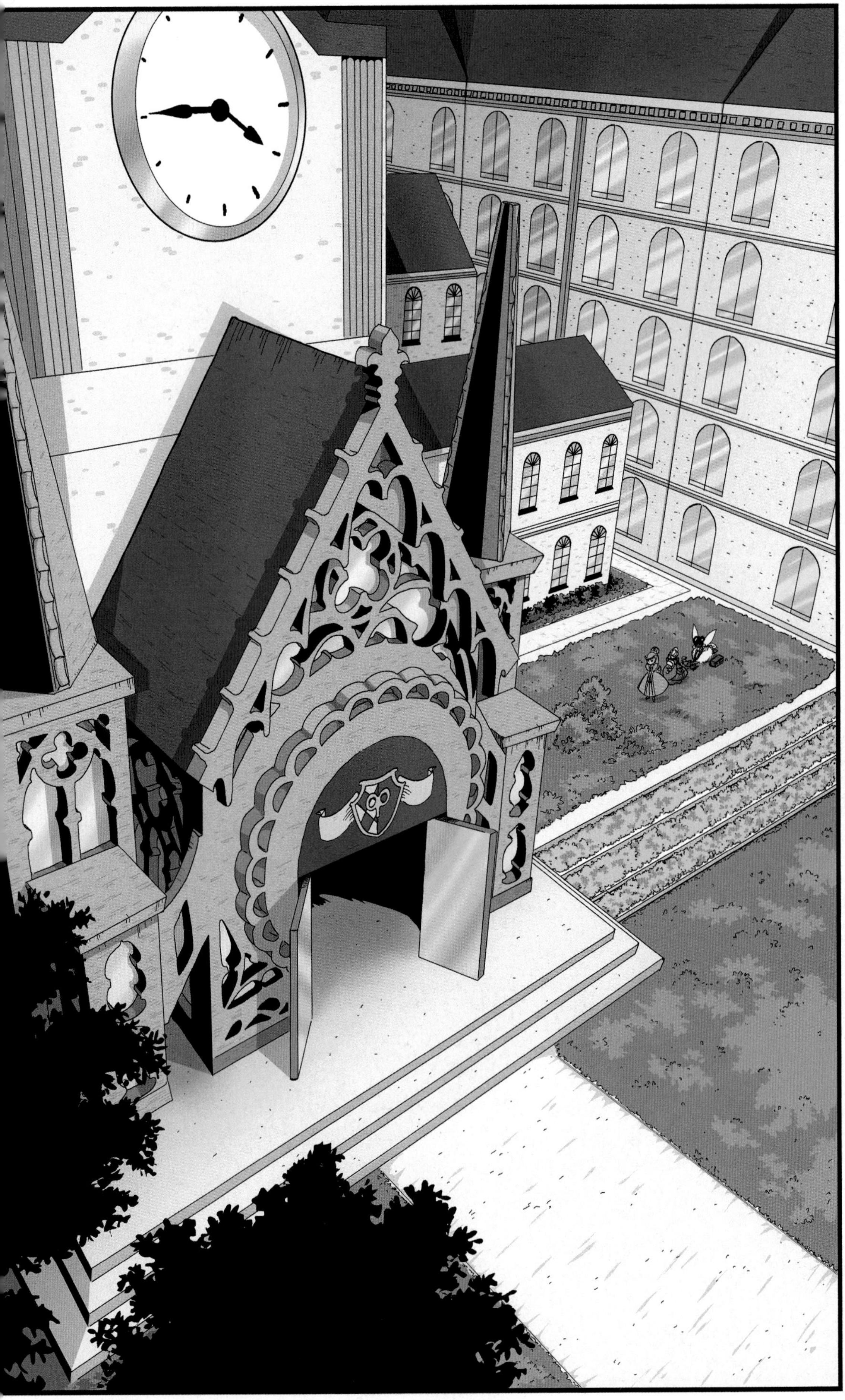

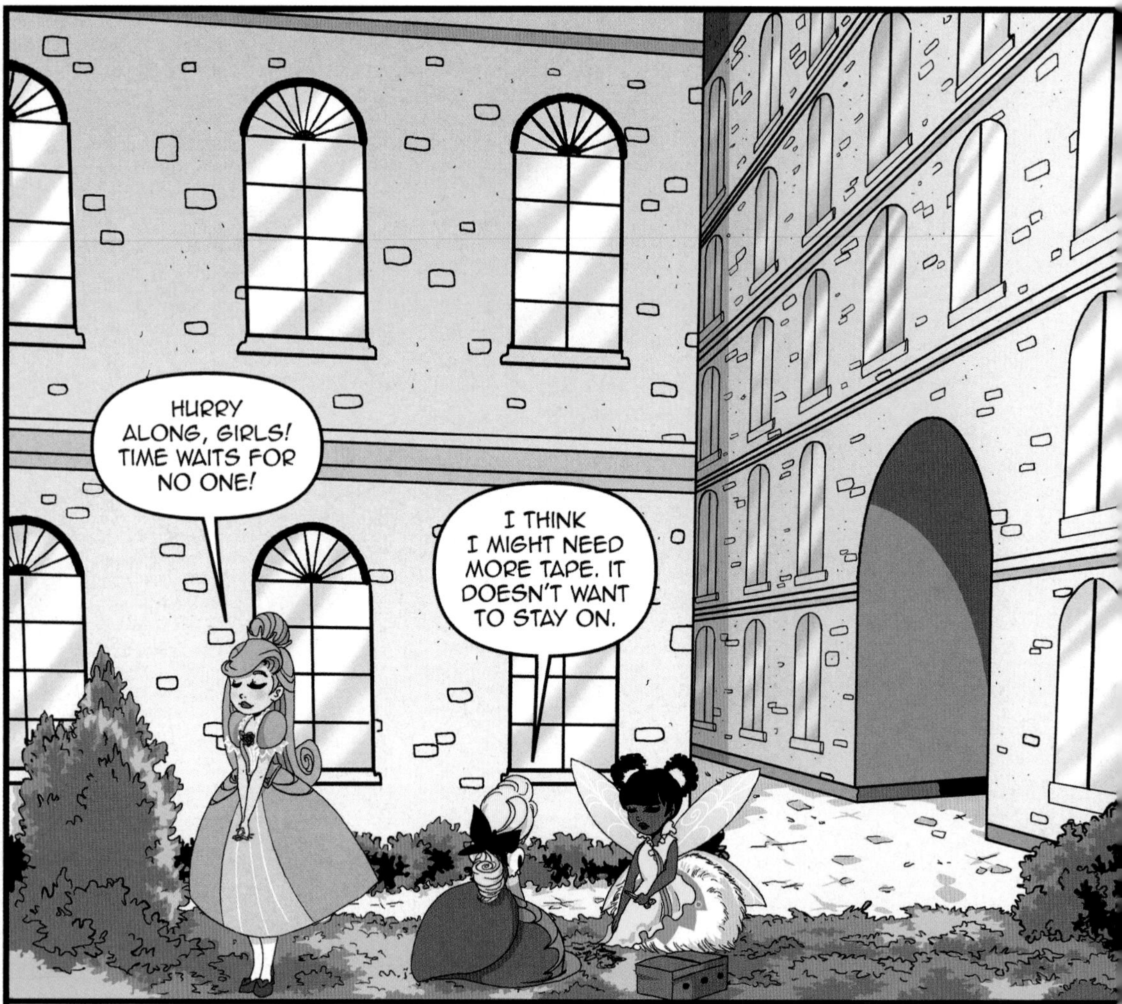
HURRY ALONG, GIRLS! TIME WAITS FOR NO ONE!
I THINK I MIGHT NEED MORE TAPE. IT DOESN'T WANT TO STAY ON.

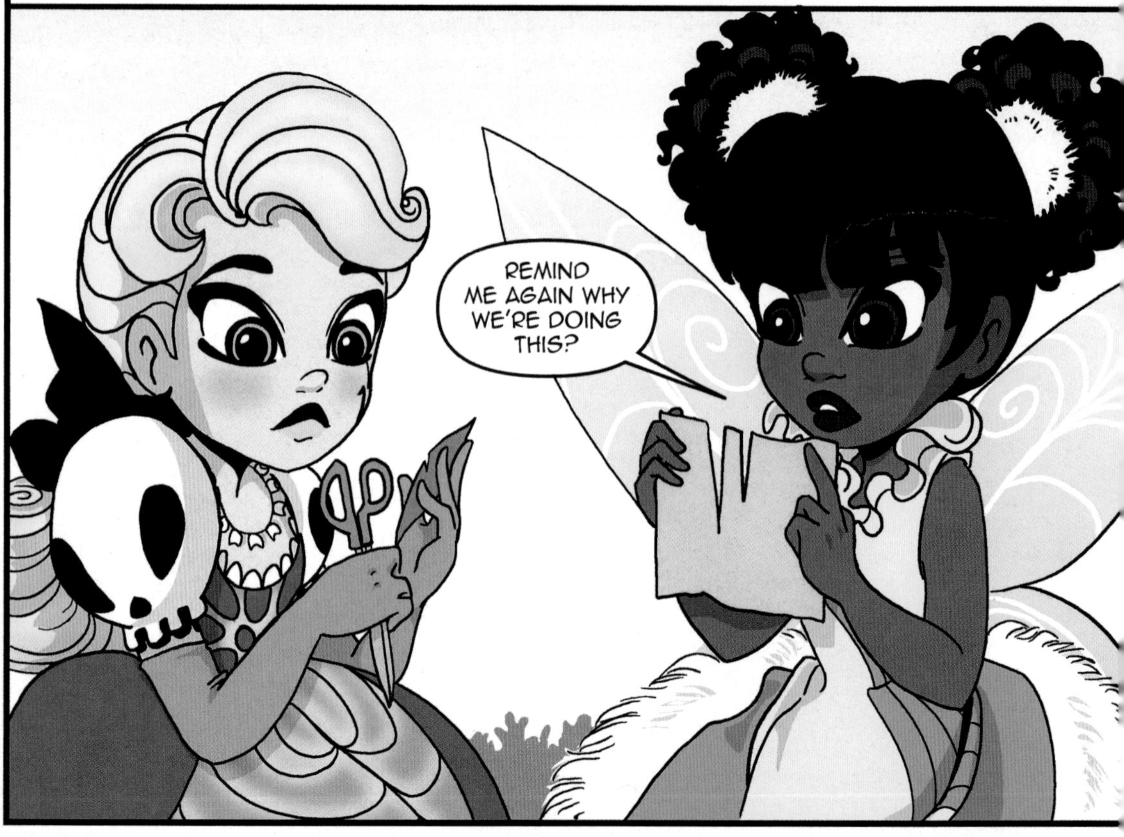
REMIND ME AGAIN WHY WE'RE DOING THIS?

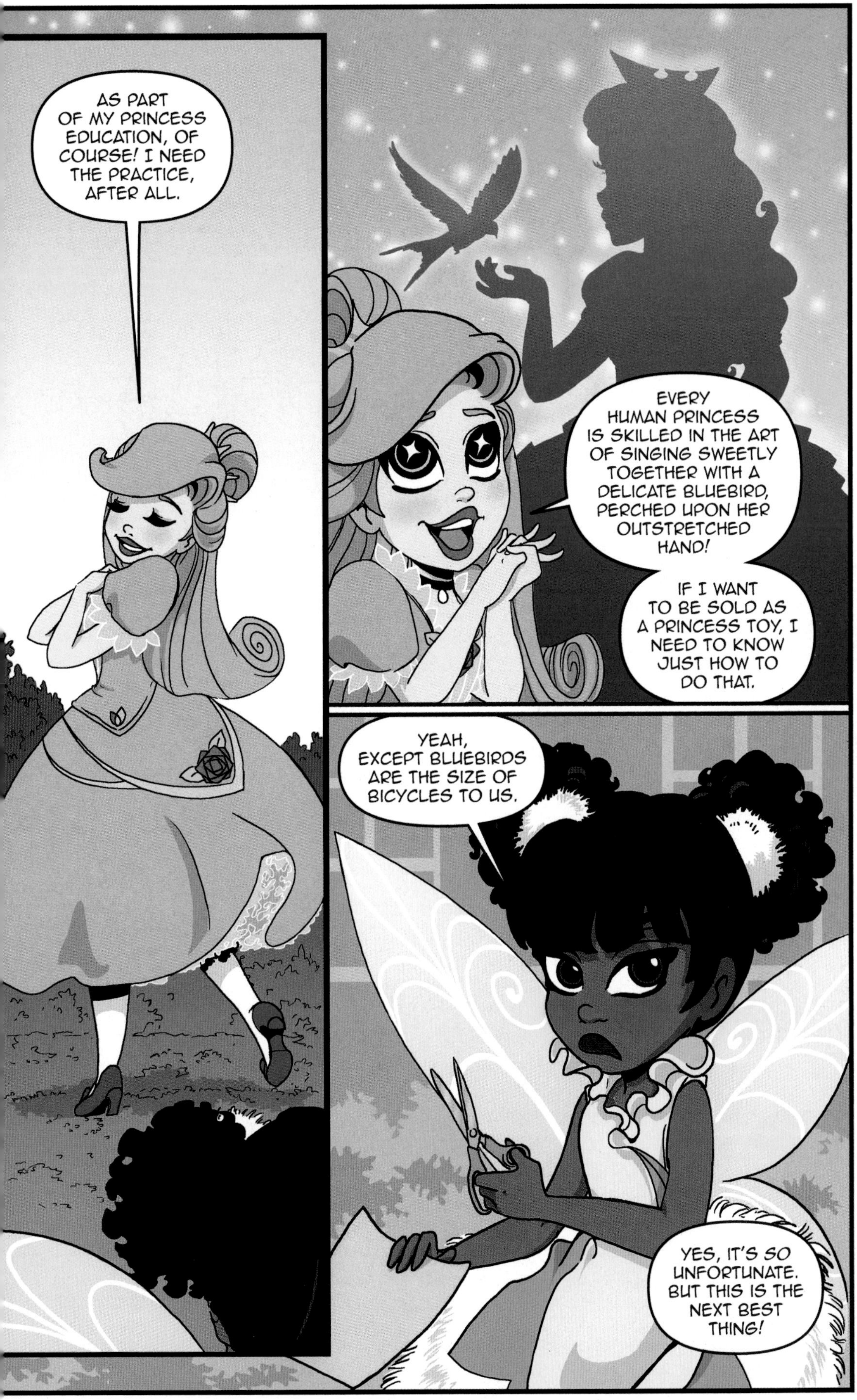
AS PART OF MY PRINCESS EDUCATION, OF COURSE! I NEED THE PRACTICE, AFTER ALL.
EVERY HUMAN PRINCESS IS SKILLED IN THE ART OF SINGING SWEETLY TOGETHER WITH A DELICATE BLUEBIRD, PERCHED UPON HER OUTSTRETCHED HAND!
IF I WANT TO BE SOLD AS A PRINCESS TOY, I NEED TO KNOW JUST HOW TO DO THAT.
YEAH, EXCEPT BLUEBIRDS ARE THE SIZE OF BICYCLES TO US.
YES, IT'S SO UNFORTUNATE. BUT THIS IS THE NEXT BEST THING!

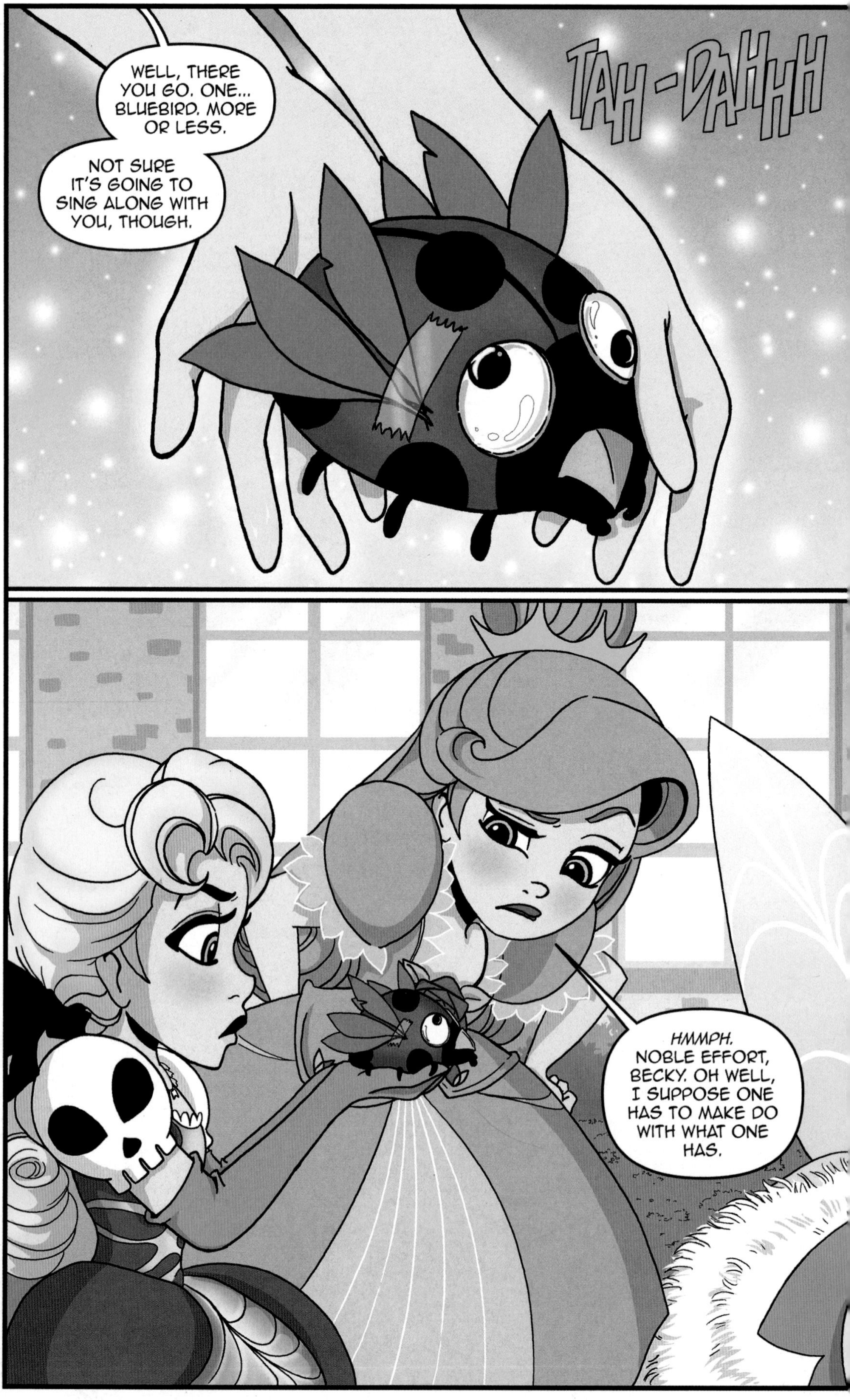
TAH-DAHHH
WELL, THERE YOU GO. ONE... BLUEBIRD. MORE OR LESS.
NOT SURE IT'S GOING TO SING ALONG WITH YOU, THOUGH.
HMMPH. NOBLE EFFORT, BECKY. OH WELL, I SUPPOSE ONE HAS TO MAKE DO WITH WHAT ONE HAS.

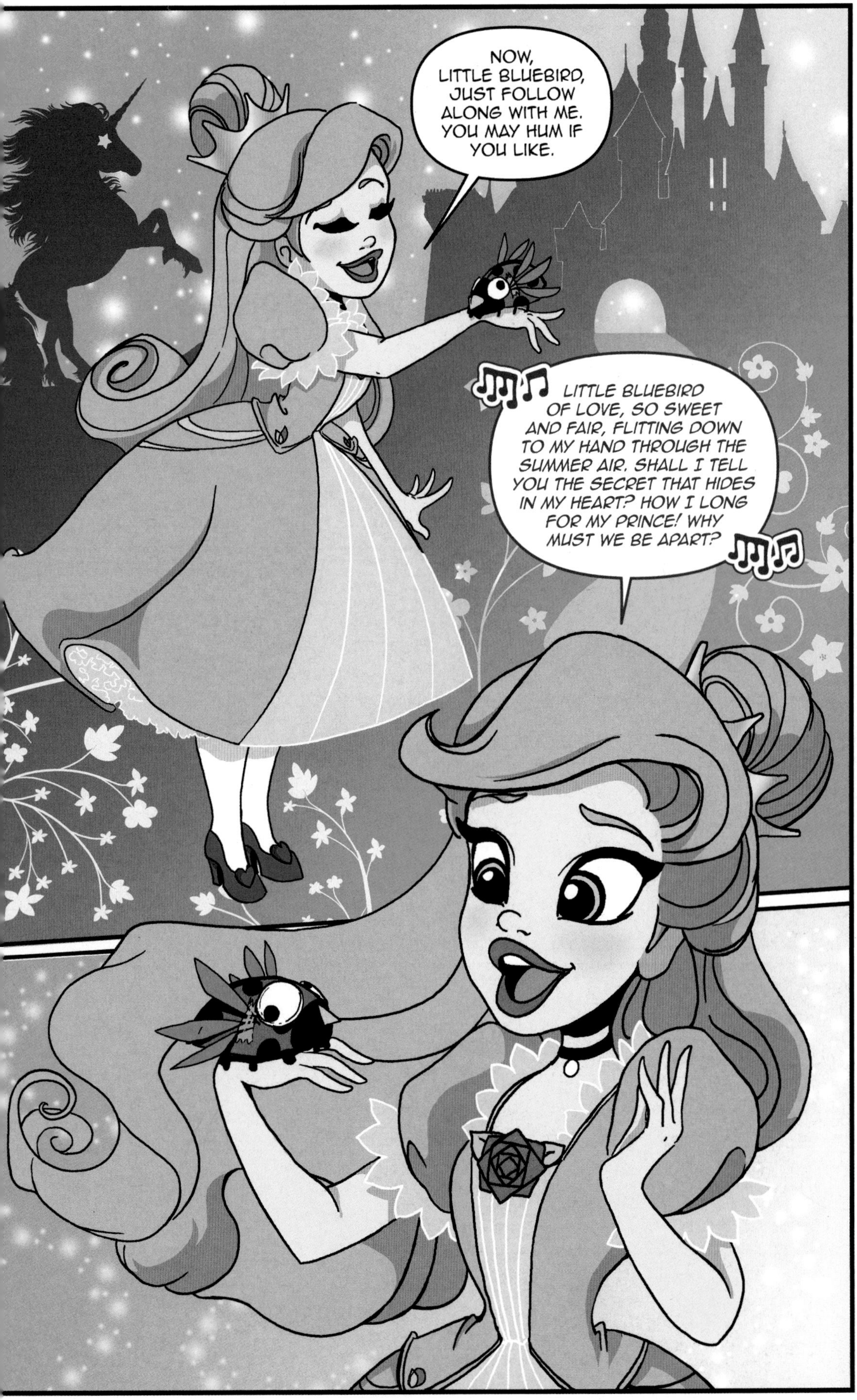
NOW, LITTLE BLUEBIRD, JUST FOLLOW ALONG WITH ME. YOU MAY HUM IF YOU LIKE.
LITTLE BLUEBIRD OF LOVE, SO SWEET AND FAIR, FLITTING DOWN TO MY HAND THROUGH THE SUMMER AIR. SHALL I TELL YOU THE SECRET THAT HIDES IN MY HEART? HOW I LONG FOR MY PRINCE! WHY MUST WE BE APART?

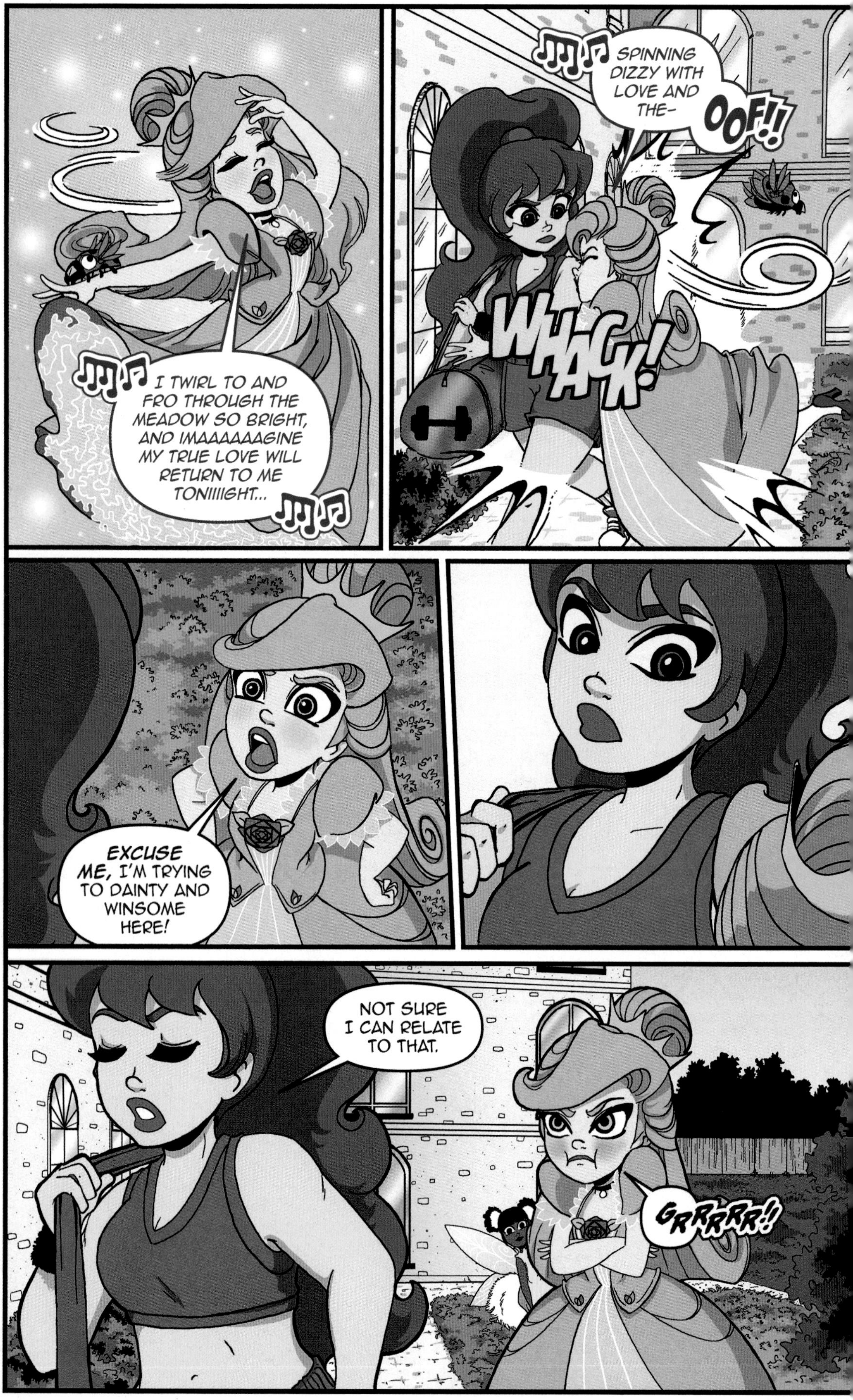
I TWIRL TO AND FRO THROUGH THE MEADOW SO BRIGHT, AND IMAAAAAAAGINE MY TRUE LOVE WILL RETURN TO ME TONIIIIGHT...
SPINNING DIZZY WITH LOVE AND THE-
OOF!!
WHACK!
EXCUSE ME, I'M TRYING TO DAINTY AND WINSOME HERE!
NOT SURE I CAN RELATE TO THAT.
GRRRRR!!

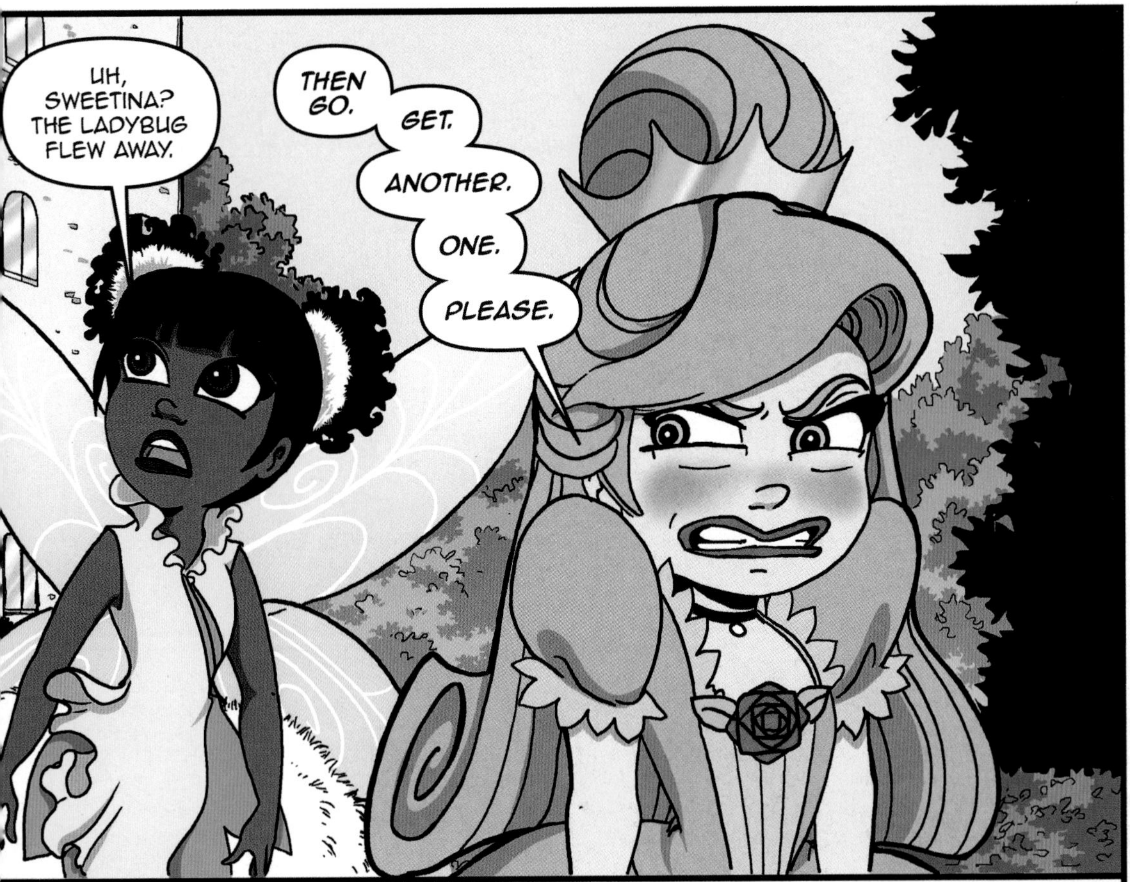
UH, SWEETINA? THE LADYBUG FLEW AWAY.
THEN GO.
GET.
ANOTHER.
ONE.
PLEASE.

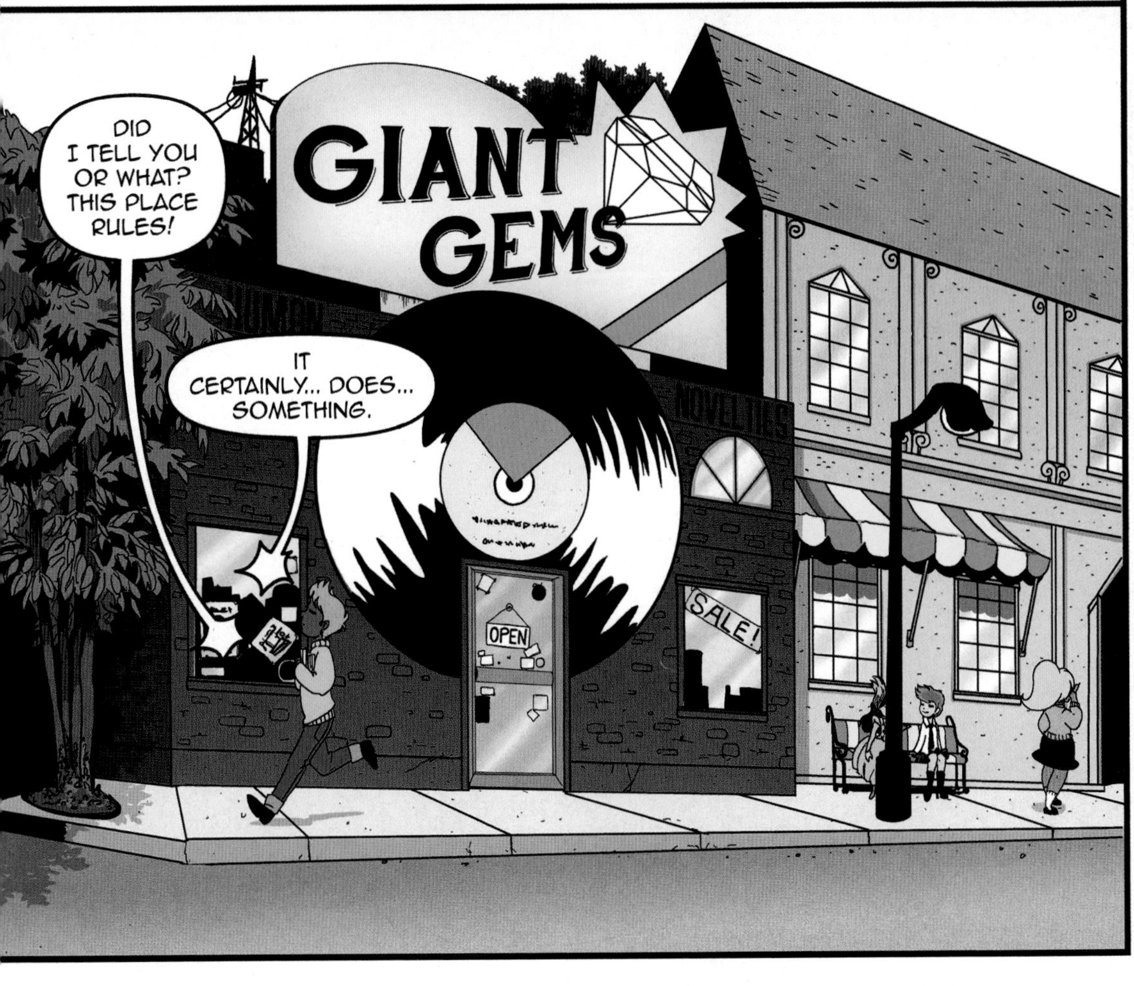
GIANT GEMS
DID I TELL YOU OR WHAT? THIS PLACE RULES!
IT CERTAINLY... DOES... SOMETHING.
NOVELTIES
OPEN
SALE!

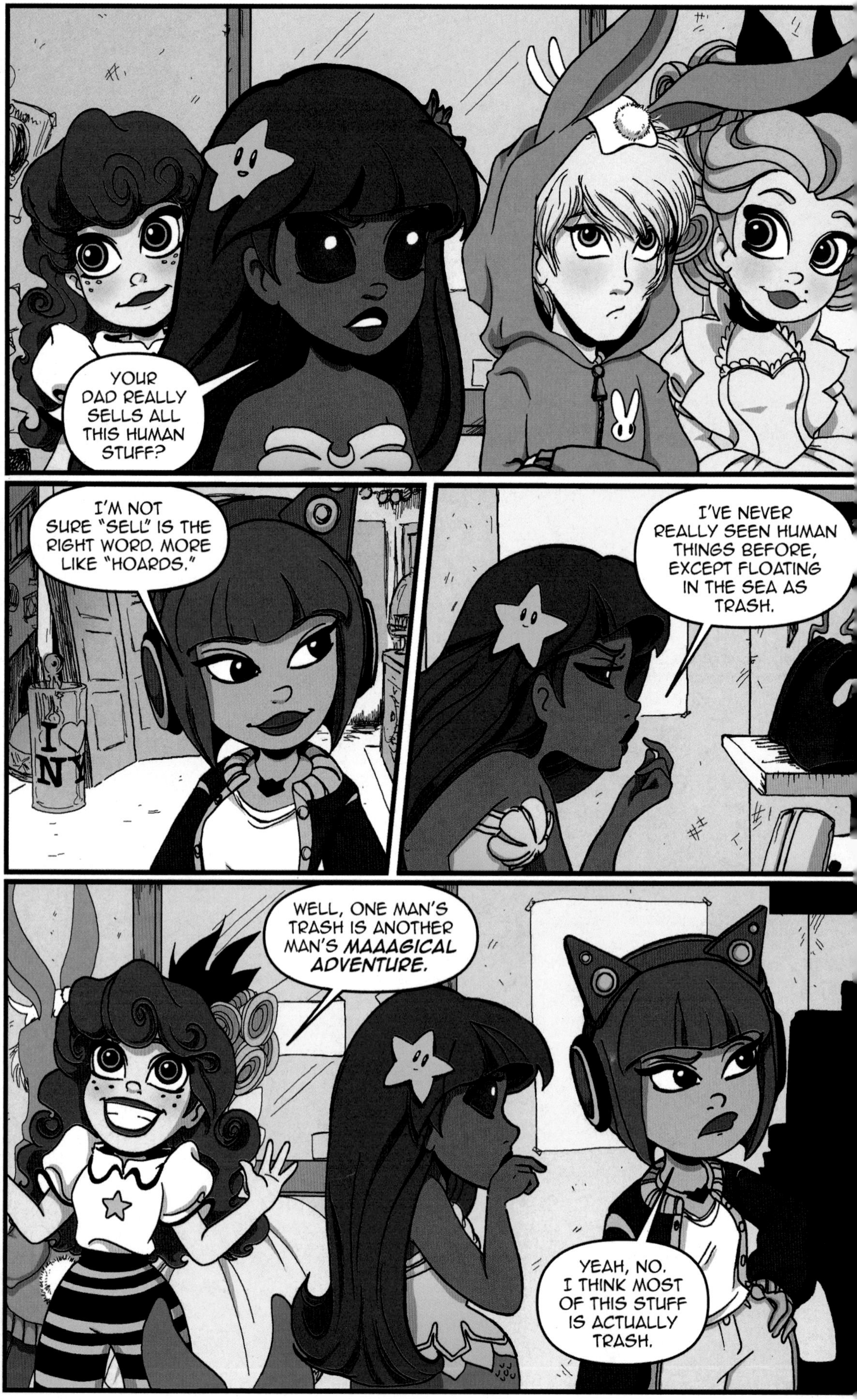
YOUR DAD REALLY SELLS ALL THIS HUMAN STUFF?
I'M NOT SURE "SELL" IS THE RIGHT WORD. MORE LIKE "HOARDS."
I ♥ NY
I'VE NEVER REALLY SEEN HUMAN THINGS BEFORE, EXCEPT FLOATING IN THE SEA AS TRASH.
WELL, ONE MAN'S TRASH IS ANOTHER MAN'S *MAAAGICAL ADVENTURE.*
YEAH, NO. I THINK MOST OF THIS STUFF IS ACTUALLY TRASH.

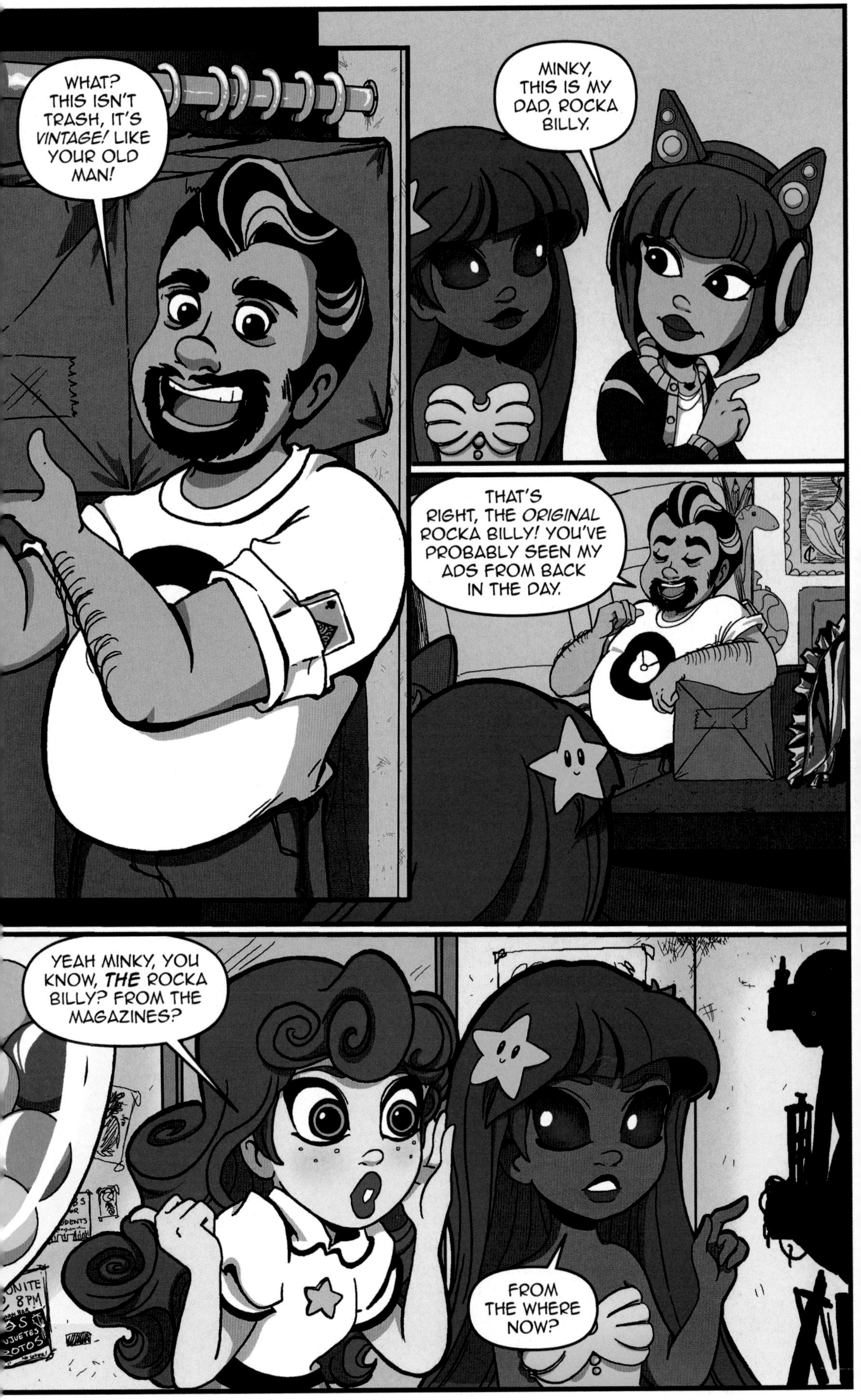
WHAT? THIS ISN'T TRASH, IT'S VINTAGE! LIKE YOUR OLD MAN!
MINKY, THIS IS MY DAD, ROCKA BILLY.
THAT'S RIGHT, THE ORIGINAL ROCKA BILLY! YOU'VE PROBABLY SEEN MY ADS FROM BACK IN THE DAY.
YEAH MINKY, YOU KNOW, THE ROCKA BILLY? FROM THE MAGAZINES?
FROM THE WHERE NOW?

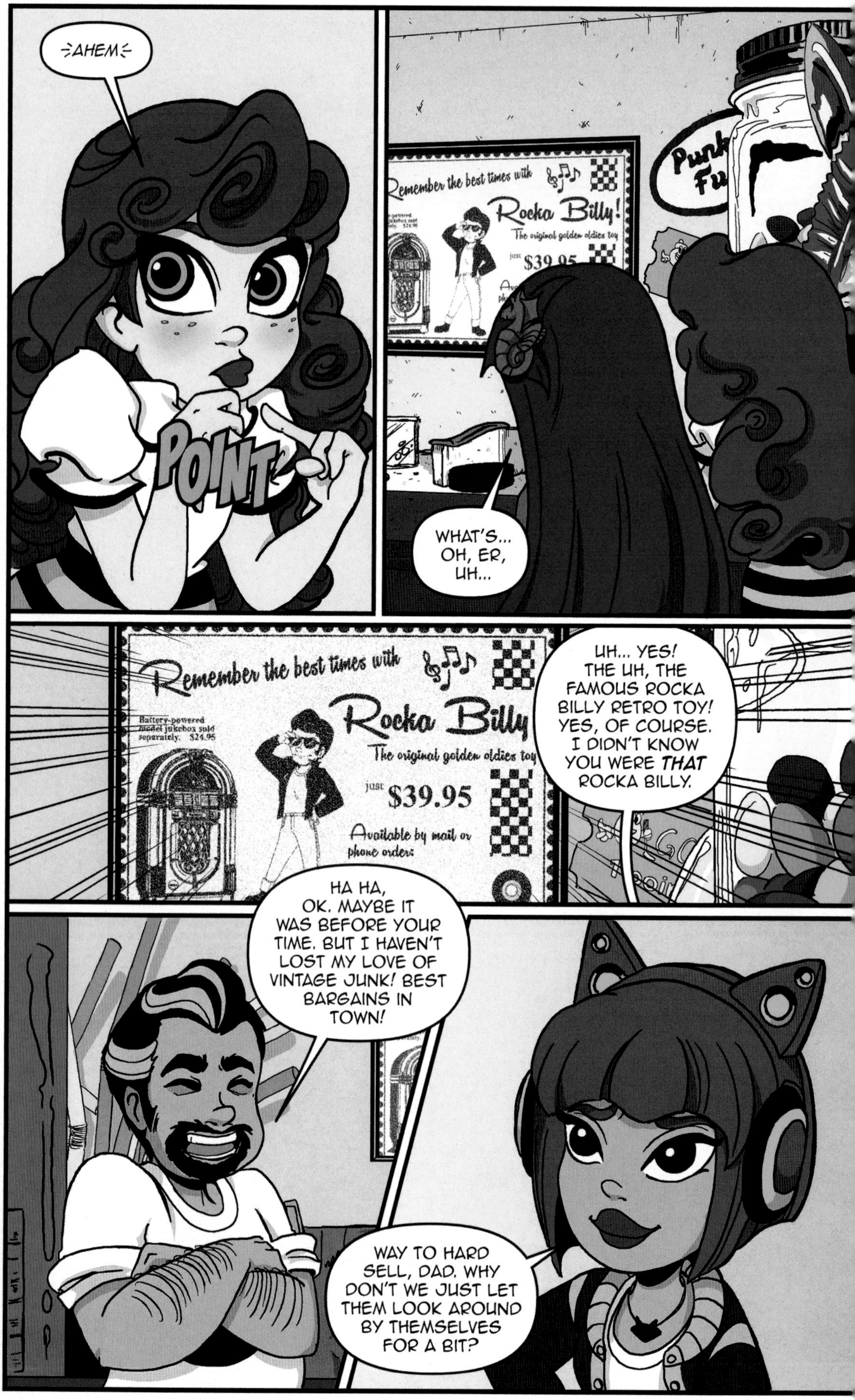
AHEM
POINT
Remember the best times with
Rocka Billy!
The original golden oldies toy
just $39.95
WHAT'S... OH, ER, UH...
Remember the best times with
Rocka Billy
Battery-powered model jukebox sold separately. $24.95
The original golden oldies toy
just $39.95
Available by mail or phone order.
UH... YES! THE UH, THE FAMOUS ROCKA BILLY RETRO TOY! YES, OF COURSE. I DIDN'T KNOW YOU WERE *THAT* ROCKA BILLY.
HA HA, OK. MAYBE IT WAS BEFORE YOUR TIME. BUT I HAVEN'T LOST MY LOVE OF VINTAGE JUNK! BEST BARGAINS IN TOWN!
WAY TO HARD SELL, DAD. WHY DON'T WE JUST LET THEM LOOK AROUND BY THEMSELVES FOR A BIT?

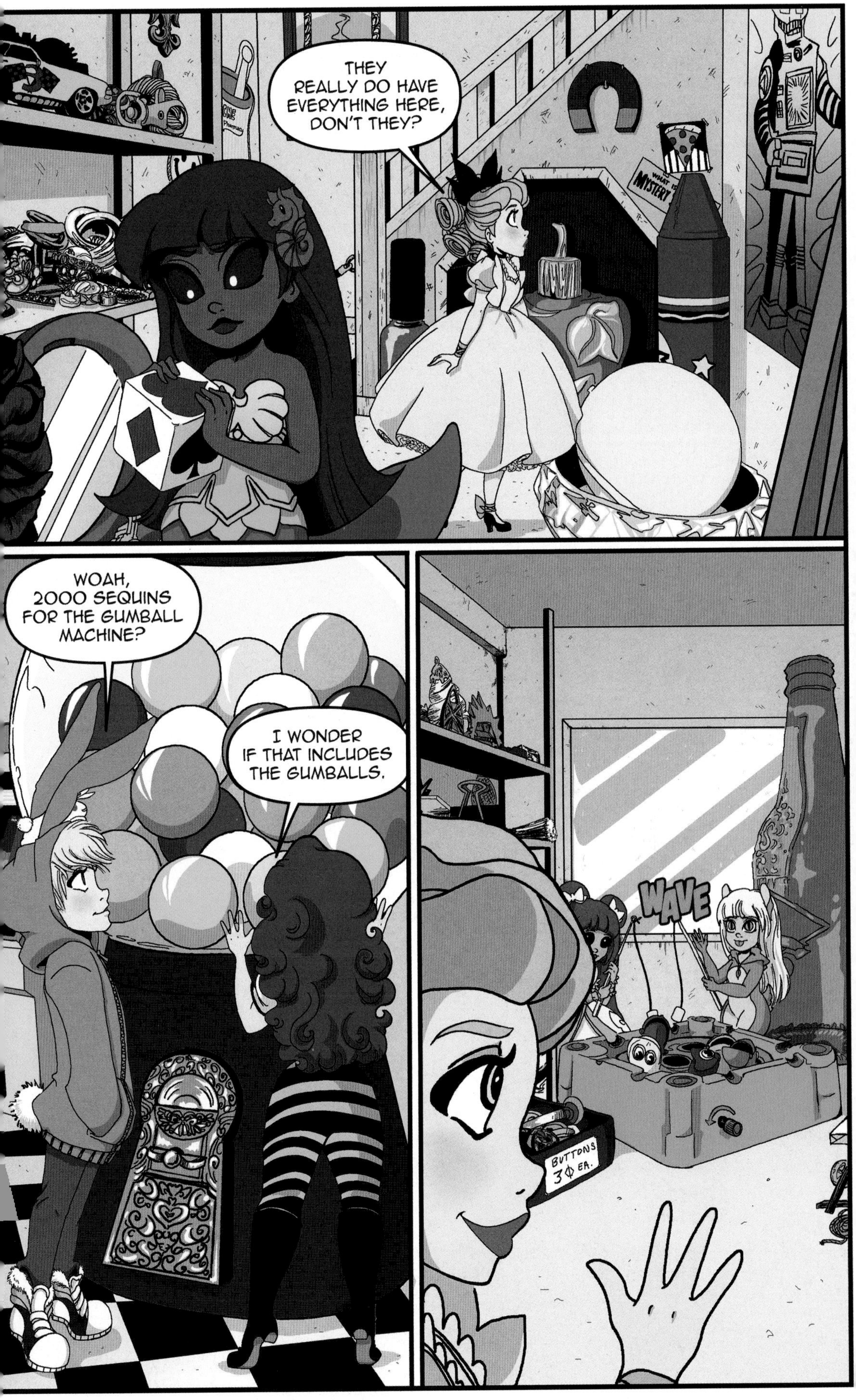
THEY REALLY DO HAVE EVERYTHING HERE, DON'T THEY?
WHAT IS MYSTERY
WOAH, 2000 SEQUINS FOR THE GUMBALL MACHINE?
I WONDER IF THAT INCLUDES THE GUMBALLS.
WAVE
BUTTONS 3¢ EA.

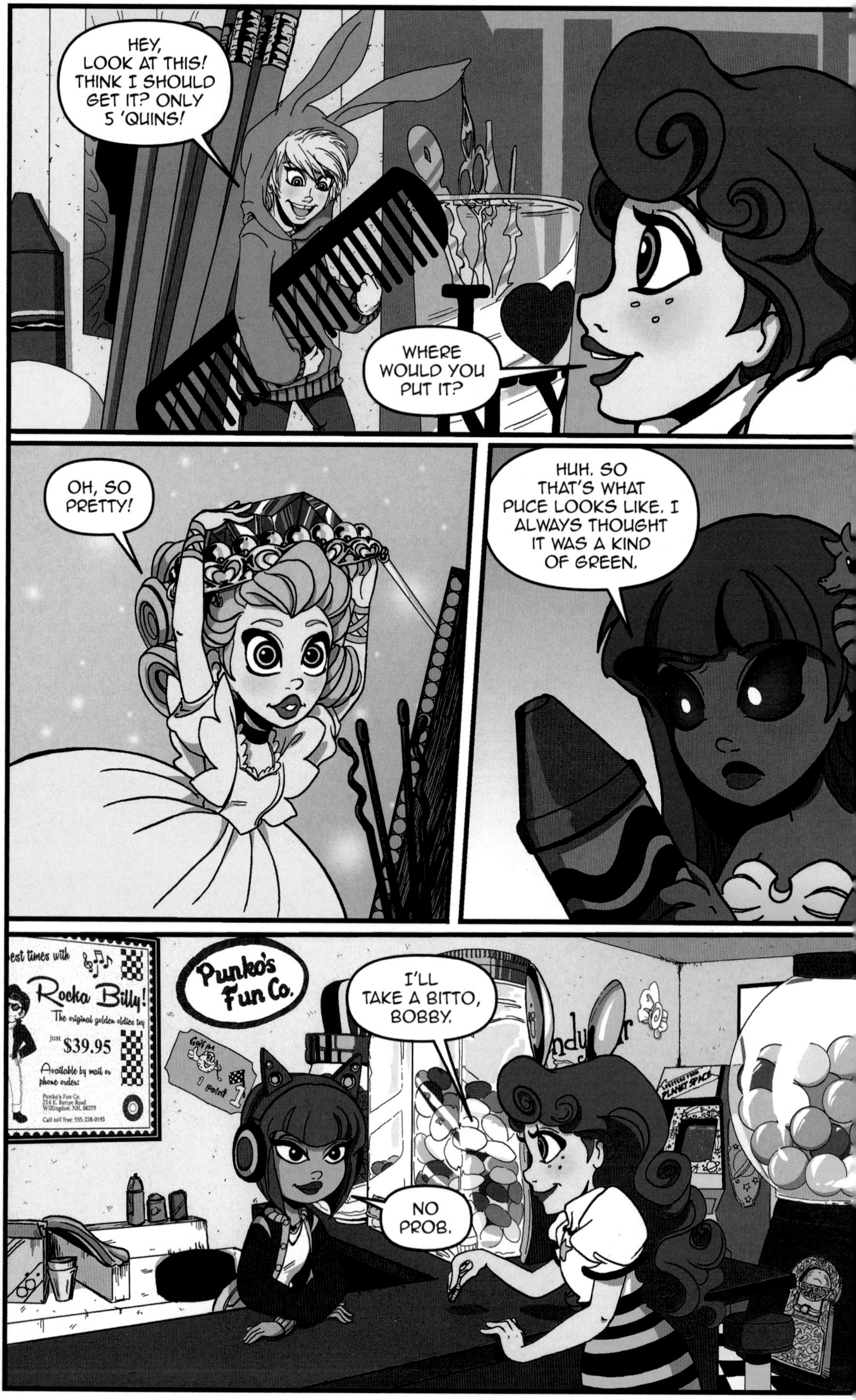
HEY, LOOK AT THIS! THINK I SHOULD GET IT? ONLY 5 'QUINS!
WHERE WOULD YOU PUT IT?
OH, SO PRETTY!
HUH. SO THAT'S WHAT PUCE LOOKS LIKE. I ALWAYS THOUGHT IT WAS A KIND OF GREEN.
est times with
Rocka Billy!
The original golden oldies toy
just $39.95
Available by mail or phone order:
Punko's Fun Co.
214 E. Battye Road
Willingdon, NH, 06279
Call toll free: 555-238-0193
Punko's Fun Co.
I'LL TAKE A BITTO, BOBBY.
NO PROB.

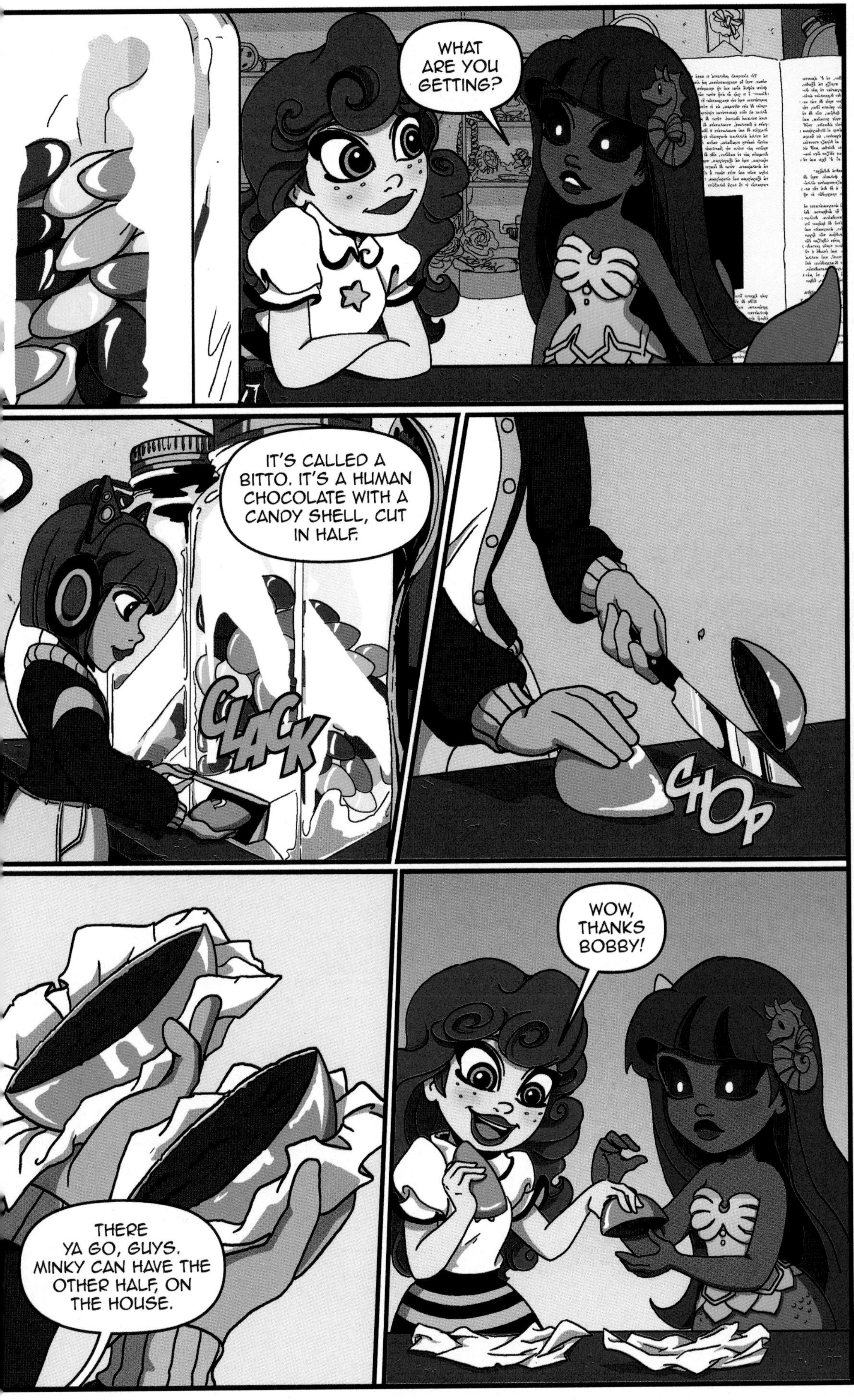
WHAT ARE YOU GETTING?
IT'S CALLED A BITTO. IT'S A HUMAN CHOCOLATE WITH A CANDY SHELL, CUT IN HALF.
CLACK
CHOP
THERE YA GO, GUYS. MINKY CAN HAVE THE OTHER HALF, ON THE HOUSE.
WOW, THANKS BOBBY!

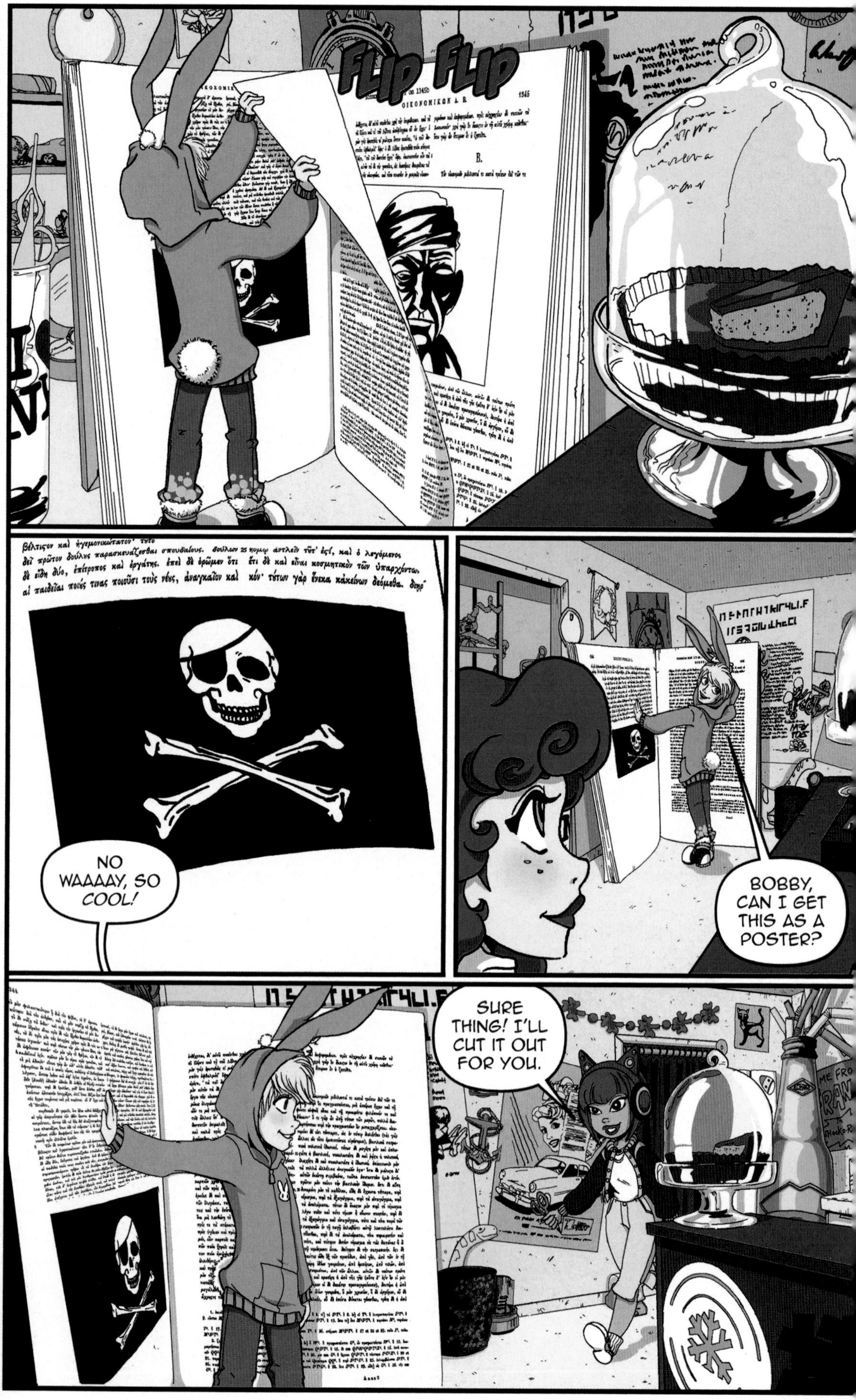
FLIP FLIP
NO WAAAAY, SO COOL!
BOBBY, CAN I GET THIS AS A POSTER?
SURE THING! I'LL CUT IT OUT FOR YOU.

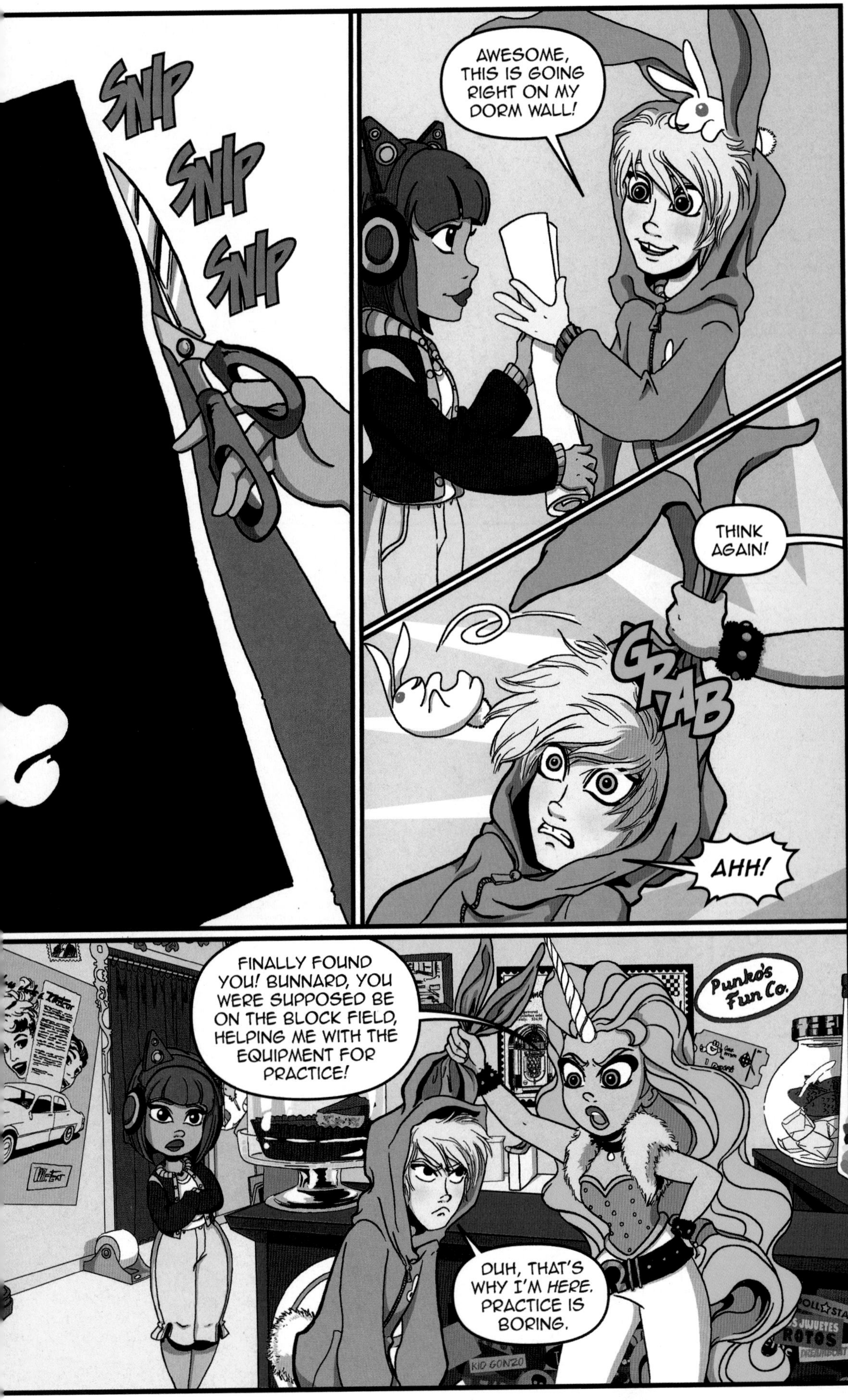
SNIP SNIP SNIP
AWESOME, THIS IS GOING RIGHT ON MY DORM WALL!
THINK AGAIN!
GRAB
AHH!
FINALLY FOUND YOU! BUNNARD, YOU WERE SUPPOSED BE ON THE BLOCK FIELD, HELPING ME WITH THE EQUIPMENT FOR PRACTICE!
Punko's Fun Co.
DUH, THAT'S WHY I'M HERE. PRACTICE IS BORING.
KID GONZO
ROTOS

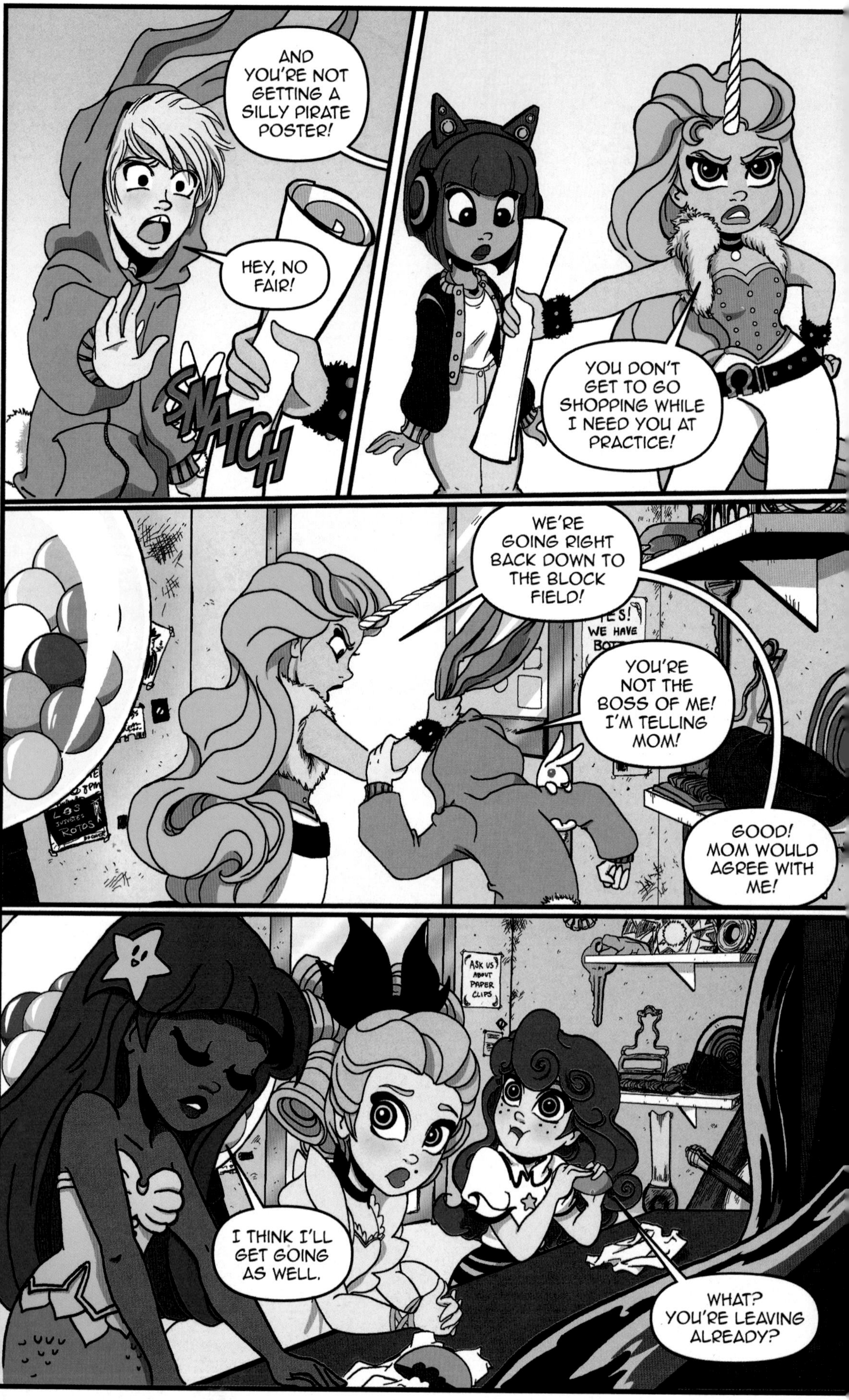
AND YOU'RE NOT GETTING A SILLY PIRATE POSTER!
HEY, NO FAIR!
SNATCH
YOU DON'T GET TO GO SHOPPING WHILE I NEED YOU AT PRACTICE!
WE'RE GOING RIGHT BACK DOWN TO THE BLOCK FIELD!
YOU'RE NOT THE BOSS OF ME! I'M TELLING MOM!
GOOD! MOM WOULD AGREE WITH ME!
ASK US ABOUT PAPER CLIPS
I THINK I'LL GET GOING AS WELL.
WHAT? YOU'RE LEAVING ALREADY?

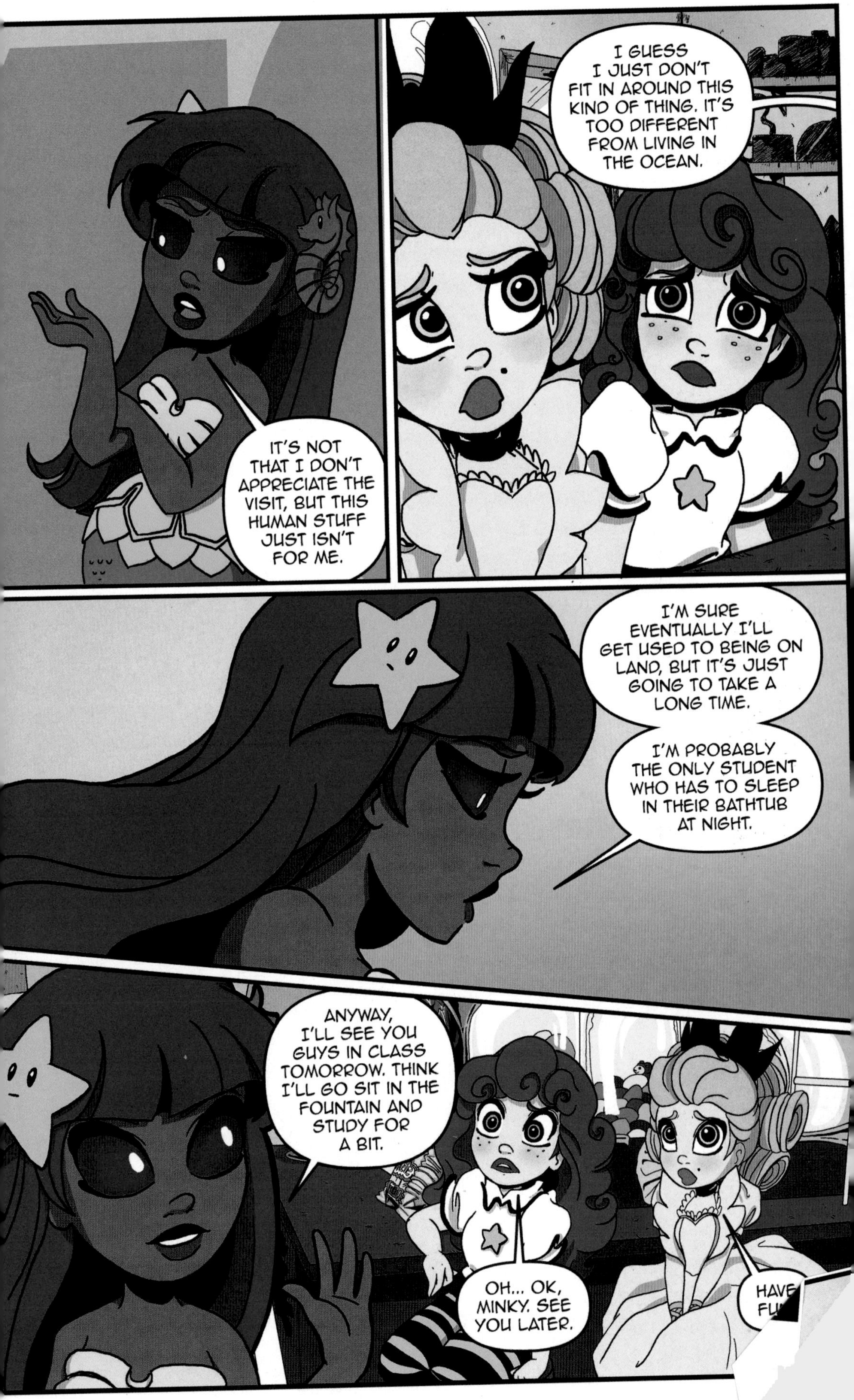
IT'S NOT THAT I DON'T APPRECIATE THE VISIT, BUT THIS HUMAN STUFF JUST ISN'T FOR ME.
I GUESS I JUST DON'T FIT IN AROUND THIS KIND OF THING. IT'S TOO DIFFERENT FROM LIVING IN THE OCEAN.
I'M SURE EVENTUALLY I'LL GET USED TO BEING ON LAND, BUT IT'S JUST GOING TO TAKE A LONG TIME.
I'M PROBABLY THE ONLY STUDENT WHO HAS TO SLEEP IN THEIR BATHTUB AT NIGHT.
ANYWAY, I'LL SEE YOU GUYS IN CLASS TOMORROW. THINK I'LL GO SIT IN THE FOUNTAIN AND STUDY FOR A BIT.
OH... OK, MINKY. SEE YOU LATER.
HAVE

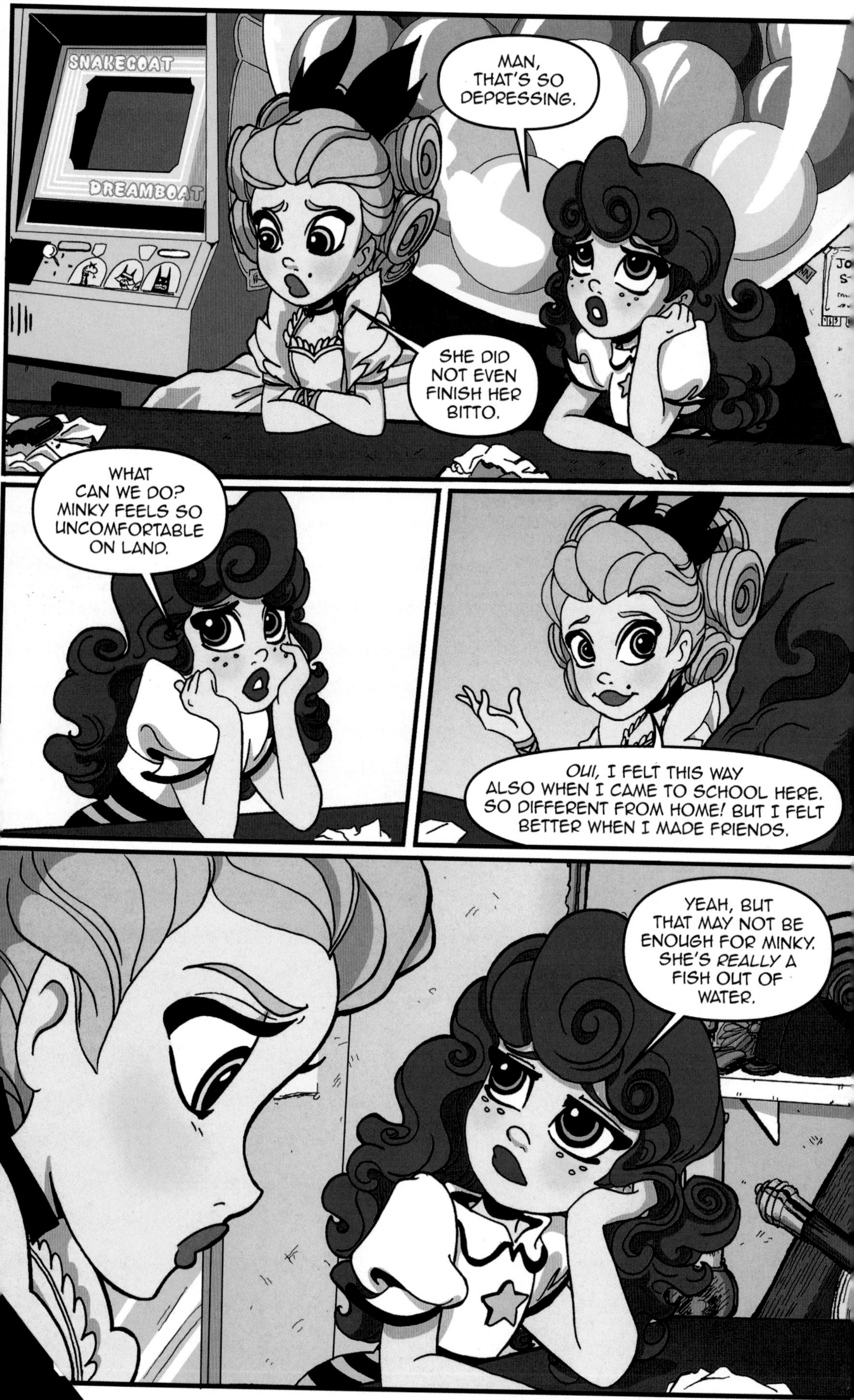
SNAKECOAT
DREAMBOAT
MAN, THAT'S SO DEPRESSING.
SHE DID NOT EVEN FINISH HER BITTO.
WHAT CAN WE DO? MINKY FEELS SO UNCOMFORTABLE ON LAND.
OUI, I FELT THIS WAY ALSO WHEN I CAME TO SCHOOL HERE. SO DIFFERENT FROM HOME! BUT I FELT BETTER WHEN I MADE FRIENDS.
YEAH, BUT THAT MAY NOT BE ENOUGH FOR MINKY. SHE'S *REALLY* A FISH OUT OF WATER.

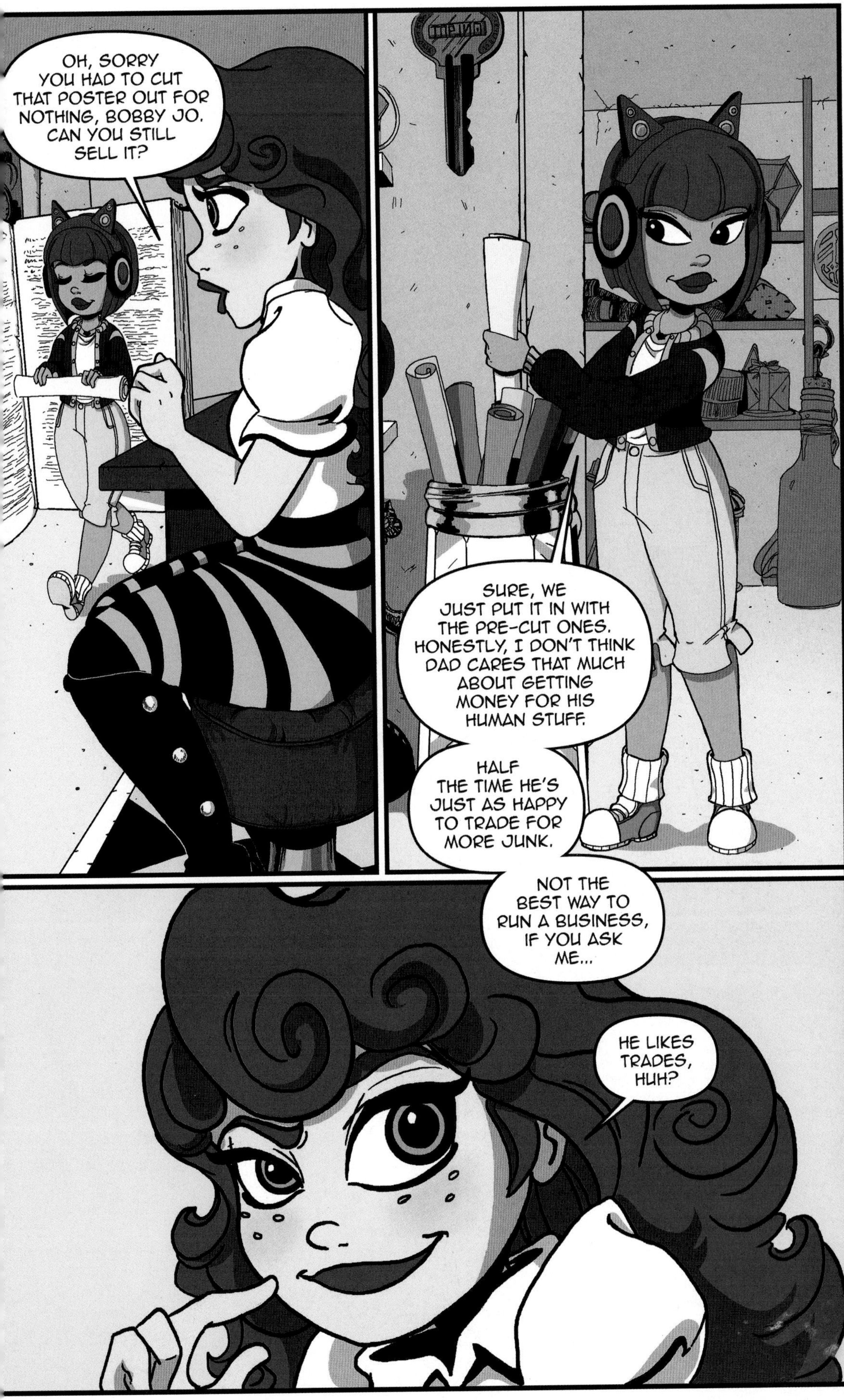
OH, SORRY YOU HAD TO CUT THAT POSTER OUT FOR NOTHING, BOBBY JO. CAN YOU STILL SELL IT?
SURE, WE JUST PUT IT IN WITH THE PRE-CUT ONES. HONESTLY, I DON'T THINK DAD CARES THAT MUCH ABOUT GETTING MONEY FOR HIS HUMAN STUFF.
HALF THE TIME HE'S JUST AS HAPPY TO TRADE FOR MORE JUNK.
NOT THE BEST WAY TO RUN A BUSINESS, IF YOU ASK ME...
HE LIKES TRADES, HUH?

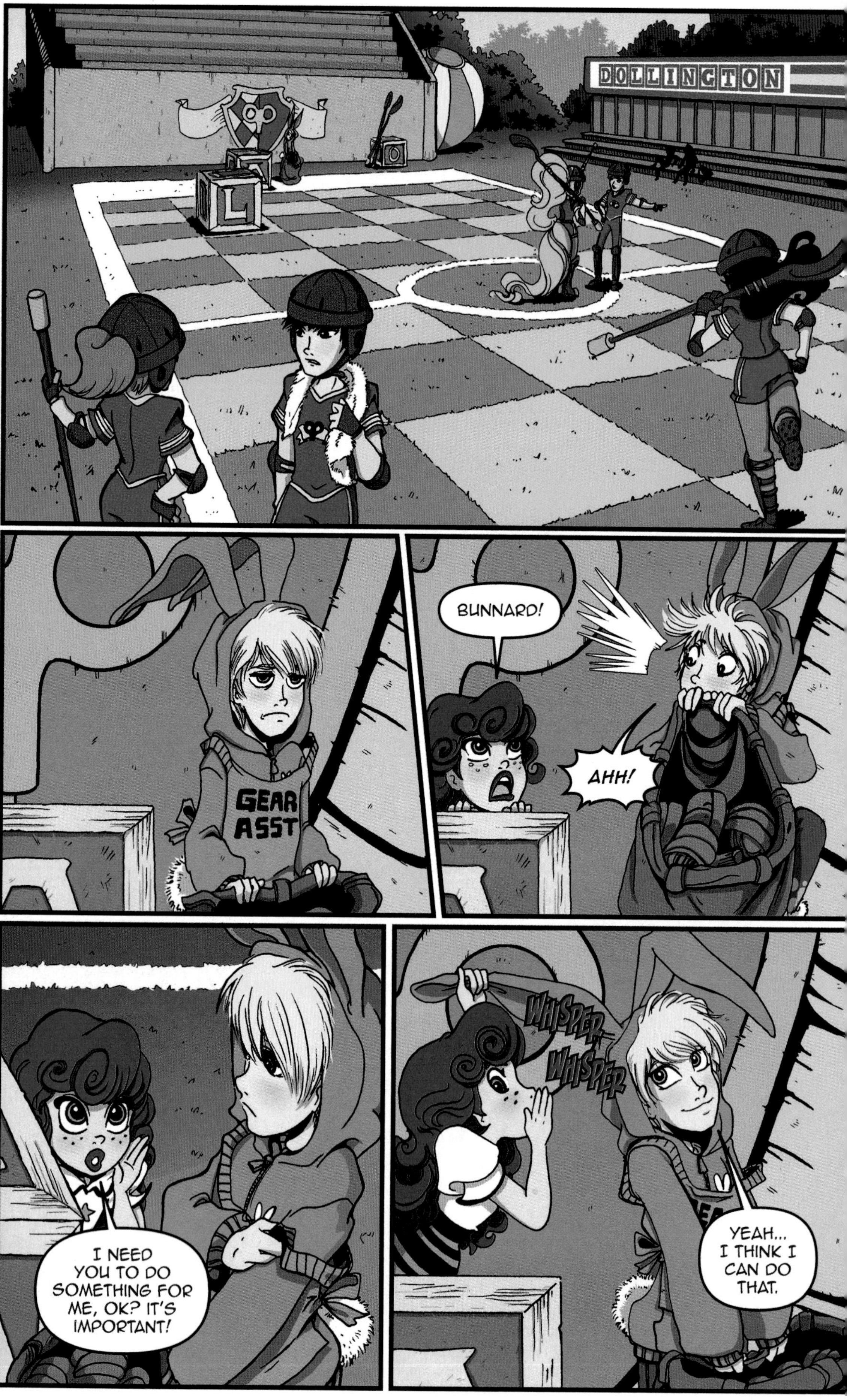
DOLLINGTON
GEAR ASST
BUNNARD!
AHH!
I NEED YOU TO DO SOMETHING FOR ME, OK? IT'S IMPORTANT!
WHISPER WHISPER
YEAH... I THINK I CAN DO THAT.

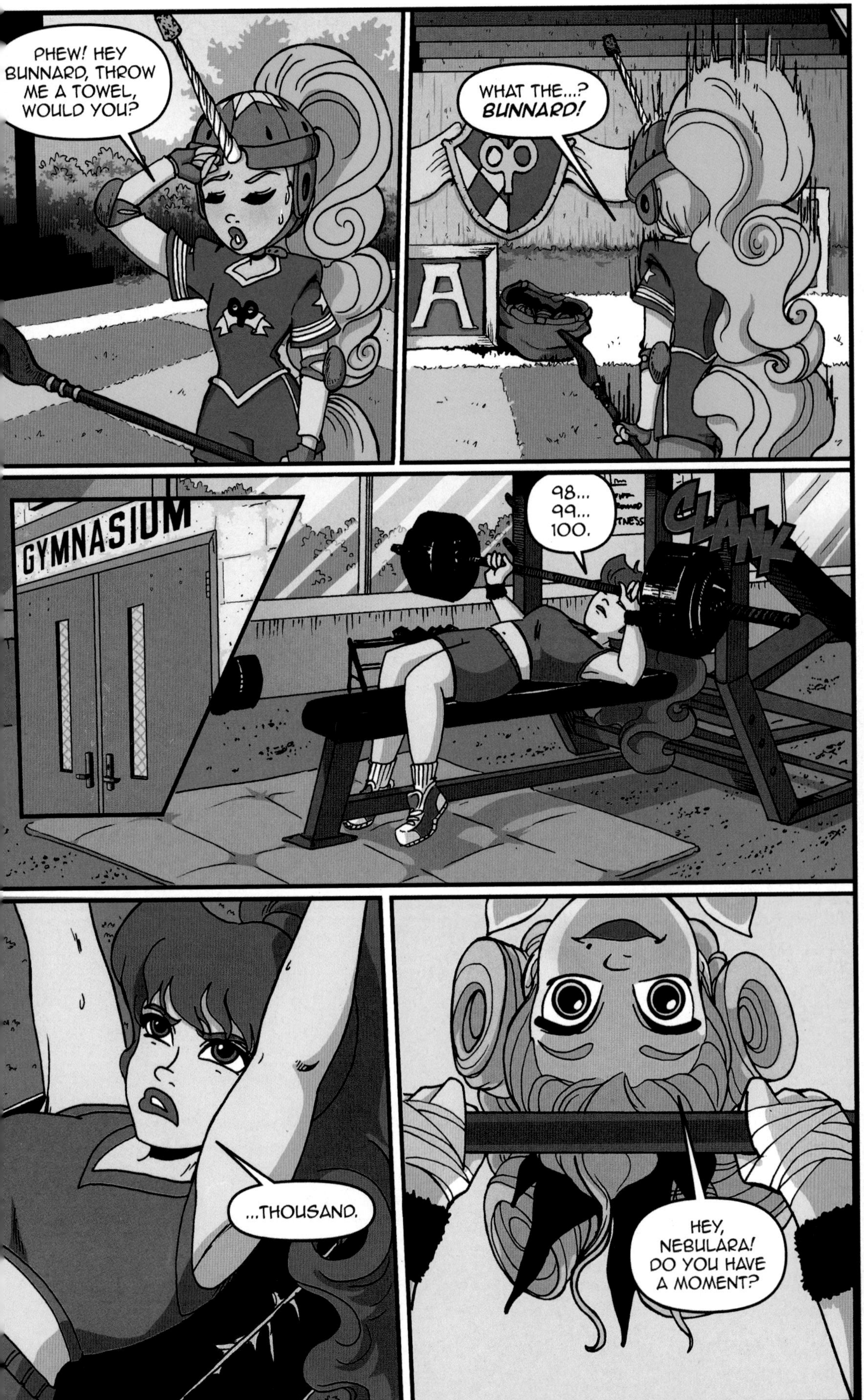
PHEW! HEY BUNNARD, THROW ME A TOWEL, WOULD YOU?
WHAT THE...? BUNNARD!
A
GYMNASIUM
98... 99... 100.
CLANK
...THOUSAND.
HEY, NEBULARA! DO YOU HAVE A MOMENT?

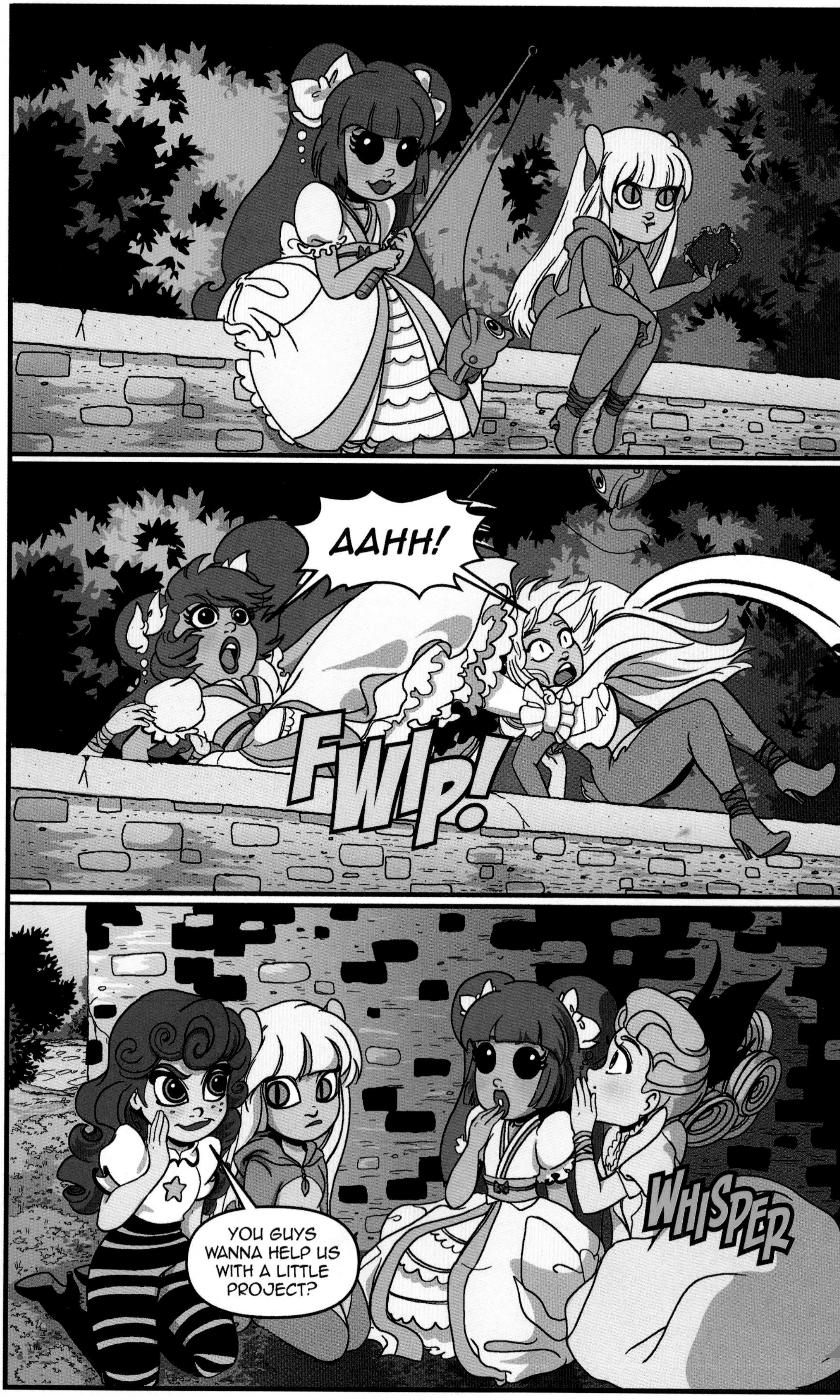
AAHH!
FWIP!
WHISPER
YOU GUYS WANNA HELP US WITH A LITTLE PROJECT?

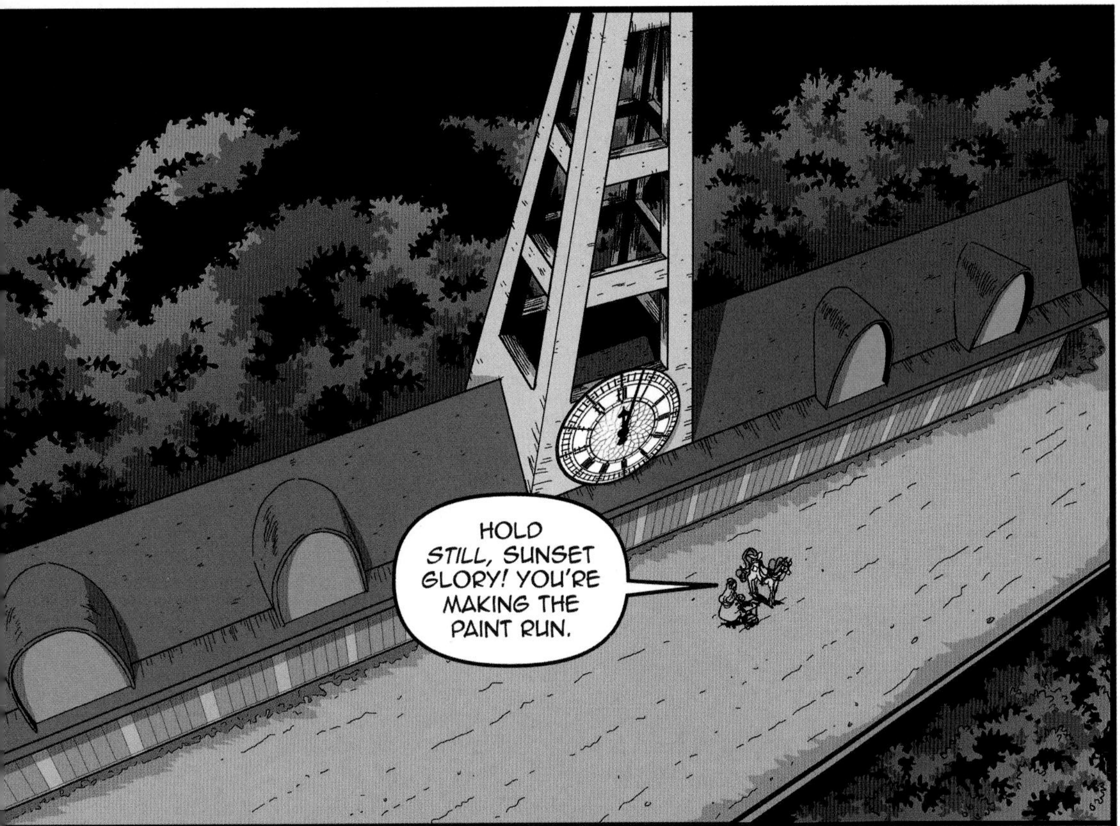
HOLD STILL, SUNSET GLORY! YOU'RE MAKING THE PAINT RUN.

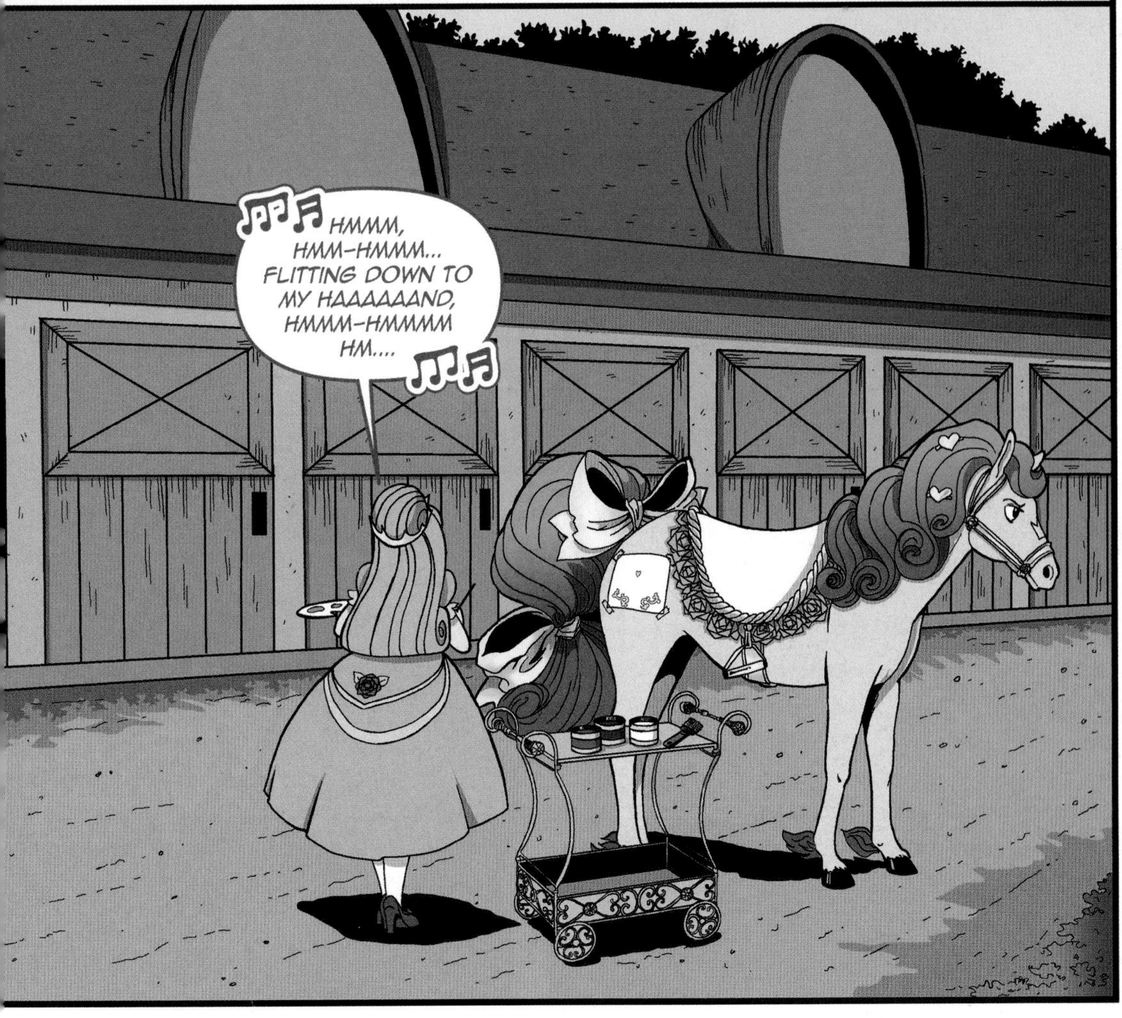
HMMM, HMM-HMMM... FLITTING DOWN TO MY HAAAAAAND, HMMM-HMMMM HM....

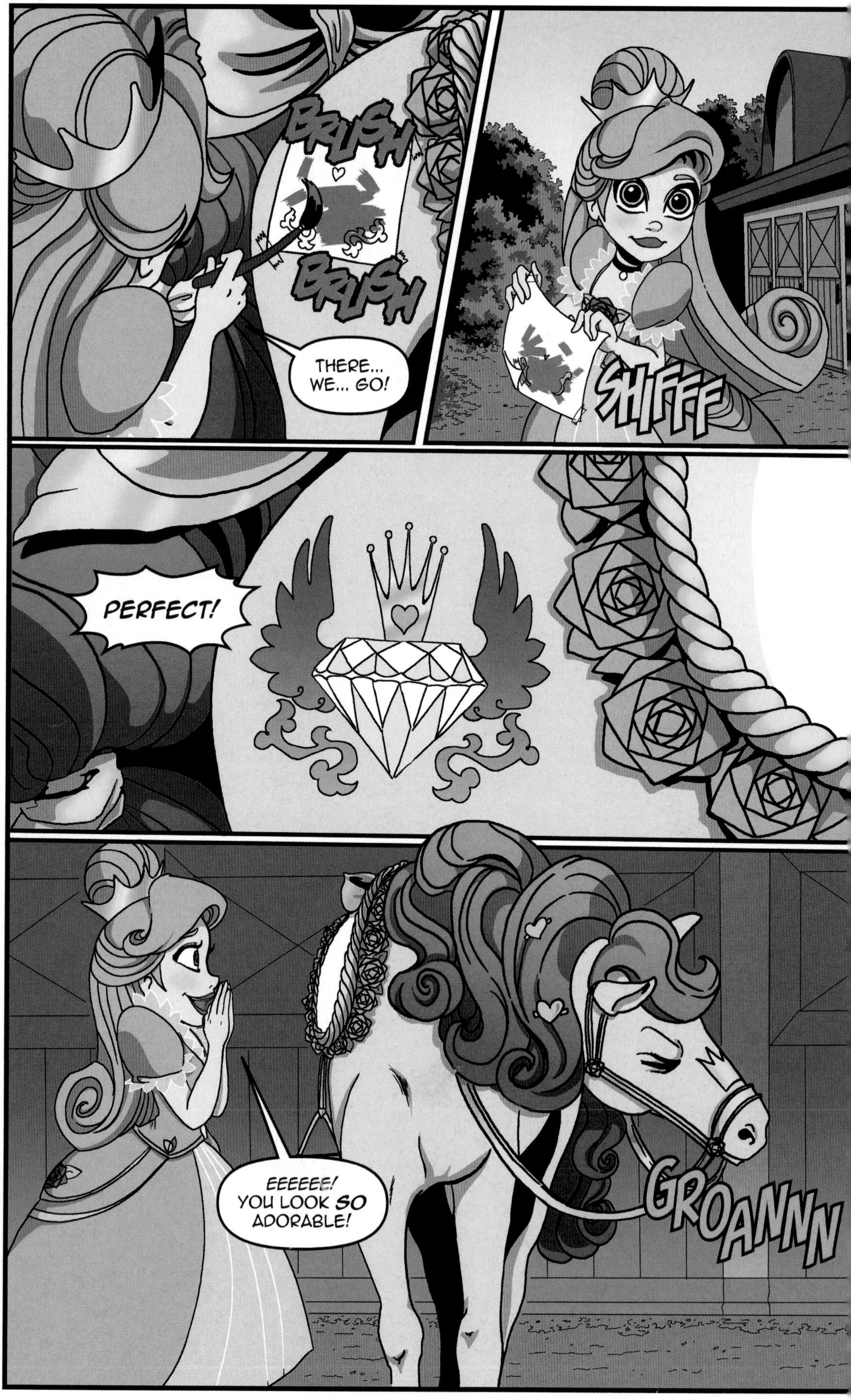
BRUSH
BRUSH
THERE... WE... GO!
SHIFFF
PERFECT!
EEEEEE! YOU LOOK SO ADORABLE!
GROANNN

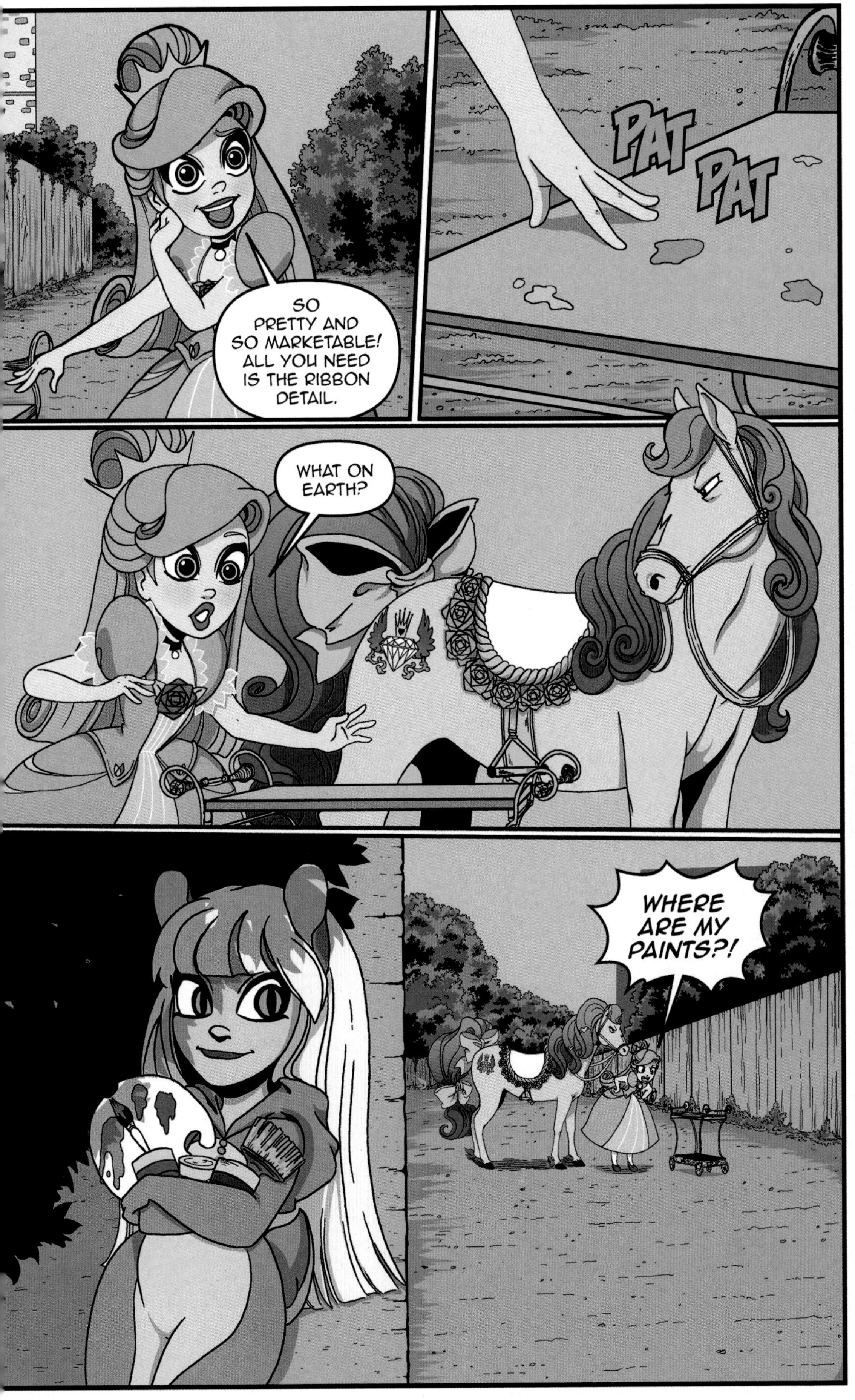
SO PRETTY AND SO MARKETABLE! ALL YOU NEED IS THE RIBBON DETAIL.
PAT PAT
WHAT ON EARTH?
WHERE ARE MY PAINTS?!

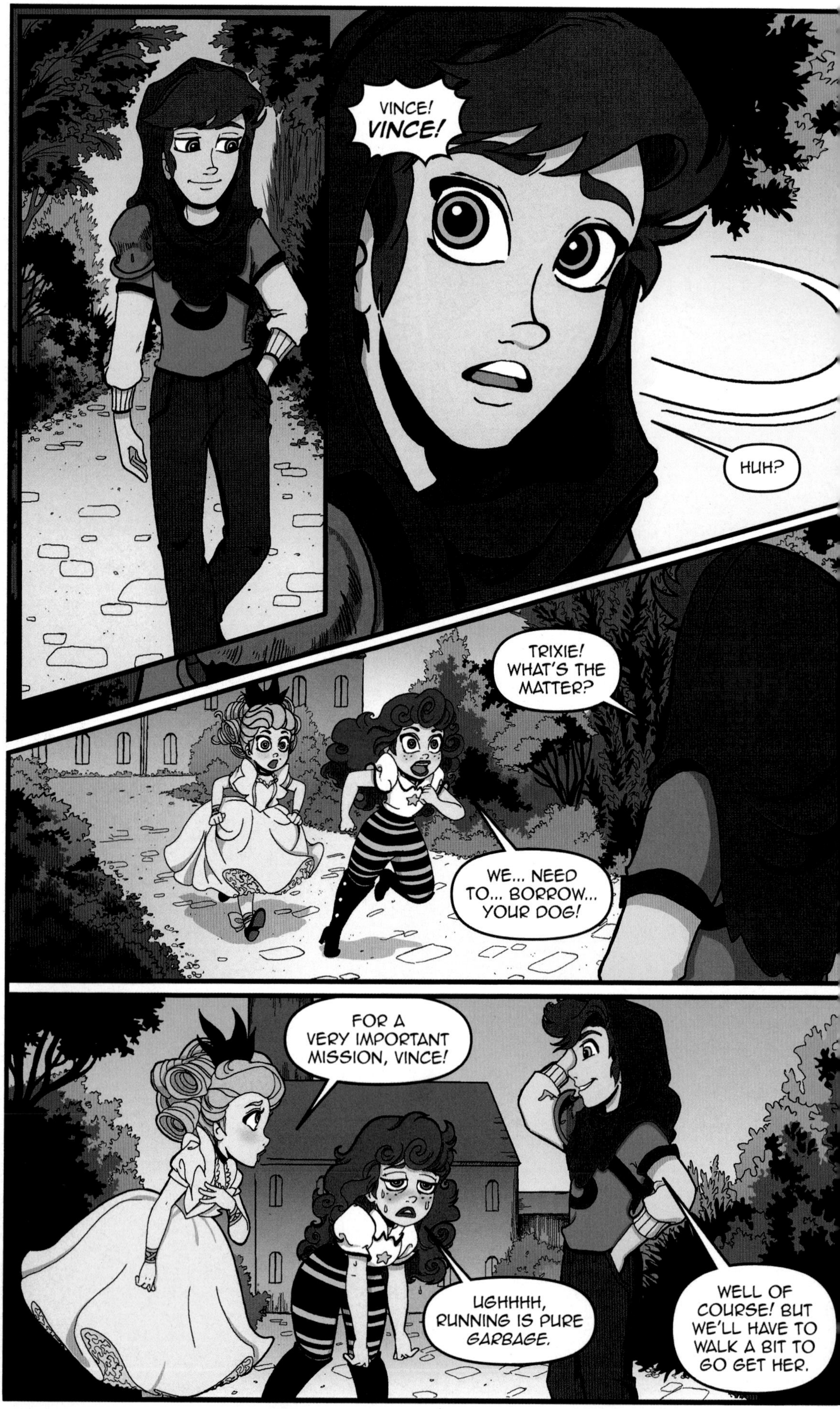
VINCE! VINCE!
HUH?
TRIXIE! WHAT'S THE MATTER?
WE... NEED TO... BORROW... YOUR DOG!
FOR A VERY IMPORTANT MISSION, VINCE!
UGHHHH, RUNNING IS PURE GARBAGE.
WELL OF COURSE! BUT WE'LL HAVE TO WALK A BIT TO GO GET HER.

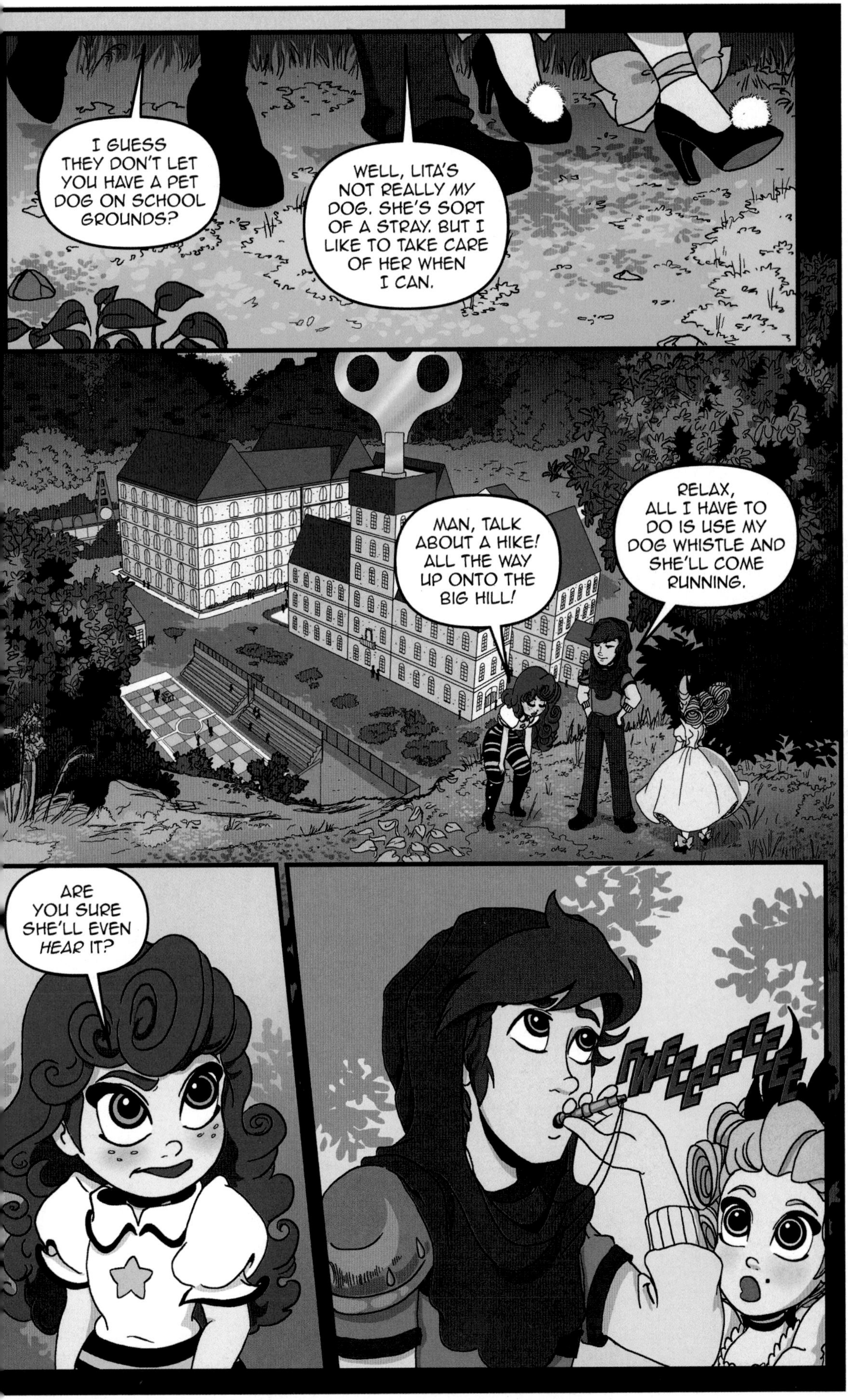
I GUESS THEY DON'T LET YOU HAVE A PET DOG ON SCHOOL GROUNDS?
WELL, LITA'S NOT REALLY *MY* DOG. SHE'S SORT OF A STRAY. BUT I LIKE TO TAKE CARE OF HER WHEN I CAN.
MAN, TALK ABOUT A HIKE! ALL THE WAY UP ONTO THE BIG HILL!
RELAX, ALL I HAVE TO DO IS USE MY DOG WHISTLE AND SHE'LL COME RUNNING.
ARE YOU SURE SHE'LL EVEN *HEAR* IT?
FWEEEEEEEEEEE

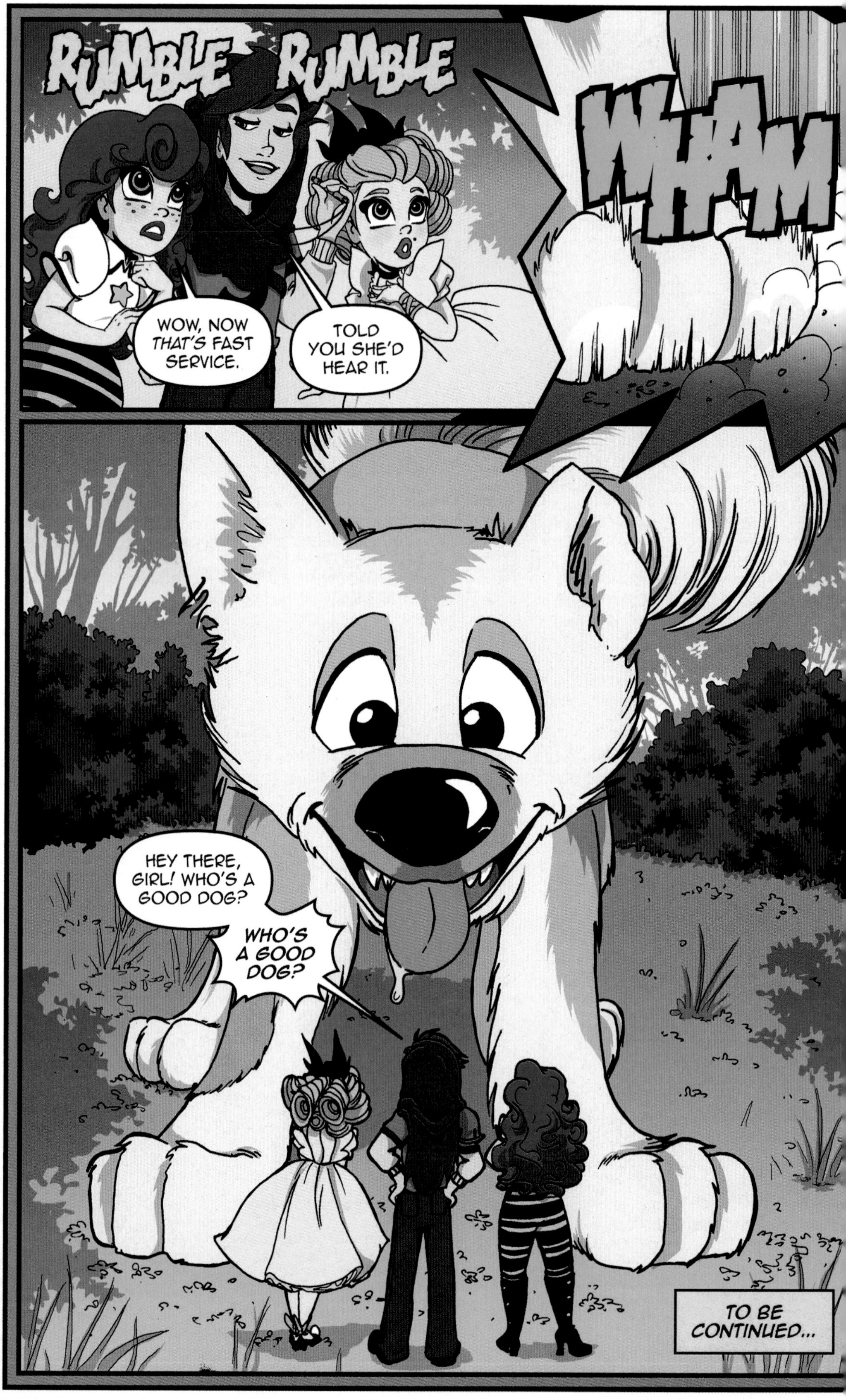
RUMBLE RUMBLE
WHAM
WOW, NOW THAT'S FAST SERVICE.
TOLD YOU SHE'D HEAR IT.
HEY THERE, GIRL! WHO'S A GOOD DOG?
WHO'S A GOOD DOG?
TO BE CONTINUED...

pages in progress

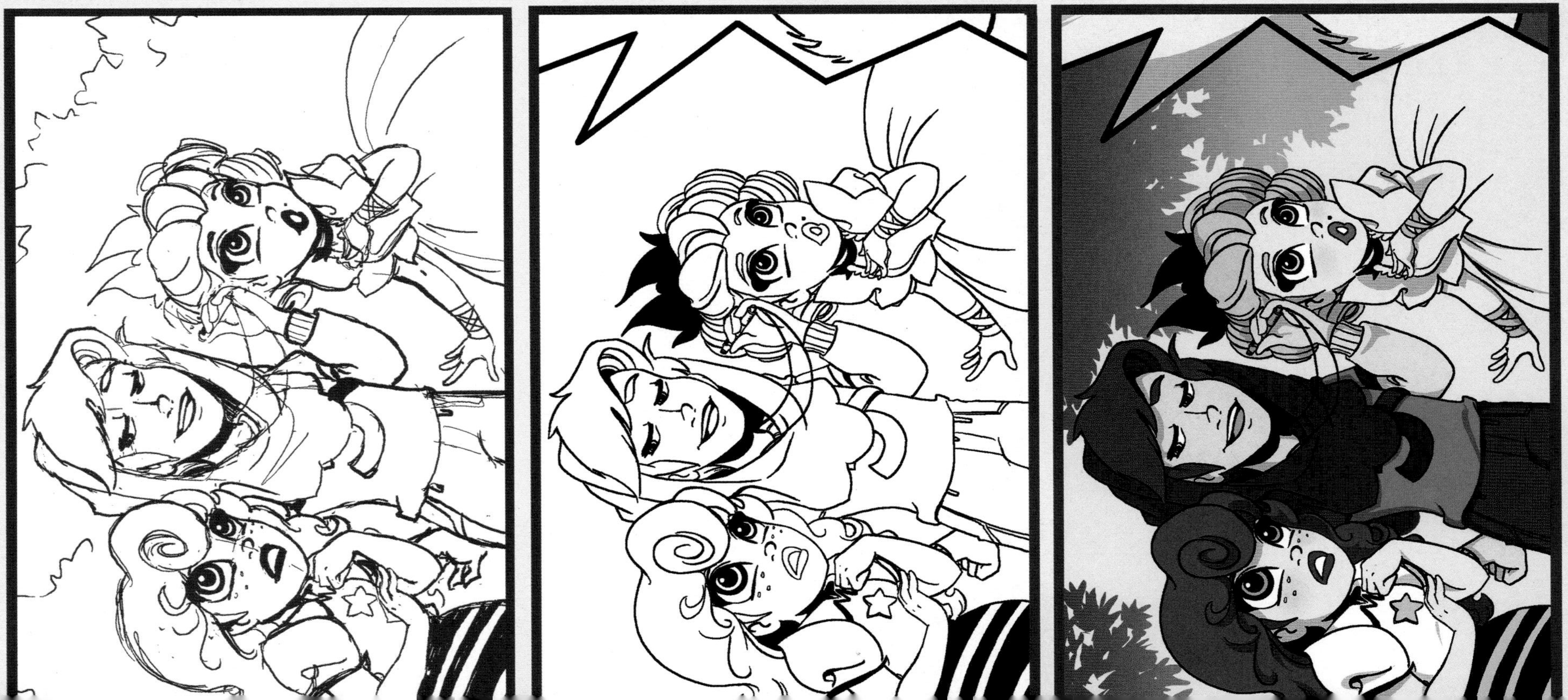

pages in progress

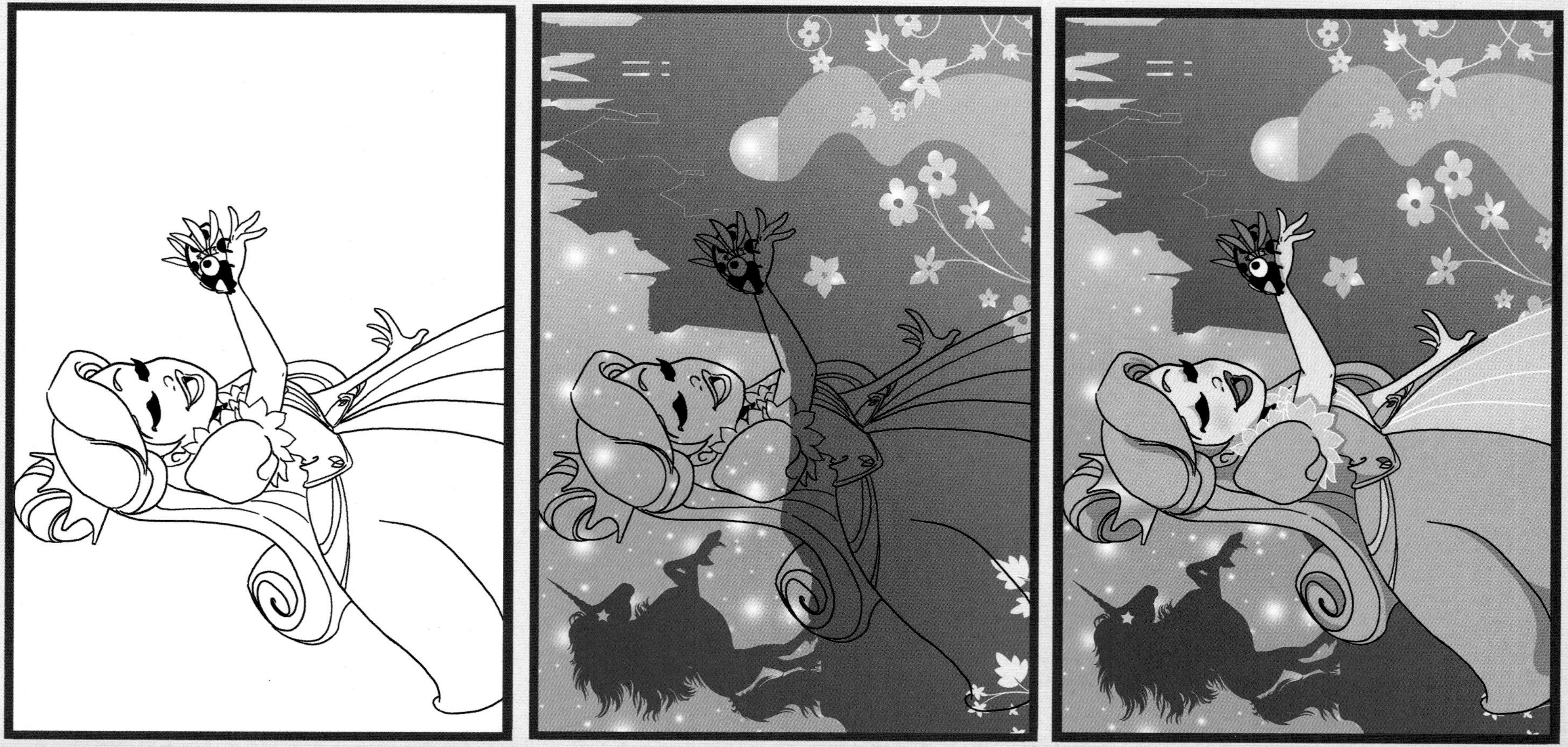

GIANTS

PART THREE

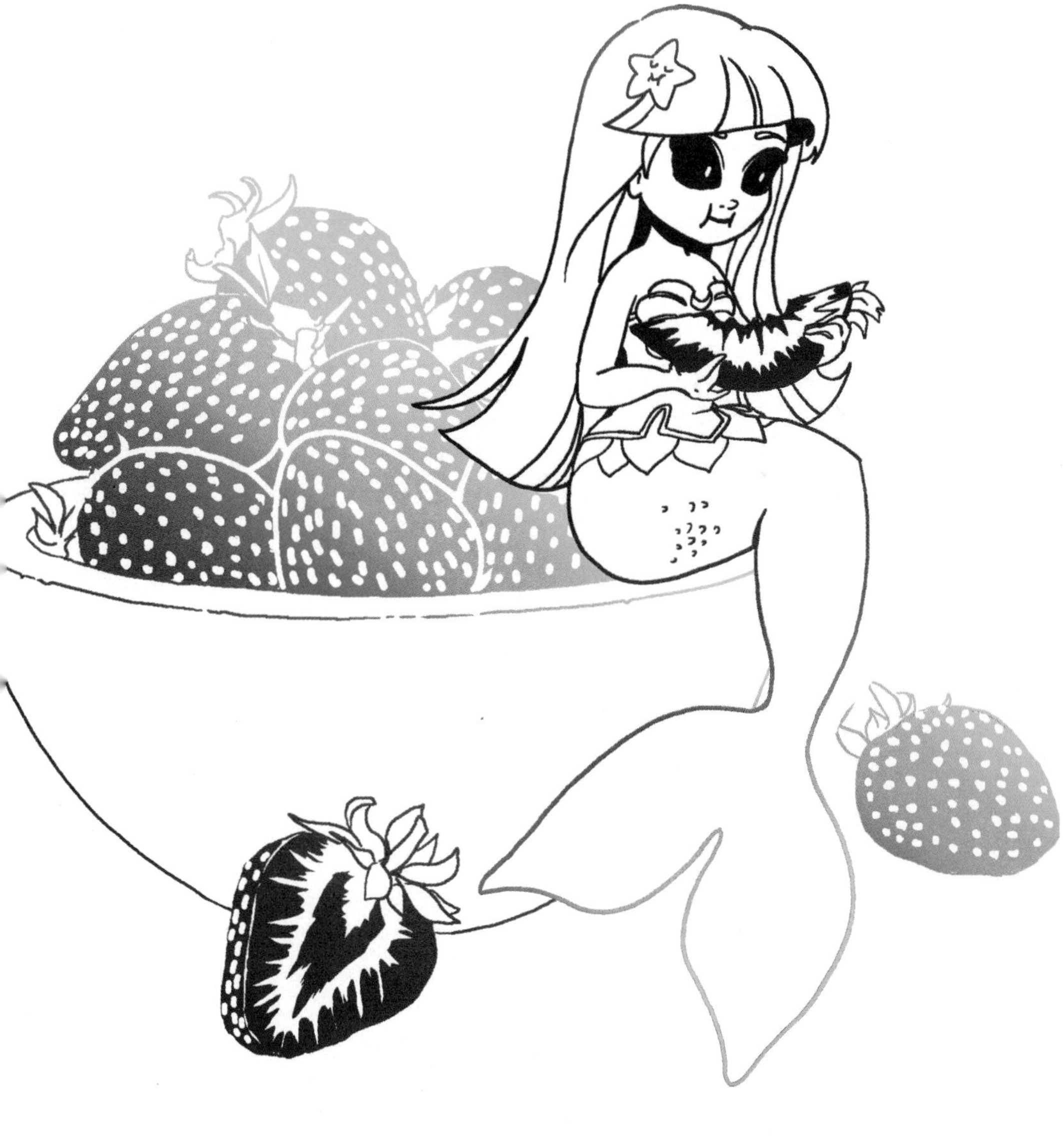

TOYETICA 7

STORY AND ART BY MARTY LEGROW

LETTERING
Justin Birch

HAVE YOU FOUND
the mouse yet?

Bryan Seaton: Publisher/ CEO • Shawn Gabborin: Editor In Chief • Jason Martin: Publisher-Danger Zone • Nicole D'Andria: Marketing Director/Editor
Danielle Davison: Executive Administrator • Chad Cicconi: Action Lawyer • Shawn Pryor: President of Creator Relations

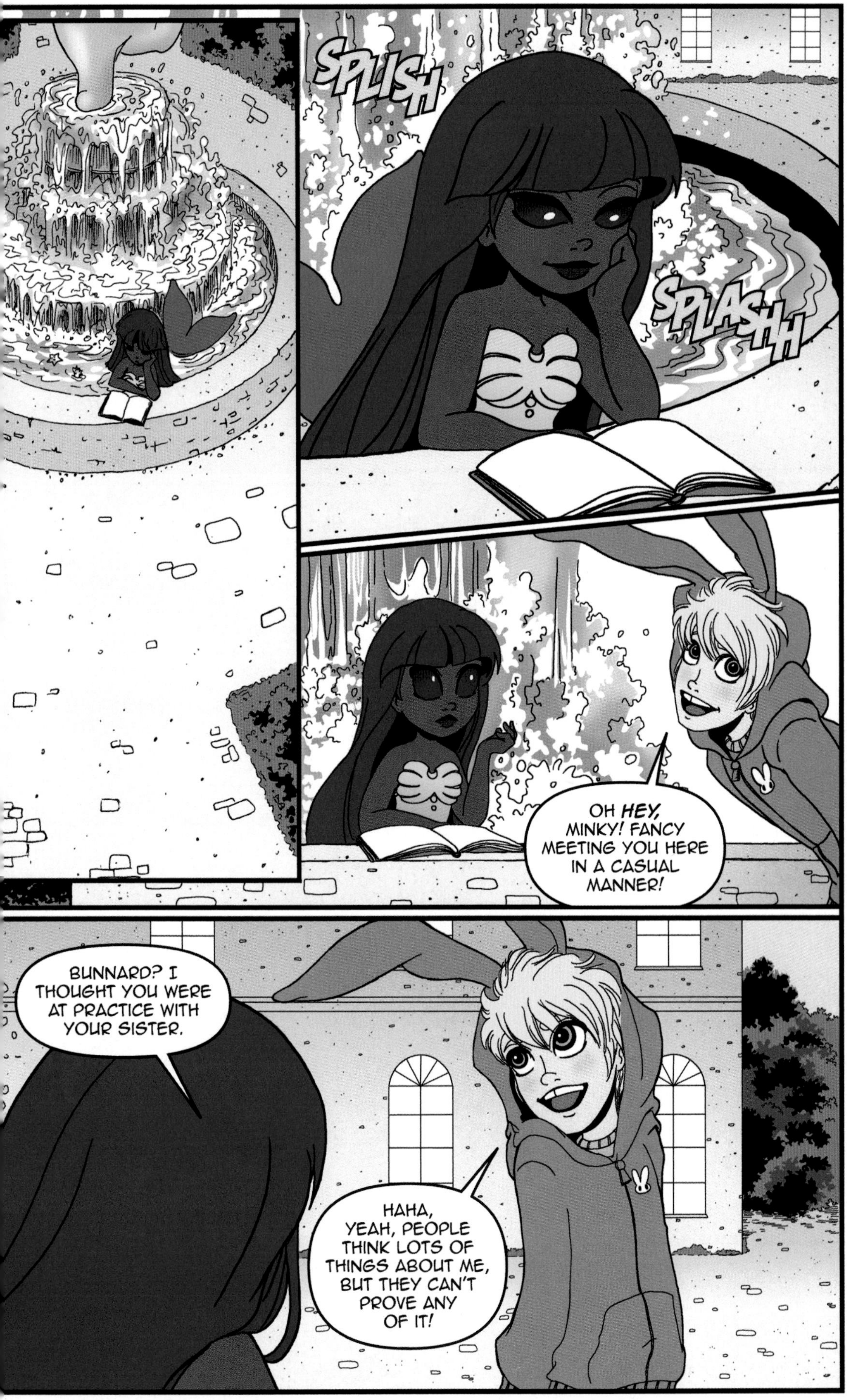
SPLISH
SPLASHH
OH HEY, MINKY! FANCY MEETING YOU HERE IN A CASUAL MANNER!
BUNNARD? I THOUGHT YOU WERE AT PRACTICE WITH YOUR SISTER.
HAHA, YEAH, PEOPLE THINK LOTS OF THINGS ABOUT ME, BUT THEY CAN'T PROVE ANY OF IT!

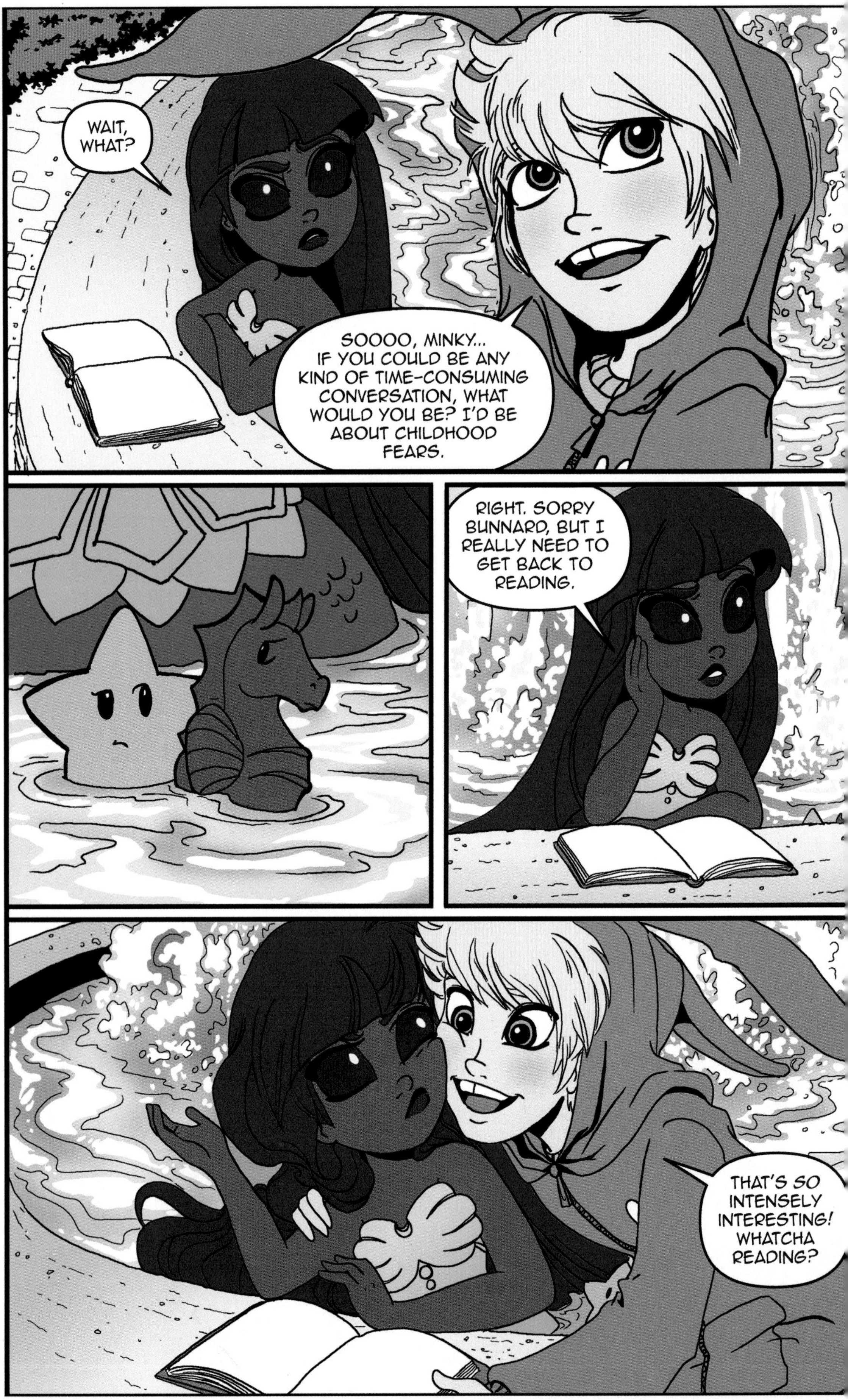
WAIT, WHAT?
SOOOO, MINKY... IF YOU COULD BE ANY KIND OF TIME-CONSUMING CONVERSATION, WHAT WOULD YOU BE? I'D BE ABOUT CHILDHOOD FEARS.
RIGHT. SORRY BUNNARD, BUT I REALLY NEED TO GET BACK TO READING.
THAT'S SO INTENSELY INTERESTING! WHATCHA READING?

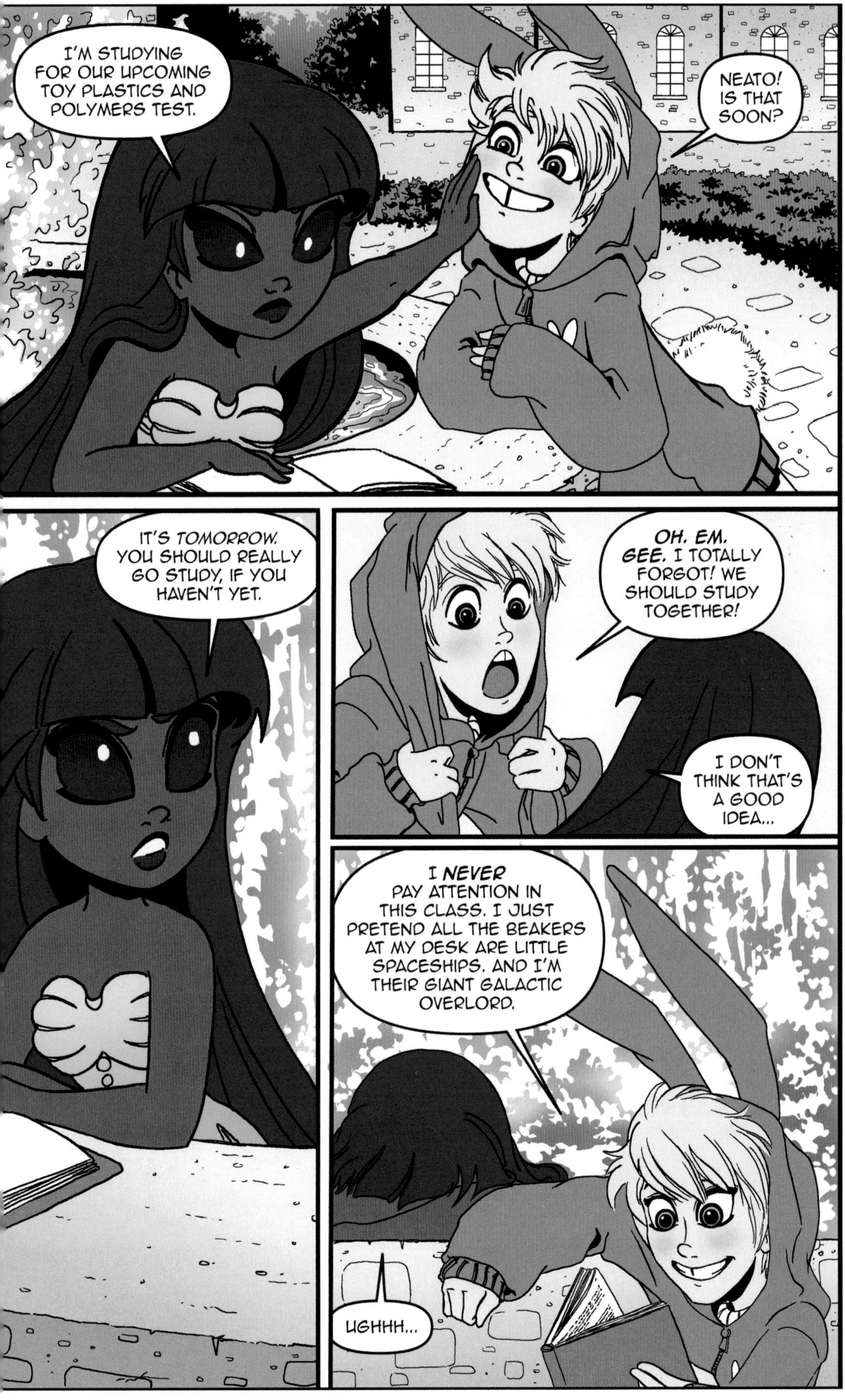
I'M STUDYING FOR OUR UPCOMING TOY PLASTICS AND POLYMERS TEST.
NEATO! IS THAT SOON?
IT'S *TOMORROW.* YOU SHOULD REALLY GO STUDY, IF YOU HAVEN'T YET.
OH. EM. GEE. I TOTALLY FORGOT! WE SHOULD STUDY TOGETHER!
I DON'T THINK THAT'S A GOOD IDEA...
I ***NEVER*** PAY ATTENTION IN THIS CLASS. I JUST PRETEND ALL THE BEAKERS AT MY DESK ARE LITTLE SPACESHIPS. AND I'M THEIR GIANT GALACTIC OVERLORD.
UGHHH...

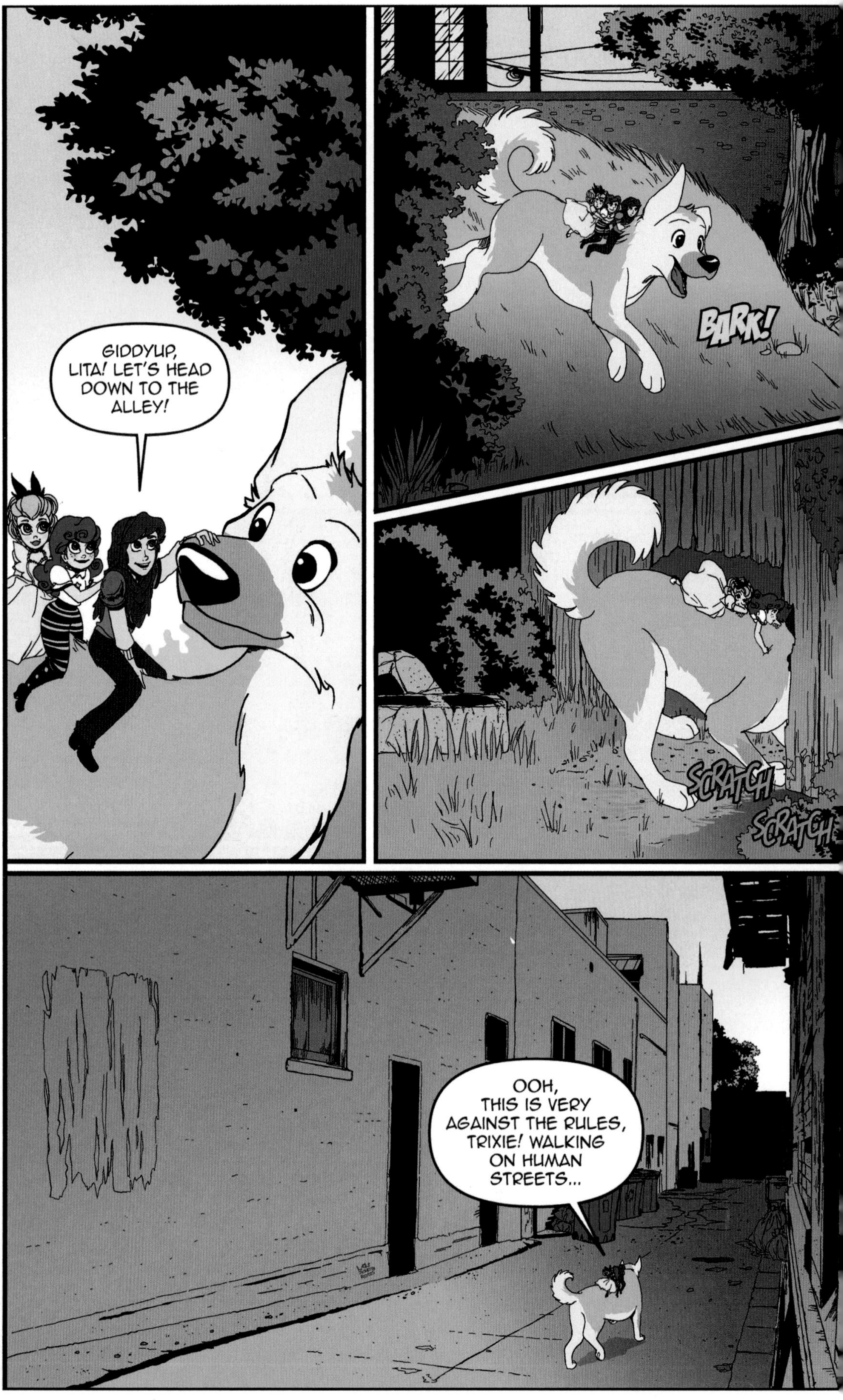
GIDDYUP, LITA! LET'S HEAD DOWN TO THE ALLEY!
BARK!
SCRATCH
SCRATCH
OOH, THIS IS VERY AGAINST THE RULES, TRIXIE! WALKING ON HUMAN STREETS...

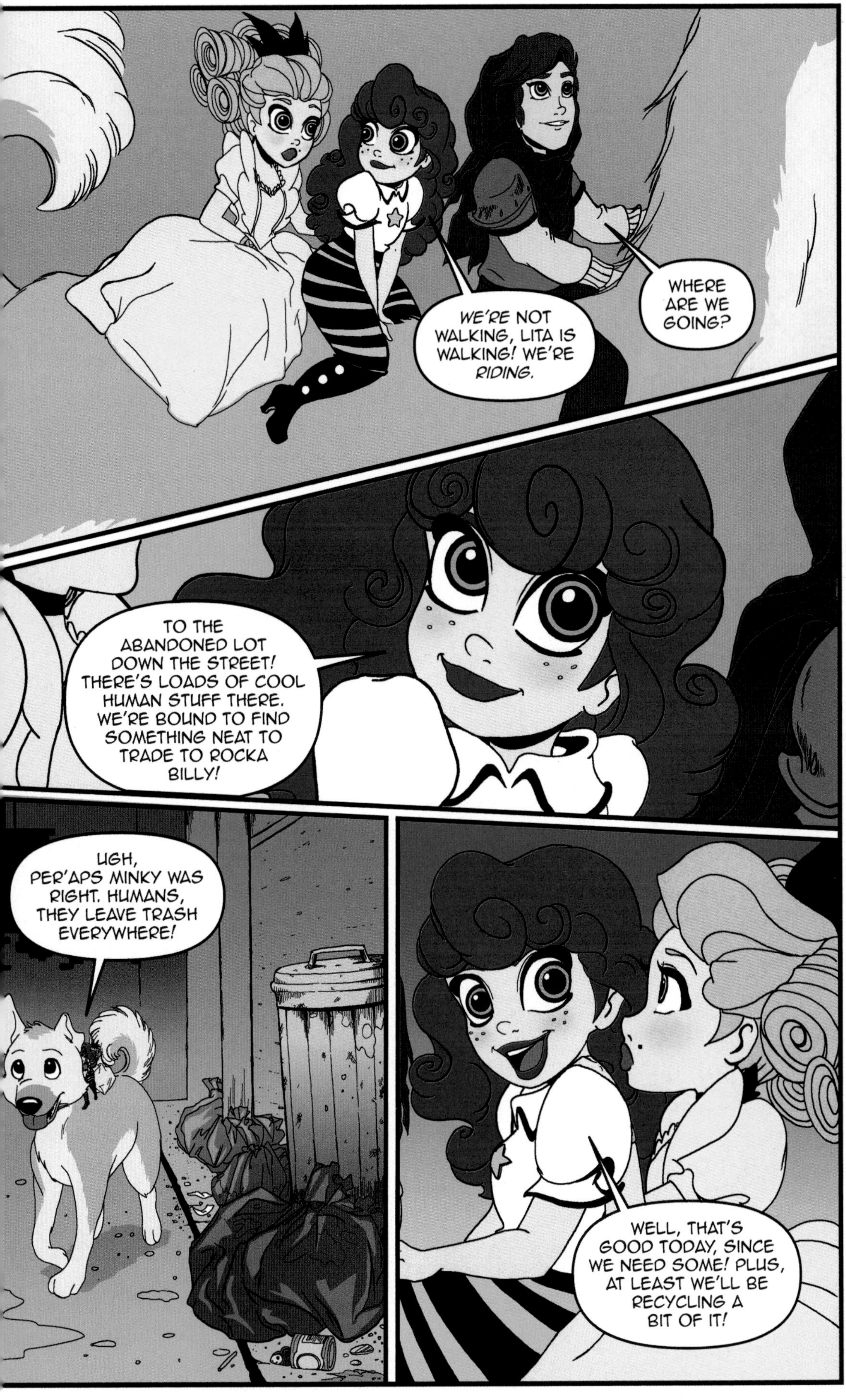
WHERE ARE WE GOING?
WE'RE NOT WALKING, LITA IS WALKING! WE'RE RIDING.
TO THE ABANDONED LOT DOWN THE STREET! THERE'S LOADS OF COOL HUMAN STUFF THERE. WE'RE BOUND TO FIND SOMETHING NEAT TO TRADE TO ROCKA BILLY!
UGH, PER'APS MINKY WAS RIGHT. HUMANS, THEY LEAVE TRASH EVERYWHERE!
WELL, THAT'S GOOD TODAY, SINCE WE NEED SOME! PLUS, AT LEAST WE'LL BE RECYCLING A BIT OF IT!

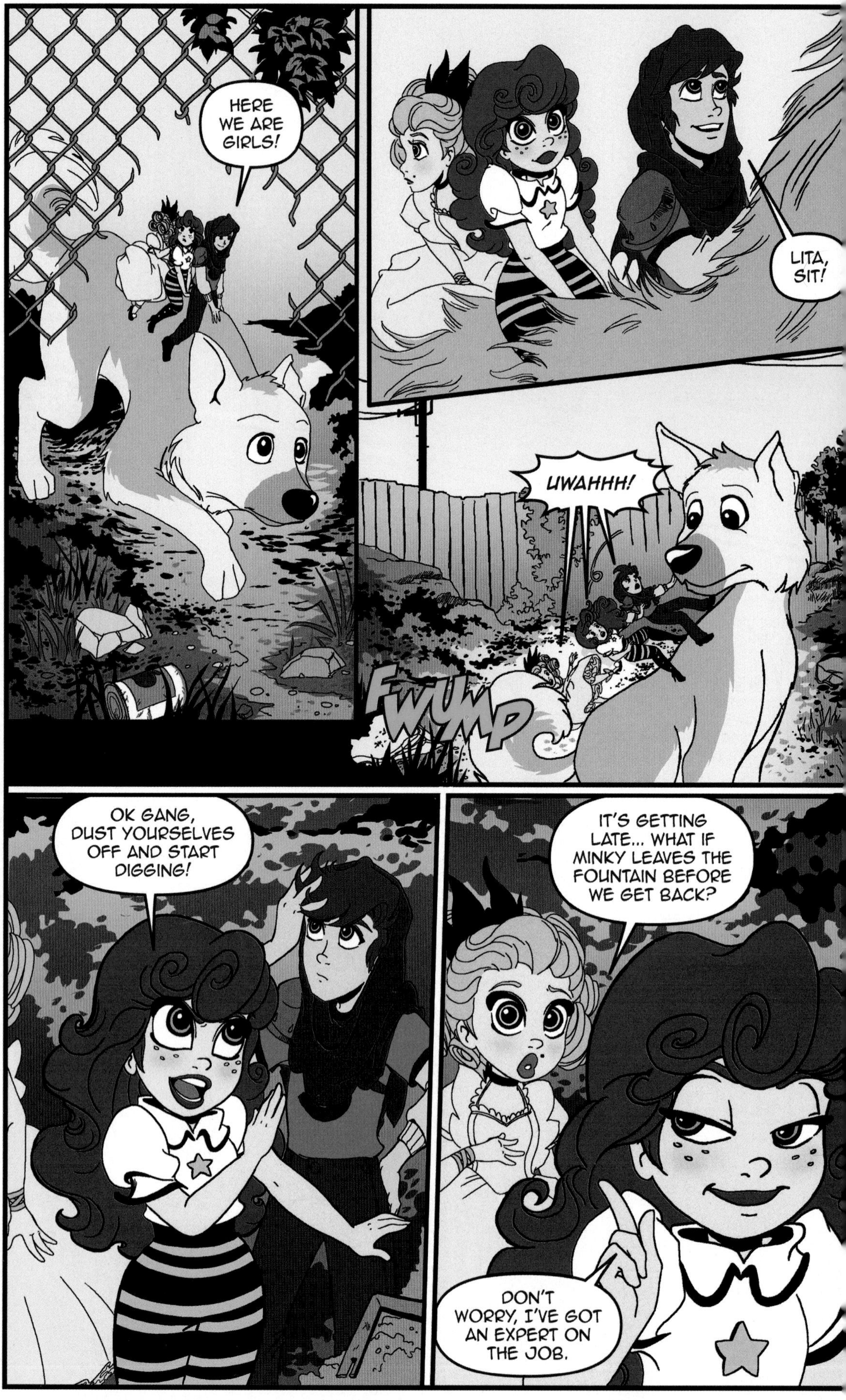
HERE WE ARE GIRLS!
LITA, SIT!
UWAHHH!
FWUMP
OK GANG, DUST YOURSELVES OFF AND START DIGGING!
IT'S GETTING LATE... WHAT IF MINKY LEAVES THE FOUNTAIN BEFORE WE GET BACK?
DON'T WORRY, I'VE GOT AN EXPERT ON THE JOB.

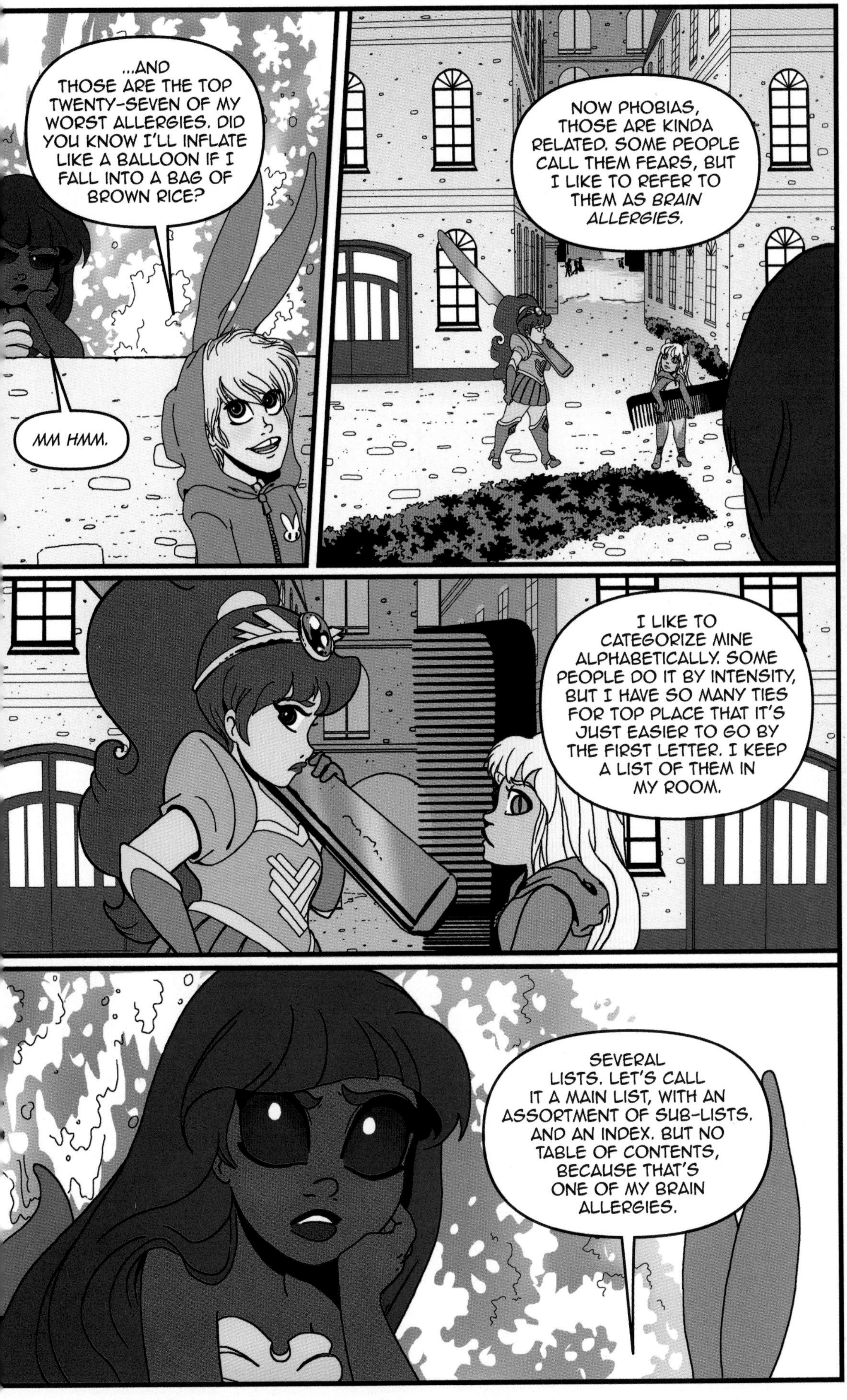
...AND THOSE ARE THE TOP TWENTY-SEVEN OF MY WORST ALLERGIES. DID YOU KNOW I'LL INFLATE LIKE A BALLOON IF I FALL INTO A BAG OF BROWN RICE?
MM HMM.
NOW PHOBIAS, THOSE ARE KINDA RELATED. SOME PEOPLE CALL THEM FEARS, BUT I LIKE TO REFER TO THEM AS *BRAIN ALLERGIES*.
I LIKE TO CATEGORIZE MINE ALPHABETICALLY. SOME PEOPLE DO IT BY INTENSITY, BUT I HAVE SO MANY TIES FOR TOP PLACE THAT IT'S JUST EASIER TO GO BY THE FIRST LETTER. I KEEP A LIST OF THEM IN MY ROOM.
SEVERAL LISTS. LET'S CALL IT A MAIN LIST, WITH AN ASSORTMENT OF SUB-LISTS. AND AN INDEX. BUT NO TABLE OF CONTENTS, BECAUSE THAT'S ONE OF MY BRAIN ALLERGIES.

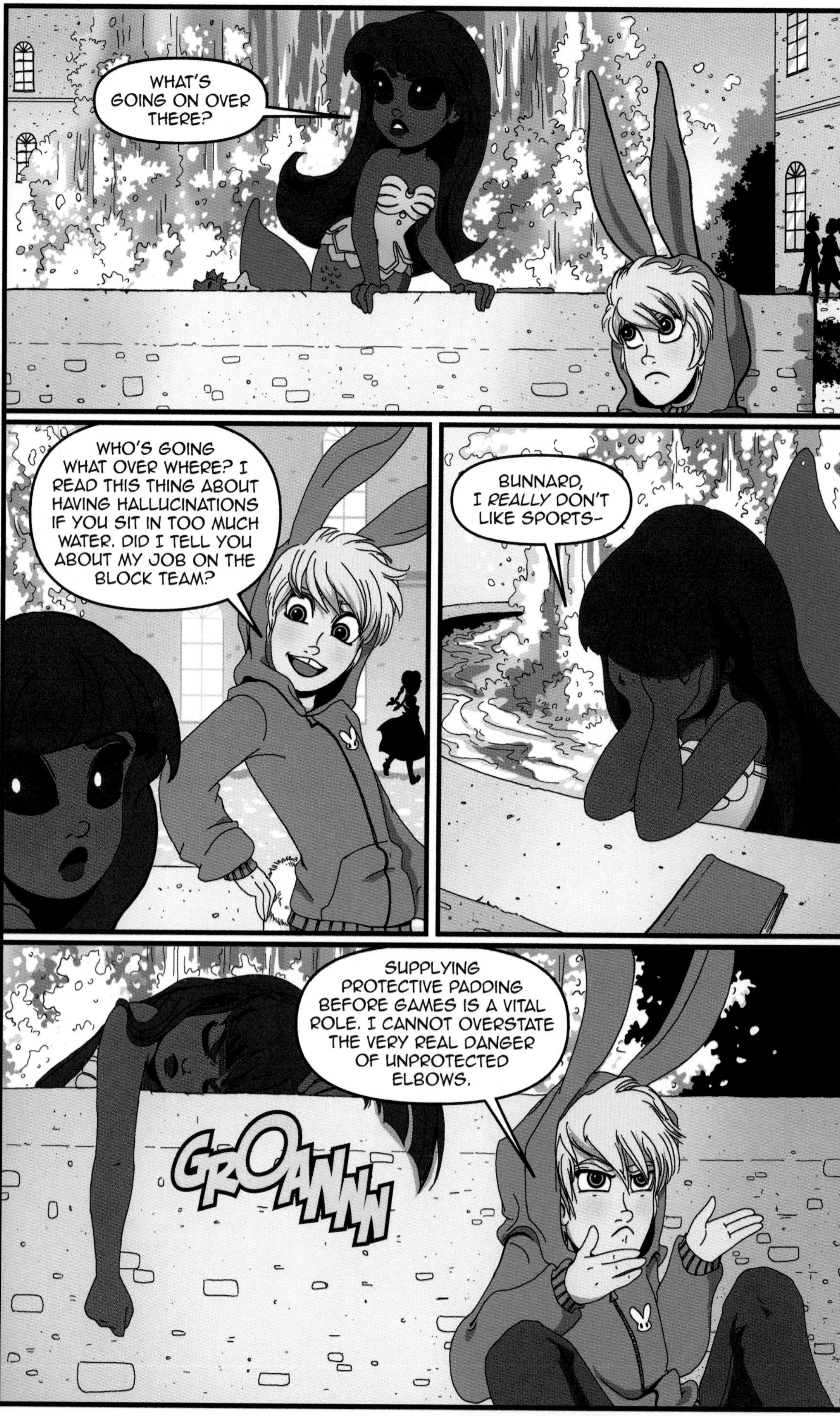
WHAT'S GOING ON OVER THERE?
WHO'S GOING WHAT OVER WHERE? I READ THIS THING ABOUT HAVING HALLUCINATIONS IF YOU SIT IN TOO MUCH WATER. DID I TELL YOU ABOUT MY JOB ON THE BLOCK TEAM?
BUNNARD, I *REALLY* DON'T LIKE SPORTS-
SUPPLYING PROTECTIVE PADDING BEFORE GAMES IS A VITAL ROLE. I CANNOT OVERSTATE THE VERY REAL DANGER OF UNPROTECTED ELBOWS.
GROANNNN

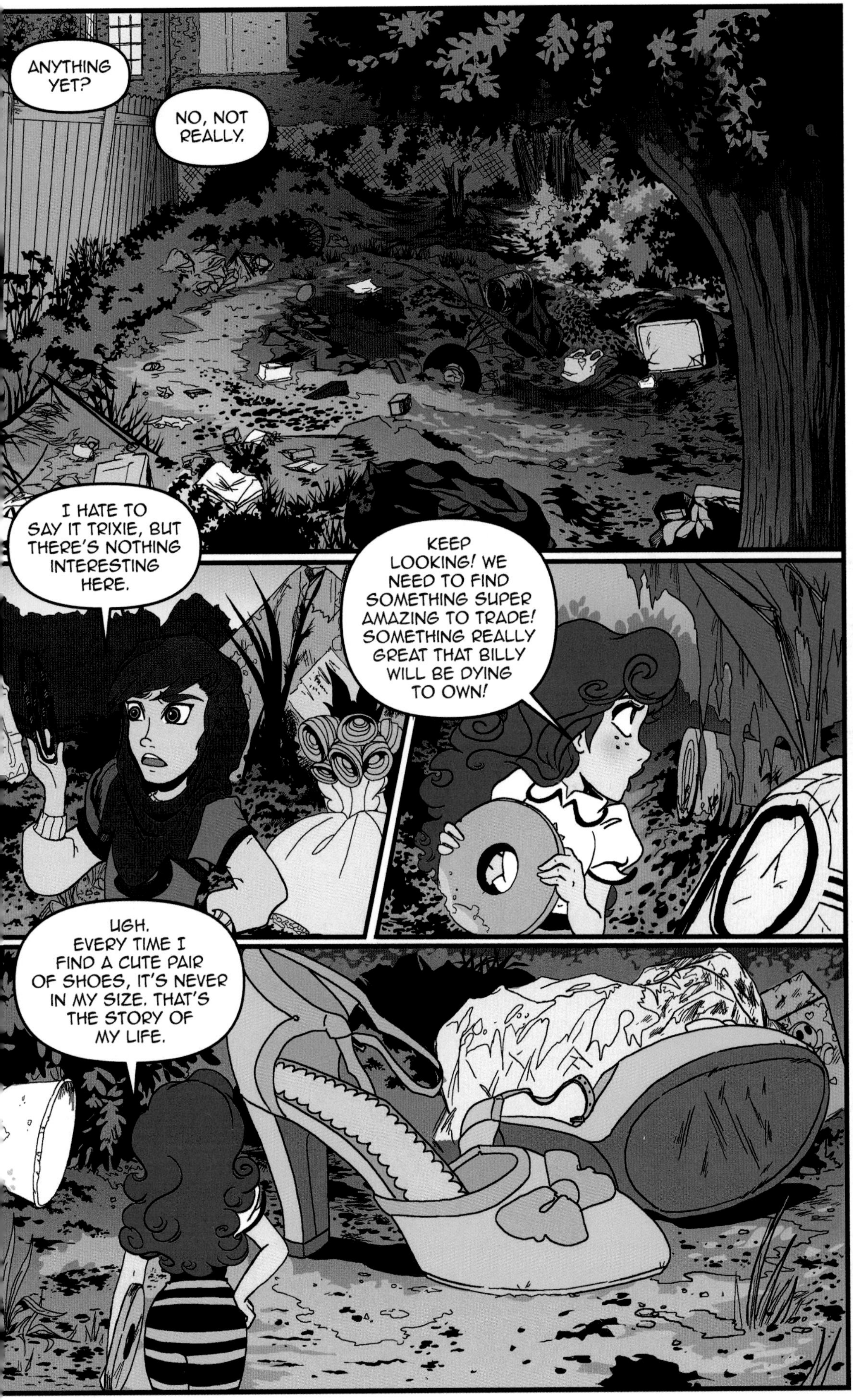
ANYTHING YET?
NO, NOT REALLY.
I HATE TO SAY IT TRIXIE, BUT THERE'S NOTHING INTERESTING HERE.
KEEP LOOKING! WE NEED TO FIND SOMETHING SUPER AMAZING TO TRADE! SOMETHING REALLY GREAT THAT BILLY WILL BE DYING TO OWN!
UGH. EVERY TIME I FIND A CUTE PAIR OF SHOES, IT'S NEVER IN MY SIZE. THAT'S THE STORY OF MY LIFE.

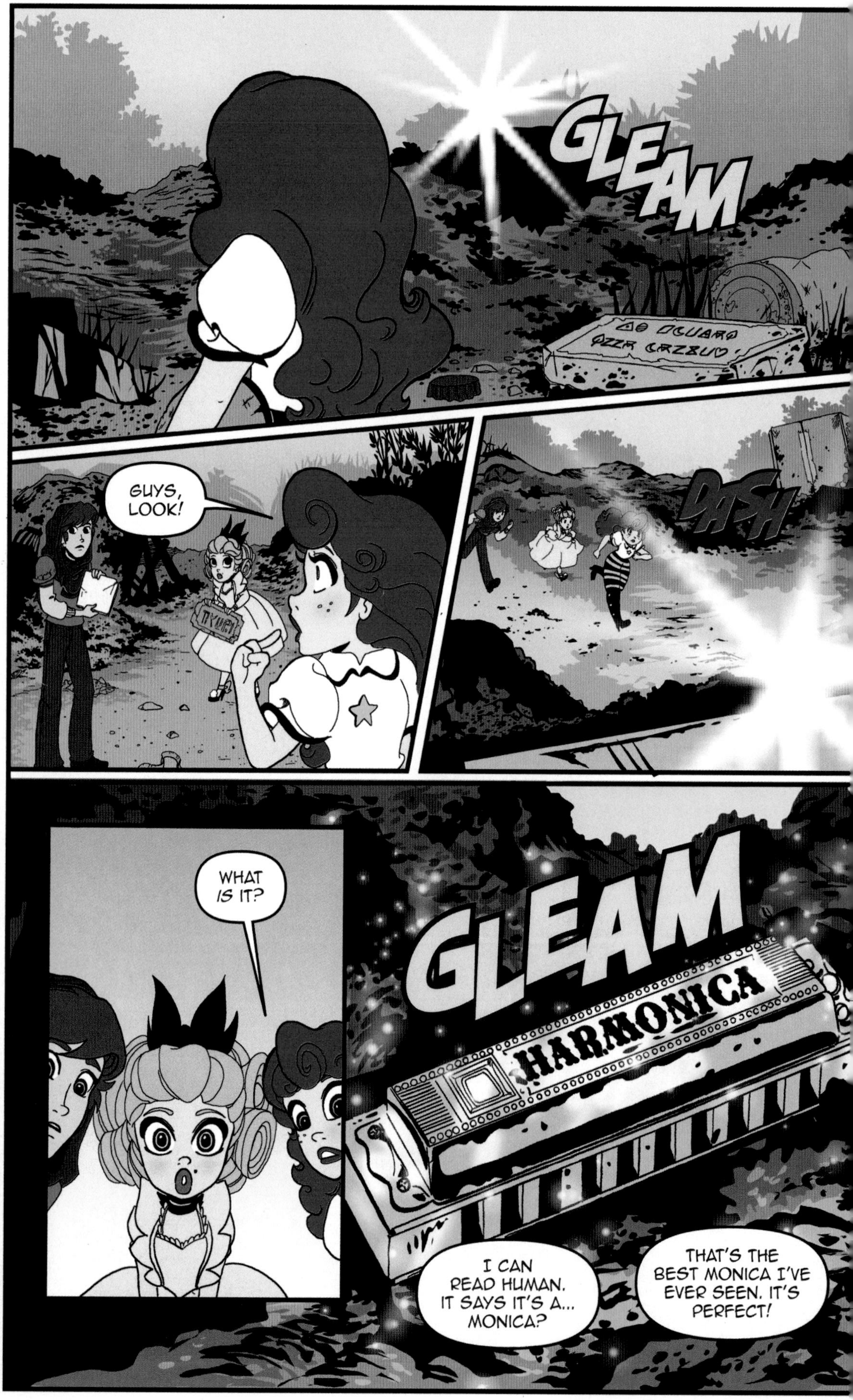
GLEAM
GUYS, LOOK!
DASH
WHAT IS IT?
GLEAM
HARMONICA
I CAN READ HUMAN. IT SAYS IT'S A... MONICA?
THAT'S THE BEST MONICA I'VE EVER SEEN. IT'S PERFECT!

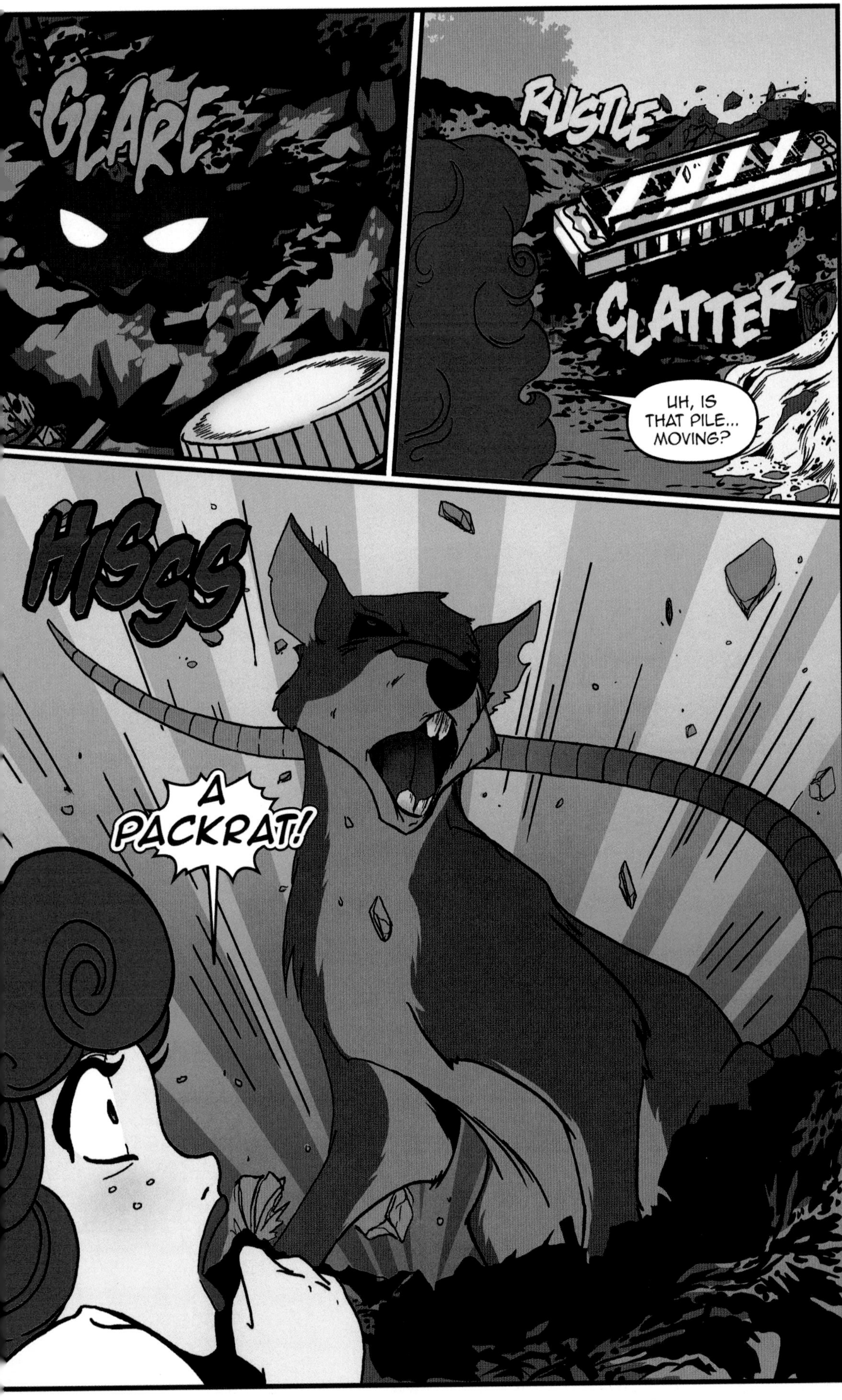
GLARE
RUSTLE
CLATTER
UH, IS THAT PILE... MOVING?
HISSS
A PACKRAT!

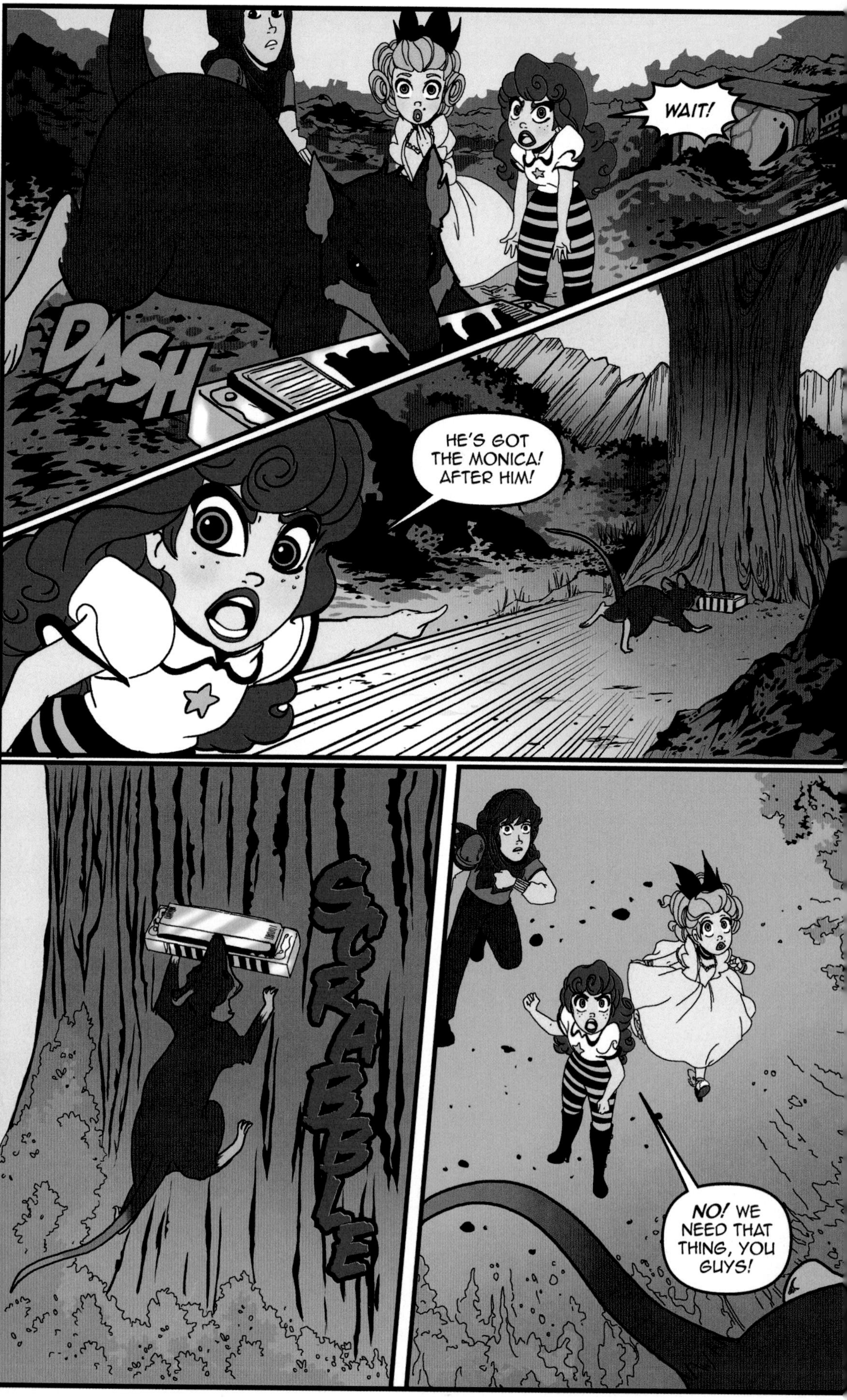
WAIT!
DASH
HE'S GOT THE MONICA! AFTER HIM!
SCRABBLE
NO! WE NEED THAT THING, YOU GUYS!

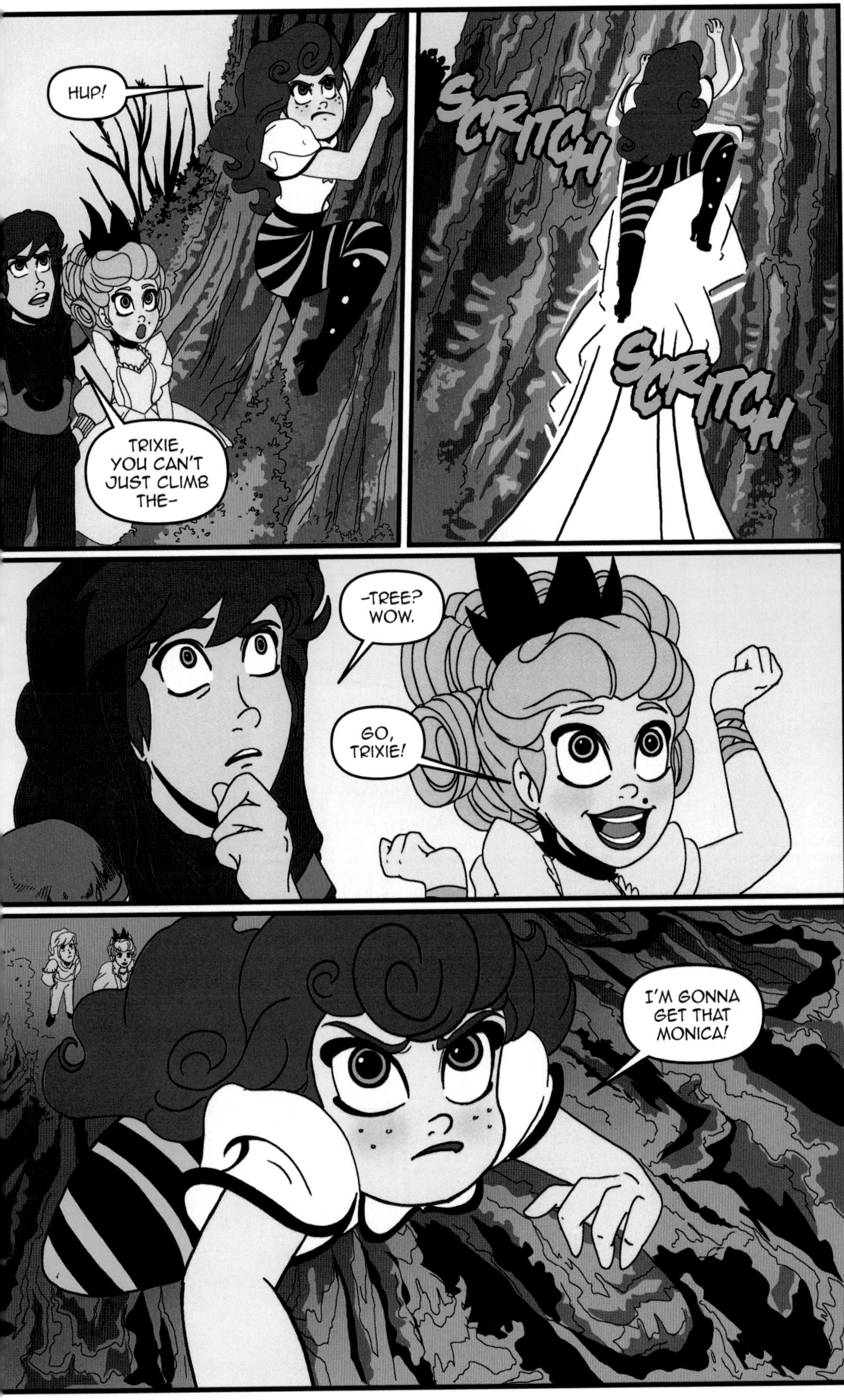
HUP!
TRIXIE, YOU CAN'T JUST CLIMB THE-
SCRITCH
SCRITCH
-TREE? WOW.
GO, TRIXIE!
I'M GONNA GET THAT MONICA!

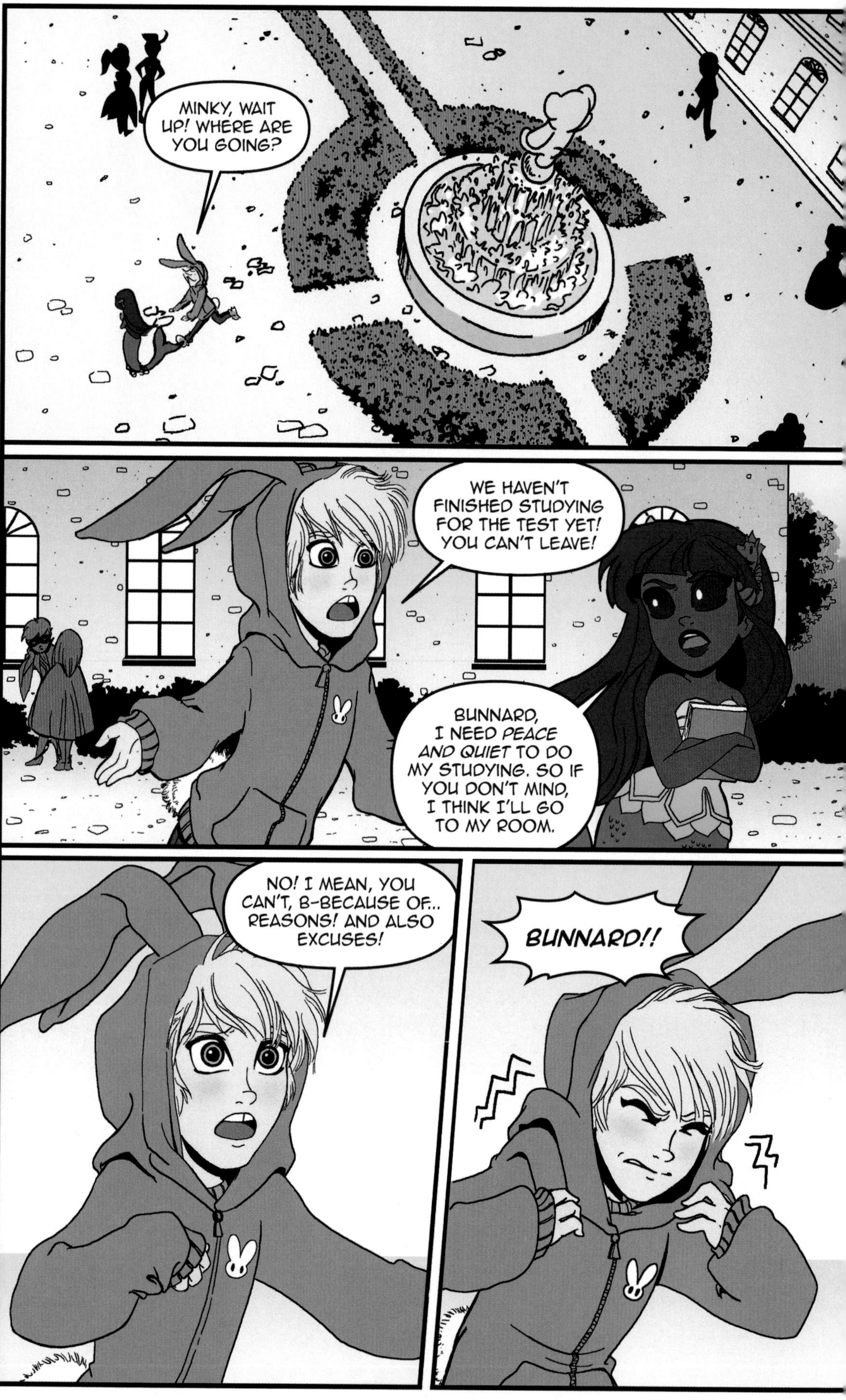
MINKY, WAIT UP! WHERE ARE YOU GOING?
WE HAVEN'T FINISHED STUDYING FOR THE TEST YET! YOU CAN'T LEAVE!
BUNNARD, I NEED *PEACE AND QUIET* TO DO MY STUDYING. SO IF YOU DON'T MIND, I THINK I'LL GO TO MY ROOM.
NO! I MEAN, YOU CAN'T, B-BECAUSE OF... REASONS! AND ALSO EXCUSES!
BUNNARD!!

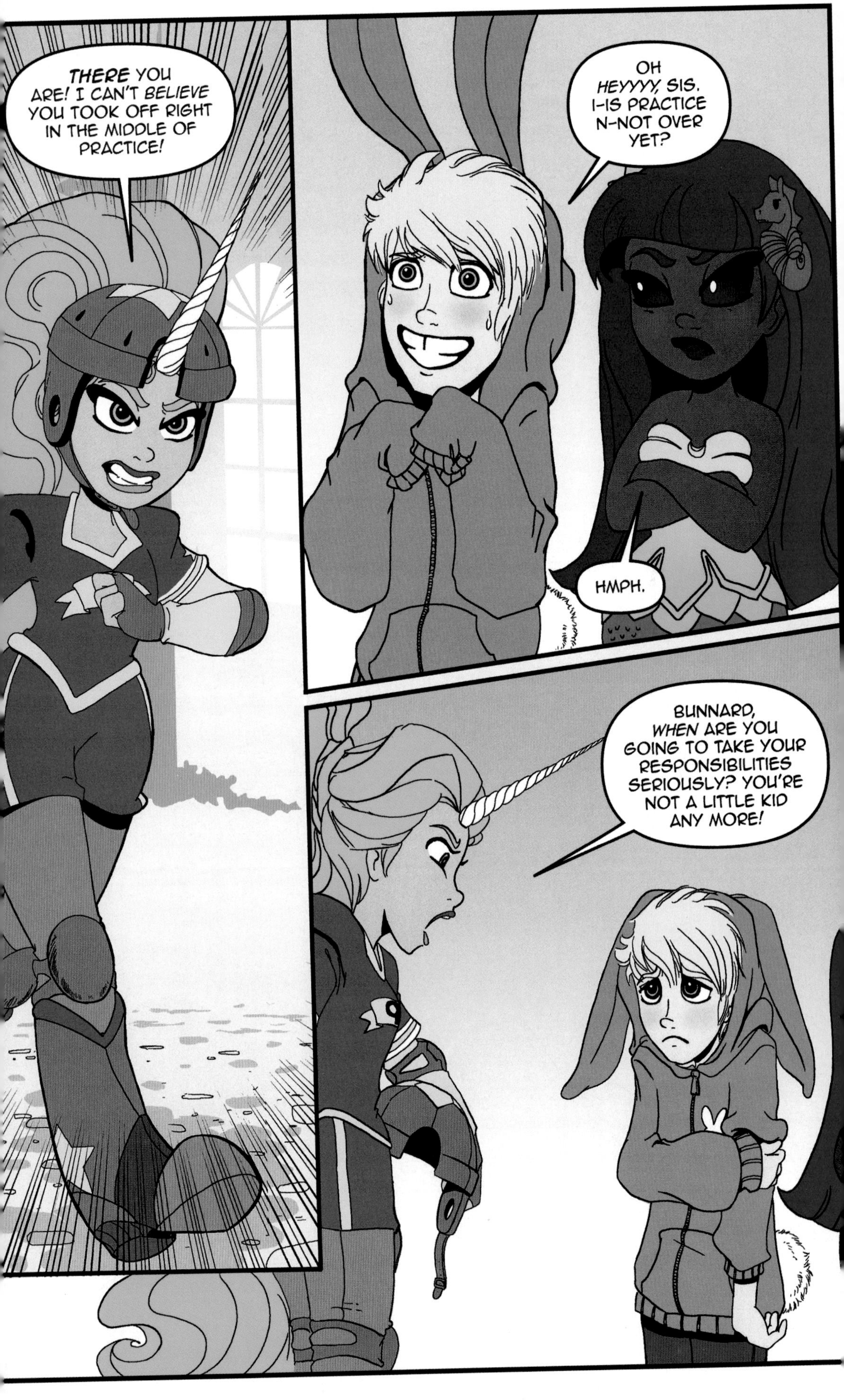
THERE YOU ARE! I CAN'T BELIEVE YOU TOOK OFF RIGHT IN THE MIDDLE OF PRACTICE!
OH HEYYYY, SIS. I-IS PRACTICE N-NOT OVER YET?
HMPH.
BUNNARD, WHEN ARE YOU GOING TO TAKE YOUR RESPONSIBILITIES SERIOUSLY? YOU'RE NOT A LITTLE KID ANY MORE!

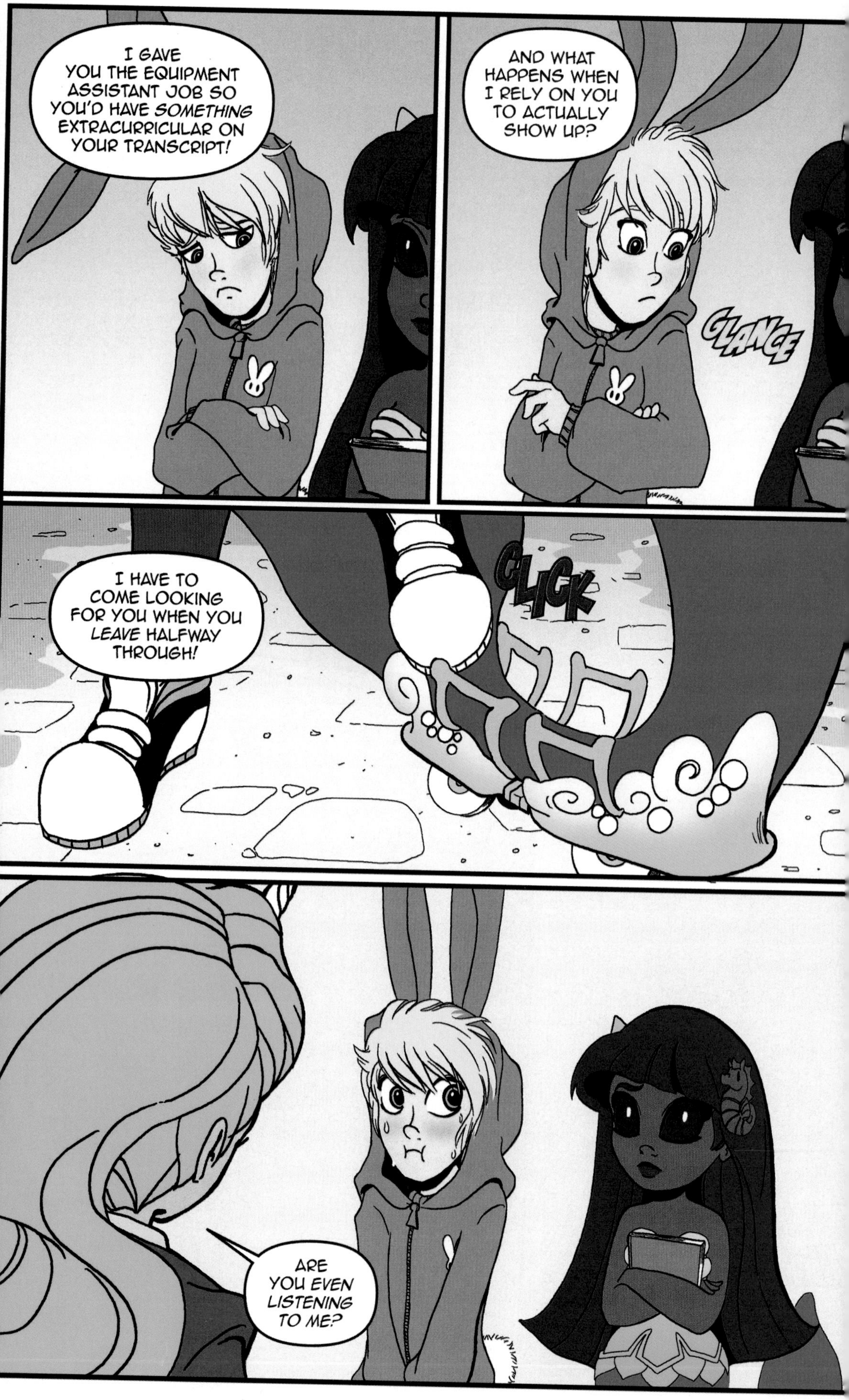

I GAVE YOU THE EQUIPMENT ASSISTANT JOB SO YOU'D HAVE *SOMETHING* EXTRACURRICULAR ON YOUR TRANSCRIPT!
AND WHAT HAPPENS WHEN I RELY ON YOU TO ACTUALLY SHOW UP?
GLANCE
I HAVE TO COME LOOKING FOR YOU WHEN YOU *LEAVE* HALFWAY THROUGH!
CLICK
ARE YOU EVEN LISTENING TO ME?

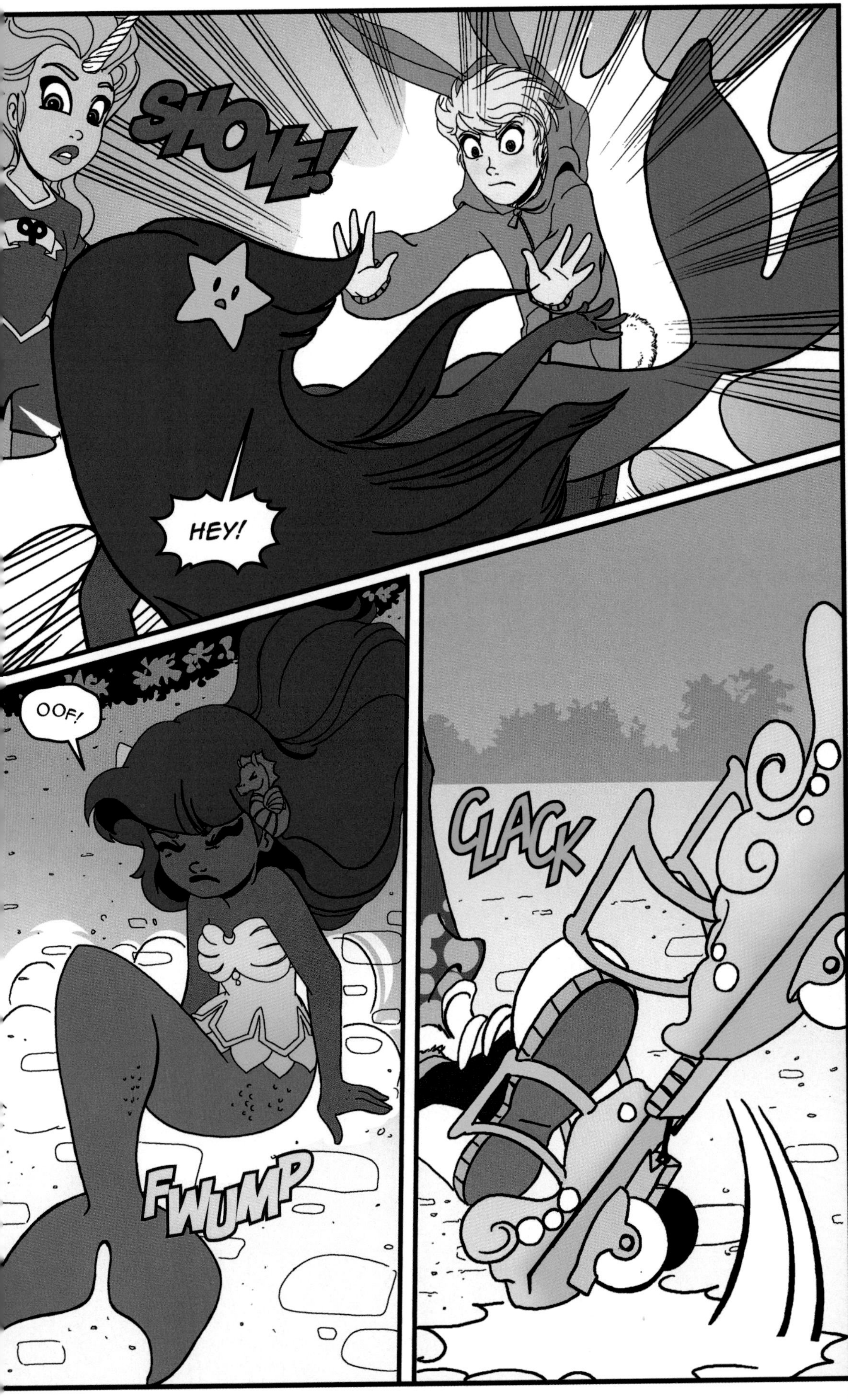
SHOVE!
HEY!
OOF!
FWUMP
CLACK

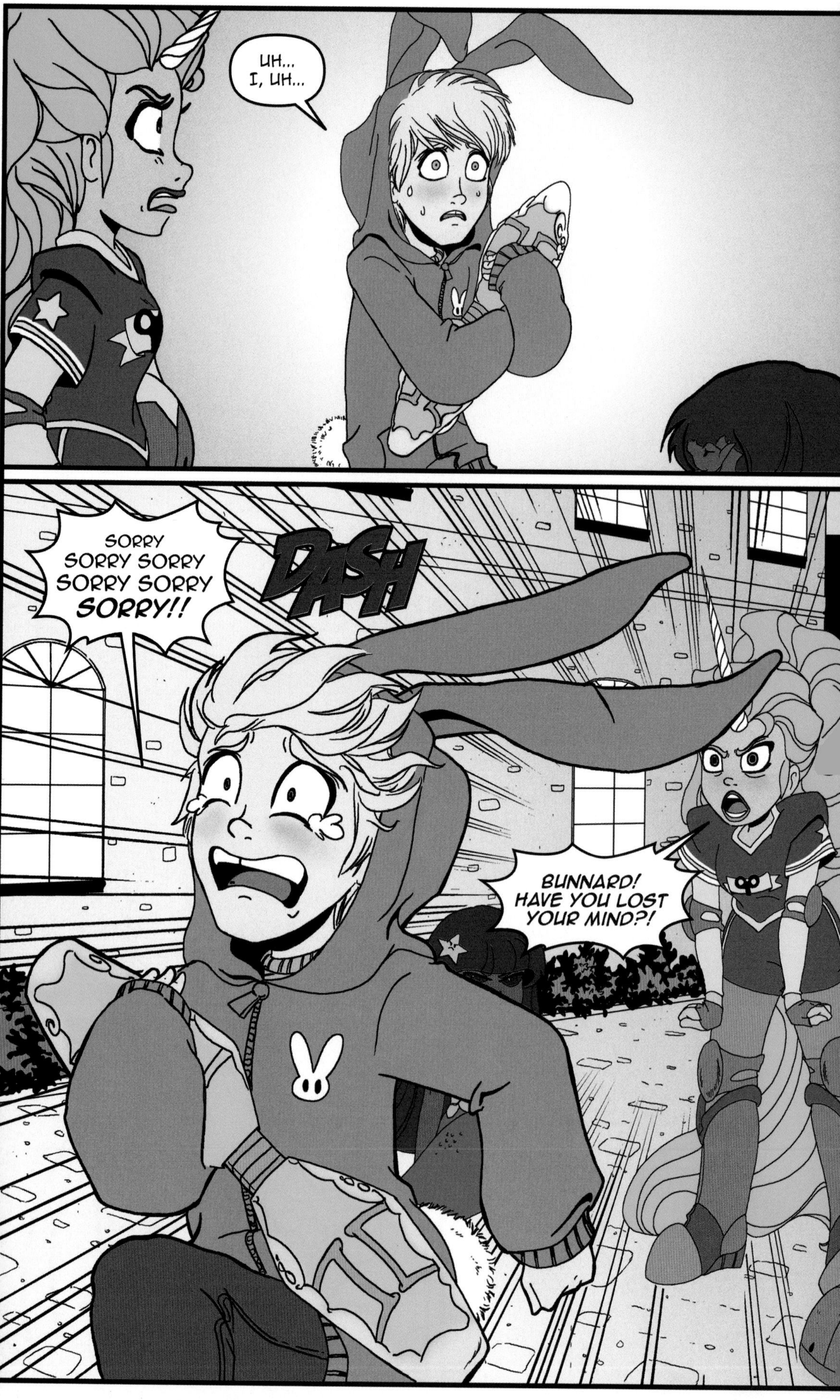
UH...
I, UH...
SORRY
SORRY SORRY
SORRY SORRY
SORRY!!
DASH
BUNNARD!
HAVE YOU LOST
YOUR MIND?!

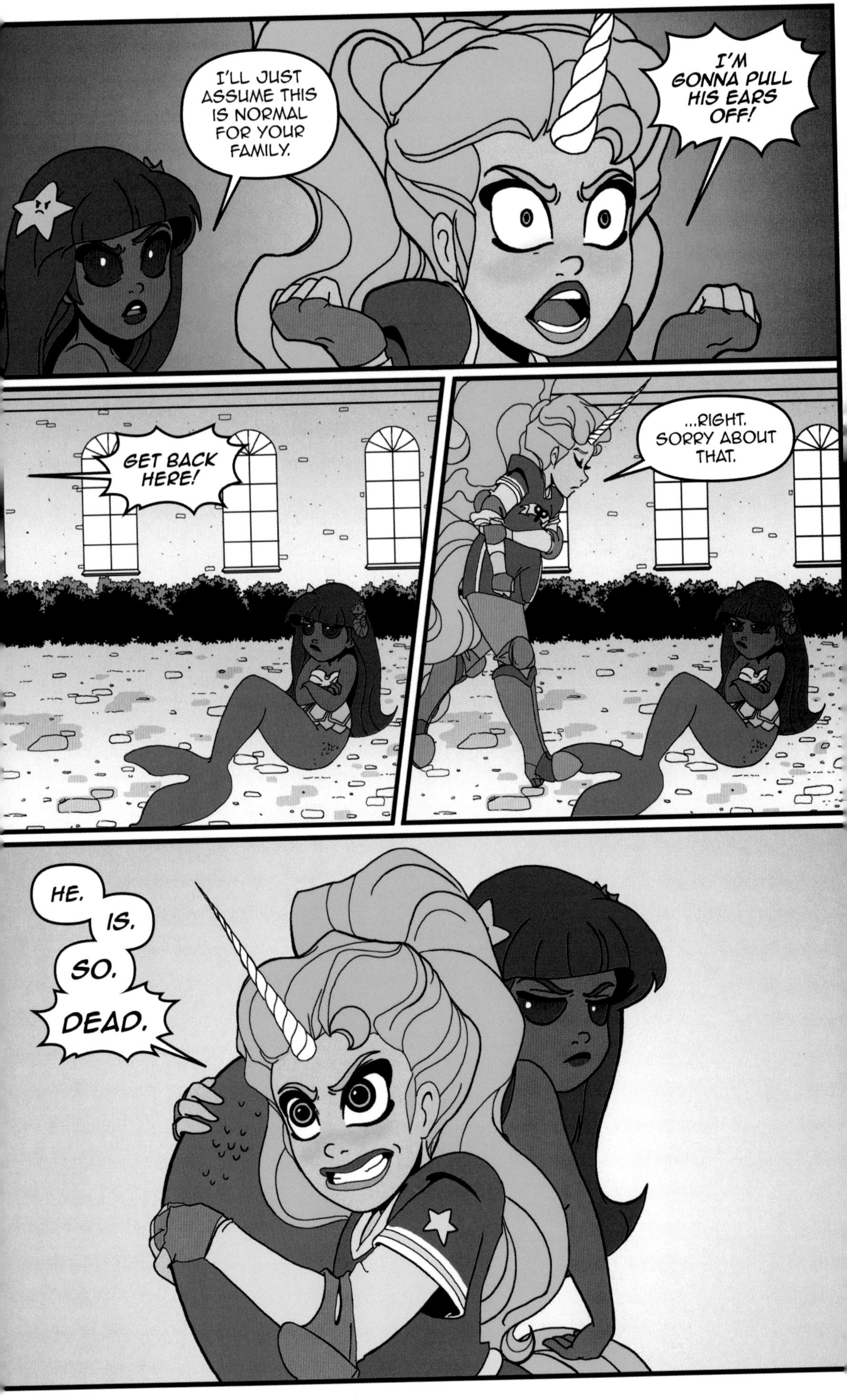
I'LL JUST ASSUME THIS IS NORMAL FOR YOUR FAMILY.
I'M GONNA PULL HIS EARS OFF!
GET BACK HERE!
...RIGHT. SORRY ABOUT THAT.
HE.
IS.
SO.
DEAD.

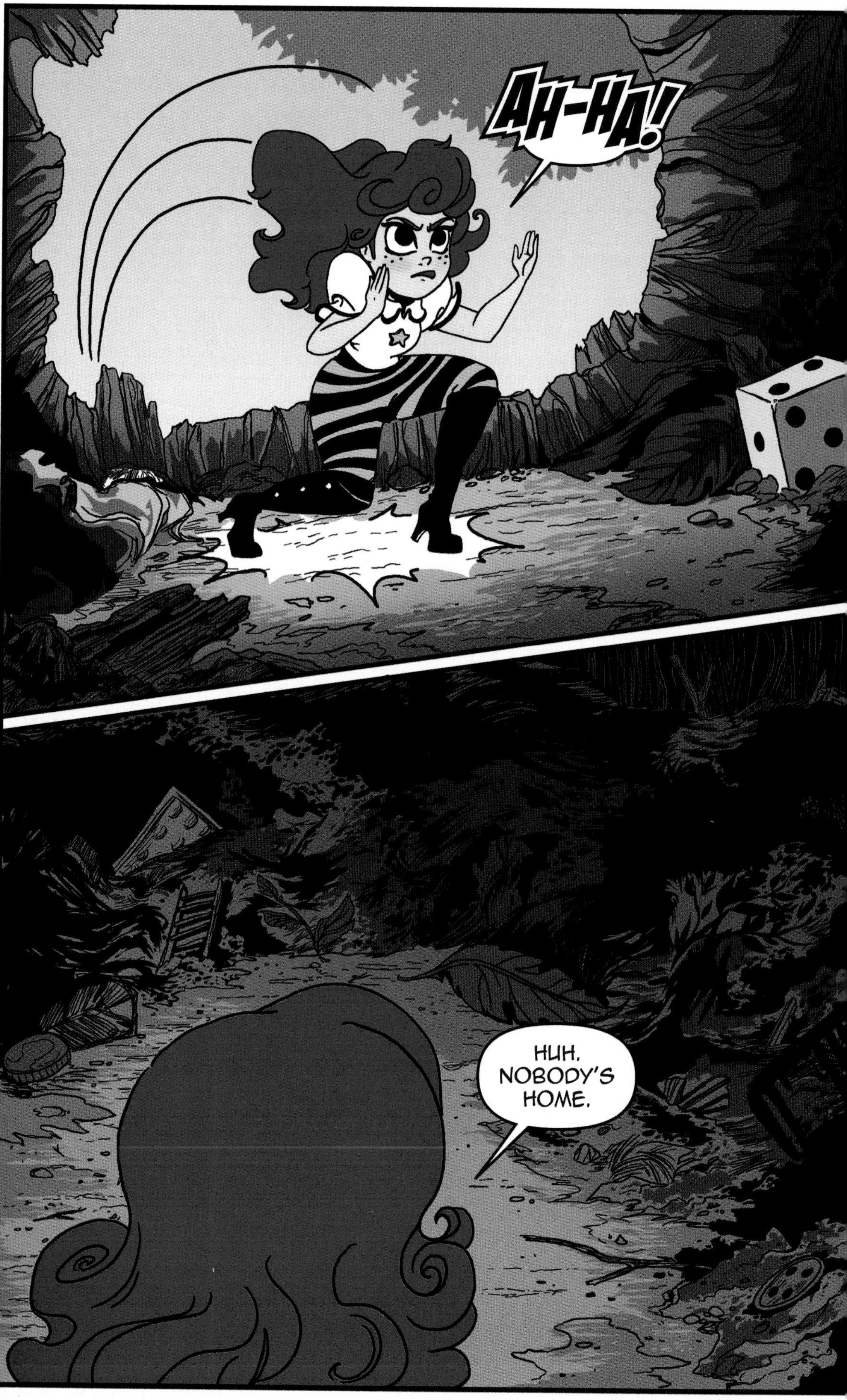
AH-HA!
HUH. NOBODY'S HOME.

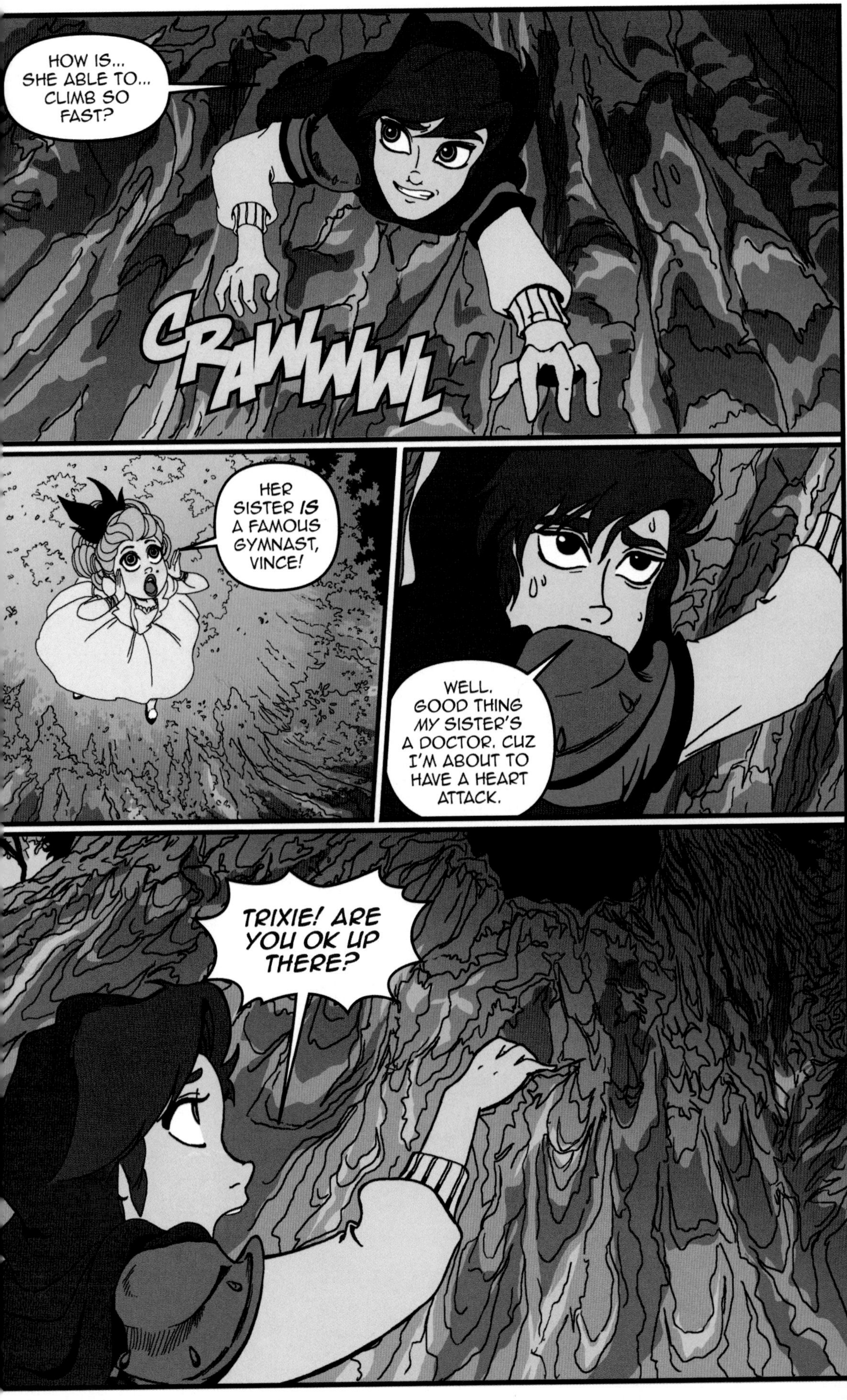
HOW IS... SHE ABLE TO... CLIMB SO FAST?
CRAWWWL
HER SISTER *IS* A FAMOUS GYMNAST, VINCE!
WELL. GOOD THING *MY* SISTER'S A DOCTOR. CUZ I'M ABOUT TO HAVE A HEART ATTACK.
TRIXIE! ARE YOU OK UP THERE?

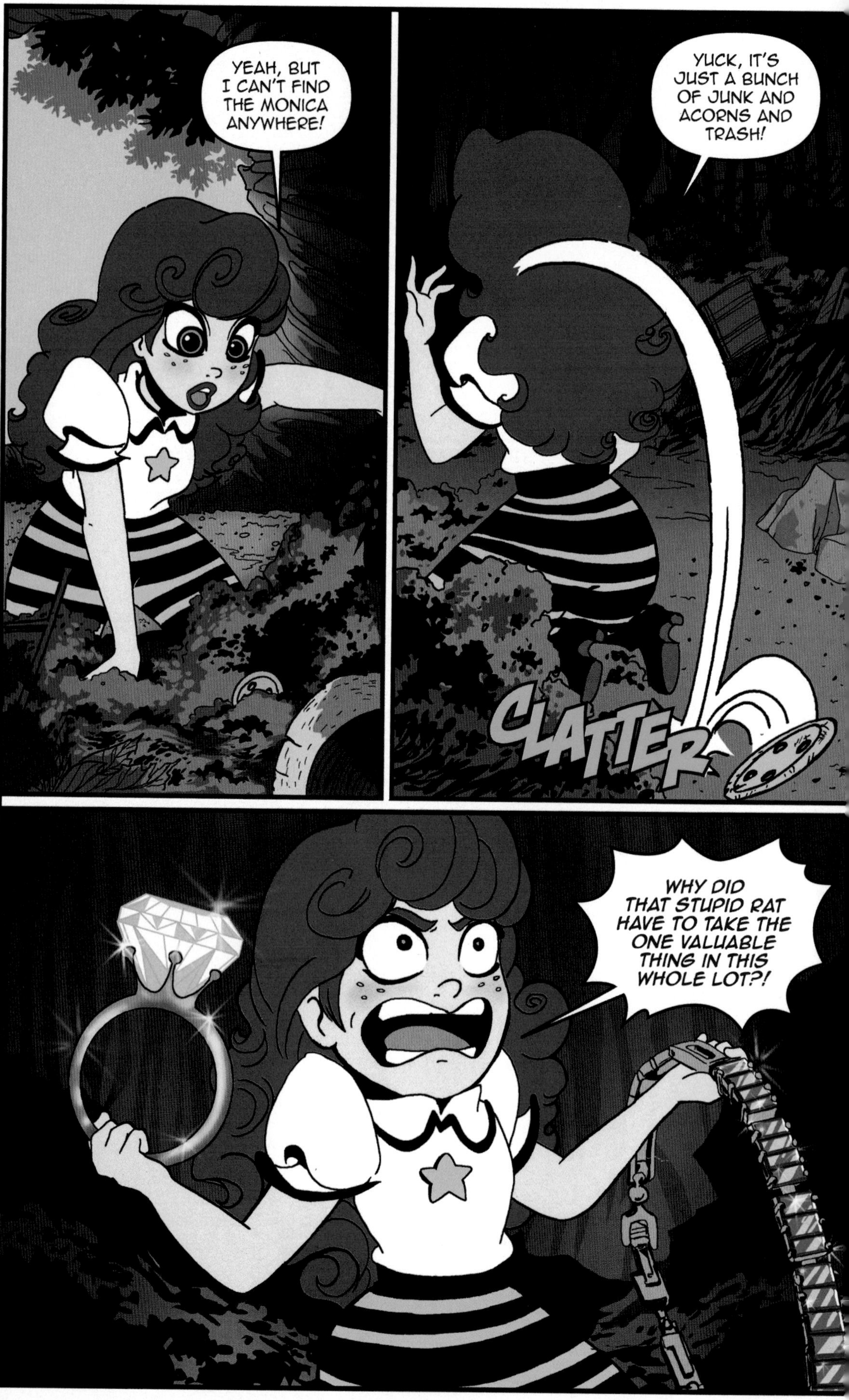
YEAH, BUT I CAN'T FIND THE MONICA ANYWHERE!
YUCK, IT'S JUST A BUNCH OF JUNK AND ACORNS AND TRASH!
CLATTER
WHY DID THAT STUPID RAT HAVE TO TAKE THE ONE VALUABLE THING IN THIS WHOLE LOT?!

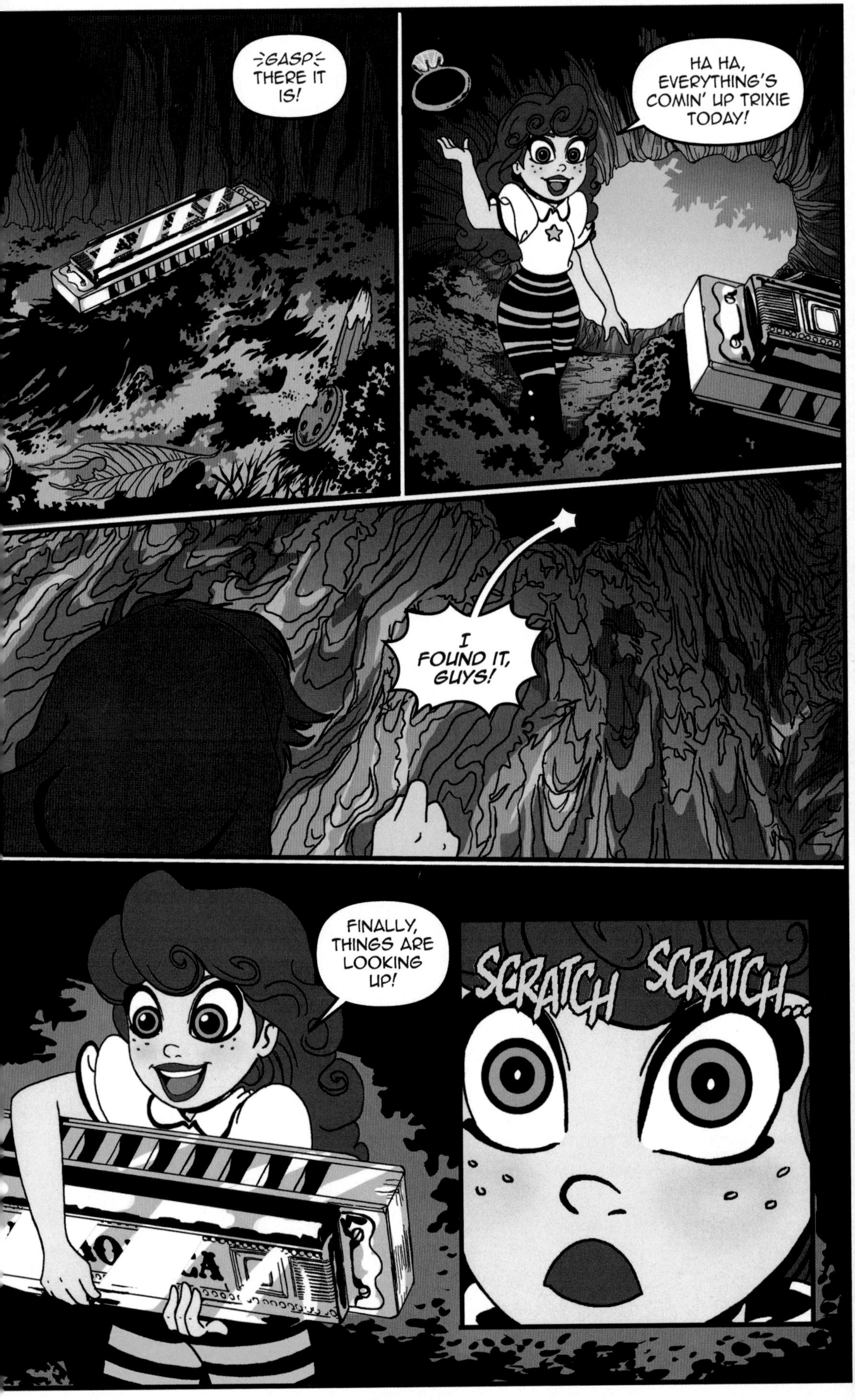

GASP THERE IT IS!
HA HA, EVERYTHING'S COMIN' UP TRIXIE TODAY!
I FOUND IT, GUYS!
FINALLY, THINGS ARE LOOKING UP!
SCRATCH SCRATCH...

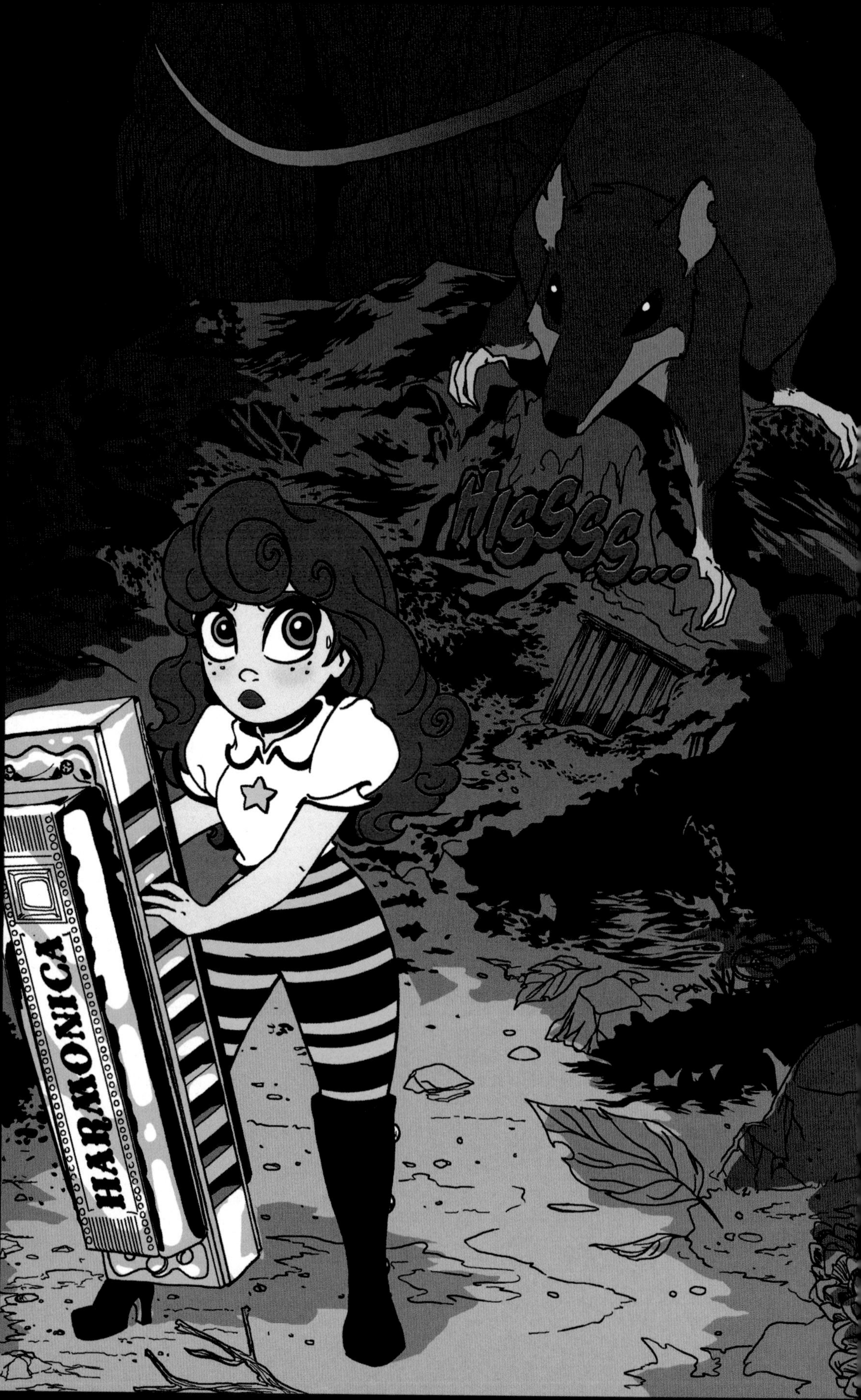
HISSSS...
HARMONICA

pages in progress

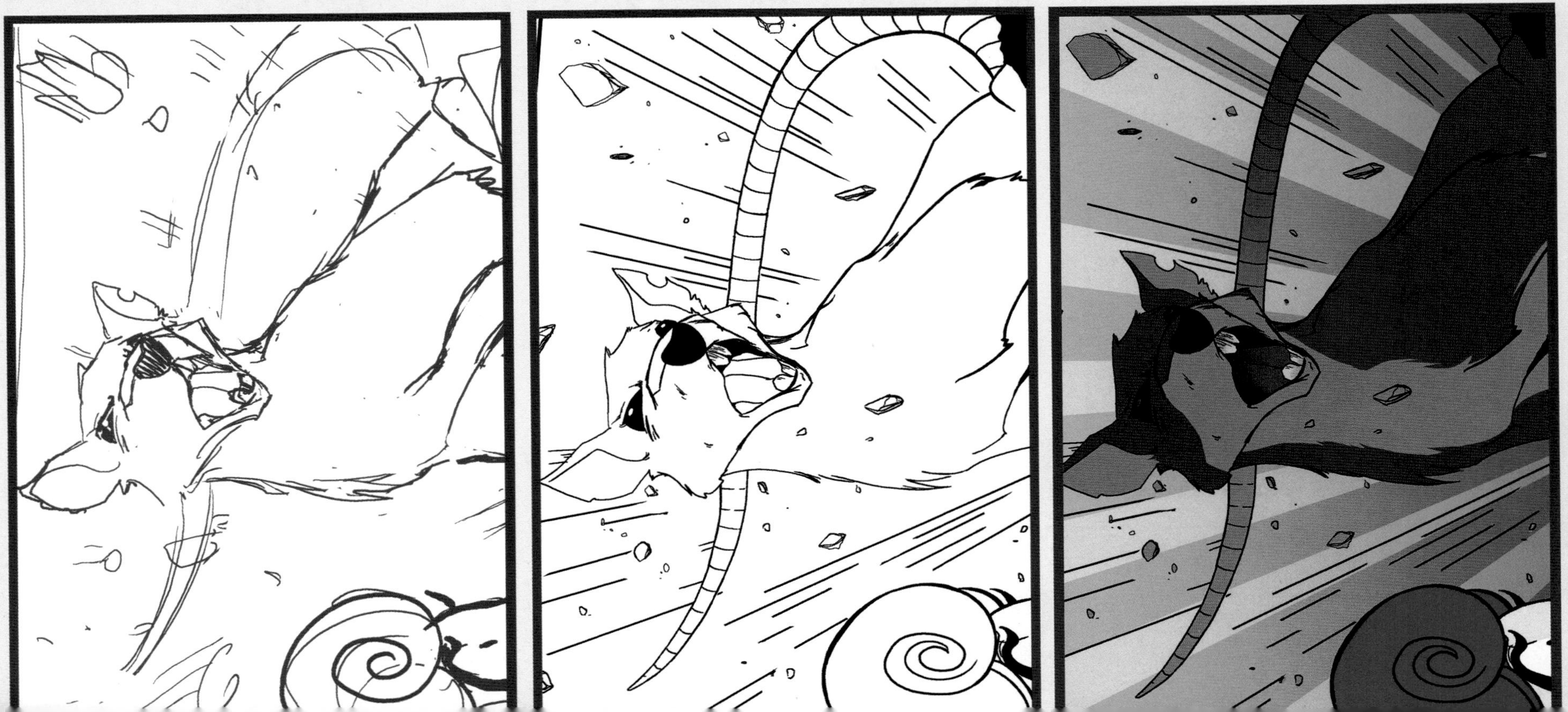

pages in progress

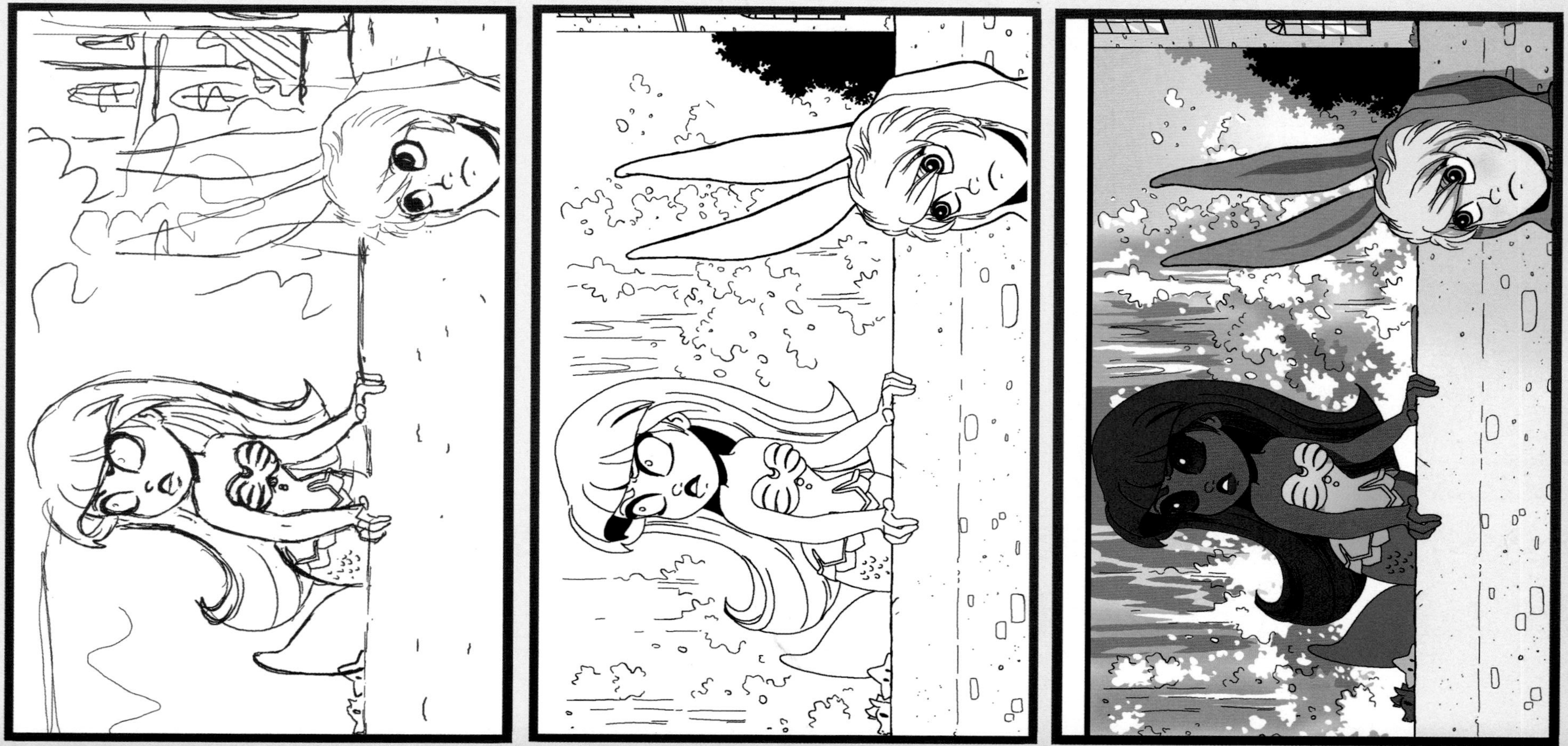

pages in progress

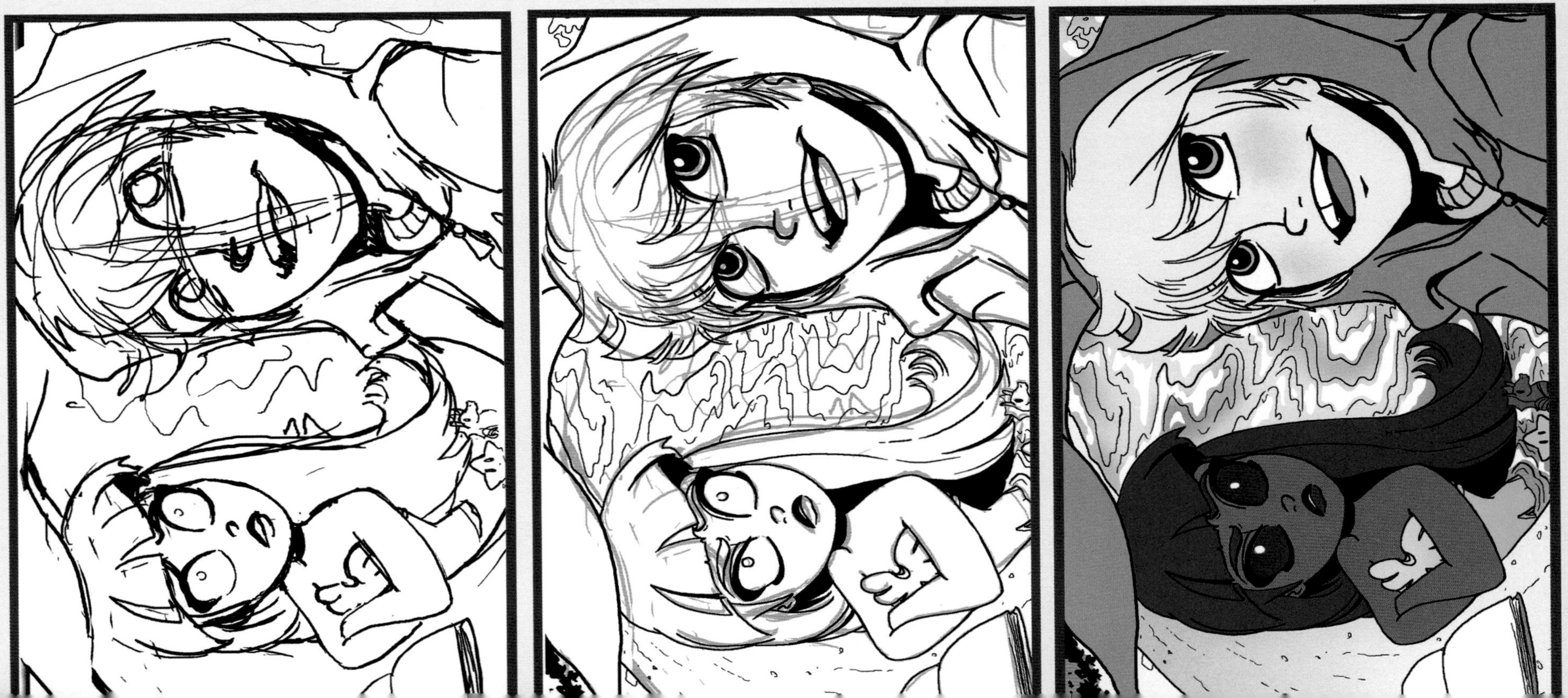

pages in progress

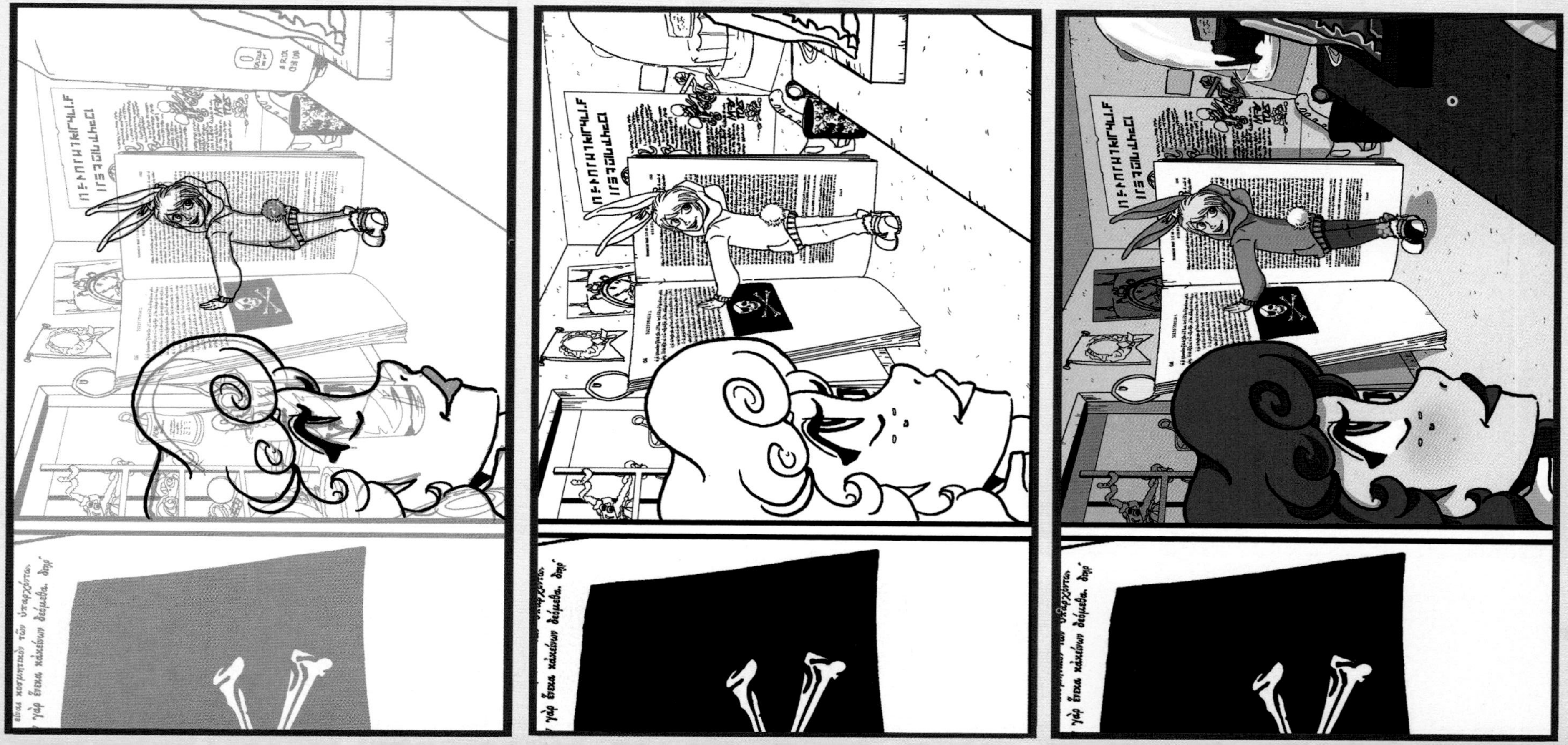
εἶναι κοσμητικὸν τῶν ὑπαρχόντων
γὰρ ἕνεκα κἀκείνων δεόμεθα. διὸ

pages in progress

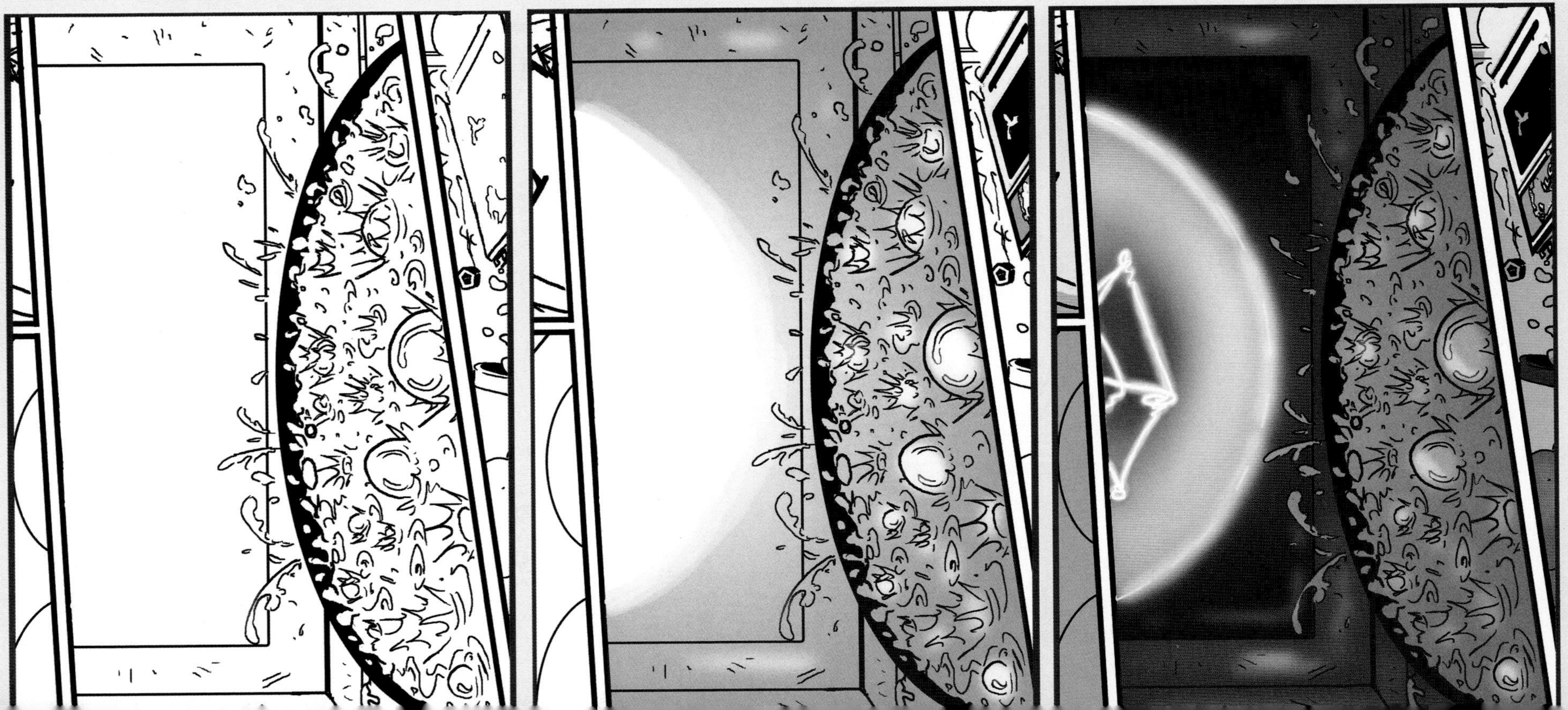

Live on Twitch.tv!

WANT MORE TOYETICA DOODLES AND COMICS **DRAWN LIVE?**

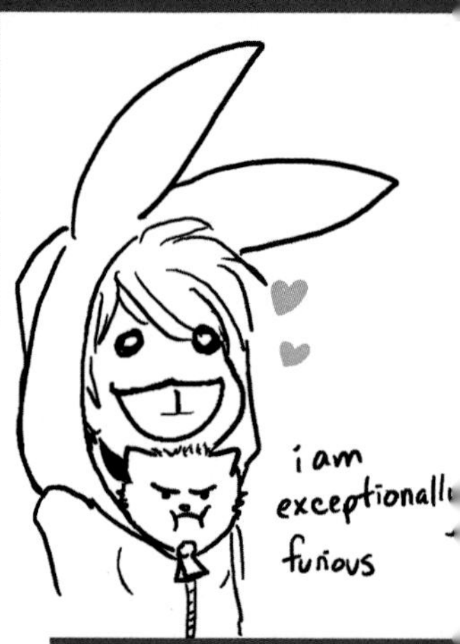

i am exceptionally furious

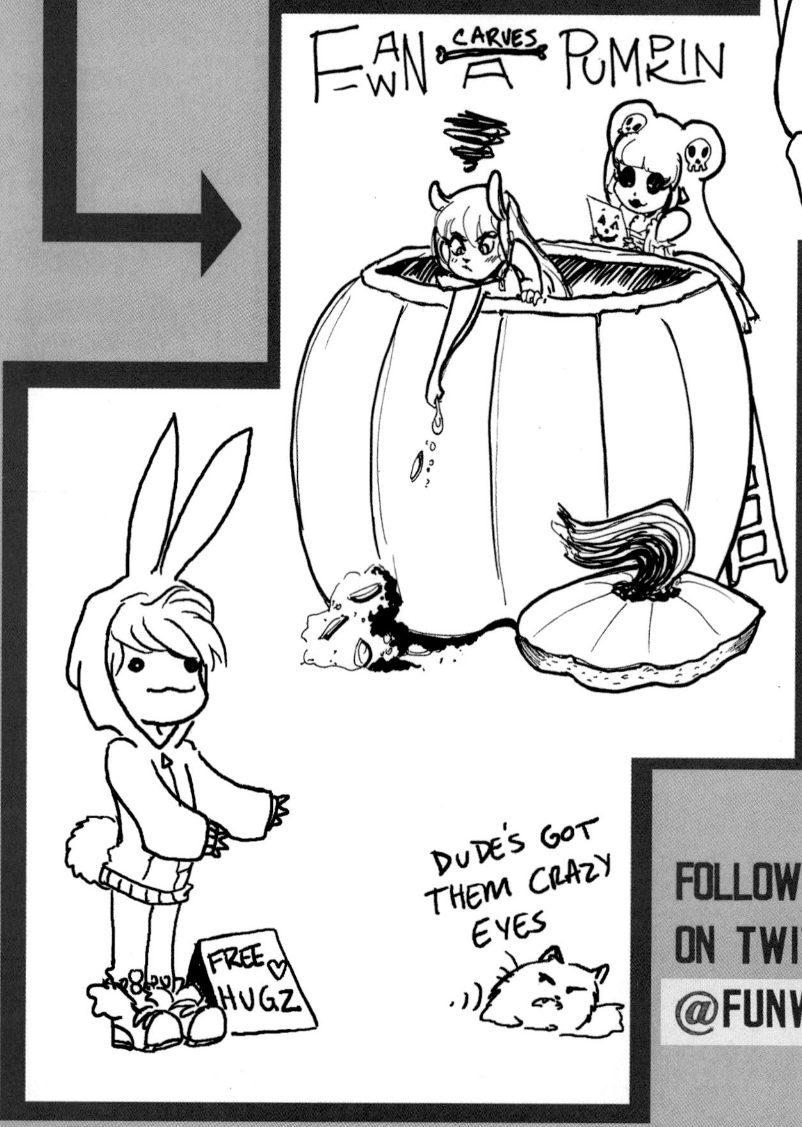

FAWN CARVES A PUMPKIN
FREE HUGZ
DUDE'S GOT THEM CRAZY EYES

Heck yeah dumb stu like this!

FOLLOW ME ON TWITCH

@FUNWITHPUNKO

@MartyLegrow FunWithPunko

GIANTS

PART FOUR

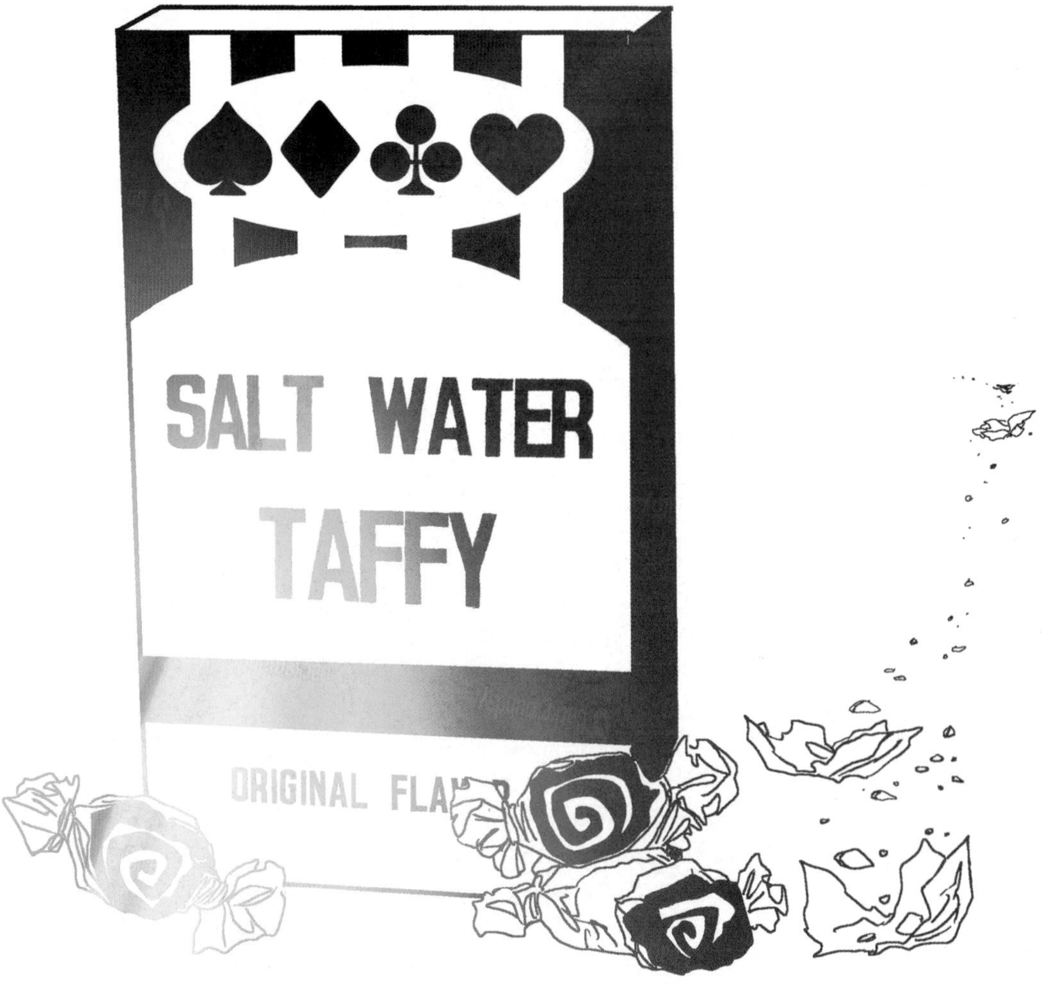
SALT WATER
TAFFY
ORIGINAL

TOYETICA 8

STORY AND ART BY MARTY LEGROW

LETTERING
Justin Birch

LIKE A SNAKE
IN A LEG FACTORY

Bryan Seaton: Publisher/ CEO • Shawn Gabborin: Editor In Chief • Jason Martin: Publisher-Danger Zone • Nicole D'Andria: Marketing Director/Editor
Danielle Davison: Executive Administrator • Chad Cicconi: Action Lawyer • Shawn Pryor: President of Creator Relations

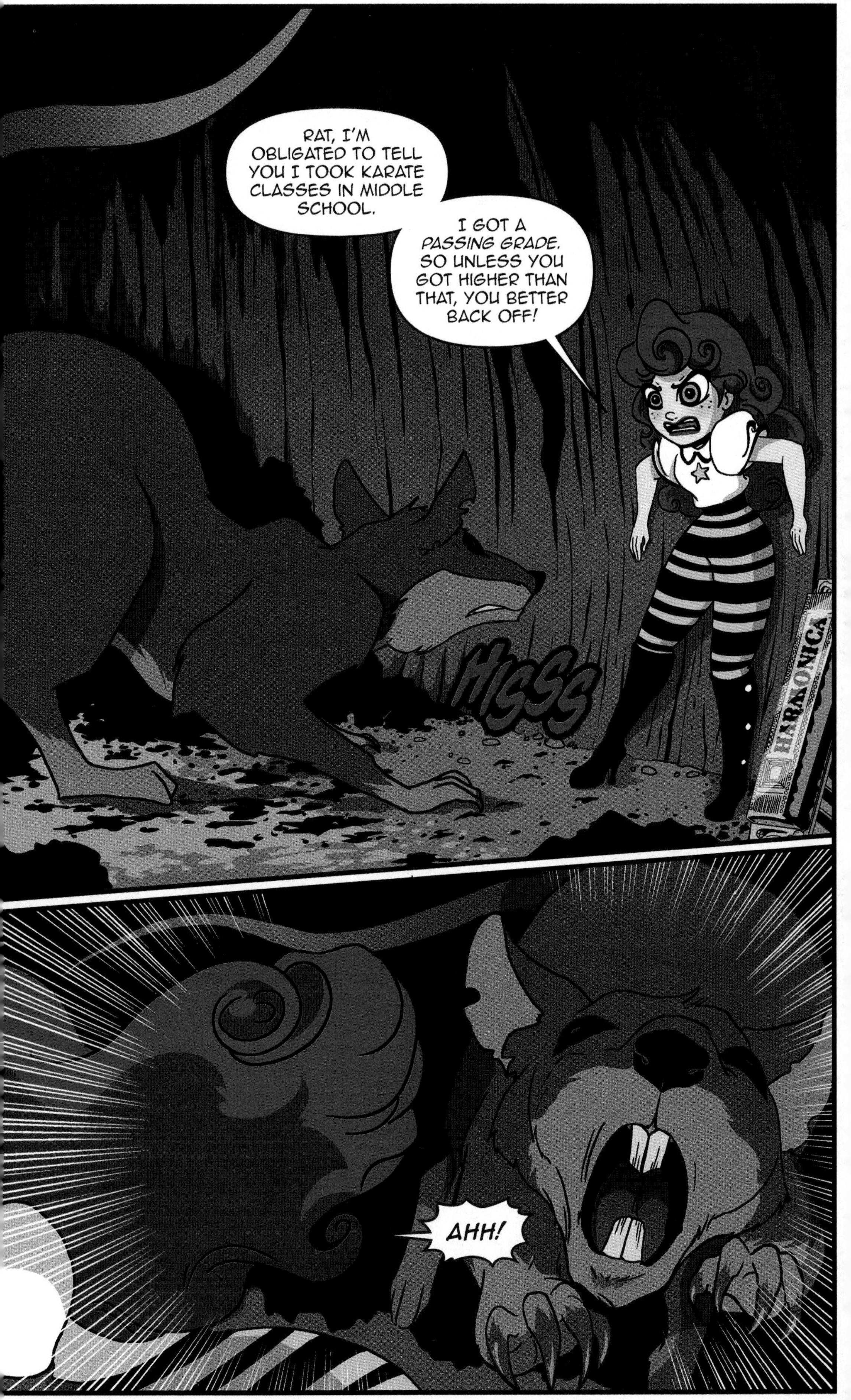
RAT, I'M OBLIGATED TO TELL YOU I TOOK KARATE CLASSES IN MIDDLE SCHOOL.
I GOT A *PASSING GRADE.* SO UNLESS YOU GOT HIGHER THAN THAT, YOU BETTER BACK OFF!
HISSS
HARMONICA
AHH!

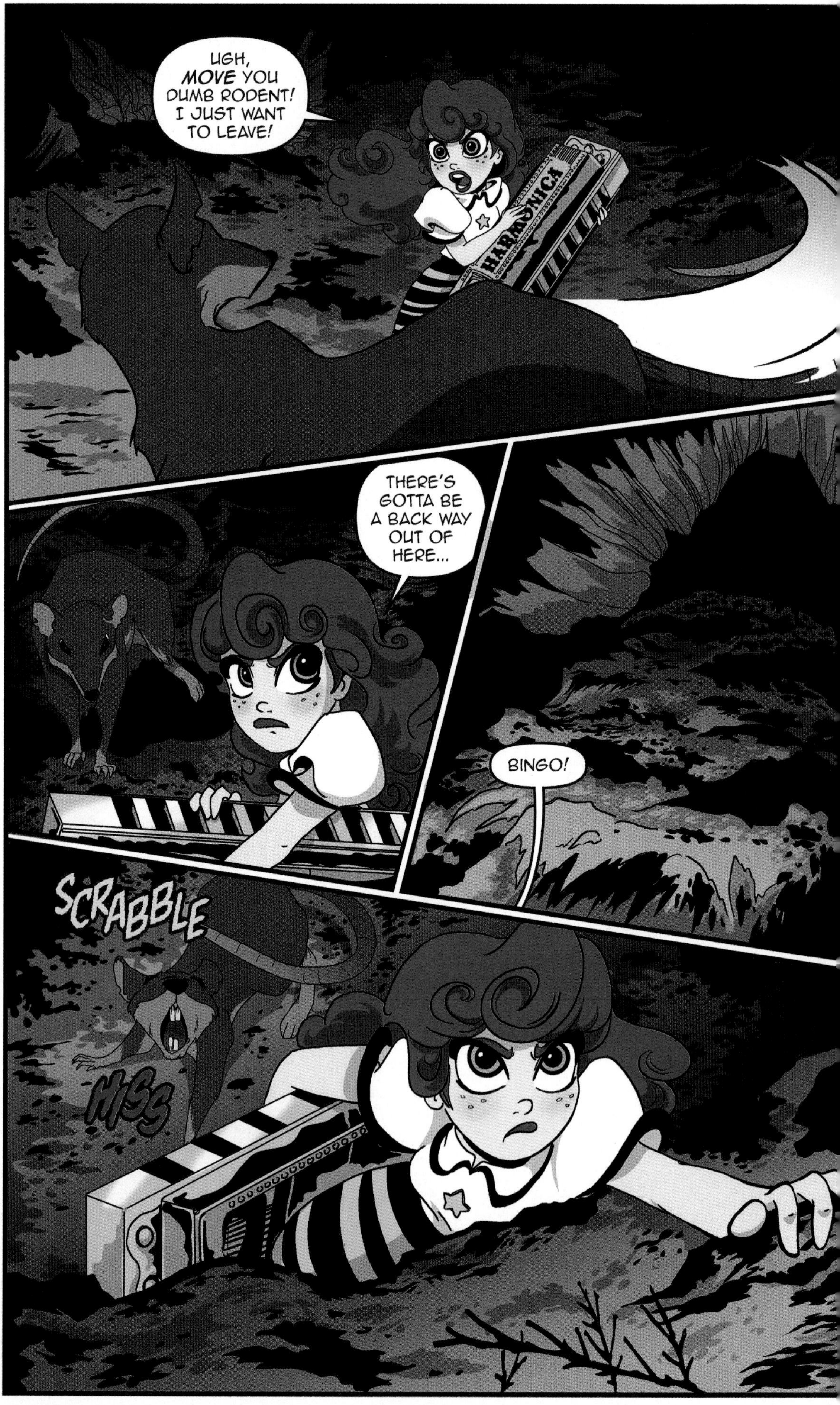
UGH, MOVE YOU DUMB RODENT! I JUST WANT TO LEAVE!
HARMONICA
THERE'S GOTTA BE A BACK WAY OUT OF HERE...
BINGO!
SCRABBLE
HISS

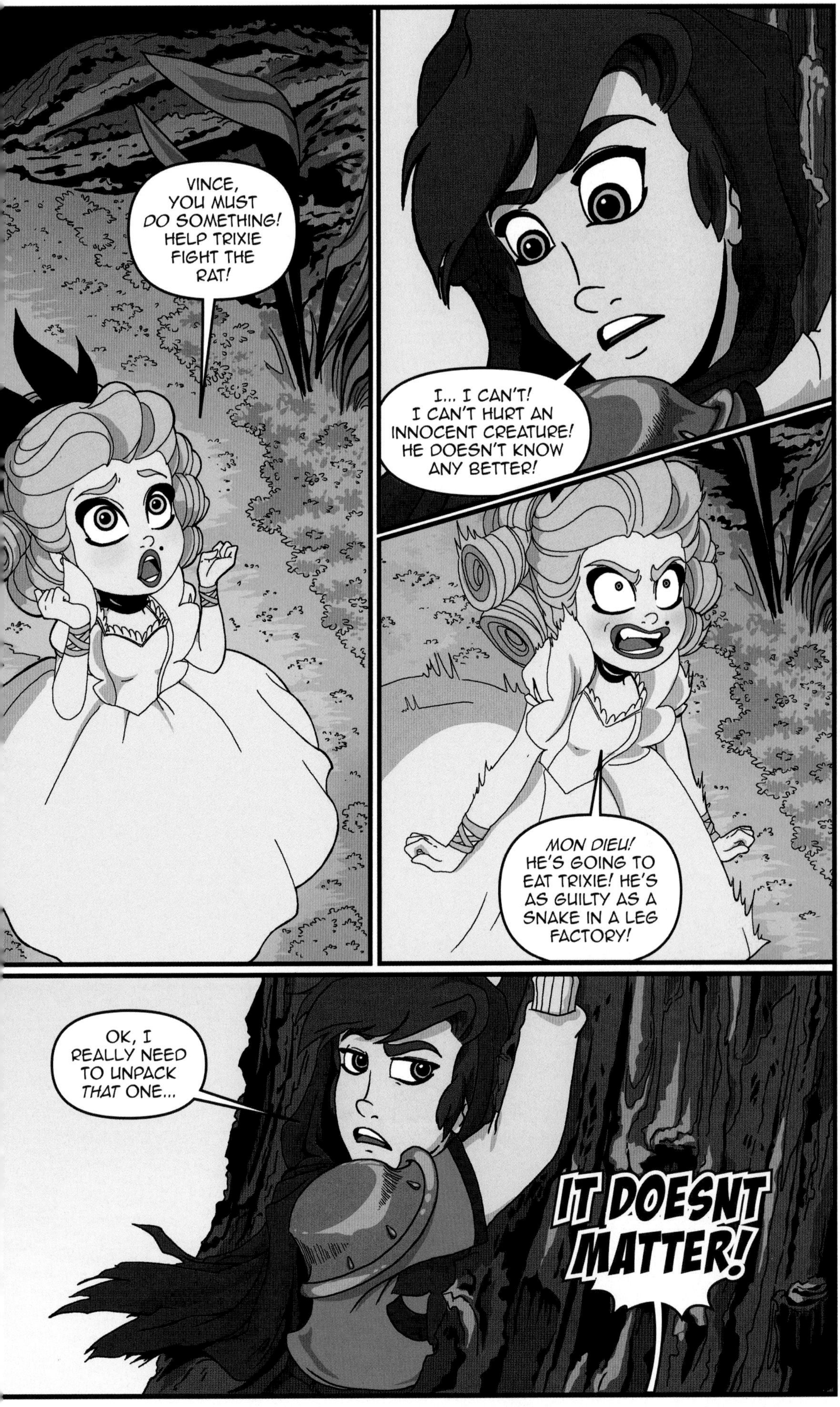
VINCE, YOU MUST *DO* SOMETHING! HELP TRIXIE FIGHT THE RAT!
I... I CAN'T! I CAN'T HURT AN INNOCENT CREATURE! HE DOESN'T KNOW ANY BETTER!
MON DIEU! HE'S GOING TO EAT TRIXIE! HE'S AS GUILTY AS A SNAKE IN A LEG FACTORY!
OK, I REALLY NEED TO UNPACK *THAT* ONE...
IT DOESNT MATTER!

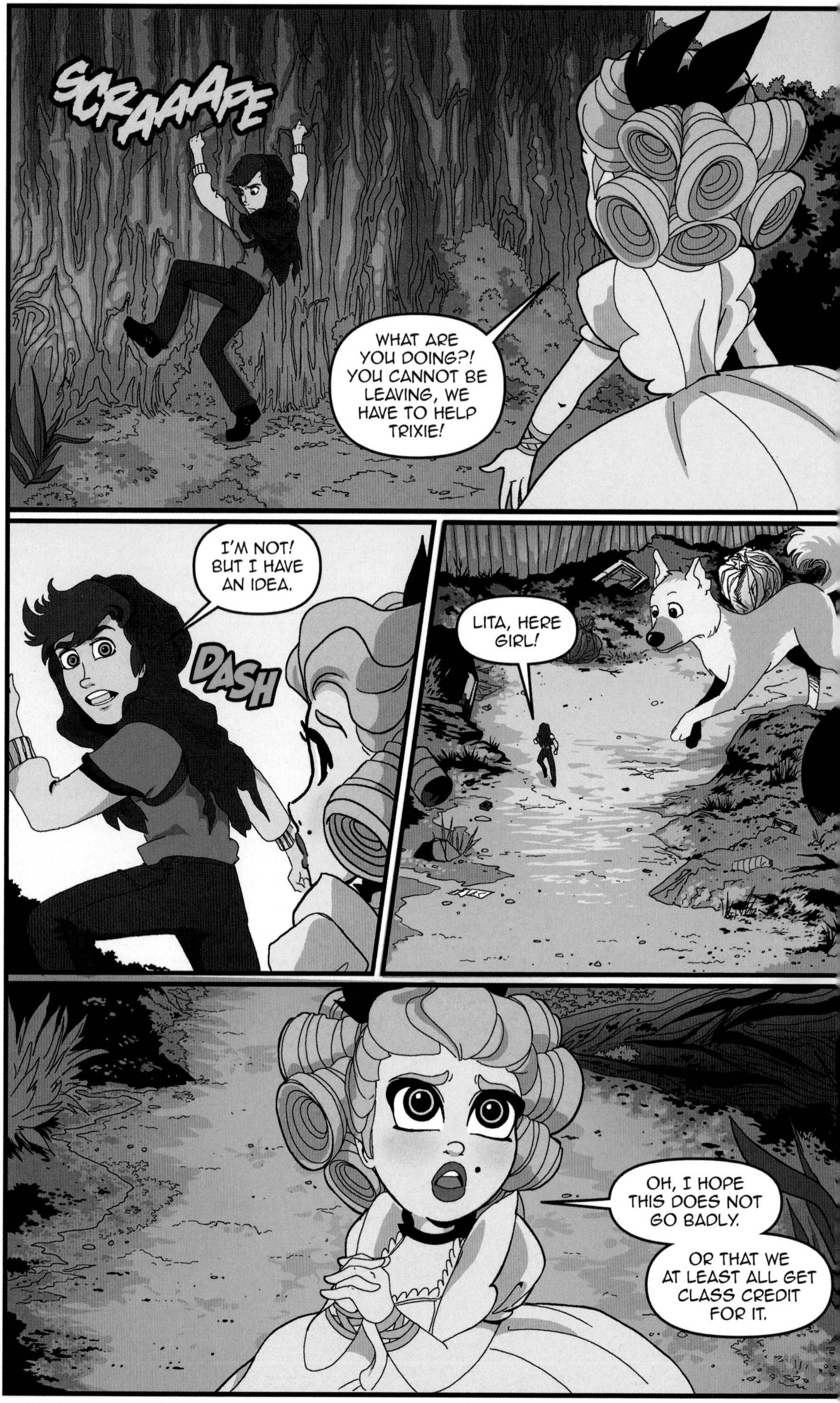
SCRAAAAPE
WHAT ARE YOU DOING?! YOU CANNOT BE LEAVING, WE HAVE TO HELP TRIXIE!
I'M NOT! BUT I HAVE AN IDEA.
DASH
LITA, HERE GIRL!
OH, I HOPE THIS DOES NOT GO BADLY.
OR THAT WE AT LEAST ALL GET CLASS CREDIT FOR IT.

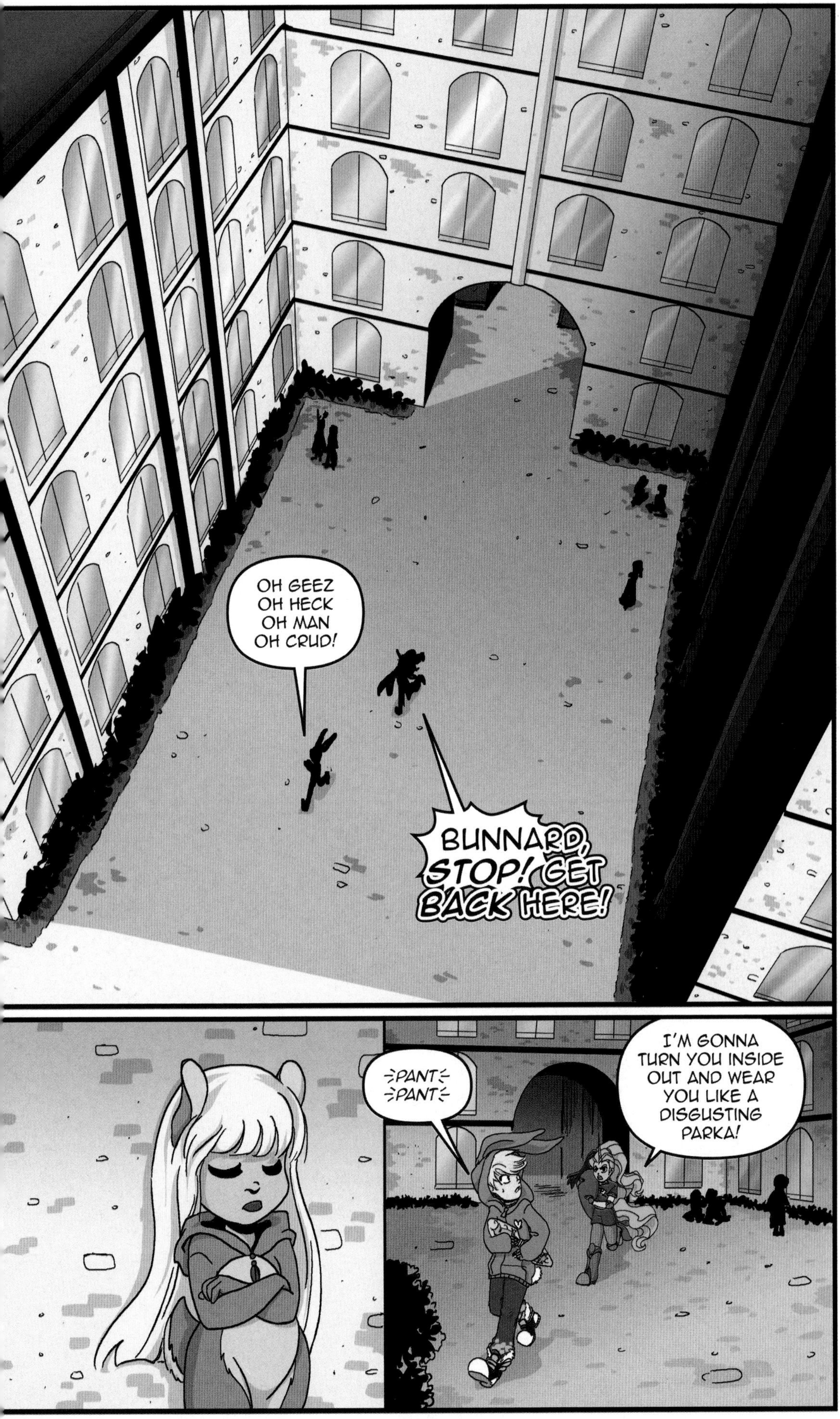
OH GEEZ OH HECK OH MAN OH CRUD!
BUNNARD, STOP! GET BACK HERE!
=PANT= =PANT=
I'M GONNA TURN YOU INSIDE OUT AND WEAR YOU LIKE A DISGUSTING PARKA!

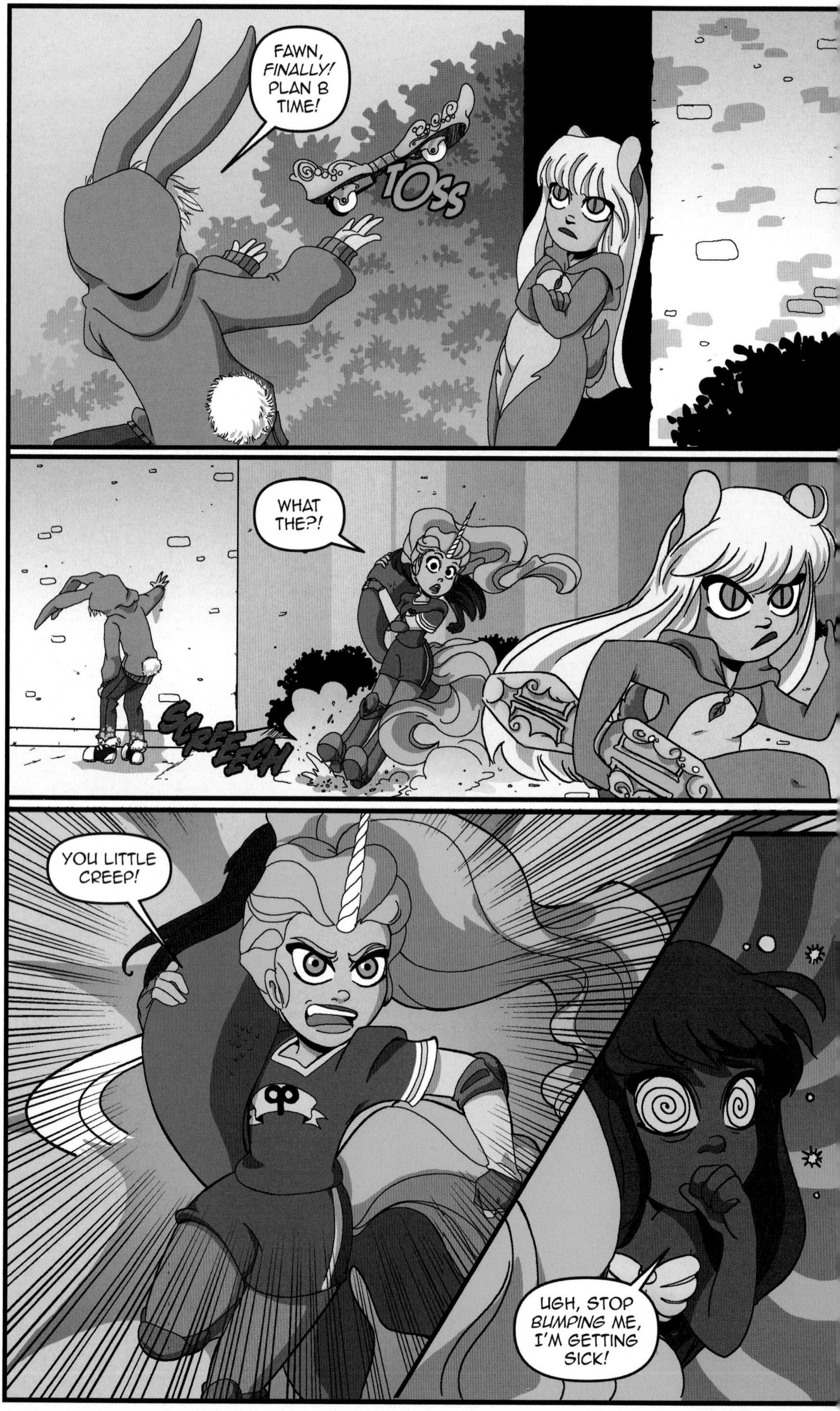
FAWN, FINALLY! PLAN B TIME!
TOSS
WHAT THE?!
SCREEECH
YOU LITTLE CREEP!
UGH, STOP BUMPING ME, I'M GETTING SICK!

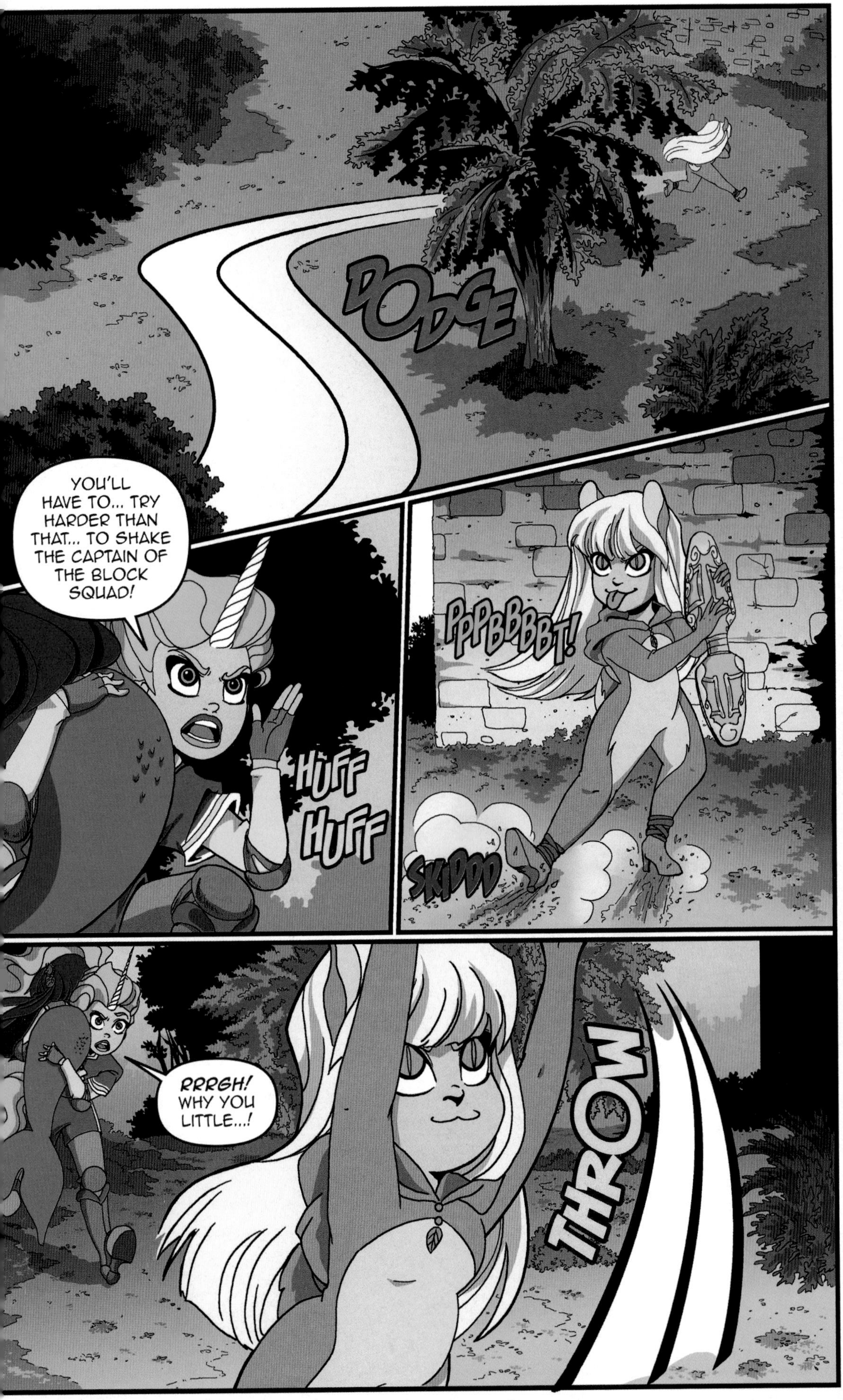
DODGE
YOU'LL HAVE TO... TRY HARDER THAN THAT... TO SHAKE THE CAPTAIN OF THE BLOCK SQUAD!
HUFF HUFF
PPPBBBBT!
SKIDDD
RRRGH! WHY YOU LITTLE...!
THROW

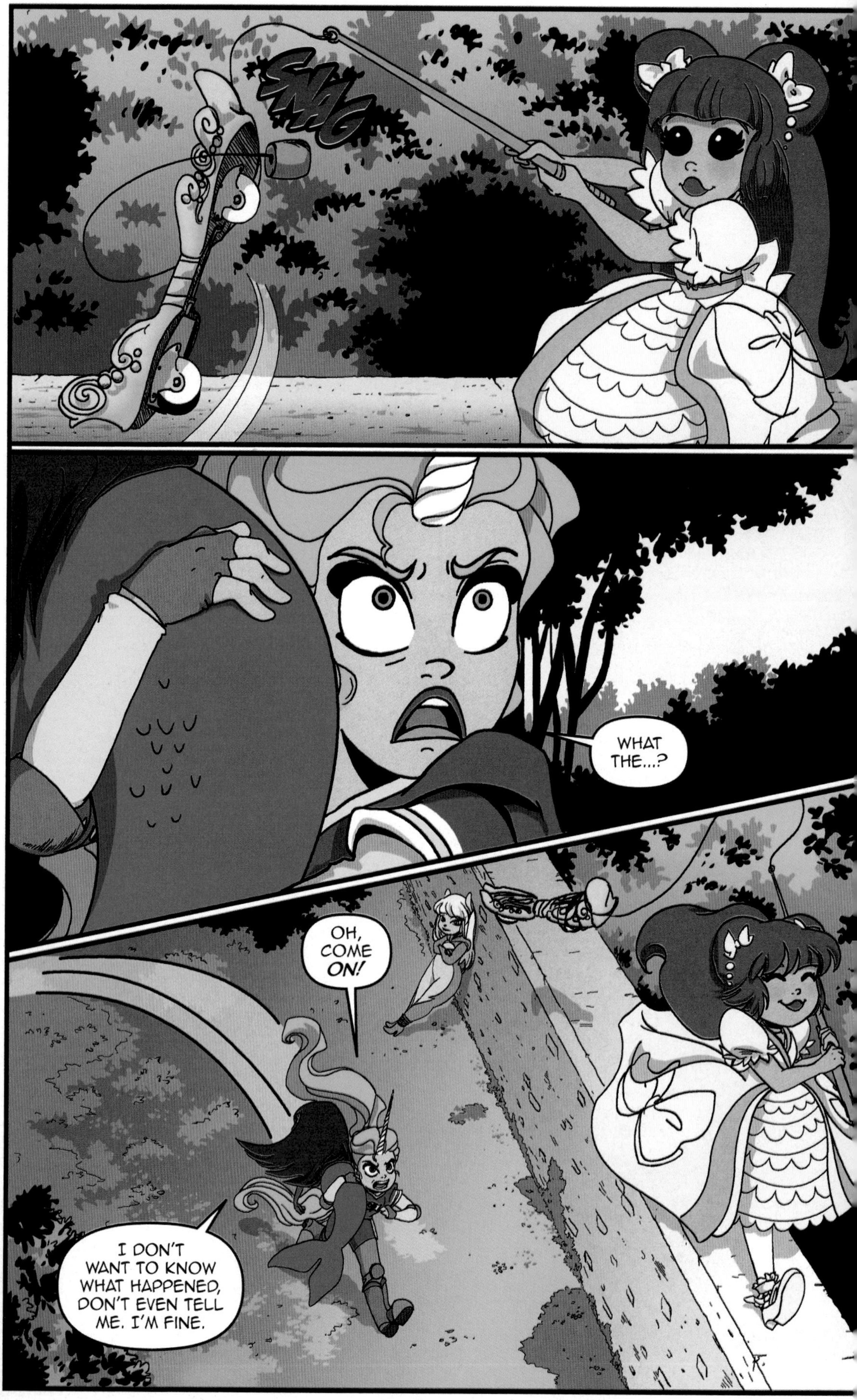
SNAG
WHAT THE...?
OH, COME ON!
I DON'T WANT TO KNOW WHAT HAPPENED, DON'T EVEN TELL ME. I'M FINE.

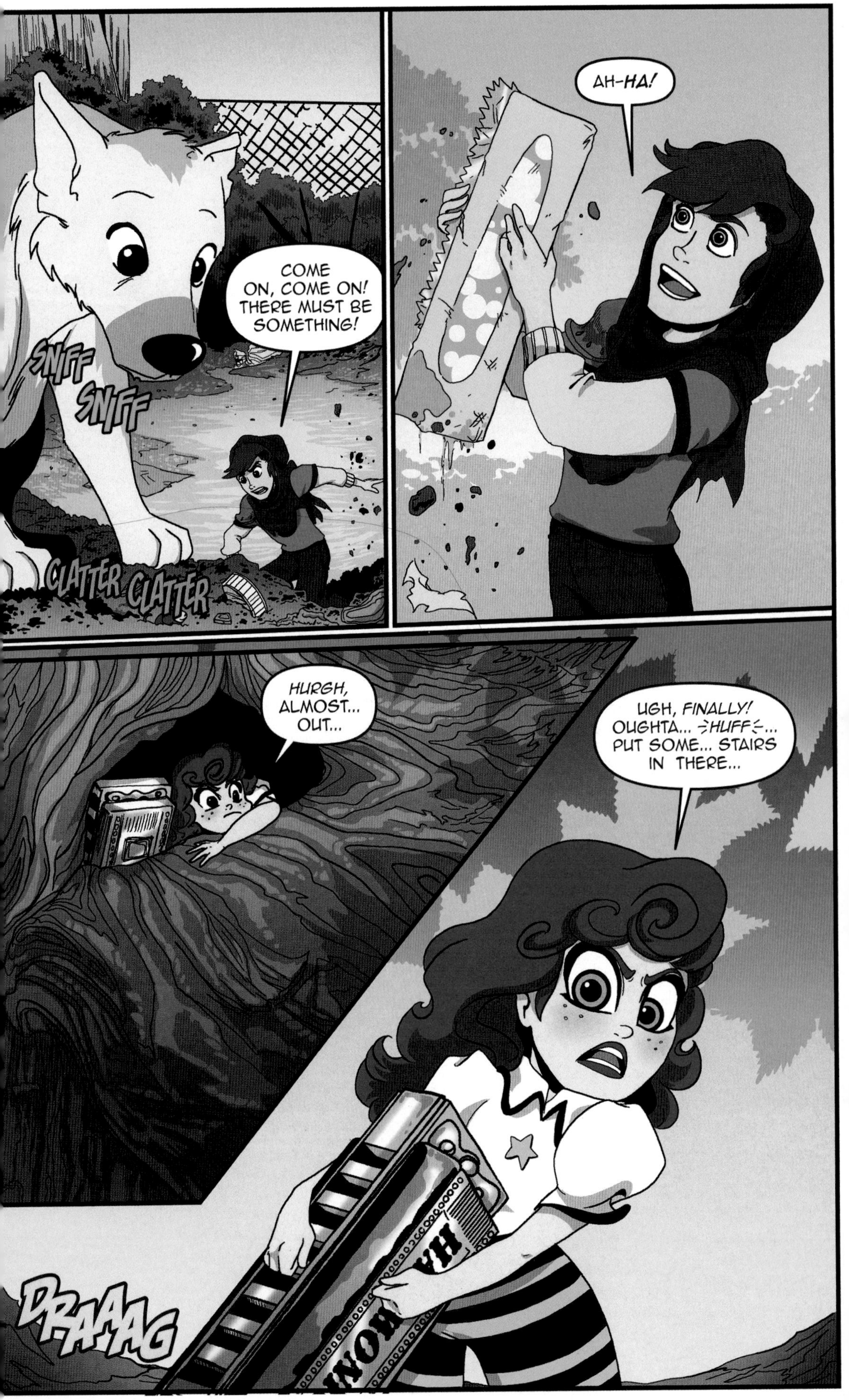
SNIFF SNIFF
COME ON, COME ON! THERE MUST BE SOMETHING!
CLATTER CLATTER
AH-HA!
HURGH, ALMOST... OUT...
UGH, FINALLY! OUGHTA... HUFF... PUT SOME... STAIRS IN THERE...
DRAAAG

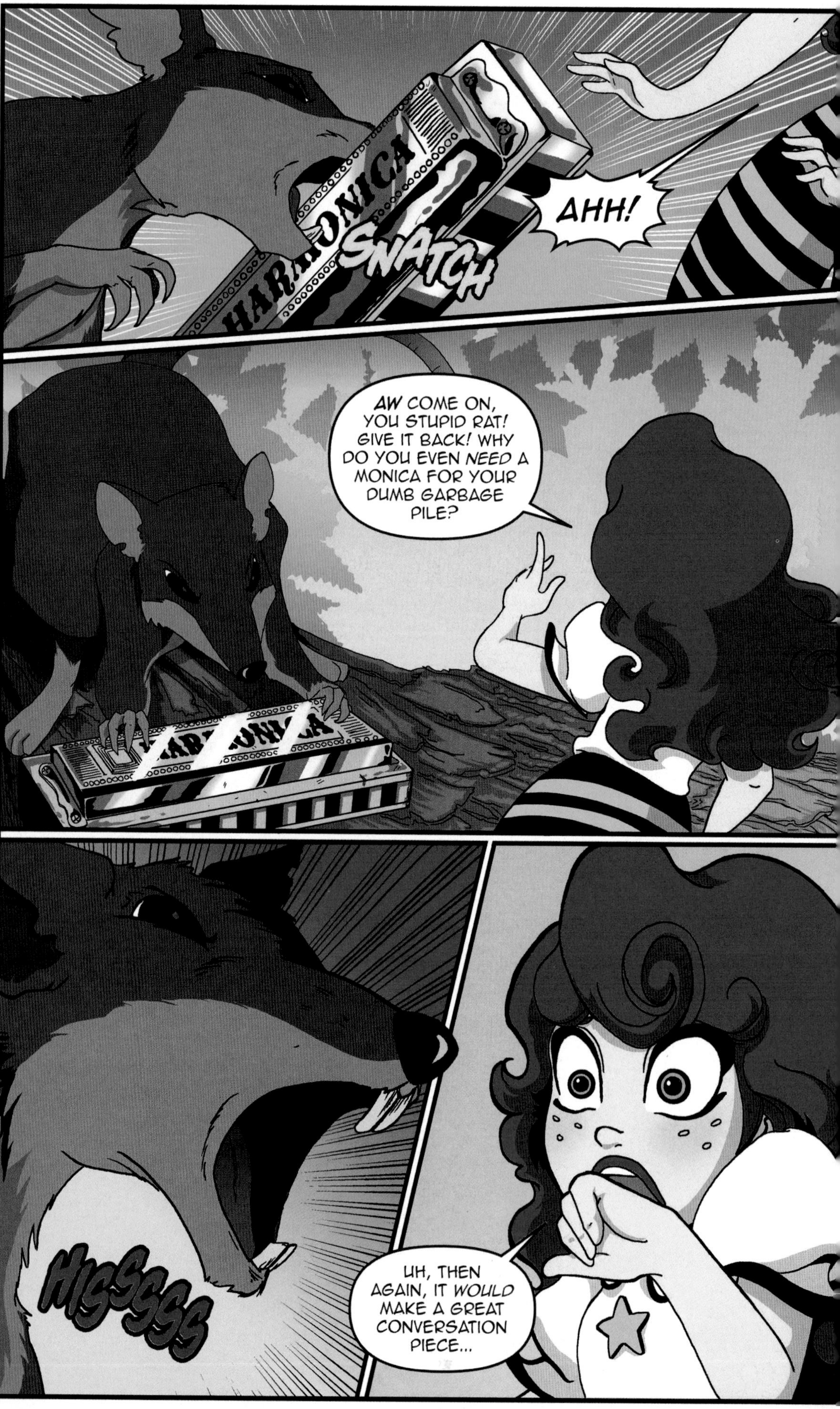
HARMONICA
SNATCH
AHH!
AW COME ON, YOU STUPID RAT! GIVE IT BACK! WHY DO YOU EVEN NEED A MONICA FOR YOUR DUMB GARBAGE PILE?
HISSSSS
UH, THEN AGAIN, IT WOULD MAKE A GREAT CONVERSATION PIECE...

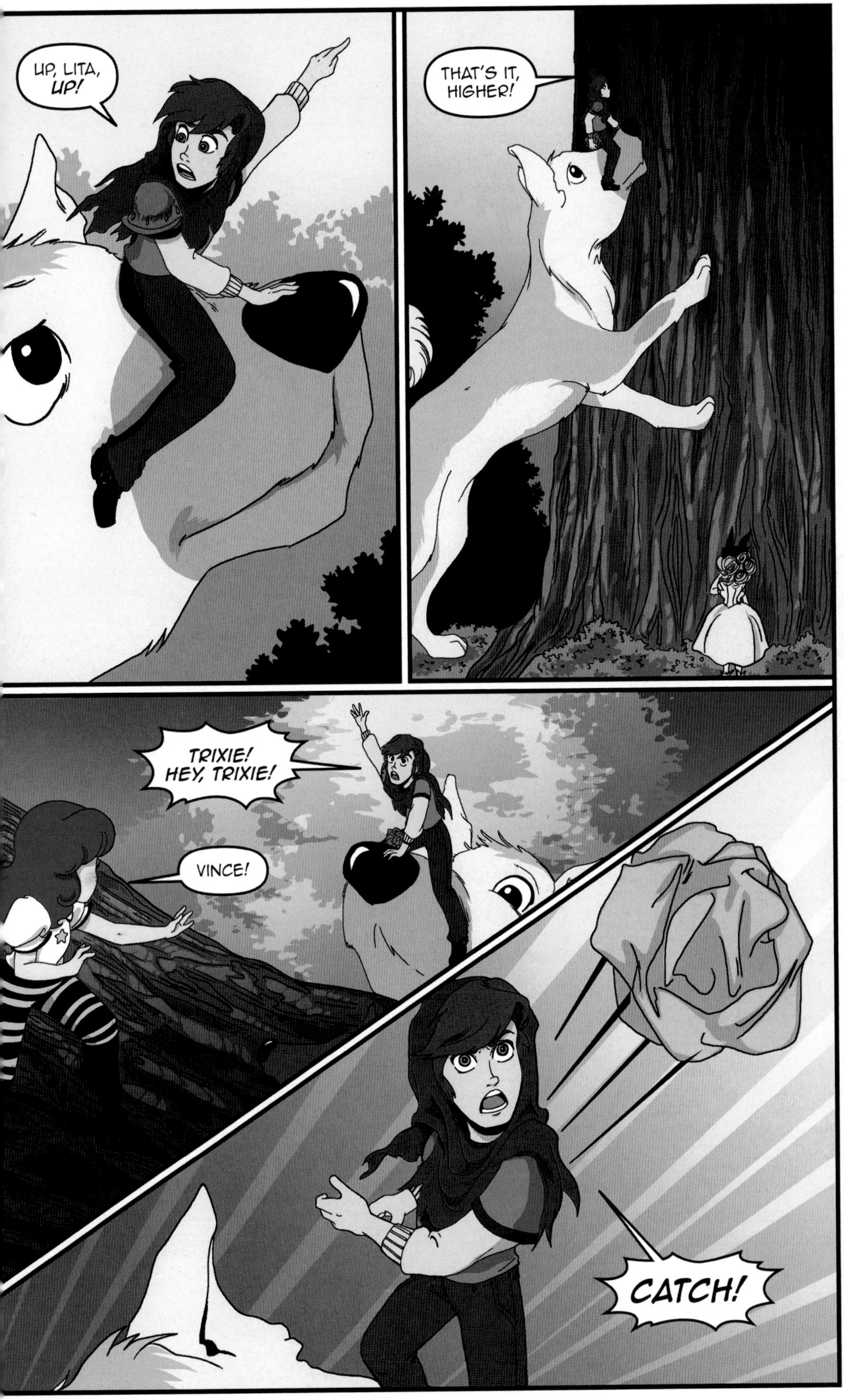
UP, LITA, UP!
THAT'S IT, HIGHER!
TRIXIE! HEY, TRIXIE!
VINCE!
CATCH!

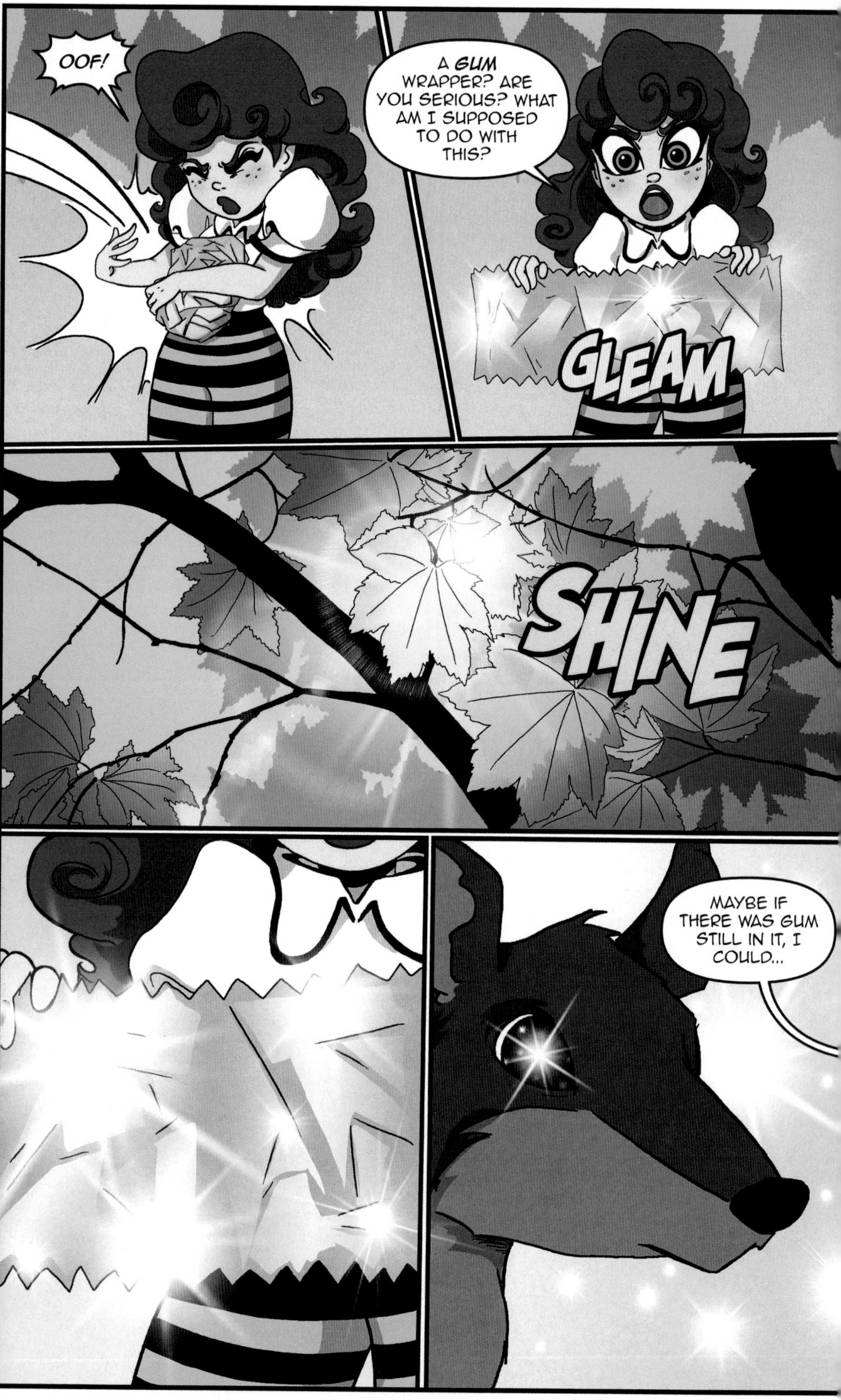
OOF!
A GUM WRAPPER? ARE YOU SERIOUS? WHAT AM I SUPPOSED TO DO WITH THIS?
GLEAM
SHINE
MAYBE IF THERE WAS GUM STILL IN IT, I COULD...

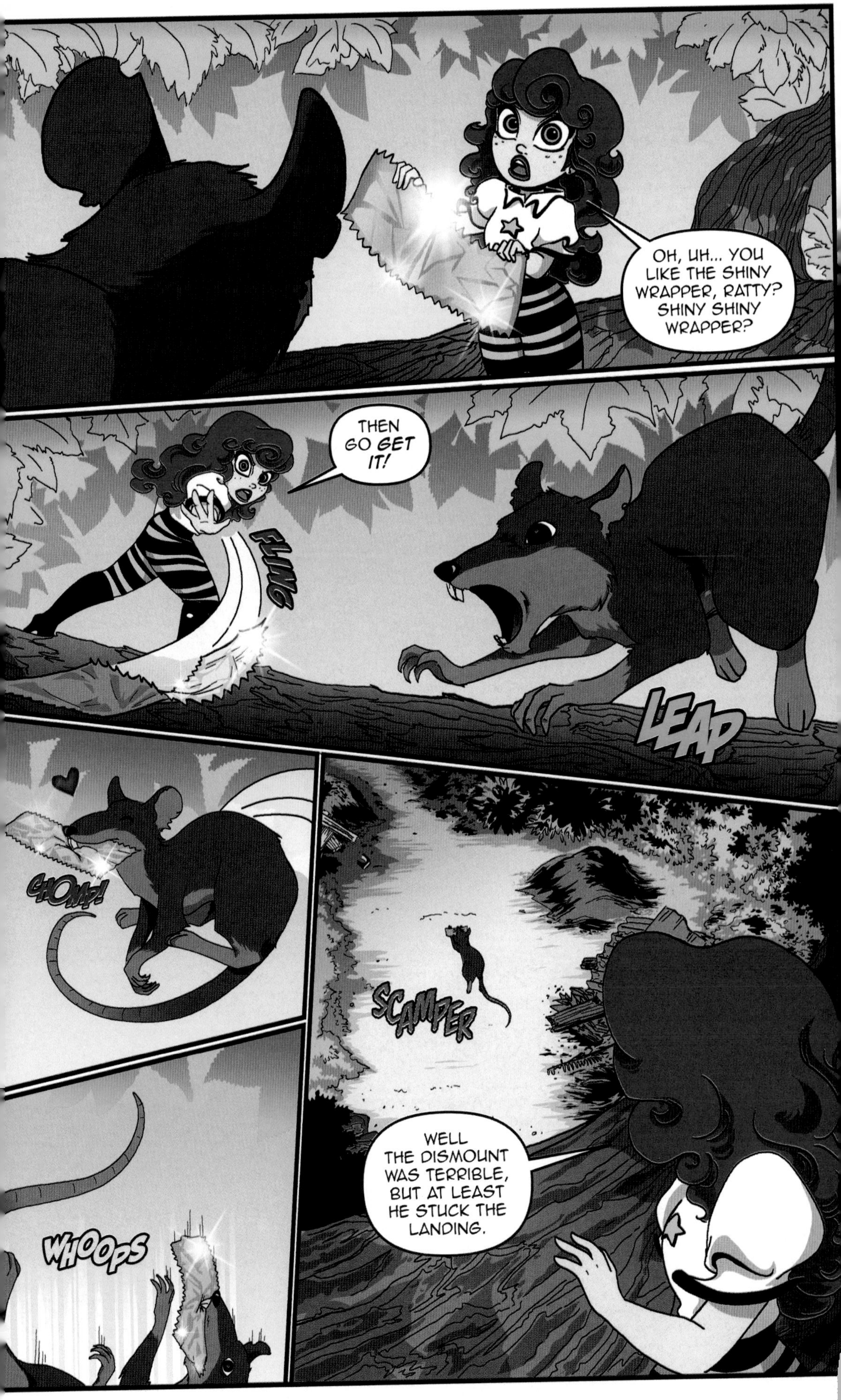
OH, UH... YOU LIKE THE SHINY WRAPPER, RATTY? SHINY SHINY WRAPPER?
THEN GO GET IT!
FLING
LEAP
CHOMP!
WHOOPS
SCAMPER
WELL THE DISMOUNT WAS TERRIBLE, BUT AT LEAST HE STUCK THE LANDING.

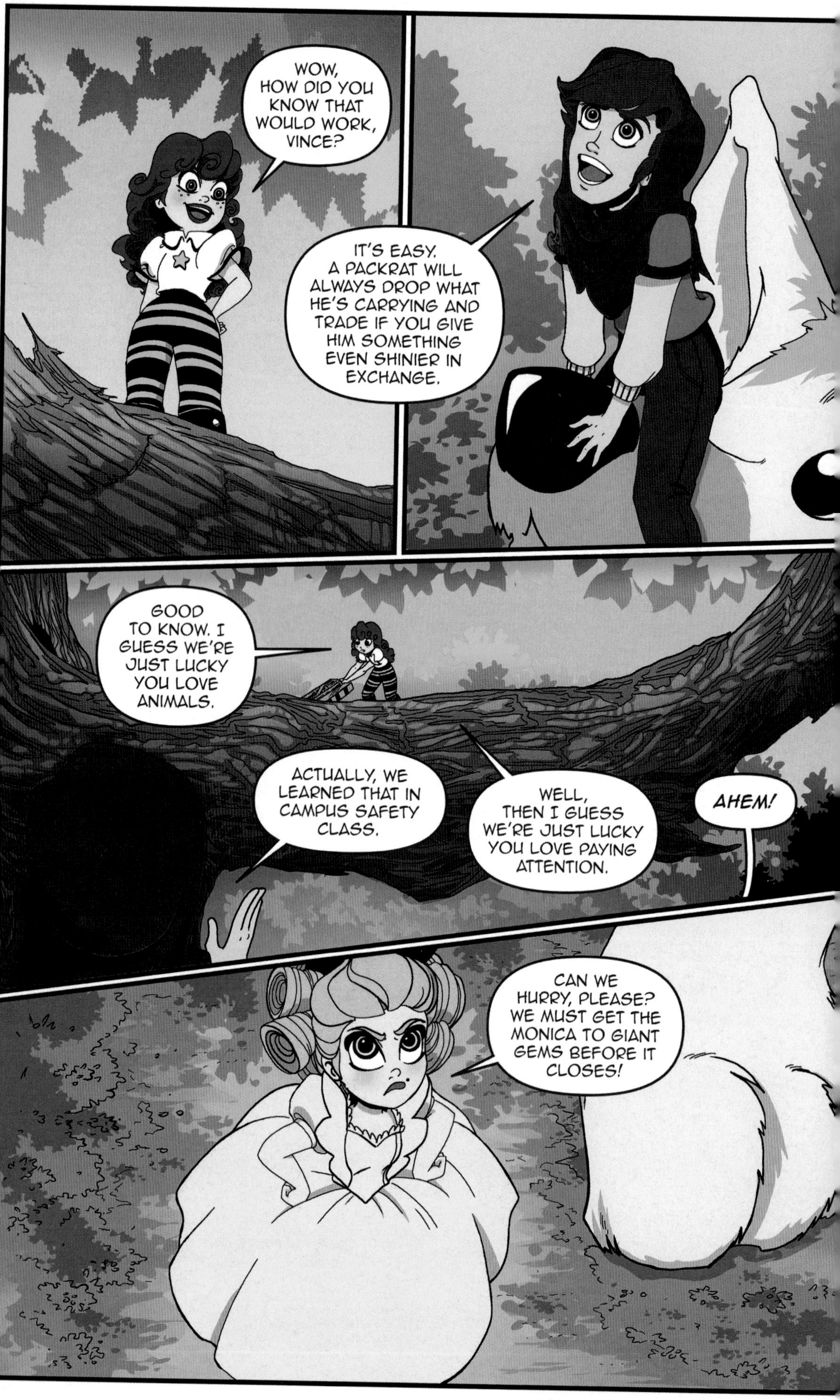
WOW, HOW DID YOU KNOW THAT WOULD WORK, VINCE?
IT'S EASY. A PACKRAT WILL ALWAYS DROP WHAT HE'S CARRYING AND TRADE IF YOU GIVE HIM SOMETHING EVEN SHINIER IN EXCHANGE.
GOOD TO KNOW. I GUESS WE'RE JUST LUCKY YOU LOVE ANIMALS.
ACTUALLY, WE LEARNED THAT IN CAMPUS SAFETY CLASS.
WELL, THEN I GUESS WE'RE JUST LUCKY YOU LOVE PAYING ATTENTION.
AHEM!
CAN WE HURRY, PLEASE? WE MUST GET THE MONICA TO GIANT GEMS BEFORE IT CLOSES!

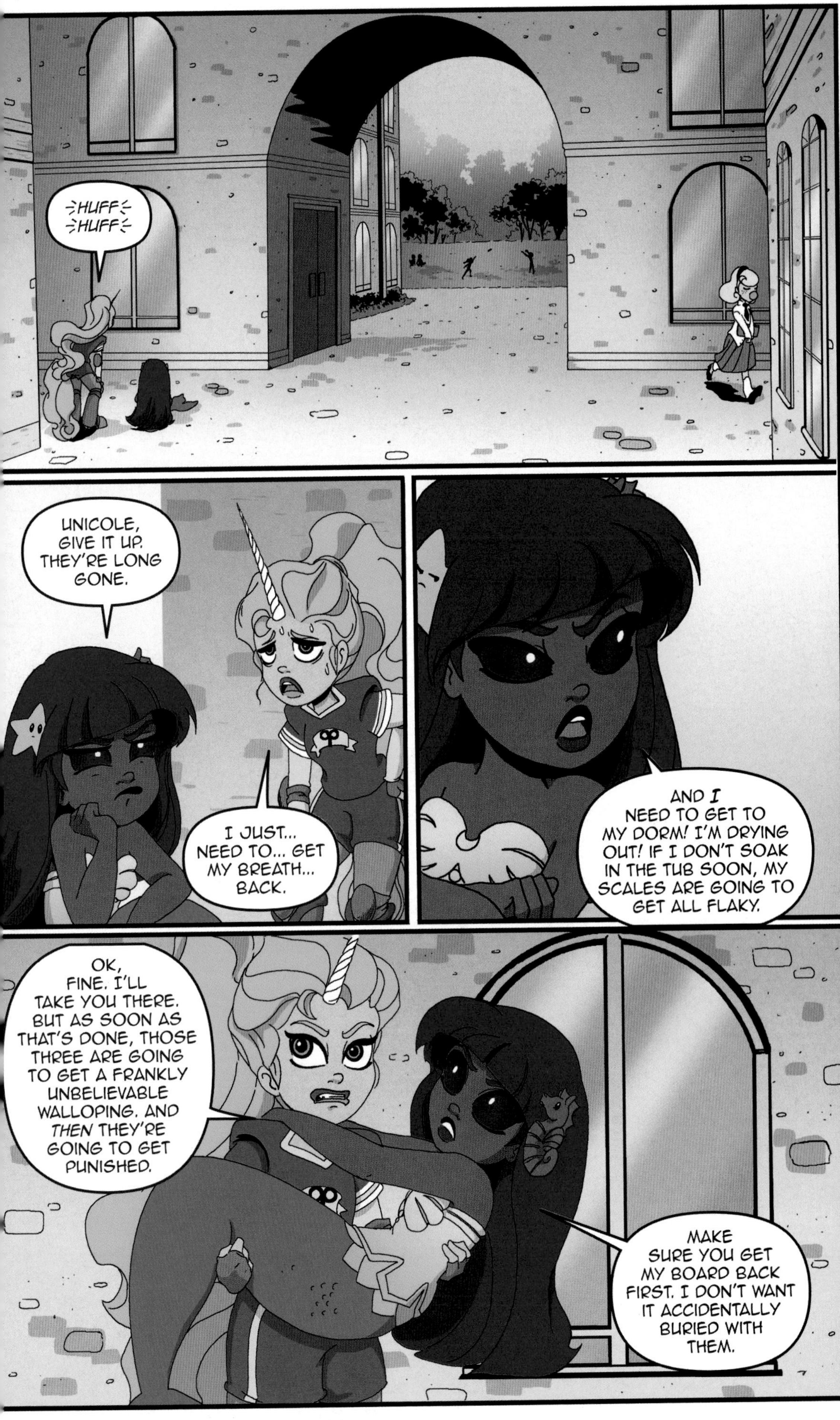

HUFF HUFF
UNICOLE, GIVE IT UP. THEY'RE LONG GONE.
I JUST... NEED TO... GET MY BREATH... BACK.
AND I NEED TO GET TO MY DORM! I'M DRYING OUT! IF I DON'T SOAK IN THE TUB SOON, MY SCALES ARE GOING TO GET ALL FLAKY.
OK, FINE. I'LL TAKE YOU THERE. BUT AS SOON AS THAT'S DONE, THOSE THREE ARE GOING TO GET A FRANKLY UNBELIEVABLE WALLOPING. AND THEN THEY'RE GOING TO GET PUNISHED.
MAKE SURE YOU GET MY BOARD BACK FIRST. I DON'T WANT IT ACCIDENTALLY BURIED WITH THEM.

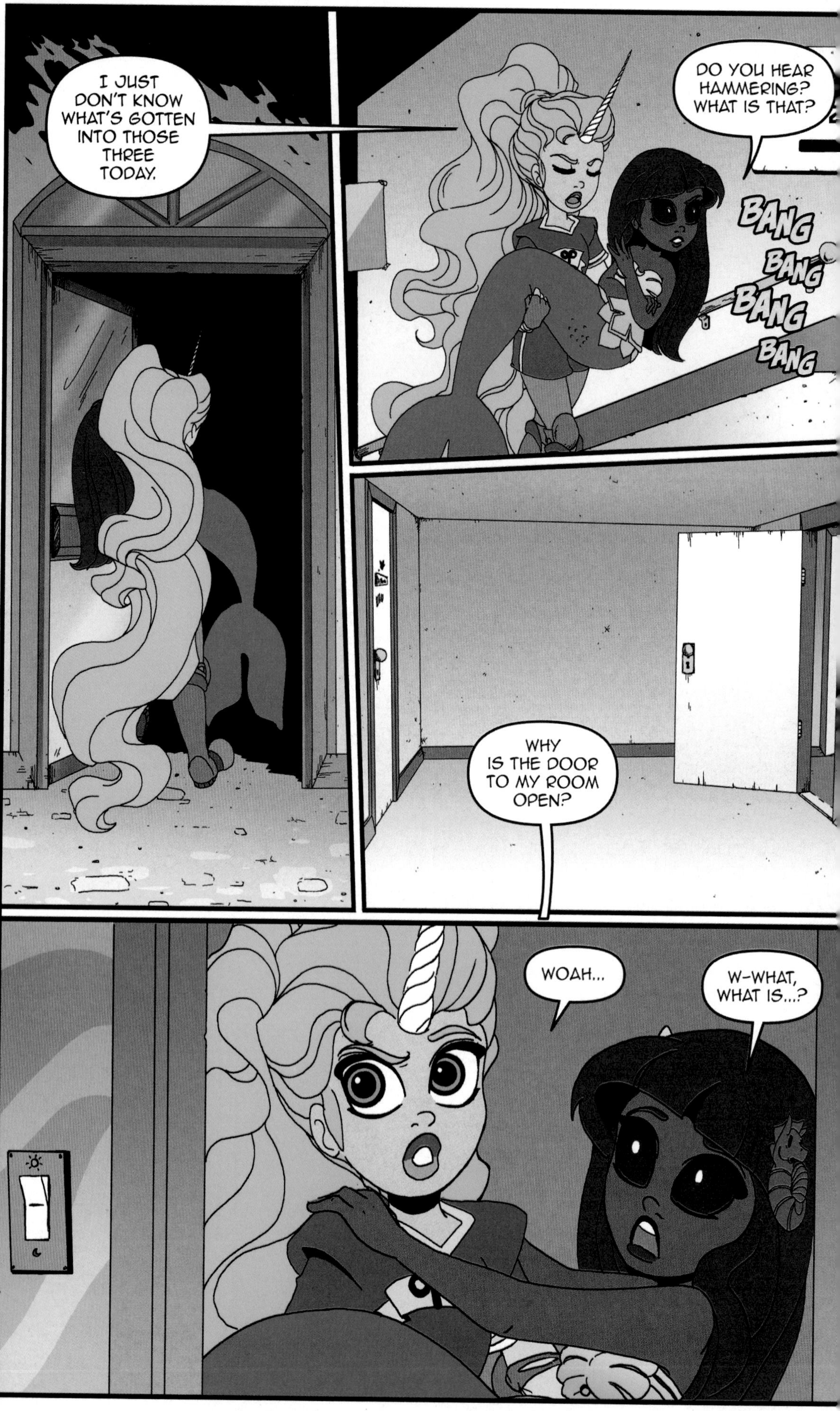
I JUST DON'T KNOW WHAT'S GOTTEN INTO THOSE THREE TODAY.
DO YOU HEAR HAMMERING? WHAT IS THAT?
BANG
BANG
BANG
BANG
WHY IS THE DOOR TO MY ROOM OPEN?
WOAH...
W-WHAT, WHAT IS...?

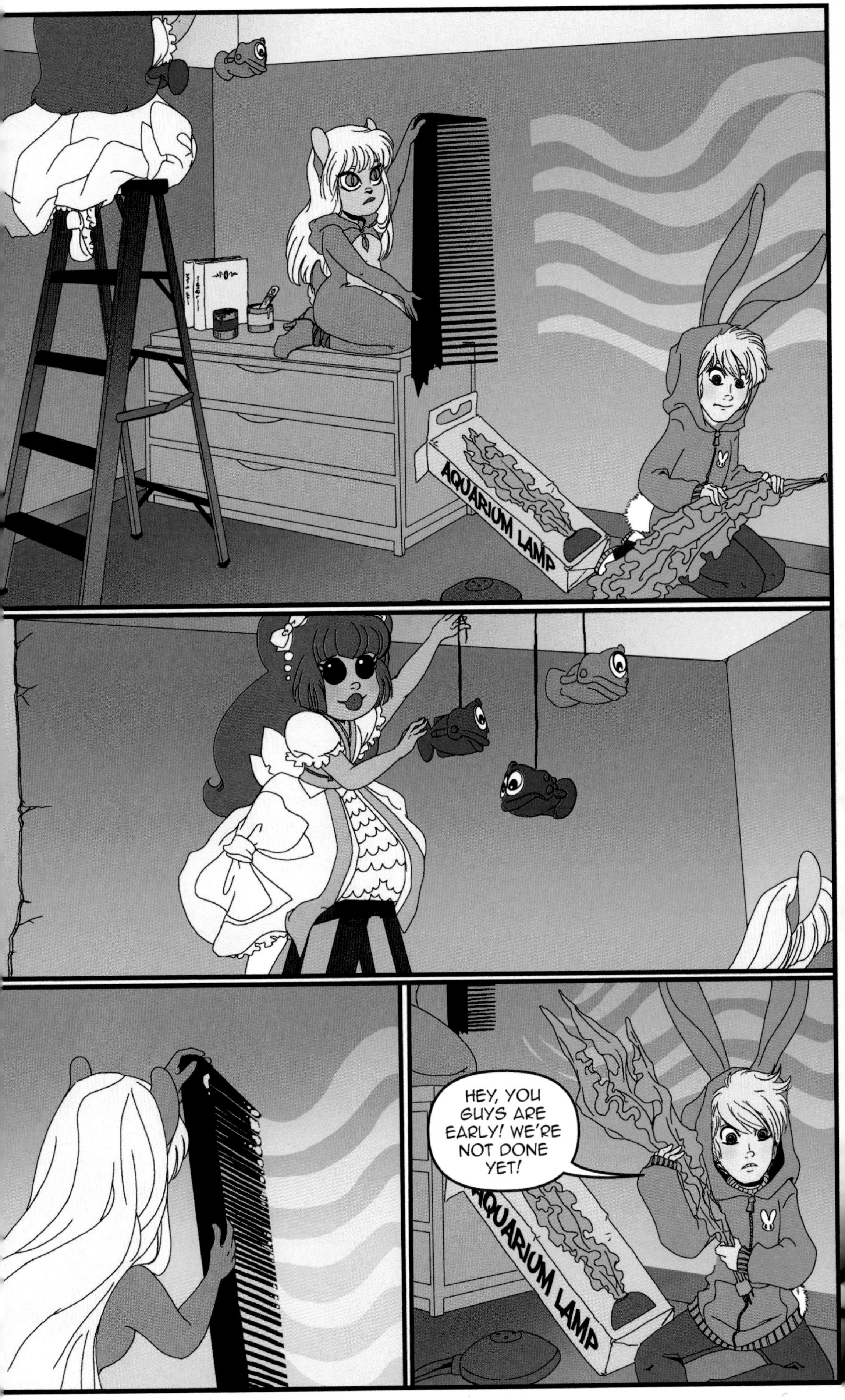
AQUARIUM LAMP
HEY, YOU GUYS ARE EARLY! WE'RE NOT DONE YET!
AQUARIUM LAMP

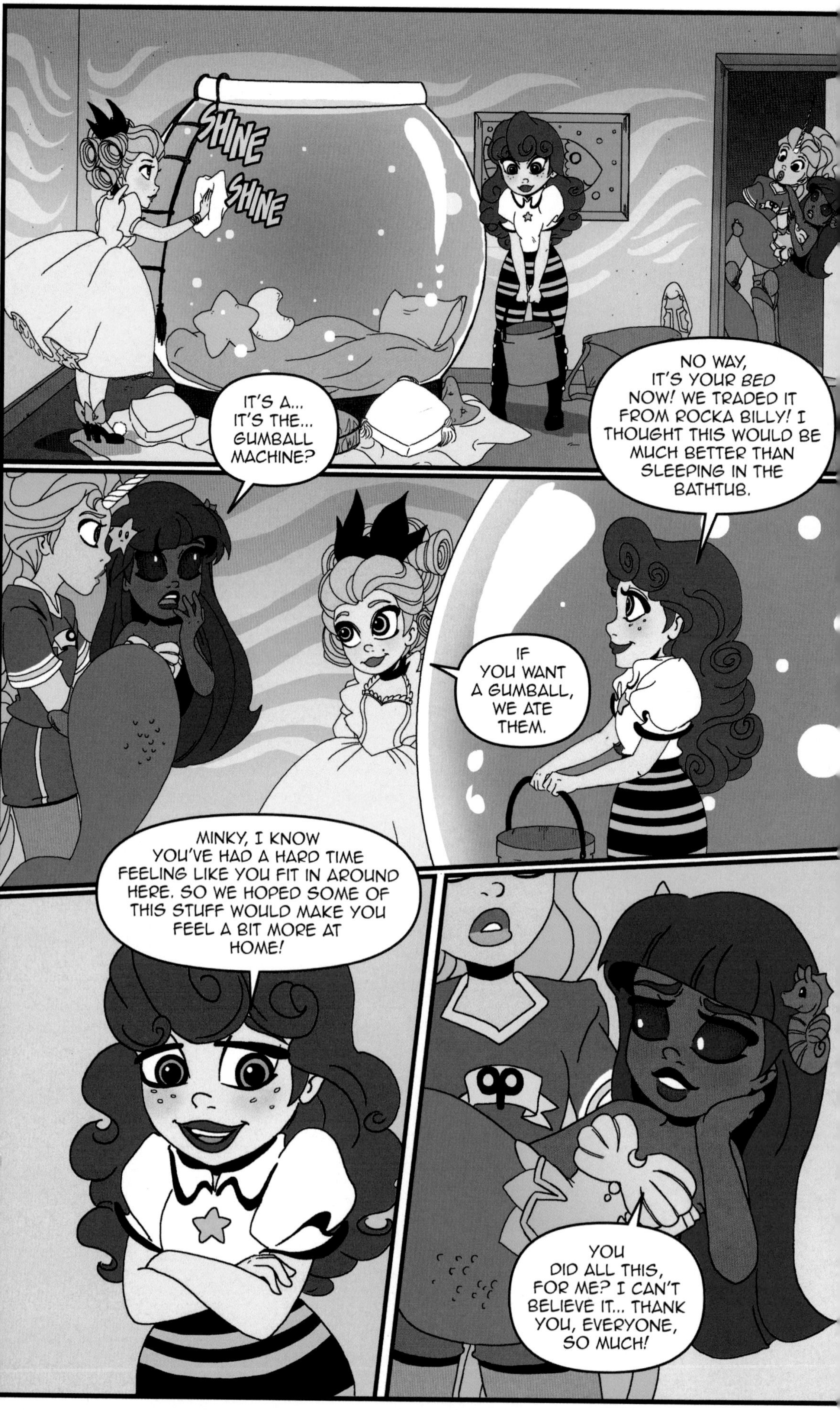
SHINE
SHINE
IT'S A... IT'S THE... GUMBALL MACHINE?
NO WAY, IT'S YOUR *BED* NOW! WE TRADED IT FROM ROCKA BILLY! I THOUGHT THIS WOULD BE MUCH BETTER THAN SLEEPING IN THE BATHTUB.
IF YOU WANT A GUMBALL, WE ATE THEM.
MINKY, I KNOW YOU'VE HAD A HARD TIME FEELING LIKE YOU FIT IN AROUND HERE. SO WE HOPED SOME OF THIS STUFF WOULD MAKE YOU FEEL A BIT MORE AT HOME!
YOU DID ALL THIS, FOR ME? I CAN'T BELIEVE IT... THANK YOU, EVERYONE, SO MUCH!

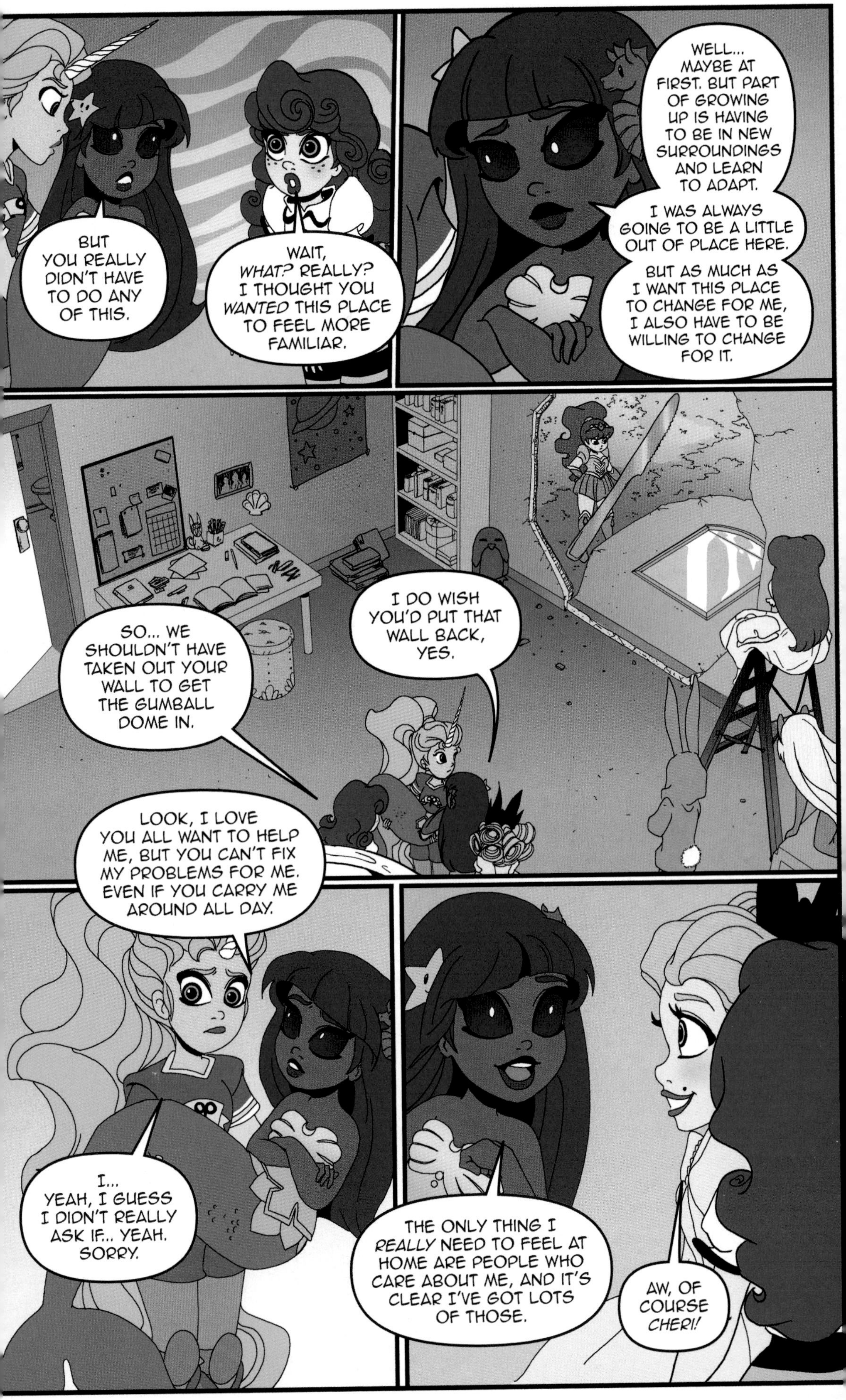
BUT YOU REALLY DIDN'T HAVE TO DO ANY OF THIS.
WAIT, *WHAT?* REALLY? I THOUGHT YOU *WANTED* THIS PLACE TO FEEL MORE FAMILIAR.
WELL... MAYBE AT FIRST. BUT PART OF GROWING UP IS HAVING TO BE IN NEW SURROUNDINGS AND LEARN TO ADAPT.
I WAS ALWAYS GOING TO BE A LITTLE OUT OF PLACE HERE.
BUT AS MUCH AS I WANT THIS PLACE TO CHANGE FOR ME, I ALSO HAVE TO BE WILLING TO CHANGE FOR IT.
SO... WE SHOULDN'T HAVE TAKEN OUT YOUR WALL TO GET THE GUMBALL DOME IN.
I DO WISH YOU'D PUT THAT WALL BACK, YES.
LOOK, I LOVE YOU ALL WANT TO HELP ME, BUT YOU CAN'T FIX MY PROBLEMS FOR ME. EVEN IF YOU CARRY ME AROUND ALL DAY.
I... YEAH, I GUESS I DIDN'T REALLY ASK IF... YEAH. SORRY.
THE ONLY THING I *REALLY* NEED TO FEEL AT HOME ARE PEOPLE WHO CARE ABOUT ME, AND IT'S CLEAR I'VE GOT LOTS OF THOSE.
AW, OF COURSE *CHERI!*

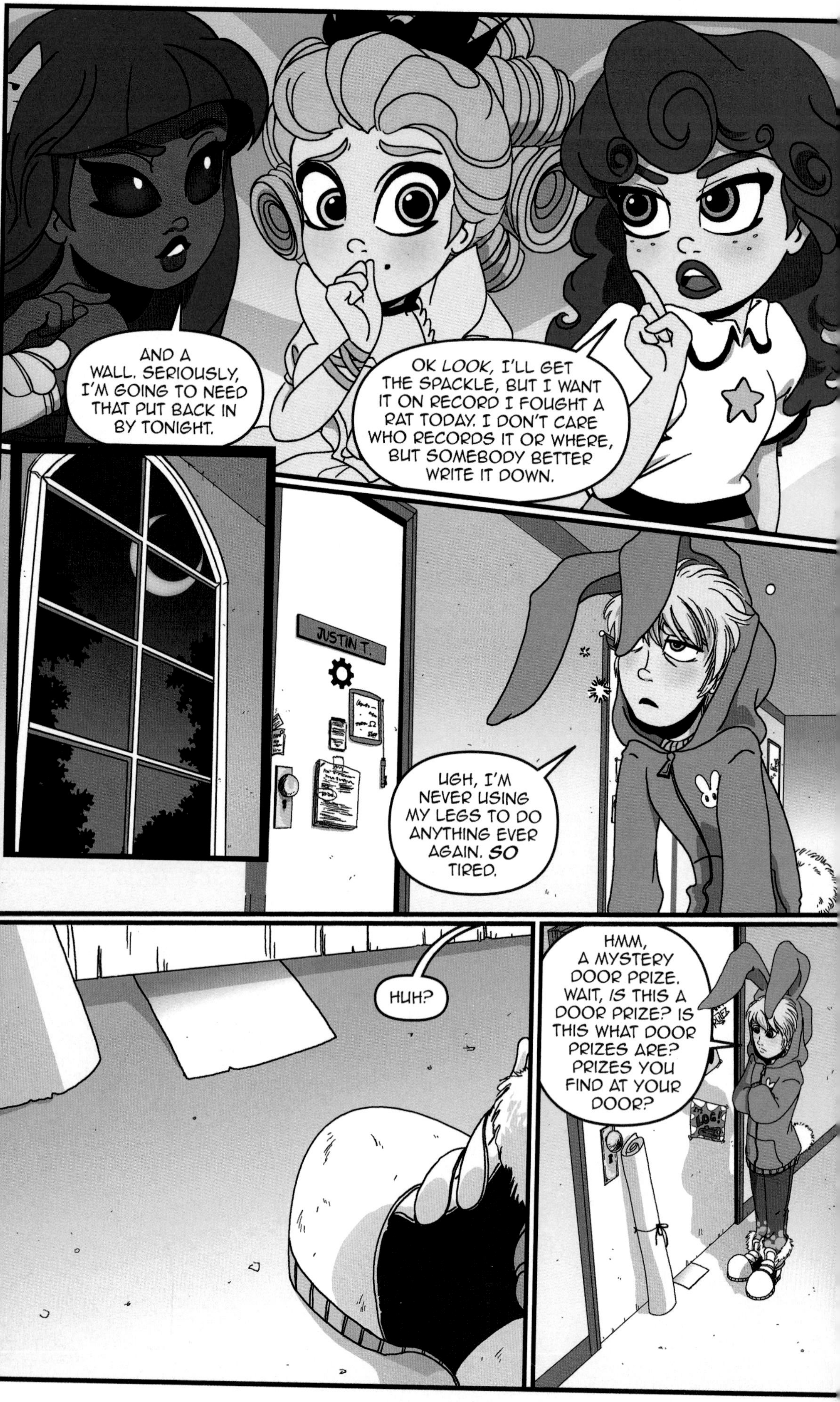
AND A WALL. SERIOUSLY, I'M GOING TO NEED THAT PUT BACK IN BY TONIGHT.
OK *LOOK*, I'LL GET THE SPACKLE, BUT I WANT IT ON RECORD I FOUGHT A RAT TODAY. I DON'T CARE WHO RECORDS IT OR WHERE, BUT SOMEBODY BETTER WRITE IT DOWN.
JUSTIN T.
UGH, I'M NEVER USING MY LEGS TO DO ANYTHING EVER AGAIN. ***SO*** TIRED.
HUH?
HMM, A MYSTERY DOOR PRIZE. WAIT, *IS* THIS A DOOR PRIZE? IS THIS WHAT DOOR PRIZES ARE? PRIZES YOU FIND AT YOUR DOOR?

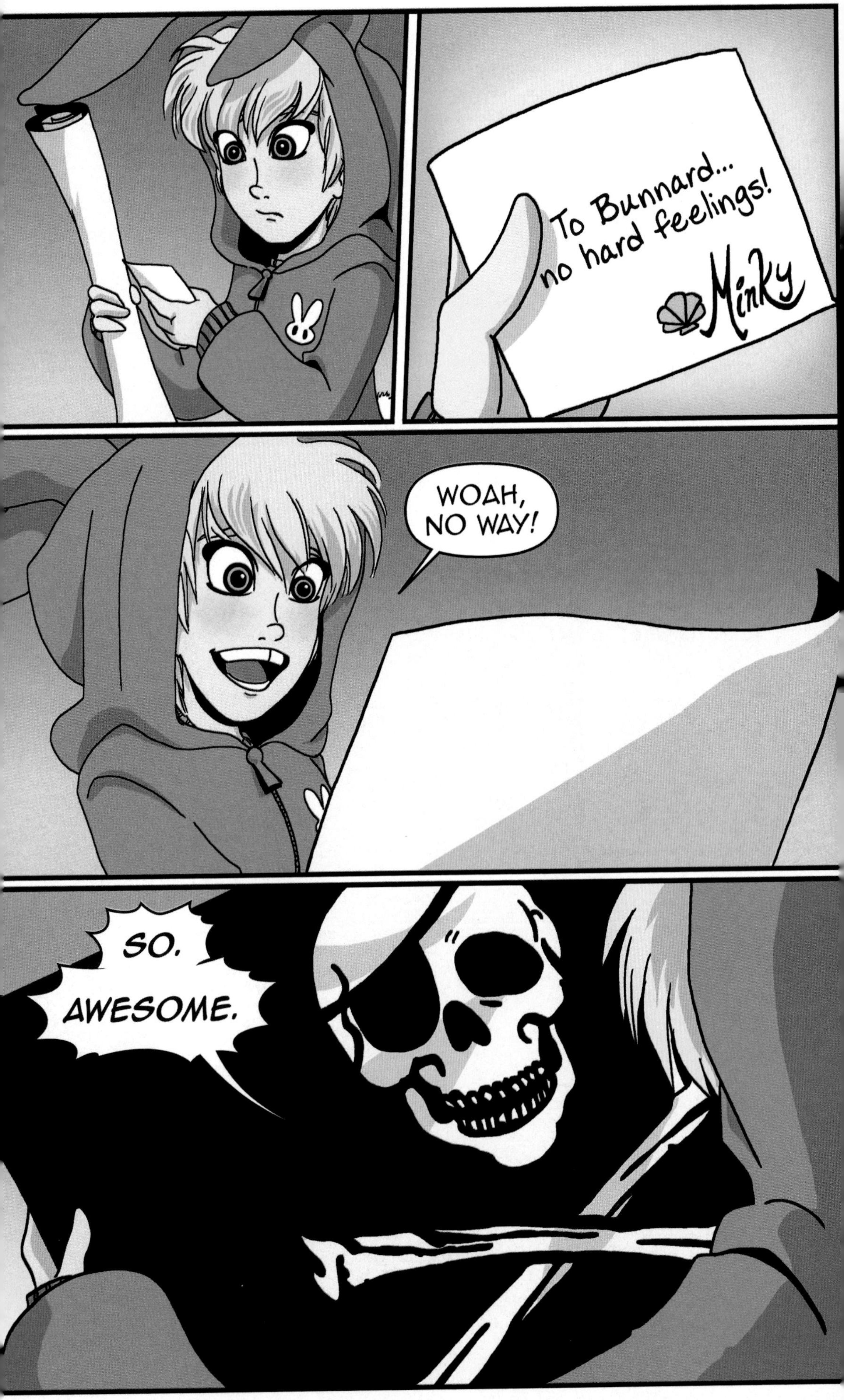
To Bunnard...
no hard feelings!
Minky
WOAH, NO WAY!
SO.
AWESOME.

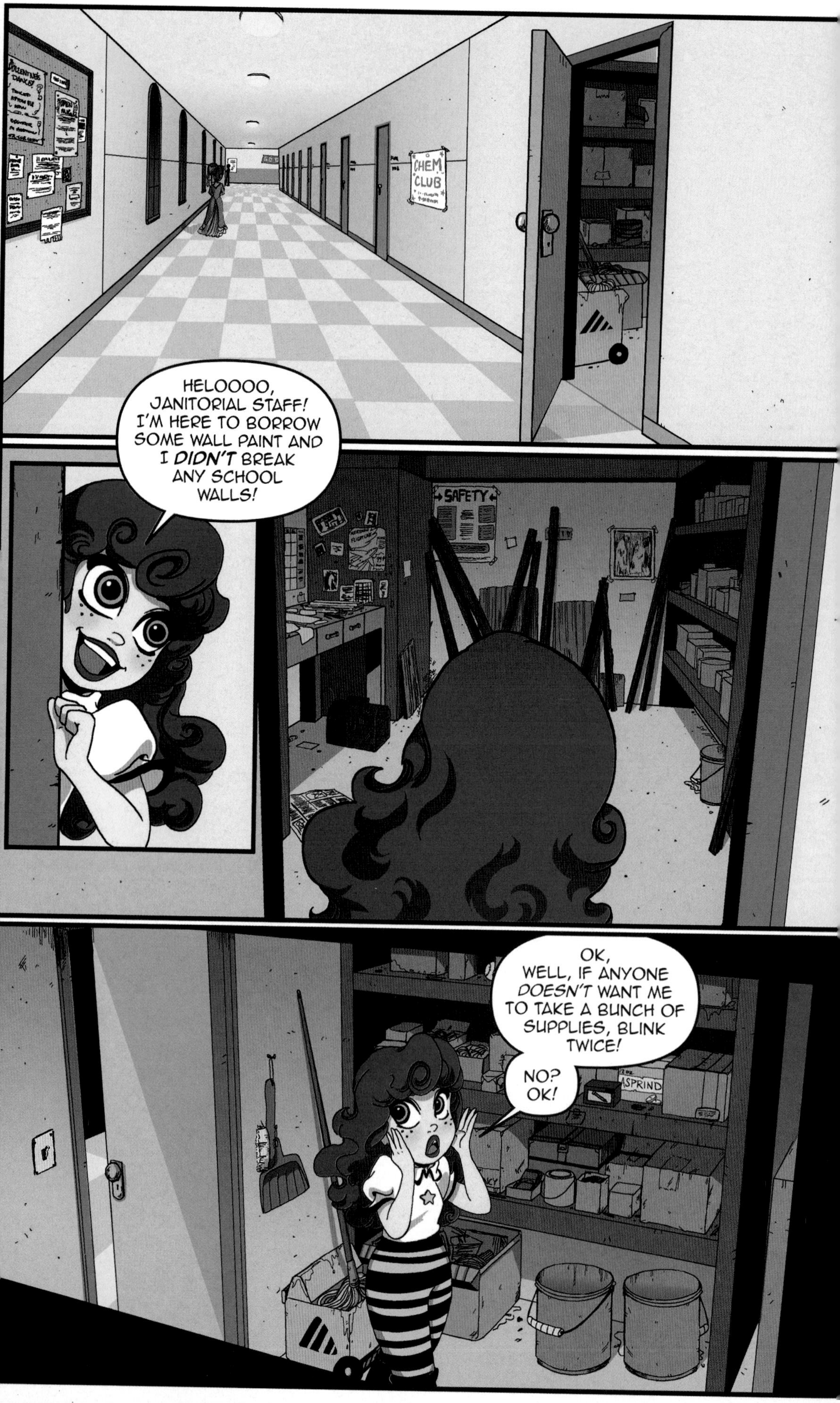
CHEM CLUB
HELOOOO, JANITORIAL STAFF! I'M HERE TO BORROW SOME WALL PAINT AND I *DIDN'T* BREAK ANY SCHOOL WALLS!
SAFETY
OK, WELL, IF ANYONE *DOESN'T* WANT ME TO TAKE A BUNCH OF SUPPLIES, BLINK TWICE!
NO? OK!

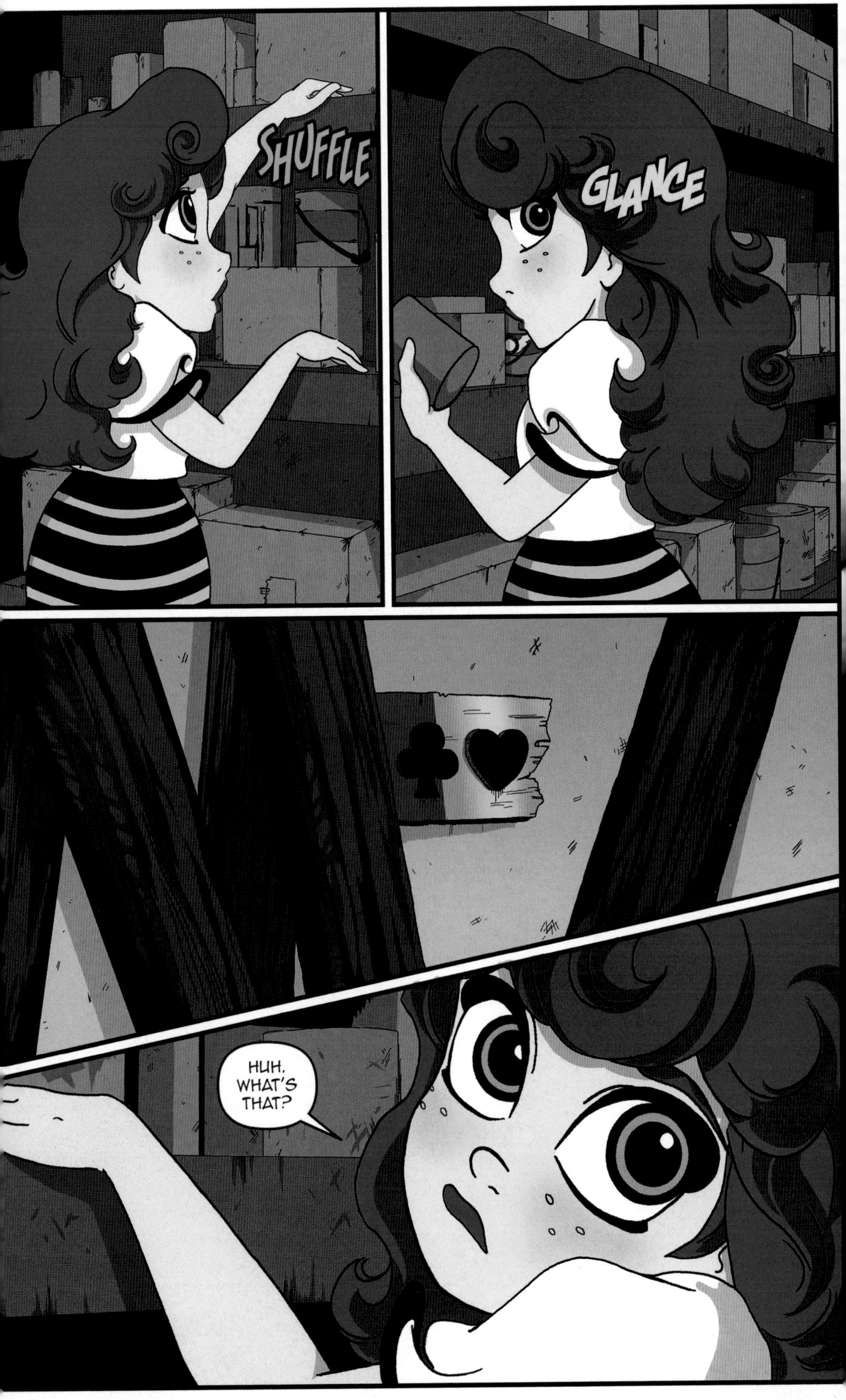
SHUFFLE
GLANCE
HUH, WHAT'S THAT?

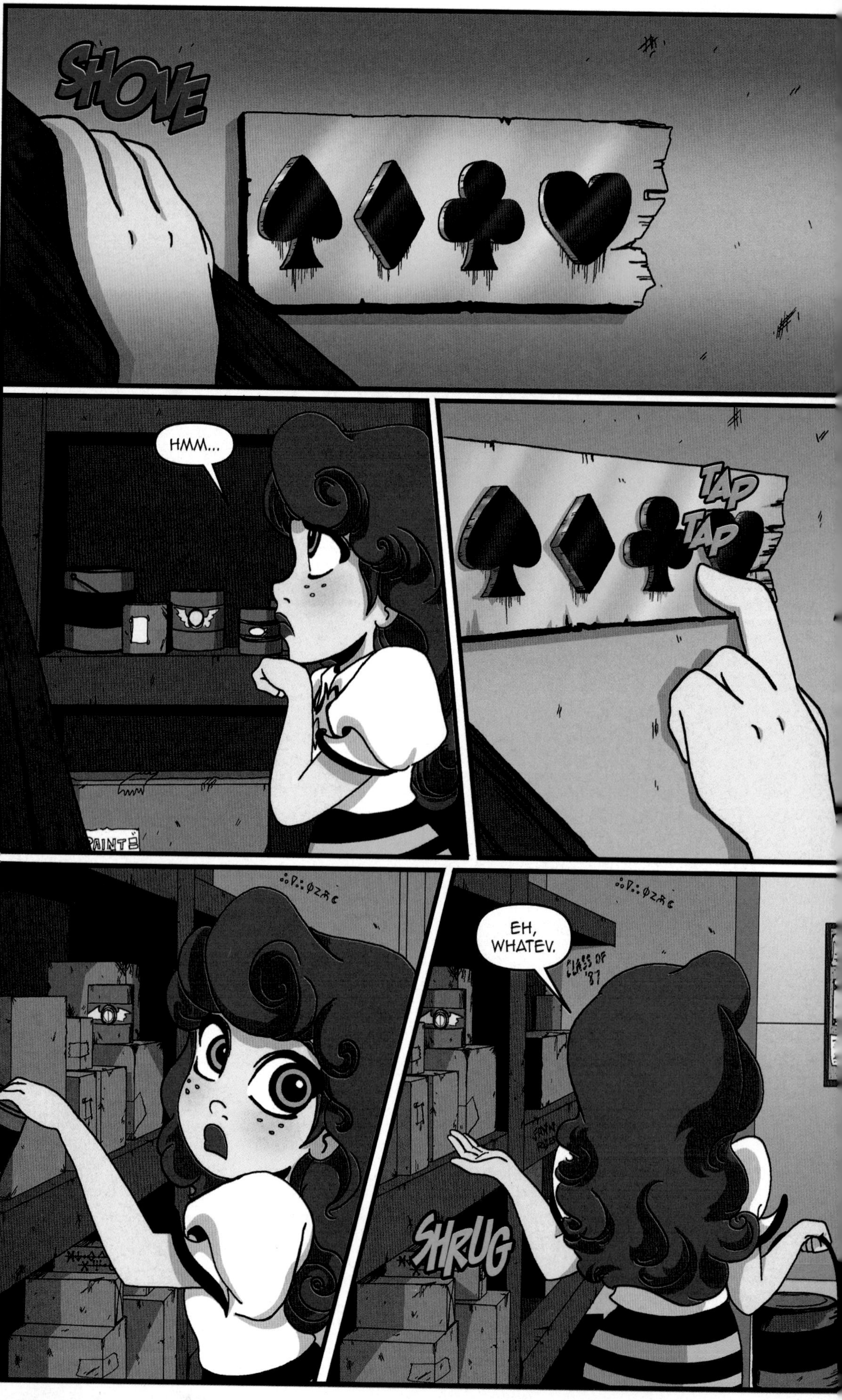
SHOVE
HMM...
TAP
TAP
PAINT
EH, WHATEV.
CLASS OF '87
SHRUG

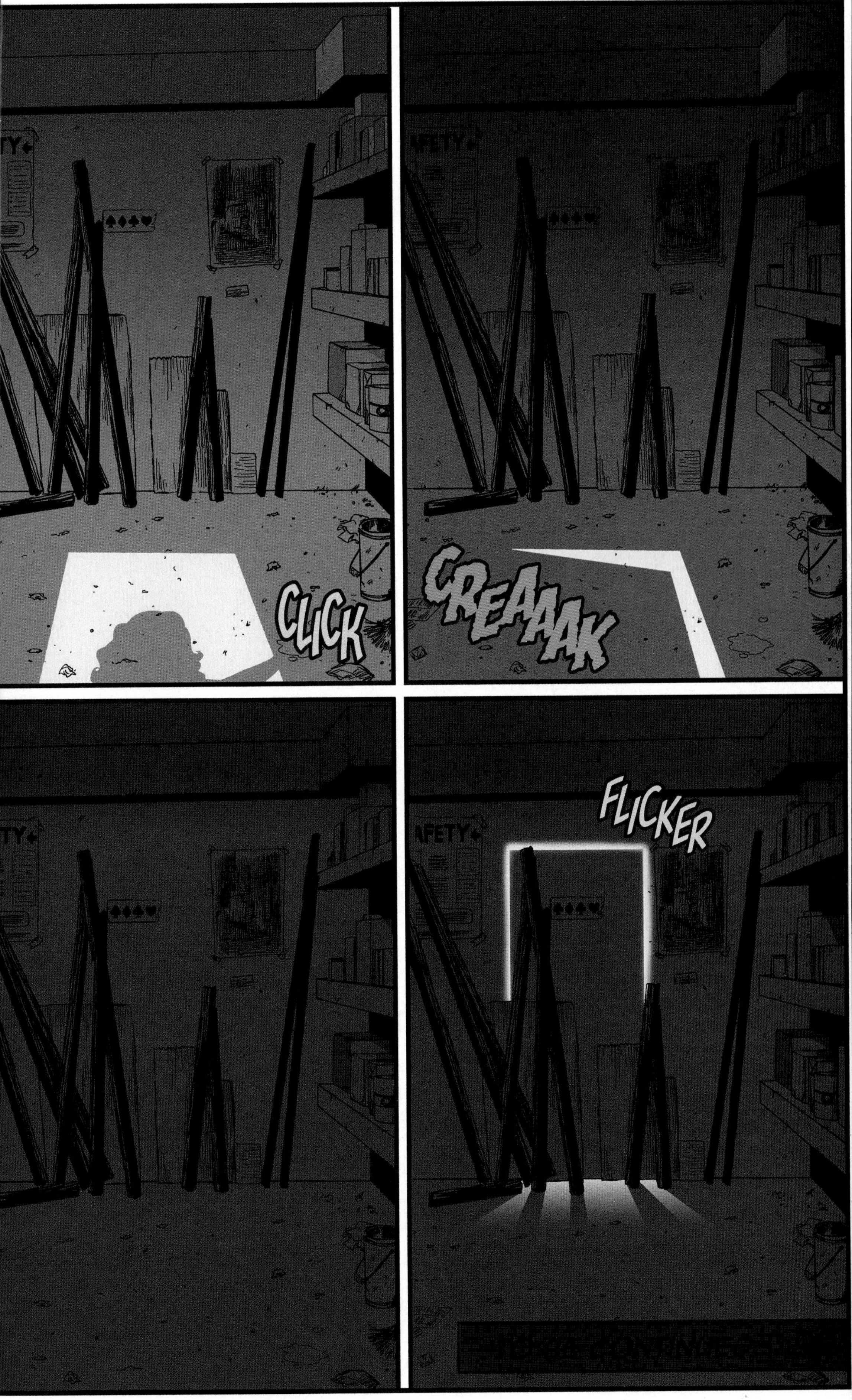
CLICK
CREAAAK
FLICKER

TOYETICA MODELS

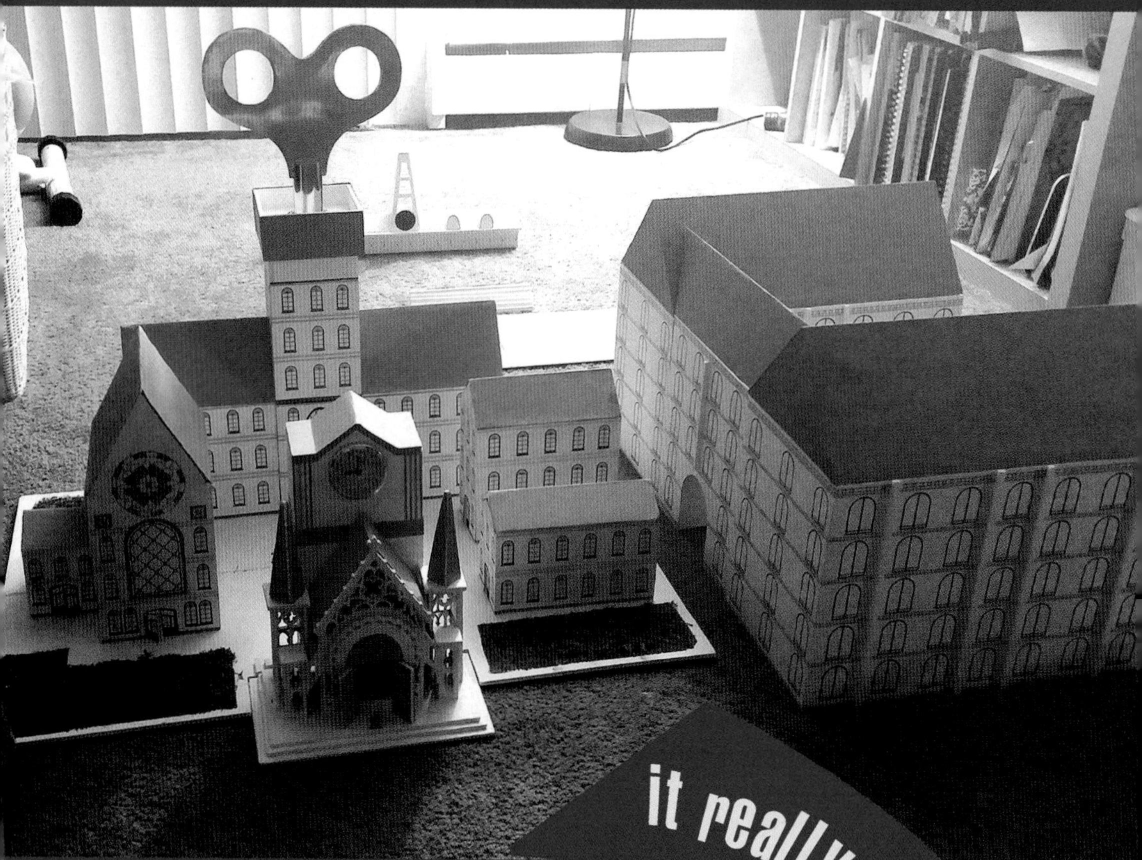

it really spins!

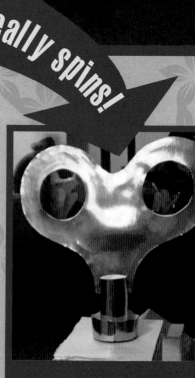

DID YOU KNOW THAT I HAVE A SET BUILT FOR ALMOST EVERY SCENE IN TOYETICA? IT'S ONE OF MY FAVE HOBBIES...MAKING LITTLE MODELS OUT OF FOAMCORE AND PAPER! I USE THEM TO ENVISION THE WORLD OF TOYETICA BETTER AND PLAN OUT SCENES. THIS SCHOOL MODEL IS SO BIG IT WON'T FIT ON MY DESK!

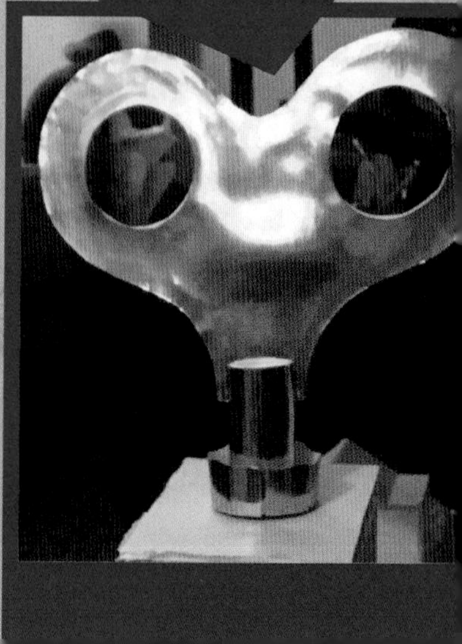

MS. WHEATLEY'S CLASSROOM

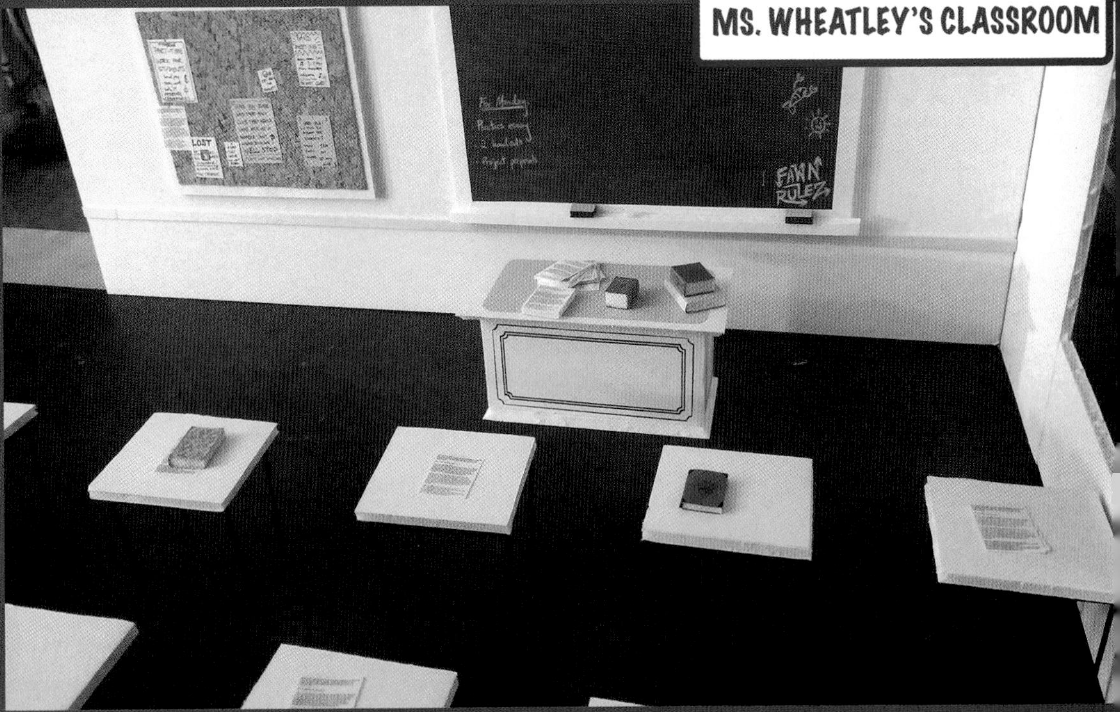

For Monday:
Plastics essay
2 handouts
Project proposals
FAWN RULEZ

Making little prop books like these is easy…just get a white square eraser and cut little slices off the end with a knife or scissors, then wrap them in colored paper for a cover! Glue the papers down and decorate with pen or paint.

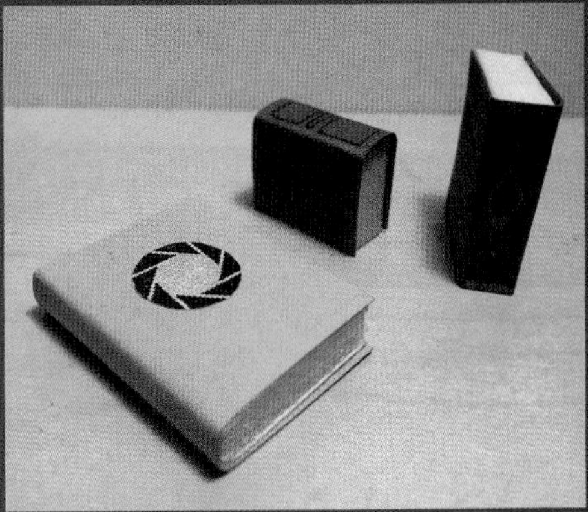

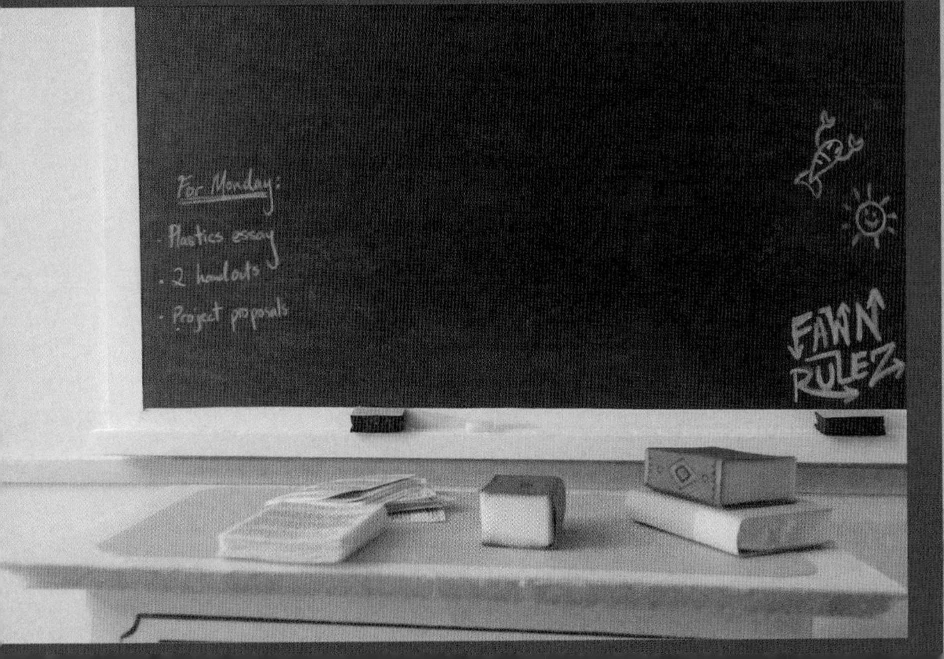

For Monday:
- Plastics essay
- 2 handouts
- Project proposals
FAWN RULEZ

FAWN LOVES TO TAG HER NAME ON THINGS (LIKE THE CHALK BOARD)

Giant Gems

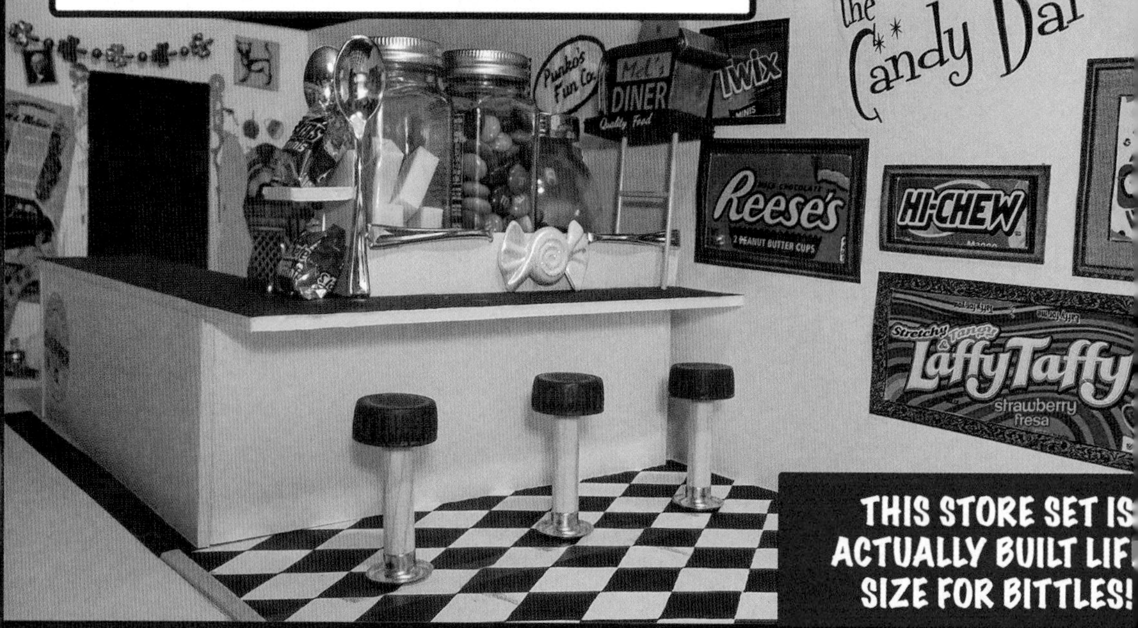

the Candy Bar
DINER
TWIX
Reese's
HI-CHEW
Laffy Taffy
strawberry
fresa

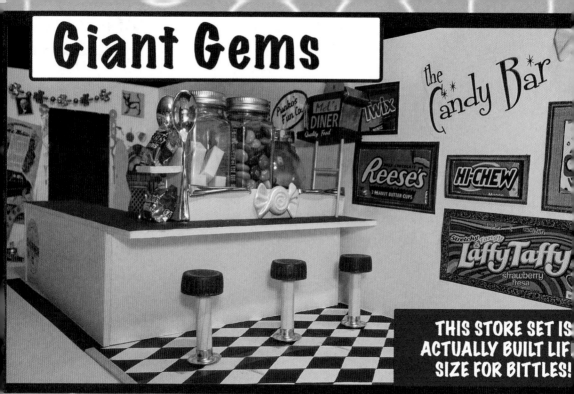

THIS STORE SET IS ACTUALLY BUILT LIF SIZE FOR BITTLES!

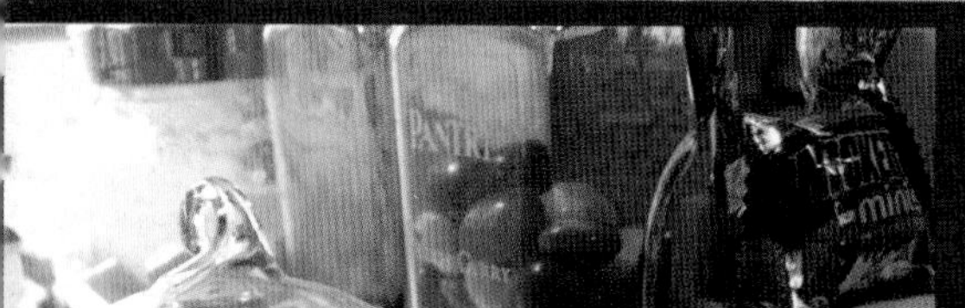

REAL CANDY DECORATES THE WHOLE SET!

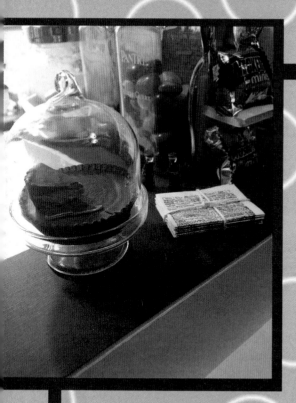

AN ARCADE CABINET MADE FROM PAPER MAKES A PERFECT GAME FOR BITTLES TO PLAY!

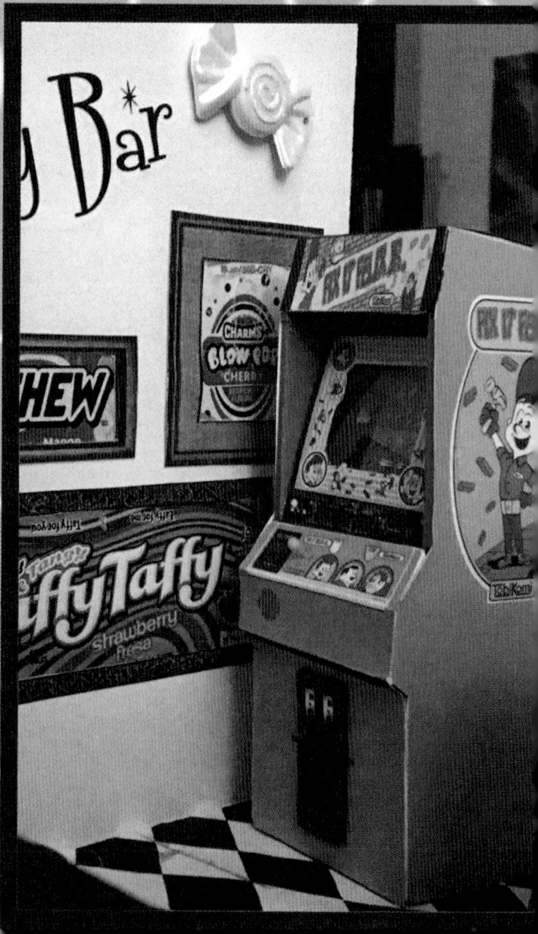

Bar
HEW
Laffy Taffy
strawberry
fresa

pages in progress

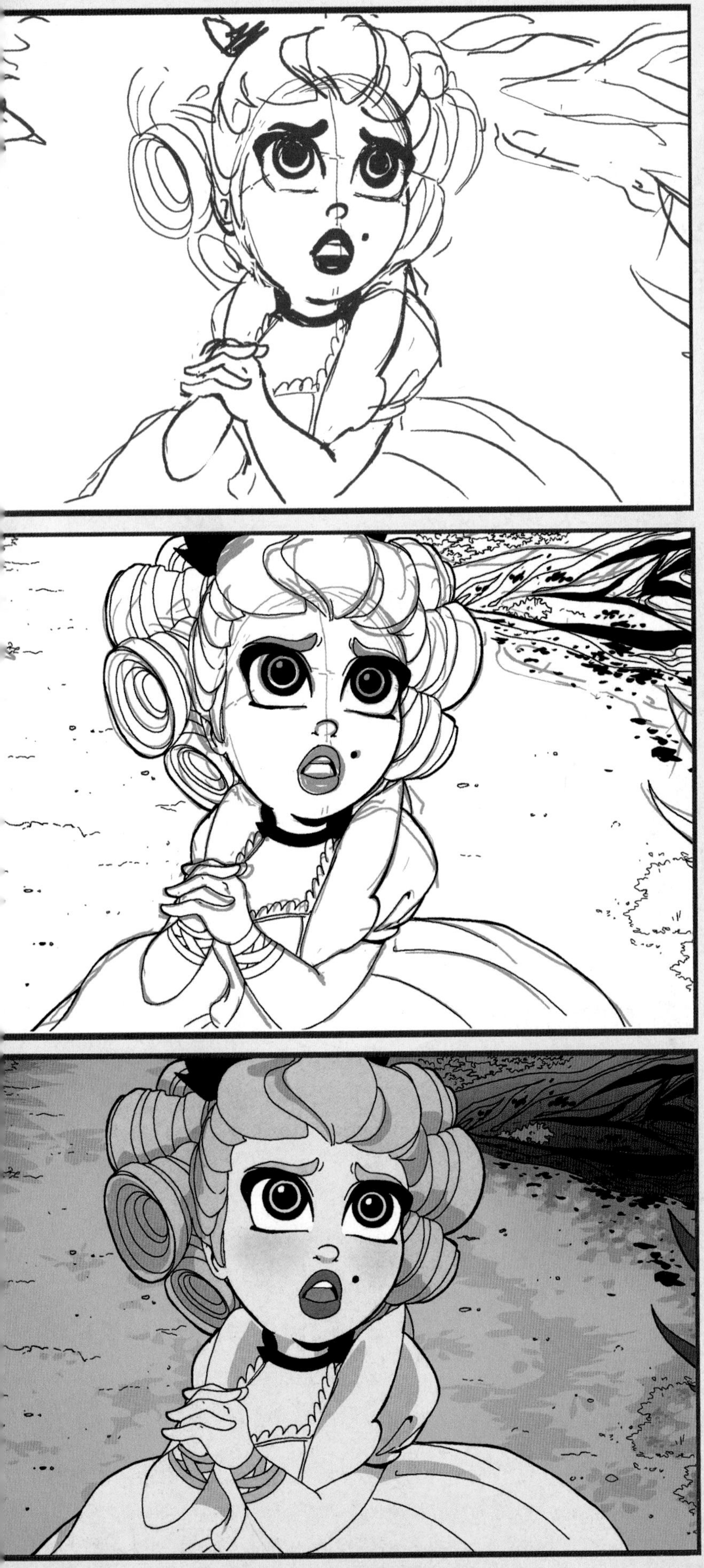

Live on Twitch.tv!

WANT MORE TOYETICA DOODLES AND COMICS **DRAWN LIVE?**

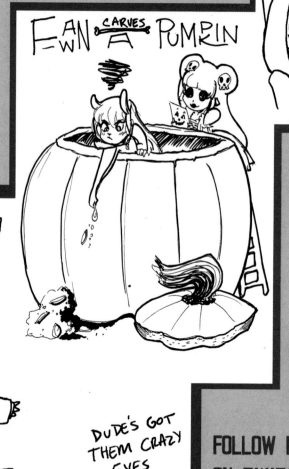

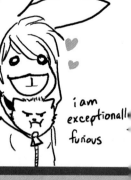

i am
exceptionall
furious

FAWN CARVES A PUMKIN
FREE HUGZ
DUDE'S GOT THEM CRAZY EYES

Heck yeah dumb stu like this!

FOLLOW ME ON TWITCH
@FUNWITHPUNKO

@MartyLegrow FunWithPunko

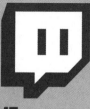